To Mum

*I was hoping to .
for your birthday
published took ...... writer*

I hope you find this a good read

Your son

Abalus

In the Beginning

by
Stephen L. Padley

Strategic Book Publishing and Rights Co.

Strategic Book Publishing and Rights Co.
12620 FM 1960, Suite A4-507
Houston, TX 77065
www.sbpra.com

ISBN: 978-1-61204-316-6

Design: Dedicated Book Services, Inc. (www.netdbs.com)

Dedication

This book is dedicated to the DGS (Dead Goat Society), a small group of good friends, like me, in the second half of our short lives on this earth. As the DGS, we walk, run, or cycle for charities. We hike, climb, camp, bush bash, kayak, and snorkel the West Australian countryside and coastal waters. May our bodies continue to hold out as we delight in nature's diversity.

Acknowledgements

I would like to thank longtime friend and member of the DGS, Barbara Edwards, who in no small way, through her encouragement, proofreading, constructive critique, and constant verbal poke in the ribs for the next chapter, brought his book into being.

Contents

In the Beginning

When I opened my eyes, the first thing I saw
Was a gnarled, grey hand with bloody claws.
My neck was pressed against a wooden beam,
Throat sticky and wet; was I in a dream?
Thin, cold steel pressed against my spine.
Was this to be my last moment, end of time?
I turned and glanced sideways to where he stood,
The dark, heavy monster in black leather hood,
An evil grin spread across his twisted face,
As the axe he lifted, my heart picked up pace.
Tongue dried, lips cracked, last breath did I take,
Final thought of forgiveness for their mistake.
Body freed of head, and all went black.
I look down where the axe did hack.
No sight, no sound, silent scream from within,
Why do I feel this is not the end?
The shell I lived in lies in two parts.
But, my sense of self exists as my heart departs.
My thoughts, they float in the damp, misty air.
I sense a feeling of love and care.
It's all around me, embracing each thought.
The executioner's axe all for naught,
My mind open, to wander, for all to know
As I find my spirit begin to grow.
I understand things I never knew
And yearn to be part of this spirit true.
My thoughts are expanded and spirit immersed.
I am part of this limitless universe.
Memories of earth-bound time grow hazy.
Confined to one planet now seems crazy.
Free of the womb of Mother Earth spinning,
For the spirit released, this is just the beginning.

Preface

This novel came into being following the creation of a picture from an image in my mind. When I showed the picture to family and friends, they were puzzled by the drawing that seemed to be in contradiction of the three words within it, "In the Beginning." In explanation, I wrote the poem that was inspired by the picture. But, it did not seem enough for those who read the poem and had seen the picture. So, I decided to write a short story to provide a background to the picture. It was intended to be only a short story, but it took on a life of its own and evolved over a period of time. It got me thinking about the constant war of intellect and belief over the subject of creation or evolution and about some of the most astute minds within their fields of study or research sitting on one side or the other. The god in my mind's eye is far cleverer than either side of this coin, in that if life and this universe are indeed a creation, it was created to evolve. Evolution was built into the whole model. Man's evolution is not just that of our physical adaptability to the environment to which we are subjected but also of the mind. Our greatest and most powerful tool for this evolution is our curiosity. Armed with it, we explore, discover, and learn about our physical world and that which lies beyond it.

From the human imagination bursts creativity, expressed in the forms of music, literature, and the arts, not to forget architecture and design. But, collectively or individually, to think that we know all there is to know about what has been taught us or that which we are prepared to believe from dogmatic institutions dulls the curiosity by which we can evolve and understand the part we play in this universe. Of course, there are many influences in civilization that distract the majority of us from this. I'm sure many of you can work out what these are.

Many years ago I came across a saying by W. Clement Stone, "Whatever the mind can conceive and believe will be achieved." This principle is adequately demonstrated in a lot

of science fiction novels of the past. When science and technology catch up with the ideas expressed in some of these
novels and even films, then it becomes a reality. Science fact
tends to follow science fiction. Does a similar mechanism
work in the realm of religion, whereupon our ancestors, in an
effort to explain our existence, conceived of the idea of some
kind of supreme beings or God? Can the principle expressed
in the above quote then influence the growth of individual
cultures with some form of belief structure embedded?

Is there a message in this novel? Maybe, I leave that for
the reader to find out.

"Once you've come to the conclusion that what you know
already is all you need to know, you have a degree in disin-
terest."— John Dobson

Chapter 1—The Cardinals Visit

A loud knock on the heavy, wooden door reverberated through the house, followed by the deep commanding voice, "Open in the name of his Eminence, the Cardinal of Surrendom."

Mother looked at Father with a worried, puzzled frown on her face. Father quickly closed the book he was reading to us, turned to the fireplace, and removed the left-hand hearthstone to reveal the small recess holding several books that we were not supposed to be reading. It was not our place to enquire of any knowledge outside the teachings of the Lord Master of Surrendom. The Cardinal was renowned for his dogged pursuit to seek out those citizens like my father, who thought there was more to understand than the church had ever told us. The likes of us had a tendency to disappear. Having replaced the book in the secret recess, he repositioned the stone and scuffled ash and old embers into the cracks. Unless you looked really hard, it was almost undetectable in the flickering light of the burning logs. Father picked up the Holy Writings issued to all Surrendom households. The book, leather bound with gold-leaf embossing, was to always be in a place of prominence in each house by commandment of the Lord Master.

Visits by clergy of each town were frequent and unannounced under the guise of fatherly concern for the well-being of the flock in his care. But, everyone knew that these visits were more about ensuring the dwellers were following the path laid out for them in the writings of the good book. It was the Father's duty to report any doubts about a family's devotion to the Faith. A visit from the Cardinal was not entirely unexpected since the last unannounced call from the Father became a somewhat animated discussion between my father and the Father. Part of the ritual of these visits was a compulsory tithe collection that demonstrated one's devotion to the Faith. My father, in an unguarded moment, questioned the necessity for the third increase in the tithe this season. The Father simply reminded him that it was not

1

for him to question what the Lord Master's servants required the money for. My father could not let it go at that and glibly remarked that an omnipotent Lord Master would have no need of money; indeed, the creator of all things did not create for profit. The Father, shocked by this remark, retorted with some vehemence that the Lord Master could see into the minds and hearts of all his flock and would seek out those found untrue. He quietly left.

That was two days ago.

The second knock on the door was followed by a more impatient demand for the door to be opened. The Holy Writings were placed on the table. My father walked over to his chair, sat, picked up his pipe, and began to refill it.

"Go open the door, Evey. It'll be OK."

Mother brushed down her dress, patted her hair into place, glanced into the mirror, and smiled falsely. I sat down by the fire on my stool, picked up my knife, and continued to whittle my stick into the fireplace. Mother crossed the room to the door and, with a sharp deep sigh of breath, opened it and stepped back as two of the Cardinal's guards strode in and gave the room the once-over to ensure there were no potential threats to the Cardinal. Once satisfied, the taller guard nodded back toward the door, and his Eminence strode in. His heavy, blue velvet cape with hood was held close to his body by a jeweled chain and clasp across his upper chest, and he was clearly clutching the lower section of the cape with his hands. He was tall, almost as tall as my father, but thin and wispy looking, with piercing dark eyes that reminded me of a cat focused on its prey and ready to pounce. Two bony hands opened the cape and unclasped the gold chain, and with a wide sweep of his left hand, he removed the cape and held it out to my mother to relieve him of it. Father stood respectfully and bowed his head without taking his eyes off the Cardinal.

"Welcome to our humble home, your Eminence. I trust you are well."

Without a word, the Cardinal strode into the center of the living area and slowly cast his intense gaze around the room, taking in every detail, turning slowly on the balls of his feet in full circle.

After several seconds, his intense gaze returned to my father, still standing by his chair with pipe in hand.

"Can I offer you some refreshment? Some wine perhaps, or would you prefer a warm beverage this chilly evening?"

"No, I have brought my own refreshment, but you can provide me with a chair by the fire."

"Abalus, move the rocker by the fire for his Eminence," Father gestured toward the heavy oak rocker.

I quickly put down my knife and stick, went over to Mother's small sewing area, and moved the rocker to the fire. Without his cape, the Cardinal looked quite frail, but each movement and posture seemed precise, calculated somehow. Dressed in a loose, plain-black, full-length tunic, what he lacked in bulk was made up by the volume of his clothes. He sat in the rocker and waved at the two guards to remove themselves from his presence. They turned, walked out the door, and closed it behind them. Presumably, that was where they would remain unless called upon.

"You are Rider, Adiemus Rider, are you not?" The Cardinal's voice was deeper than I had expected from this thin, frail frame.

"Yes, your Eminence, I am, and this is my wife, Evey and my son Abalus," Father responded, casting an open palm toward each of us in turn. Mother sat by the table and rested her hands in her lap. I could see in her face she was very uncomfortable with this man in her house.

"Be seated, Rider." The Cardinal's voice had all the force of command.

I returned to my stool, picked up my knife, and whittled stick. Father gave me a stern look. I instantly put the stick down and placed the knife in the pigskin scabbard on my belt. From where I sat, I could see that the rocker was placed over the hearth stone that concealed our books. I smiled gently to myself and immediately regretted it as the intense eyes bored into mine from just across the fireplace. I looked down into the fire so I did not have to have my thoughts ripped out of my head. The Cardinal's attention returned to my father. "I understand from the Father of this district that you had questioned the increases in the tithe; is this true?"

"My apologies, your Eminence, they were words born out of frustration. It has been a difficult year for blacksmiths with the loss of so many horses to the equine phage and the increasing rarity of good metal. Much of my business revolves around horses and the needs of farmers. I have barely been able to put food in the mouths of my family, let alone pay increases in tithes."

I knew this was only partly the truth; Father had indeed lost trade with the farming community, but he turned his hand to making swords and axes. Although not a master in these weapons, his reputation was beginning to grow, each new weapon an improvement on the last. Knowing this was at least a part truth allowed my father to return his Eminence's gaze by looking him straight in the eye without a flinch.

"Hmm," his Eminence responded. "It has also been noted that your attendance to worship has been somewhat erratic over the last six months."

"I have not been well, and neither have my wife and son. In times of need, we take care of each other."

"Hmm, I see," the Cardinal responded. He began to gently rock in the chair.

"I see you have the Good Book on the table there. Do you read this to your family every night?"

After a brief pause that would only have been the merest time to blink, my father replied, "Yes, your Eminence."

The Cardinal did not miss the pause before the response. He had been a Pursuer of the faith long enough to know when he was being lied to. The Cardinal turned to me and fixed his eyes to mine. My heart began to race, and I caught my breath, waiting for what was to come next. My fifteen years of life had not been enough to know how to lie when the needs of the family demanded it. Indeed, my father had always told me to tell the truth regardless of the consequences. A noble attribute, but now my father's life might depend on a lie.

The Cardinal continued to rock the chair. "Son, what was the last passage your father read to you out of the Book?"

I turned my eyes down to the rocking chair and saw the hearthstone move under the weight of the rocker as it tipped forward. "Well, tonight we read the story of how the mighty armies of the Northern provinces were overcome by the chosen warriors of the Lord Master in the ancient land of Hedonim."

"Really, and who was the leader of the Warriors, and what prayer was spoken before battle?" his Eminence replied with a sickly smile on his face.

My mind went blank; it was almost a month ago when we read this story. "It was . . . It was . . ." My eyes looked up, and I found myself caught in the intense eyes of his Eminence.

"Come now, son, surely you have not forgotten such an exciting story. Who was the leader of the Warriors?"

My eyes dropped back to the hearthstone, which was now looking distinctly loose. With alarm, I turned my eyes to my father and back to the stone. This did not escape the intense gaze of his Eminence. He followed my eyes downward to the stone, leaned forward in the chair, and saw the stone move with his weight.

"Well, Mr. Rider, what have we here? It seems your fireplace holds a little mystery maybe, or is it just in need of repair?"

His Eminence had documented past visitations and recorded some of the more novel ways in which citizens had attempted to secrete banned knowledge. The fireplace had provided several places in the past. In the chimney, the shelf over the fireplace, under the grate, a false bottom of the wood basket, even behind pictures above the fireplace were all recorded.

Father took a step forward. His Eminence reminded him of the guards just outside the door. Removing a short dagger with a red, jeweled handle from his belt, the Cardinal stooped down, shoved the rocker away from the hearth, stuck his blade into the gap between the stones, and levered the loose stone up. Then, he jammed his knife underneath so the stone did not fall back into gap. He released the knife and thrust his fingers under the stone to lift it out of the hole. At this moment, he took his eyes off my father and me.

Without even thinking about it, I dove across the hearth, withdrawing my knife from its scabbard at the same time, swung it around, and buried the blade into his neck. He was totally caught by surprise and looked round into my face, mouth open but no sound coming out. I looked into his eyes; the intense gaze was still there, boring into my mind. I looked at his neck. The knife had gone right through where his voice box would have been. He could not yell the alarm, just give a sort of grated cackle. I looked again more closely, something was not quite right.

"Father . . . Father, he does not bleed. There's no blood!"

Father was by my side in two strides, squatted down, and looked for himself. Mother was still at the table with her hands held up to her face, trying to blot out the scene before her.

Father leaned forward to reach out for the knife. The Cardinal's reactions were quick and precise as his left hand swept round and grasped my father's wrist. I could see the pain in his face as the grip was crushing the bones in his forearm together. Still maintaining the grip, the Cardinal got to his feet and, with seemingly little effort, pushed my father across the room, where he fell against the table and was barely able to prevent himself pushing over my mother. With careful and deliberate motion, his fingers clasped round the knife stuck in his throat, and as we gazed in amazement, unable to speak, he withdrew the knife. No blood. No pain showed on his face. The Cardinal turned his attention to me, his attacker, and his right arm slashed across the space—his bony fingers sunk into my neck. I could feel the pressure of the blood in my temple and could barely breathe.

My mother was the first to react. I guess a mother's instinct to protect her young spurred her into action as she grabbed a cast-iron saucepan from the stove and swung it menacingly across the side of his skull. It would surely have crushed bone, but instead of the dull crunching sound, there was a sound more like metal on metal. As I looked up into the Cardinal's face in terror, I could see the skin of his left ear had turned sort off hazy and indistinct, and underneath, there was a crimson, metallic glint in the firelight. His grip did not relax, and my eyes became unfocused. There was another metallic thud and a third. The iron grip was gone, and I fell to the floor, gasping for breath. The Cardinal's head looked misshapen and flatter on the left-hand side, and the intense gaze, which was the hallmark of his presence, was gone; the dark eyes held no focus as he fell to the floor. Just as he dropped to the floor, there was a loud clatter as my mother released her grip on the saucepan, which landed on the stone floor as she stood in shock at what she had done. The noise was followed by the front door being flung open as two guards, alerted by the noise, took in the scene before them. The shorter of the two guards leveled a stubby, single-handed crossbow directly at my father and pulled the trigger. The next instant, the shaft of a six-inch bolt appeared in my father's chest, and he went limp and sank to his knees.

"Adiemus . . . nooo!" my mother screamed as she rushed over to where he fell, dropped to her knees, and cradled his head with shaking hands, stroking his face. The tall guard grabbed me by the hair, forced me to stand up, and pushed my face against the wall; strong hands grabbed both my arms, and I felt my wrists being bound behind my back with a leather lace. The second of the Cardinal's guard had moved over to where my father had fallen and checked his pulse for life; he was gone. Turning to my mother, he dragged her away and pushed her to bend forward over the table, face planted into the wood with a firm hand on the back of her head. My captor yanked me over to the door and pushed me so hard that I fell outside, and he followed, slamming the door behind him.

I heard mother cry out in pain and anguish, "Forgive me, Adiemus. I know not what I do . . ." There was a loud clatter of furniture. "Mother! Mother!" I shouted, struggling against the guard to run back toward the house.

The guard caught me a swift backhand across the face. "Silence, you wretched sinner!"

I looked across the street to see a horse-drawn cart. The guard dragged me over to the side. The cart was a fully enclosed box with a small door in the back just big enough for an adult to crawl or be pushed into.

"Get in," the guard commanded.

"Where are you taking me?" I blurted. "I want my mother."

"You are to be judged and convicted by the Lord Master. Your mother will be . . . judged as well, shortly." The guard's face showed some kind of masked pleasure, a slim smile on his lips.

I heard no further noise come from the house apart from stifled sobs. My incarceration alone in the box, which a person could just about sit up in, seemed like an age, but it was probably as long as it takes to read the Lord Master's prayer. I heard the door of the house open and footsteps to the back of the cart. The bolt was unlatched, and the door opened. The guard with dark smudges on his face and hands stood in its frame with my mother over his shoulder. She was bundled through the door, and it was secured into place. I pushed myself forward to her side, but I could not even lift her head up as my wrists were still bound behind my back. I could only whisper in her ear, but there was no response. She lay bunched up just as she was pushed in. I tried to move her into what I thought to be a more comfortable position, but without the use of my hands, it was difficult to maneuver the dead weight of her body. In the little light of the setting sun coming from the cracks in the planks of the box, I could see her face was cut and grazed across the right cheek, and I saw bruises around her eyes. Her apron was gone, and her dress was ripped as was her white blouse. Tears began to form in my eyes, and I felt their warmth run down my face.

There was a sudden lurch, and the sound of the horses' hooves as the box began its journey to wherever the Lord Master ruled from. I knew not where.

Chapter 2—Incarceration

We must have traveled in the confines of the cart for most of the night. As I awoke with a start from dozing when the cart hit a large pothole, the glimmer of dawn light could be seen in between the planks of wood that made the walls of the box. Mother did not seem to have moved at all. I leaned over her face and could feel the shallow breath on my cheek. I tried to rouse her but to no avail. Suddenly, the cart came to a halt, and I heard the guard call out to some unseen person to open the gates in the name of his Eminence. There was the sound of heavy metal drawbolts and a chain being manipulated, and we moved forward again with a lurch of the cart.

Shortly afterwards, we came to a stop again, and I heard the footfalls of the guards jump down from the cart and move round to the door of this small prison I was in. With a loud thud, the bolt was drawn, and sunlight streamed into the aperture. Then, the dark form of a guard's arm reached in, grabbed my ankle, and hauled me out into the bright sunlight.

I looked around to see myself surrounded by four large walls about the height of four people standing on each others' shoulders, at least eighty paces each in length, and small stone buildings down by the gate that we had just come through. There seemed to be no other entrance or exit. The ground beneath my feet was solid stone, and there were four circular, low stone walls with a stairwell going down under the ground. In the center of the space was a wooden platform wide enough for two or three people to stand on. On the platform stood a block of wood held up from the platform by a trestle at each end. The block of wood had a U-shaped section carved out at the center. The wood was stained dark red all around the U-shaped section. A sharp push in the back from one of the guards set me stumbling toward one of the stairwells. I turned round to see what was happening to Mother. The shorter of the two guards had her curled over his shoulder and was walking across the space toward another of the stairwells. Another shove in the back sent me further toward the stairwell. There was nowhere to run and hide even if I had the thought to try. As we descended down the stairwell, the darkness enveloped us. As my eyes got used to the dim light, I began to see my surroundings for the first time. We were in an open space lit by lanterns in the ceiling glowing with a whitish-yellow light. There were no flames as one would expect from a rag lantern like we used back in town. The light was constant, not flickering.

As my eyes accustomed more to this light, I could see that the boundary walls of this space had regularly spaced doors around the walls. The space was circular, about fifteen paces across. In the center sat another guard at a table, staring intently at a small tablet in his grasp, with his thumbs moving rapidly over the surface of each end. There were strange noises emanating from the tablet in his hand. He glanced up, looking slightly annoyed at the interruption. He put down his tablet and picked up another with neat rows of buttons on it. Above each button was a number. He pressed one of the buttons, and there was a loud click from one of the doors in the wall to my left. As I looked over, I could see into a small room with a bed and sink, a small table with chair, and a pot under the bed. As I was guided toward the cell, I could see a small shelf on the back wall on which stood a copy of the Holy Writings, as could be found in each family home.

It was lit by another small light similar to the one in the main area.

"What have you done with my mother? Where have you taken her?" I demanded.

"I'd be more concerned about yourself if I were you; your mother is to be realigned with the Lord Master."

"What are you going to do with me?" I replied.

"I'm not going to do anything; I just find sinners and bring them here for judgment." He grinned, pulled out a knife, grabbed me by the hair, and brought the knife against my throat.

"Son, you should start saying your prayers." He took the knife from my throat and placed it on the leather thong binding my wrists. With a quick movement, he cut the bond, pushed me into the small room, and shut the door. A few seconds later, I heard the same click. I rushed to the door and bounced back off it. It didn't even rattle on the hinges. I stared at the door with a desolate feeling. What was to become of me now?

I looked around the room, about two paces across and five paces in length. For some reason, what light there was seemed to be directed to the Holy Writings, the meager light caught in the gold-leaf embossing drawing the eye to the book. I sat on the bed and just stared at the opposite wall, wondering what the guard had meant about my mother was to be realigned with the Lord Master.

In the silence with only my thoughts, a low whisper of a human voice pierced into my awareness. I got up from the bed to try and track down the direction it was coming from. It was coming from low down the wall somewhere by the table. I moved the table further along the wall close to the door, got down on all fours, and ran my fingers around the seams between the stones.

"Hello, hello . . . Who's there? Can anyone hear me?"

"Hello, yes, I hear you," a hopeful whisper replied.

I continued to trace the wall with my fingers, and at about knee height, I discovered a small hole about the size of my finger. I brought my eye down to the hole.

"Hello," I whispered.

In the dim light, I saw the blink of another eye gazing back at me.

"What is your name?" whispered the eye.

"Abalus, and yours?"

"Magdalin, call me Mags. Why are you here? Where are you from?" The young girl's voice raised slightly above a whisper.

"I come from the province of Balgara, a town called Dealton. Our house got visited by his Eminence. I— I think we may have killed him," I replied in a low whisper.

I heard her whistle between her teeth, "Wow, are you serious? I heard that he could not be killed. There are stories of people having tried before, but he always seemed turn up again."

"What about you? Why are you here? What's to become of us?" I whispered.

"My mum and dad were reading some stuff from an old book my dad dug up when readying the fields for planting. Dad was trying to teach me some stuff he was beginning to understand from the book. The Father visited our farm one day and spied the book on the side dresser. Dad had forgotten to put it out of sight." She paused briefly and said as if in explanation, "We don't often get visitors out on the farm as our home is so far from the village of Hasley."

I responded, "My dad complained about the tithe increases; that's why we got visited. But, it was the discovery of our books that his Eminence . . . It was my fault, my fault, and now Father is dead." Tears began to well up in my eyes as the memory of last night's events came to the fore again. "They've got my mother as well. They took her down into another one of these places, I think."

Mags whispered, "They keep all family members separate. You don't get to see them again."

"How long you been here, Mags?"

"Not sure, but we seem to get two meals a day, a sort of porridgy thing when they wake us up and some sort of soup later. I've had six sets of meals, so I think I've been here six days."

"What are they going to do to us?" I asked.

"It depends on what you've done. If you are charged with false education, you are given the option to be realigned to the Lord Master, or you will be executed for believing false knowledge." Her voice kept to a low whisper still.

Taking her cue, I whispered back, "Well, I'll probably be executed cos' I stabbed the Cardinal in the throat with my knife, but I didn't kill him."

There was a long silence from the other side of the wall then I heard just a single, "Wowww."

At that moment, a low voice came shockingly loud into my cell as well as everyone else's. "All right you young sinners, time for your stroll in the yard, and get rid of your excrement from your cell."

I heard several door seals click open and the sound of metal pots being picked up off the stone floor. I paced over to my door and pulled it toward me. A cool breeze met my exit into the main space. I looked to my left to see if Mags was out of her cell. I found myself looking at a thin girl with long, dark hair, not surprisingly rather tangled. She was about my age, perhaps a year or two older; it was hard to tell. She had a pretty face with dark brown eyes and high cheekbones. Her skirt was disheveled and was probably bright red in color a few days ago, but it was now covered in grime from her manky cell as was her collar-high shirt—well, it would be collar high if some of the buttons were not missing. I wondered if our captors had molested her as had happened to my mother. If she had been, she did not seem to show it. In fact, she smiled at me like a long-lost friend. Her whole face lit up, but it was brief as the guard approached with a short metal stick in hand. I looked further around the chamber to see about another dozen kids, some as young as five. There was one boy who looked about seventeen or eighteen. He looked as if he had been beaten a few times. There were bruises on his face and his bare arms. But, what struck me most of all was the look on his face. Defiance and a burning anger raged as he looked toward the guards approaching, metal sticks waved at chest height. I got the impression he was well familiar with the sticks.

"Do you know him, Mags?" I asked gesturing his way.

"His name is Shaun. He came here the same day I did." She paused as a second guard approached the front of the line.

"All right you lot, you know the drill. Move!" the guard shouted. The line around the chamber turned, and we moved off toward the stairs, one behind the other.

"While we were being transported here, he told me that he . . ." she paused again, "he had killed the Cardinal!"

"Silence, you two, unless you wish to feel this stick on your throat," the guard shouted at the front and side of the line.

I waited as the guard at the front of the line began the ascent and whispered tensely, "But, that's not possible. He was at our house last night. Are you sure that's what he said?"

"Yes, Abalus, now shh! Otherwise, you'll get the stick."

With my mind trying to grasp this bit of information, I climbed the stairs out into the sunlight of the stone courtyard, now warming in the midmorning sun. I had to talk to Shaun somehow. I resolved to find a way to get to talk with him as soon as possible.

The line moved to the nearest wall. As we approached closer, I could see a small trapdoor with a sliding bolt embedded in the wall. I had not noticed it before as it was no bigger than one of the medium-sized stones used for the wall, and it was a very similar color. As I watched, the front guard unbolted the access, opened the flap upward, and secured it up with a small chain dangling from the wall. The line moved forward again, and as each kid in front of me approached, they tipped the contents of their pots down the chute. Then turned to the left and started walking around the perimeter of the wall.

"What's on the other side of the chute, Mags?"

"A small stream runs below. Why?"

"Oh, never mind, just thinking," I replied.

The walk around the wall lasted only three circuits, and then we were returned to the chamber and directed back to our cells. As I entered my cell, on the table stood a bowl of pale, creamy, white porridgy stuff and a small spoon. What was puzzling was how did it get there? I saw no one go down into our chamber from the courtyard while we were up there emptying our pots and walking round the walls. I was sure I would have noticed. There must be another way into the underground prison besides the stairwell; it was the only explanation I could think off. I resolved the next day when we were let out to pay more attention to my prison surroundings.

For now, I decided to pay close attention to my own cell; it might reveal how the porridge appeared. Starting with the bed, I looked underneath—no spring supports, only wooden battens. Nothing but the pot was underneath. The floor was smooth stone, no seams from wall to wall. The table and chair were made of some smooth, seamless material with a slightly mottled surface, like it was made out of a single piece—no joints or screws or pegs. They were both lightweight; I could pick them up with one hand. Probably wouldn't hurt a guard if I threw one at him. The walls were made of stone, but this was the first time I had seen stone that was so neatly carved into very regular rectangles about the size of my foot. Back on my knees, I returned to the small hole in the wall between my cell and Mags's. The hole, on closer inspection, was in a seam between these square stones. I scratched around the hole with my fingernail, and I felt it crumble into small bits. I grabbed the spoon off the table and scraped at the seam with the end. The seam gave way slowly. With a little effort, I might be able to remove a stone. At least Mags and I could talk to each other easier than through the small hole. Plus, it gave me something to do. I tore off the bottom section of my shirt and laid it on the ground under the part of the wall where the dust fell. As a small pile collected, I transferred it into the pot under the bed. Before tomorrow's exercise walk, I would take a pee and cover up the collected dust and hope the guards would not look too closely in my pot before I had a chance to discard it down the chute in the courtyard.

Mags heard my efforts, and after I explained what I was doing, she copied my actions on the other side of the stone block. After some while and several shirt tales of dirt into the pot later, the square stone showed signs of working loose. I stood up, went to the door, turned, and faced into my cell. Looking down toward the table, I checked to see if a guard could see the stone under the table from the doorway. A guard would have to stoop to be at the right level to see the brick. The table obscured the brick.

Crouching back under the table, I called for Mags in a low whisper. I needn't have bothered as she was already there waiting for me so we could ease the brick out and talk some more.

"Abalus, what books did you have?"

"The last one Father was reading from was called *The Guinness Book of Records*. It had all sorts of stuff in it about people's achievements and all sorts of strange things. It had pictures of strange machines that flew or went underwater or moved along the ground. Some time in the past, it seemed we had done all sorts of things, but what happened? We don't have those things now."

"You mean we built things that flew?" Mags queried.

"Yes I think so, or some people like us—it was a long time ago. The book was made in 2004 [1]BLM."

"That would be about a hundred and fifty years ago. What did the flying machine look like?"

I closed my eyes to draw on my memory. "It was thin and white, and it had wings, but they did not fold back like a bird, and it had small wheels underneath. The writing said it was 'three dot seven m' long and 'five dot seven m' wingspan. It was the world's smallest jet aircraft, and one man could fly in it. I don't know what an m is, but it seems to be some measurement of its size."

"I think I know what that might be," replied Mags.

"You do? How? What does it mean?" I said, puzzled.

"My dad had a book on carpentry. It showed how to make chairs and tables and cupboards and things. It was weird because it showed pictures of different tools, but some you plugged into the wall by a piece of thick string. Some of the plans for the furniture had measurements to cut pieces of wood, and these measurements were in ms as well, but another measurement would follow it inside curves with 'ft' or 'in.' My dad figured that ft might stand for the length of a foot. So, you can measure by pacing your feet one in front of the other. Dad tried it with a plan for a table, and lengths

---

[1]BLM-before the coming of Lord Master. The Lord Master became manifest in the Holy Writings. The Cardinal uses this book to teach the population. When the Cardinal appeared, the calendar was reset to 1.

measured using feet sort of worked to the size one might build a table for your home. From what I remember, three feet lengths equaled about one m."

"Hang on a moment," I said as I stood up and walked over to the end wall of my cell. Starting with my heel against the wall, I counted my foot lengths one in front of the other. It came to thirteen. I then did the same across the cell; it came to seven foot lengths. My guess was the length of the jet air-craft in the book was just about the length of my cell.

I returned to the hole in the wall, "The aircraft in the book would have been as long as our cells!"

"What other stuff was in your book, Abalus?" Mags whis-pered excitedly through our small portal.

"You ever heard of radio?"

"No"

"Nor had I, but I read in the *Guinness Book of Records* about a man called Oscar who talked and played music on the radio for the longest time. There used be something called television as well. People would perform plays and other stuff, and lots of people could watch them on television."

There was a moment of silence from the other side of the wall. "Where are these things now? What happened to them?" Mags's questions had been in my thoughts for some time, but I had no answers. Mags attempted to answer her own question. "Perhaps all those things are still around somewhere—we just haven't found them."

"Mags, some time ago we had a book called *In Six Days*. It was written by lots of people. Some were called scien-tists; others were engineers. They all seemed to have a lot of knowledge about different things that I didn't understand. I think perhaps these were the people who built some of the stuff written about in the Guinness book. They all seemed to be talking about why they thought that we were created by some higher being called God."

Mags cut in, "Is that the same as our Lord Master?"

"Probably," I replied.

"Why do you think they don't teach us this stuff in the Lord Master's schools? All we get taught is to read the Holy

Writings and to count, and that's it. Why don't they teach us more about our world?" Mags sounded a little angry as she said this through gritted teeth. She continued, "Here we are imprisoned for trying to find out more. Why is this so bad? Why is this knowledge forbidden?"

"Perhaps it's the reason it's all gone, somehow. Something must have happened; perhaps someone learned something or made something so terrible that they fought over it," I replied.

There was silence between us for a while as we both got lost in our thoughts. I could hear low murmurings going on around us and wondered whether other cells had adjoining crevices that kids were talking through to each other, or perhaps they were just talking to themselves to break the solitude. It struck me that, if our brick was easy to remove, other cells could also dig out the seams to make holes in the walls. I remembered that Shaun was four cells down from me.

"Mags, is there another hole on the other wall in your cell?"

"No."

"Do you think you can make one and get the kid in that one to make a hole on the other side as well?"

"Why?"

"I want to talk to Shaun four cells down. We could get others to relay messages back and forth. I need to find out how he killed the Cardinal."

"OK," she replied.

"Mags, wait a moment—did you have any other books besides the carpentry one?"

"Yes, we had one called *The Origin of Species*. It was very old; some pages were missing, and lots were loose and falling out, but my father put them in count order as best he could."

"What was it about?"

"Well, we only read little bits and pieces, and I didn't understand most of what Father read. He could not explain it any better either. But, it seemed to be saying that all the animals evolved and adapted. Some died out; others didn't."

I cut in before she went on further, "What does evolve mean?"

"I'm not sure, but it's like we sort of grew up and changed over time to adapt to the world as it was or is—does that make sense?"

I puzzled over this, "Well no . . . yes . . . sort of, I think. Sort of the opposite of being created?"

Mags responded with enthusiasm, "Yes, that's it—I think."

I continued, "Perhaps that's what caused the trouble. All those people with a lot of knowledge could not agree which was right."

I bent down a little further so I could look through our hole in the wall. This little tunnel that allowed us to share our experiences and thoughts now became a connection of minds. Eyes were already there staring back. Through the gloom and the grime on her cheeks, I knew she was smiling at me.

"You know," she said, "if we were created in the beginning to evolve over time, and seasons change, that would have made the God a pretty clever being, and there would have been no arguments."

I pushed my hand through the wall and felt the warmth of her fingers close over mine, and my heart beat a little faster as I said, "Can you see if you can make a hole in the other wall?"

"OK," she replied, but she did not move away immediately, keeping her hand in mine for a few seconds longer. When she released my hand, I retreated from under the table and lay on the bed with my hands cradling my head, fingers interlocked. My mind drifted back to the night the Cardinal visited and the vision of my father with a crossbow bolt buried in his chest dropping to the floor and my mother's cries in the house as I stared out of the cart box in the street. And for the first time since that night, I cried.

Chapter 3—Shaun

I must have laid there for some time, drifting off to sleep and waking with a start from a dream. I can only vaguely remember fleeting images, the Cardinal's piercing, dark eyes moving toward me, no face or body; a large, curved blade dropping from the sky; black ravens picking at bones. Why these images, I don't know, but they frightened me. I had no idea what time of day it was, but my stomach was beginning to rumble. It must be close to the second meal of the day that Mags mentioned. Moving off the bed, I returned to our brick portal under the table.

"Mags, you there?"

"Not now, Abalus, the next meal should be here any moment. Get out from under the table."

I quickly replaced the brick in the wall and returned to my bed. I had barely settled my head back on the pillow when there was the now-familiar click of the door lock. The door swung open. I was expecting a guard to walk in, but that was not the case. A low, whirring noise came from outside the door. As the noise approached, two small red orbs embedded in a black cylinder floated into my cell. I stayed frozen on my bed and just followed this cylinder with my eyes, barely moving my head. The cylinder was black and smooth with the exception of indentations where the red light emitted. I could not see any other moving parts, although it might have had wheels underneath, but the cylinder was so low to the ground. The only sound was the low, whirring noise. The cylinder stood slightly higher than the tabletop, and as I watched with frightened curiosity, the cylinder stopped in front of the table and turned so the red orbs were facing the table. It seemed to adjust its position so it was central to the table. I leaned over to get a better view of what it was doing. There was a gentle click, and a small aperture opened in the front just above the two red orbs. A thin arm with two fingers and a thumb extended out of the aperture and gripped round the empty plate on the table and drew the plate into itself. As soon as the empty plate disappeared, the small arm extended with a fresh plate of food. The arm withdrew, the aperture closed, and the cylinder whirred round and floated back out of the cell. The door closed, and the click of the lock secured the cell once more. Now I knew why I had not seen anyone taking food down into the cells previously, but I still didn't know where the black cylinders came from. What were they? Were they machines from our past? Come to think of it, what was that strange tablet making odd noises in the hands of the guard at the desk when I first got here? The more I saw of this place, the stranger it seemed to be.

I moved over to the table to inspect the food on the plate. Picking up the spoon, somewhat misshapen by its use to carve away the seams in the wall, I took a scoop of the dull—brown, fibrous-looking stuff and gingerly stuck my tongue out to sample the flavor. It was slightly warm and tasted a bit like pumpkin with something else added. I was hungry, so I took the plate back to my bed, sat, and finished off the meal. Returning the plate back to the table, I crouched back underneath, removed the brick, and quietly called Mags's name.

"How's the digging going in the other cells—any news?"

"Well, the cell next to me has got through to the one on the other side—that's Sarai; she's thirteen. But, the cell on the other side of her is taking a bit longer. It's occupied by a young boy. He's only nine, but he is doing his best." Mags stopped briefly to take a breath.

I cut in, "OK, let me know as soon as we have a link to Shaun."

Mags bent down to peer through the hole, "Did you see the black food delivery thingy?"

"Yes, where does it come from?"

"I don't know. No one has seen its arrival because, at breakfast time, we are all out of the cells up in the courtyard, and the evening meal, we are all in here. No one has seen it at any other time."

Mags continued, "Don't touch it, whatever you do. I've heard other kids say, if you touch it, it causes your muscles to twitch uncontrollably, and you go all weak. Don't try run-ning out the door either, as it can fire a thin wire at you, and the same thing happens. There was a commotion a couple of nights ago, and I heard that it was Shaun. He had tried to run out."

"Mags, did you ever find anything else on the farm be-sides books?"

"Well, we found bits and pieces of rusty machinery. I think our land has been a farm for a very long time. Some of the machinery, Dad figured out by the shape of it that they could have been used for digging up the soil and turning it over. Dad tried to pull it apart and fix it, but most of it was so rotten that it just fell apart. There was some smaller stuff as well. There was one thing; it had a circular stone attached to a round case. The case had a piece of metal string coming out of it with prongs on the end. Dad took the stone off the end and used it to sharpen blades and things.

There were other bits and pieces, but most seemed to fall apart in your hands as soon as you touched it."

She paused as if in thought and then continued, "There was one curious thing we did find that was almost as if it were deliberately hidden."

"Deliberately hidden?" I repeated.

She continued, "It was buried in a wooden box wrapped in this black, shiny cloth bag. The bag was not made of woven thread, and it was sort of stretchy. My dad threw a piece of it into the fire, and rather than burn, it sort of shrank into a tiny ball and gave off this really black smoke with an awful smell. Inside the box was something wrapped really tightly in a clear film type of cloth, similar to the black bag, but you could see through it. The thing was wrapped so tightly that it took ages to get it unwrapped. It was about the size of a large book. It unfolded and opened to show a set of small buttons, each with a letter of the alphabet and numbers on them. Dad pressed all the different buttons. When he hit one, a gentle whirring noise came from the book, and the blank lid started showing words and numbers that flicked on and off. After a while, the screen just went blue, and everything stopped. Then, a little light on the front started flashing red, and above it were the words 'Batt low.' After that, it just went all blank and quiet again. We never got it to show any more words after that."

"I'd like to see that," I said. "Have you still got it?"

"Yes, Dad wrapped it back up, put it back in the box, and hid it in the barn."

Mags pulled away from our small portal, and all was quiet for a moment. Her face returned into view. "Sarai says the little boy has made a hole through to Shaun's cell."

"Great, pass this message to Shaun—tell him my name is Abalus and I want to speak with him. Tell him I think I know how we could escape from here." *That should get his attention,* I thought.

Mags disappeared from the hole in the wall, and over the other side of her cell, I could hear her whispering to Sarai. I hoped the young boy on the other side of her did not muddle up the message. The wait for a reply felt like forever, but eventually, Mags reappeared in the frame of the wall.

"Shaun says tomorrow, when we get let out to the court-yard, he'll create a distraction, and you can step back down the line to him."

I smiled to myself. "OK, ask him what he was put in here for."

There was another long pause before the response came back.

Mags said, "Because I found out too much!"

"What does that mean, Mags?"

"I don't know."

"Do you think he had a big stash of books or something?" I ventured.

"Hang on; I'll ask."

Another long pause ensued as the question passed across each cell boundary. The answer came back via Mags rather more of a question than an answer.

"He found the Exhibition Center?"

I hoped that I would understand what that meant tomorrow when I got to talk to Shaun properly.

Mags and I talked some more about our homes and parents. She made one comment that both puzzled and disturbed me. Each family in the town of Malahim only had one child, which was strange, because, when I thought about it, that was the same for my own village. Why was that? Eventually, we fell into a silence, and shortly after, the lights in the cell went dim yellow. It was time to sleep, not that I felt much like sleep. My mind alive with questions about this place and about what Shaun had discovered. Mags stayed at the hole in the wall talking for a while longer but soon fell into silence. We looked at one another in the gloom, and for the second time, her hand came through the aperture and touched my face. I leaned toward it to press my skin close to hers. It felt good to have some kind of contact, warm and comforting somehow. I clasped her hand in mine, gently kissed her fingers, and said good night.

I withdrew from under the table and lay back onto the bed, wishing it was already morning and I would be able to talk to Shaun. It was going to be a long night.

"All right you young sinners, it's time for your morning jaunt in the sun." I awoke the next morning with these words ringing loud in my ears. I have no idea how long it was before I fell asleep, but I felt drowsy as if I had not been asleep for very long. Again, I heard the clanking of pots as kids in their cells retrieved them in preparation for the doors to unlock so we could all march out. As soon as my cell door clicked, I was out and immediately looked to my left to see Mags first; down the line stood Shaun. His defiant gaze was cast toward the guard, who sneered menacingly back at him but said nothing. Shaun nodded acknowledgement that he recognized me. As we formed a line like yesterday, there were three kids in front of me. Mags stood behind me, then Sarai and the young boy. Shaun was next in line, followed by another young lad and several other children after that. We turned and faced the stairs as directed and started the walk up into the sunlight. I had just taken a few paces out into the courtyard when there was a scuffle behind me. I heard Shaun's voice raised and turned to see what was going on. Shaun was giving the young lad behind him a piece of his mind as he had apparently walked into the back him and slopped his pot over the back of Shaun's pants. Shaun, after being loudly verbal, marched forward and in front of me, loudly proclaiming that he was not going to be stuck in a line with babies who can't hold onto their own pee. The guards laughed with amusement but did not object to Shaun's change of place in the line.

"What happened?" I said.

Shaun turned and smiled at me. "When the guard was not looking in our direction, I stopped walking, and the lad behind bumped straight into me. The rest you heard."

"What's the Exhibition Center?" That was the question that had been on my mind most of the night.

"It's a big building where they used to display machinery and technology," replied Shaun.

"What's technology?"

Shaun continued, "The lights in our cells, the food robot, the cell guard's panel he spends all his time looking at and fiddling with—that's all technology. Our ancestors long ago used to make all sorts of things. I saw some of what they used to make at the Exhibition Center. It's called Erls Cort; at least, that's what I could make out from the letters."

Puzzled, I asked, "So, what happened to it all?"

"I don't really know, but I think the answer might be to do with something else I found."

By now, the line had halted to wait the unlocking of the chute for us to throw out the contents of our pots.

Shaun turned fully to face me and whispered intensely, "If you want to know more, when we get to the chute, follow my lead."

I stared back blankly at him but said nothing.

The queue started moving again as the chute, like a beckoning mouth, accepted the refuse being thrown at it. As Shaun approached, I saw his body visibly tighten in preparation to spring into action. It suddenly dawned on me what he was about to do, and as this revelation struck, Shaun had ran the few short steps toward the chute and dove headlong into the gaping mouth. The guard by the wall was frozen to the spot in surprise, and then his realization sprung him into action. It was now or never—no time to think—and I ran and launched myself into the chute. The smell was terrible and the flies. But, the wet slopes assisted in the sliding down toward the outer wall. In front, I could see Shaun frantically scrambling toward the exit, and then he dropped out of sight. Light from the day streamed back up the chute. I heard Mags yell my name behind me. I stopped briefly to look back up the chute to see Mags half in and half out of the chute with large hands dragging her out by the ankles. I wished she had made it, too. I would miss her. But, the thirst for knowledge returned me to my efforts to get down the chute. A few more seconds of frantic crawling got me to the exit point, and the drop to the stream was about three people high. I hesitated and then saw Shaun pulling himself out of the stream, beckoning me to jump. I was briefly airborne, and then the chilling cold of the stream penetrated my clothes. It was just as well; coming down the chute was not a pleasant experience. A few strokes and I was at the far bank. Shaun held out his hand to haul me out. As I stood next to him, we could hear cheers of children from inside the walls of prison. I thought I heard Mags shout my name, but I couldn't be certain. Perhaps it was wishful thinking. Shaun grabbed my arm and pulled my attention back to the open run to the forest beyond.

"Come on, we have to run fast for the woods over there. It won't be long before they come out the main gate on the other side of the prison and make chase. We need to get into cover before they get round the wall and gain sight of us. We stand a better chance of avoiding capture if they don't see where we enter the woods."

He turned toward the forest and started running, I followed, barely able to keep up. A couple of hundred paces saw us to the outskirts of the forest, and as we melted into the tall bracken and shrubs, I stopped for a breather and looked back toward the prison. Just as I glanced at the walls on the gentle rise, the guards came into view on the right, rounding the edge of the wall. I ducked below the height of the bracken and turned to move deeper into the forest at a stoop to keep out of sight. I had glimpsed at least one guard on horseback. So, it would not take long for them to reach the forest outskirts. I ran to catch up with Shaun, not looking back anymore. Shaun seemed to know what direction to go and veered off to the right and up a rise toward what looked like some kind of embankment. Our path took us through blackberry bushes that tore at our clothes and scratched at our skin. Shaun, I think, was making it as hard as possible for the guards and the horse rider to follow our tracks. Our movements would sometimes scare birds in the trees; hopefully, the guards would not be too observant. As we reached the top of the rise, we skirted round what seemed to be some kind of stone wall, mostly buried in the earth. As we followed the perimeter, Shaun suddenly stopped dead in his tracks and turned to face the embankment.

"Somewhere along here is an entrance into the wall. Start looking."

"What is this place?"

"Shhh, just find the entrance," came the reply.

Moving along, I reached an area of wall covered in ivy and scrabbled about to feel the stone behind. Shaun was doing the same. Suddenly, he grabbed my arm and pulled me into a section of ivy. Behind was a tunnel, dark and narrow, and I had to walk with a stoop to keep my head from striking the roof. As we moved deeper, it all went pitch black. All we could do was keep our palms on the walls and step forward, feeling our way deeper into the tunnel. A few more steps and I lost contact with the wall as it seemed to open out. I heard Shaun ahead of me, scratching about, when suddenly, a small prick of light burst into being from his fingers.

"They're called matches," said Shaun in explanation. In the light, I could see we were in some kind of cave. Shaun picked up a small glass pot and held the match to the wick of a candle. He then used this candle to light another.

"This is where I have been hiding books since I was fourteen."

"So close to that place," I said, pointing in some arbitrary direction to indicate the prison.

"What better place than right under their noses, so to speak? They scour the towns and villages far away from here."

"What is this place?" I repeated.

"Don't really know, but this rise is made up of these tunnels and small rooms like this, and all the walls seem to be made of bags of sand and dirt. In some of the rooms, the bags are falling apart, and the walls are collapsing."

I took another look around the space now that my eyes were beginning to accustom to the candlelight. To my left was a large trunk, and next to it was a chair with padded cushions. Shaun saw where my attention was drawn, moved over to the trunk, and opened it. Placing the candle beside the chair, I looked inside the trunk, and it was full of books and papers with pictures of all sorts of things—cars, women, buildings, food, and all sorts of machinery and technology I had never seen before. I almost fell into the chair, picked out papers, and flicked through all sorts of pictures. Shaun stood by the tunnel entrance we had come down, keeping a keen ear for any voices from outside.

I kept pulling out papers, looking at pictures—women in sparkly dresses of all sorts of colors, they looked so beautiful. I tried to imagine Mags in one of the dresses and immediately felt sorry she did not make it here with us. There were even pictures of men and women with pictures all over their bodies and rings and beads of metal hanging from different parts of their bodies. I saw pictures of beautiful gardens full of flowers and houses that looked so big that the families must have been large with lots of children for such expansive dwellings; pictures of big, white boats like I had never seen before with engines—not paddles like we had—and not made of wood.

The question in my head again was, "What happened? We did all this, but where did it all go?"

"It's to do with his Eminence, I think," Shaun said in a low voice.

"What do you mean?"

"The Cardinal is a machine, a special type of machine called a robot. I have seen pictures of him or one like him at the Exhibition Center. Some of the machines were kept in sealed glass displays, so you could see them but not touch them. Whatever happened then, these machines seemed to have survived."

Shaun paused to listen for voices outside then went on, "I found some thin books and papers in a building that at some time housed thousands and thousands of books. A library . . . the British Library. Some of these books were called *New Scientist*. They had all sorts of stories of things being discovered and how they might be used to make our ancestors' lives better. I read stories like using rats' brains to control robots and even human brains to control robots."

"What are you saying? I don't understand."

Shaun continued, "There was another path of science called nanotechnology; it had to do with really tiny machines, so small you could not see them. They developed nanorobots that were made to break down waste materials left over from all the things they made. They were always making stuff and finding new ways to get things done faster or play games to entertain themselves; things were thrown away and replaced with something newer and better. These nanorobots were used together with something called bacteria, which are very small creatures that we cannot see, to break down all sorts of chemicals and rubbish. There used to be large factories where the waste materials were taken to be broken down into small particles to remove materials they could reuse. It was all tightly controlled. No one was allowed near the factories; they were completely sealed."

Shaun paused as if in thought when we heard a noise somewhere up along the tunnel. Shaun shrank back into the shadows, blowing out his candle. I dove for the second one I'd placed beside the trunk and slapped my hand over it. The pain in the center of my palm was intense, but I did not cry out. I crouched on the far side of the room in the darkness that enveloped us, not daring to breath. There was a shuffling noise as if something were coming down the tunnel. I could hear a sniffing and scratching getting closer and closer. Then, it suddenly went quiet. The silence was broken by a low, grumbling growl. I dared not move or breathe. My heart was pounding at my chest, and my legs began to quiver, ready for flight out of this dark hole, the haven of knowledge. As my eyes accustomed to the gloom, I could barely make out the shape of Shaun standing close to the tunnel. Against the small amount of light coming down the tunnel from outside, I could see the shape of what I thought was a large dog. It gave a low growl but did not move. For a couple of seconds, no one moved, then the dog gave another low grumble and sank to the floor, panting. Shaun took a step toward the creature. It pricked up its ears and raised its head off the floor but did nothing to suggest it was about to attack. Shaun approached and knelt beside the animal.

"Abalus, light the candle. I think it's injured."

Shaun tossed me the small box of matches. I took out a small stick and rubbed the nodule end down the rough side of the box. It sparked into life, and in fright, I dropped it; the match fell to the floor and went out. Knowing what to expect this time, I lit a second and stared at it in wonder as it slowly burnt toward my fingers. Feeling the heat close to my fingertips took me out of my trance, and I grabbed the candle from the floor, held the match to the center wick, and dropped the match before the heat got too intense. Moving over to Shaun, the light from my candle reflected in the animal's eyes as I approached. It was a dog of sorts, and it had a crossbow bolt stuck in the side of its belly. I looked back up the tunnel to see glistening spots of blood on the dusty floor. The dog whimpered as Shaun gently fingered the bolt.

"We've got to get this out. Hold his head firmly to stop him moving, cos' this is going to hurt him."

I knelt down and cradled the dog's head in both arms, resting it on my thighs. Shaun placed his left hand on the dog's belly with the bolt straddled by his second and third fingers. He gripped the shaft of the bolt, breathed in, held his breath, and pulled sharply upward. The dog yelped in pain and struggled to get up, but I held his head firmly. It was obvious that he was too weak to break free. The dog relaxed in my arms. Shaun breathed out heavily and tossed the bolt to one side. In the corner was a dusty black bag. Shaun went over, grabbed the bag, and returned to the side of the dog. Opening the bag, he pulled out an old shirt of sorts and placed it over the wound to soak up the blood. He began ripping up some sheets into a bandage to wrap around the dog's belly to hold the pad in place. The dog gave no resistance; it was too weak from the loss of blood.

"Nothing else we can do for him now, just wait and see if he lives," Shaun said.

I returned to the chair and the books and papers I was looking at.

"I reckon that's a bolt from the search party out looking for us. I wonder whose dog that is." Shaun stood up from his bandaging efforts and returned to his previous sentry position by the tunnel.

I said what we were both thinking, "Do you think the owner has been killed?"

"Maybe," Shaun replied.

I looked back toward the dog and where the bag lay. It was shiny in the flickering candlelight.

"You know, that bag looks like something Mags was telling me about. Her dad had dug up a small wooden box with a black shiny bag inside it. The bag was covering a something that looked like a large book, only it wasn't."

Shaun turned toward me. "The bag is made of a material called plastic. Our ancestors made an awful lot of that stuff, so much so that it became part of their waste and rubbish problem. It got used for all sorts of throwaway stuff. You could mould and shape this material into all sorts of things, but when it was no longer wanted, it was not easy to get rid off. It would end up in those factories I told you about."

It suddenly struck me that I knew nothing of Shaun's past, and I raised the question, "Where are your parents, Shaun?"

There was a long pause that felt sort of awkward as if I had said something wrong, and I was about to change the subject as a sort of apology when Shaun breathed out heavily and in a low voice said, "They're both dead."

"I'm sorry, Shaun," I was not going to venture any further but Shaun continued.

"My mum died five years ago after giving birth to my sister."

"You have a sister?" I marveled.

"No, she was stillborn—it means dead at birth; my mum died soon after that from loss of blood."

Shaun fell silent for a while, and I did not break the silence. The dog's labored breathing was the only sound I could hear.

"Dad was devastated. We would have been the only family of our village to have two children."

That indeed would have been something awesome, I thought.

Shaun continued, "From that point on, Dad was always asking why. Why this, and why that? He seemed to question everything. The visiting Father for our village became concerned, reported it back to his Eminence, and we got a visit, the first of several over that year after mother died. Dad questioned the Holy Writings. Who was the Lord Master? Why had no one ever seen Him? If what one is taught in the Book only raises further questions, why is it so bad to want to seek knowledge beyond the Writings? Surely, if the Holy Writings raise questions, then does it mean we are not being given the whole story? Anyway, Dad used to have frequent arguments with the Father."

Shaun paused in reflection.

"Go on," I said.

"One of Dad's friends in the village was a keeper of forbidden books, and he lent one to Dad. It was a book of maps, ever so detailed, of a big city called London. It shows all sorts of locations; they all had names and connecting roads. That's where the Erls Cort and British Library are. In the front of the book were pictures of some of the buildings around London. We did not know it then, but as it turns out, our village is about a six-day ride from what was London. After the second visit from the Cardinal, which surprised us a bit, as I thought we would be taken for sure, Dad decided that we should leave for a while and explore the country beyond our village. We packed a few things and food, Dad's friend lent us the map book again and a second horse for me, and we set off.

We came across a river and followed the current direction. I don't know why, but Dad thought it was the River Thames, which runs down and through the old city. You see, our village was called Cerenstor, and Dad thought it sounded so close to a place called Cirencester in the map book. So, we started traveling south, and sure enough, we came across a river. From there, we followed the river sometimes, but it tended to twist and turn a lot, but with the map, we would travel from where the sun rises—east, my dad said. Then, we came to some areas that looked as if they might have been big roads at one time. Dad seemed to think we could have traveled on one called the M4. It was not so much a road as a line through the trees where only grass and shrubs seemed to grow. Trees in some places just stopped at the border. We met a few people on the way and shared stories. We were not the only people to have traveled to find this big city."

Shaun paused, moved over to the dog, and rested a hand on his head, gently stroking down his neck and quietly talking.

"What shall we call him?" Shaun glanced my way.

"Barkley, I always wanted a dog, and I would have called it Barkley."

"Barkley it is, then." Shaun gently patted the dog's neck.

"I'm getting hungry. We have not eaten since last night," I said offhandedly.

The suggestion of food stirred the pangs of hunger in Shaun as well.

"I've got that covered; I've not only stored books here but some dried food as well."

Shaun got up from beside the dog, moved toward the back wall of the room, and pushed against the wall. It gave way to reveal another tunnel deeper into the rise. After a few moments and the sound of scrabbling about, Shaun reappeared with another black, plastic bag. He opened the bag, and inside were smaller, clear plastic bags with dried apple slices, nuts, pears, and some dried, salty meat strips that tasted smoky. Shaun explained these bags were found in London when they were there, and he brought them back with him when they returned to Cerenstor.

Shaun tried to tempt Barkley to eat some of the dried meat strips, but he was not interested in eating.

"We need to get some water, for us as well as Barkley," I said.

"We must wait for nightfall and go back to the stream outside the wall of the prison," Shaun replied. "It's not safe yet."

This day was going to be long, the wait an eternity. I hoped Barkley would get better.

Chapter 4—London, February, 2015 CE

Professor Geoffrey Short looked up from his podium and gazed at his audience of eminent scientists, engineers, and politicians. They had listened attentively to his concerns regarding the application of memrister technology into nanomachines. Providing a nanomachine with a capacity to learn without a tested framework of inhibitors would be dangerous. Professor Short believed the core functionality for which the nanomachine was designed should be not auto-modifiable, especially replicators. He proposed that this was inherently dangerous. Both technologies were still, relatively speaking, in their infancy, and until they were both fully understood, combining them, in his mind, was simply asking for trouble. He knew the pressures some of these scientists were subjected to from the political fraternity; indeed, he was subjected to them himself. Highly respected in their fields, the bulk of his audience were here because they, like himself, were working to provide innovative solutions to global warming, reclamation, and recycling of increasingly rare raw materials from waste products. Oil and other raw materials were not going to last forever. Everyone knew that. Earth's continuing expanding human population and the demands it placed on these primary resources were becoming increasingly more prevalent in the public awareness via the media and the Internet, at least in Western society. Since he was a child, Geoffrey Short realized that his existence in the modern world was surrounded by the marvels of technology. He decided at a very young age that he wanted to be a scientist. It was an ideal area for him to choose. Before his early teens, it was evident to his parents that he was smarter than the average kid. They decided to have him tested, and he scored in the 98th percentile on IQ tests and gained entry to Mensa. His career as a microbiologist gained him a reputation within the scientific community as a farsighted individual. Today, he was hoping that his concerns, along with his track record in the microbial recycling technologies, would carry enough weight to sway the political faction of this assembly to change or at least modify the policies regarding raw material reclamation. In his mind, political pressure was compromising the rigor with which much of the work in this area was being conducted.

"Professor Short," said a thin voice from the back of the theater, projected well by the acoustics of the surroundings.

"Yes sir, what is your name?" replied Geoffrey.

"I am Norman Quigley—I'm sure you are aware I am the Minister of Mineral Reclamation and Primary Resources."

As the minister stood up, Professor Short immediately recognized the thin, balding politician from his interviews on TV.

"Yes, Minister, you have a question for me?"

"Professor Short, I am sure you aware that it is of vital importance that we must develop the technology to reclaim up to fifty percent of the rare metals by 2018. Metals such as platinum, palladium, rhodium, and iridium are of key importance to the petroleum, pharmaceutical, and electronics industries, to name just the primaries. New deposits of gold and nickel of any significant size have not been found over the last decade. Surely, you understand that anything we can do to reclaim these metals is of primary concern for government for the good of the public?"

"Mr. Quigley, I agree with you a hundred percent, but I do not agree that the program of nanotechnology should be crow barred by combining infant technologies before they are sufficiently understood. The general public would not thank us for developing an invisible machine that cannot be controlled and has no limits placed on its capacity to learn."

"Yes, I daresay," Quigley said dismissively and went on, "I daresay then that the work being carried out in the USA of combining microorganisms with nanotechnology in a symbiotic structure to break down liquid organic waste products is also something you do not agree with?"

Geoffrey had heard of this work and studied the white papers that had come out of MIT. In fact, he had been in contact with the project leader and discussed at length some of the implications of this. Of course, it was unlikely that Quigley knew this.

"Minister, I have been in consultation with Dr. Sonia Alderbry on this very subject. I am confident that her team at MIT are heading in the right direction and are taking adequate measures to test and document the effects on several microorganisms with single-loop DNA structures. Dr. Alderbry is keeping me up-to-date with her findings."

The minister raised his hand to interject.

"In that case, are you also aware that her teams are looking to incorporate memristors in the development of her nanomachines?"

Geoffrey felt his face turn red as blood flushed his cheeks—this he had not been aware of. He resolved to speak with Sonia at the earliest opportunity.

"I . . . I . . . No, I was not aware of this, Minister."

"Well, it seems the Americans are going ahead of us in this area. I suggest that, if the Americans intend to proceed with this, then there should be little to stop us. After all, we have the best people working on this, including yourself." He smiled, knowing the embarrassment he had caused.

Geoffrey faced a sea of faces waiting for some answer from him. He had none to give.

"Ladies and gentlemen, if there are no further questions, I have other pressing matters to attend to." With that, he picked up his presentation papers and left the theater, voices humming in the background as people left. He needed to get straight back to his office and call the States. He had a lot to say to Dr. Alderbry.

As he reached his office, he flung open the door and tossed his presentation papers in the big, round filing cabinet beside the desk. Without moving round to be seated, he leaned over the desk, grabbed the cordless phone, and started pacing up and down the office while he punched keys and called up Dr. Alderbry's phone number from the list. Several rings on the other end resulted in his being transferred to her message bank.

At the beep, he said, "Sonia, it's Geoffrey. Call me asap. It's extremely important."

He punched the *call end* key and tossed the phone on his desk. As he paced up and down, he started to formulate what he was going to say to her.

He stopped pacing, sat down at his desk, leaned over, and retrieved his presentation papers from the bin. Placing them back in the manila folder, he marked them with the title and date label format of his filing system. Cradling his head in his palms, he fell lazily forward, placed his elbows on the desk, and rested the weight. No sooner had he settled than the phone rang and made him jump. He grabbed the phone and took a deep breath, ready to let rip.

"Geoffrey, I got your message. I'm glad you called. I have some important news to tell you."

Her voice was full of enthusiasm, and he could hear the excitement in her voice. It had a dissipating effect on his anger.

"Sonia, when were you going to tell me about incorporating memristor technology into your research?"

"Ah, you found out. Who told you?" Her voice took on a note of caution.

"I just found out during the question time after my presentation expressing the potential dangers of integrating these two technologies. The Minister of Mineral Reclamation and Primary Resources informed me of your intention. I can't tell you how embarrassing that was, Sonia."

"Geoff, I'm sorry. I really am. The decision to incorporate memristors is not mine. This is coming from higher up the food chain, bloody nose height."

Geoffrey half guessed that this was the case.

"Sonia, be extremely careful how fast and far you take this. Can you e-mail me a list of all bacteria forms you are currently working with? Also a list of other candidates you might be looking at in the future?"

"No problem—I'll do that after this call," replied Dr. Alderbry.

"Now, what is the exciting news you wanted to tell me about?"

"We've succeeded in combining a nanomachine with anaerobic bacteria. The potential in liquid waste breakdown is enormous. In the future, we should be able to manipulate the bacteria's genetic structure and speed up the cell division process. The nanomachines can target specific sections of the DNA strand in the nucleoid. We could also look at ways to increase mobility, particularly with spirillum forms. This could help in breaking down more viscous materials, and it could cut down the need for the constant agitators in chemical recycling plants. Less energy usage helps the bottom line."

Geoff began to feel a little uncomfortable.

"OK, OK, Sonia, I admire your enthusiasm; it's a great achievement, but just don't get ahead of yourself. Don't lose your objectivity."

"Geoff, I understand. I do really," she paused briefly, a little deflated by Geoff's somewhat neutral response. "Look, I've got to go. I have another meeting in fifteen minutes."

Geoff sighed, "Sure, I'll be in touch; don't forget to forward me that list of bacterium."

"You'll get it shortly. Bye, Geoff, and don't worry. I know what I'm doing."

Geoff put the phone back in its cradle, thinking to himself, *Sonia, I have confidence in you but not the narrow-minded people above you in the food chain.*

He sat down at his desk and stared at the coffee stain and biscuit crumbs on his notepad, wondering how many bacteria had set up residence in the brown, irregular ring in the paper. After several minutes passed as he mused over his presentation and whether he had been forceful enough in his warning, he picked up his pen, opened the desk draw, pulled out his personal journal, and began to make notes of this day, 12 February 2015.

Chapter 5—The Journey

"Shaun, take me to London. I want to see this library and Exhibition Center."

Darkness had fallen, and Shaun was folding up another of those black bags and stuffing it in his pocket. We were about to set off for some water.

"Are you nuts? What the hell do you want to go there for?"

"There is so much I don't understand about what happened before the Lord Master, and what about his Eminence? Mags told me you had killed him. Did you?"

"No."

"What happened?"

"It was while we were in London. The Cardinal and his personal guards must have followed us. Maybe later, OK? First, we must get some water for the dog and ourselves."

I breathed a sigh of acceptance and followed Shaun up the tunnel back out onto the top of the rise. The sun was disappearing over the horizon to our left, the last rays of the day glinting through the trees as they swayed gently in the evening breeze. Shaun backtracked the way we had come earlier, keeping quiet and stopping occasionally, listening intently to the sounds of the woods. No sounds of human voices in the distance could be heard. Eventually, we came to the track that led out of the wood to the clearing, and in the commencing gloom as the sun disappeared, the shadow of our prison imposed itself on the darkening sky.

Shaun dropped to a crouch in the bracken and surveyed the clearing toward the stream.

"We'll wait here until it is totally dark. I don't want any chance of us being seen from the prison if the guards are looking outward rather than inward from the walls." Shaun spoke in a low whisper, aware of how sound can carry on the silence of the enveloping night.

Soon, the fort could not be made out against the dark sky, and if a moon were to rise, it was most likely going to be partly obscured by the clouds still rolling across the sky.

Shaun tapped my shoulder, and we set off down the track and out of the safety of the woods into the exposed clearing.

After a while, we could hear the babbling water of the stream carried on the night air and knew we were getting close to the prison walls. Once we arrived at the bank, Shaun pulled out the plastic bag from his pocket, unfolded it, and opened the neck of the bag to the flowing water. I waded into the stream to hold the bottom of the bag as Shaun kept the neck of the bag open. The cold chill of the water made my feet go numb. The bag could hold a lot of water, but it weighed too much to carry. We would not be able to drag the bag for fear of putting a hole in it. Also, we had to be able to navigate back through brambles without spiking the bag. After some testing of the weight, Shaun emptied the bag to about a third of what it could have held. This weight he could hold above his head, even though the water slopped around and made the bag difficult to carry. A third was plenty for us and the dog for a day or so. How we were to find our way back to Shaun's refuge in total darkness, I had no idea, but Shaun seemed not to be worried about this. I guessed he was well familiar with the woods if he had been hiding stuff here for the last couple of years. Back across the clearing was easy going, but once back in the woods, it was easy to stumble over dead branches and rocks. Progress was slow. Once we had got into the depths of the woods, Shaun stopped, reached into his pocket, pulled out a small, cylindrical object, and pressed his thumb on the side. There was a burst of light from this stick. A small, tight beam of light danced on the undergrowth. Shaun aimed it downward a pace or two in front of us.

"What is that?" I marveled.

"Don't know what it's called, but it's very handy. I had two of them once, but one slowly faded and stopped working. Found them in London."

"Erls Cort?" I quizzed.

"Yep," Shaun replied and moved on with his light stick, and I followed, carrying the bag. As we reached the brambles, we swapped over, and I carried the torch while Shaun took the bag of water above his head to keep from catching on the thorns. Shaun was taller than I, so he had no trouble keeping the bag clear.

Occasionally, he would instruct me turn left or right, and eventually, we were at the top of the rise and searching for the ivy-covered entrance. As we approached a section of the ivy, the low, throaty grumbling of the dog could be heard. As we homed in on this sound, the entrance was located, and we moved down the tunnel.

Barkley, rather than lying on his side as we had left him, was now laid down on all fours with his head held up. His tail beat the dirt a couple of times in weak greeting. It was a good sign. Shaun disappeared in the back of the room and returned with a two wooden bowls. I helped him pour water into a bowl for Barkley. We both smiled to see the dog begin to drink. I picked up the dried meat strips to see if Barkley would eat. He gingerly took it from my hand and gently chewed on it. Not the usual enthusiasm and gusto I have seen dogs eat with. But, it was good that he was taking food. Shaun and I took long draughts of water from the remaining bowl. Water never tasted so good and welcome after nothing for the whole day. We ate some more with water to wash down the dried fruits and meat.

The meal finished, my thoughts returned to London and the Exhibition Center. There's so much I don't know about our past and our ancestors, what they had achieved, and what had gone wrong.

"Shaun, can you take me there . . . to London? I want to see this Exhibition Center for myself and the library."

"Why?"

"Perhaps we can find out what happened. Are you not curious about that? You've read some books and seen more than me. Don't you want to find out more?"

Shaun looked at me with a steely glint in his eye, "What do you hope to gain from knowing more? You'll be executed for sure."

"I attacked the Cardinal and stabbed him in the throat, remember? I don't think I am going to avoid being executed if I'm captured again anyway. I'd rather be executed knowing why than not knowing."

Shaun's steady gaze in the candlelight seemed to recognize himself in my response. He dropped his eyes from mine and looked across to Barkley.

"What about the dog?"

"We can take him with us; he's got nowhere else to go by the looks of it."

Shaun thought for a moment.

"We'll have to wait a couple of days for Barkley's wound to heal. In the meantime, we will have to forage for food for the journey. Find something better to carry water. The journey was six days on horseback. Unless we find horses, we'll be walking and carrying our own provisions. Of course, don't forget we are still being hunted by the prison guards."

I gave this some thought.

"After two days looking for us, they will be spread out a bit thin, so we should be able to avoid them quite easily. Have you still got the map book you told me about?"

"Yes, it's in the chest over there."

"Do you know where we are in the map book? Compared to Cirenstor or London?"

"We are east of Cirenstor in a place I think was called Oxford on the map. The closest village from here is called Garston."

Shaun went over to the trunk, rummaged around, and pulled out a book with *Maps of the British Isles* written on the crumpled cover. The book had loose pages coming out, and it was badly soiled with age, but Shaun knew what pages he was looking for. I peered over his shoulder as he sat in the chair by the trunk. His finger pointed to Oxford as shown on the map, and in the candlelight, we searched the map for Garston.

"There, look," I cried excitedly, pointing on the map a little to the right and down from Oxford, "Garsington."

Shaun followed my finger onto the page in the candlelight. "Could be. At least, it's a start point."

"If we travel east from here, we should come to a wide track with no trees growing on it. Used to be a big road called the M40. That should take us to London."

There was a grumbling from the tunnel entrance and a scuffling noise. Barkley had risen up and taken a couple steps toward us; his head came into the dim candlelight. He gave another low grumble and tentatively moved toward us. Shaun looked at me and grinned, and I returned his smile and beckoned Barkley to come forward, holding out another dried meat strip. Barkley gently took the piece of meat, sat down in front of the chair, and chewed on the morsel. We spent some time planning what we needed to gather together for the journey. The air was cold as night progressed. Shaun produced another two black plastic bags from the chest at the back of the room, cut holes—one in the top and one from each corner—slipped one of the bags over his head, and told me to do the same. I was amazed how the chill of the air seemed to lose its intensity. These plastic bags were truly very useful. They carry water, keep me warm, store food, keep clothes from dirt and damp, and protect technology buried in the ground.

I settled myself next to Barkley on the floor and threw my arm over his shoulders. Shaun settled in the chair, and we all fell asleep in the silence of our sanctuary underground.

I awoke the following morning to a wet tongue and cold nose pushing at my face. I opened my eyes to see the huge, dark eyes and snout of Barkley completely filling my field of view. And phew, what dog breath! Shaun was nowhere to be seen. I stood, looked toward the exit tunnel, and saw the glow of the day filtering through the ivy. Barkley walked tenderly toward the tunnel and looked back at me, waiting for me to follow, which I did. Casting the ivy aside, I stepped into the light. There was a dampness of morning dew hanging in the air, and as I breathed out, the cloud of moisture curled away to join the mist. Barkley disappeared off into the bracken, and I followed the path of shuddering fronds as Barkley paced through the undergrowth. Soon, I could see Shaun in the distance picking blackberries from the brambles and placing them in a black bag. Judging by the bulge in the bag, he had been here picking for a while. As I approached, Shaun said, "We can use these to eat as well as provide us with something to drink if we run out of water."

I started to pick berries as well. Barkley went off into the undergrowth and disappeared. I wondered whether he would return to us or just move on now that he was mobile. As the mist began to dissipate in the warming sun, we returned to our tunnel in the rise with a weighty amount of berries. Shaun retrieved two leather satchels from his trunk in the back of the room. Some of the berries were wrapped in cloth in small, cupful sizes, and the remainder stayed in the plastic bag, which Shaun squeezed and manipulated to make a juice. Some we set aside and ate as breakfast. As we returned to the map book to plan our trek, a rustling at the end of the tunnel saw Barkley return with a glint of victory in his eye and a rabbit clamped between his jaws. How he had managed to catch it, we will never know. He was such a large dog, and he was still recovering from a wound. Barkley dropped the rabbit on the floor in front us, sat down, and watched us. The look on his slobbery face seemed to say, "Well, cook it then."

"Shaun, I think Barkley is going to be sticking around for a while. It looks as if we have a hunter to help supply our journey."

"Well, let's cook this up. We've got a fair walk ahead of us; best start it at full strength."

There was plenty of dry twigs and kindling lying around, and with the use of matches, it was not long before we had a fire going. Shaun skinned the rabbit, and I tended the fire. It was not long before we were eating meat, and Barkley had his share as well.

"If we could find some string and hooks, we could make up some hand lines to fish with once we get to the river." The thought was spoken out loud for Shaun to hear. I wondered what else he might have contained in the trunk.

Shaun paused from stoking the fire as if pondering over a list in his head. He dropped the stick he was poking the fire with and went over to the trunk. I followed him over to peer into the container of curiosities it had become for me. There were more boxes of matches; the two wooden bowls; two mugs made of plastic; two sets of plastic knives, forks, and spoons; a crossbow and bolts; a pack of what looked a bit like pencils with the letters BIC written on the bag; a reel of clear, thin string; some books about food recipes; and a round glass that, when you looked through it, objects looked larger. "It's called a magnifying glass," Shaun said.

There was a mirror and a small, square, black object with rounded corners, a couple of knobs that turned on the top, and a short stem sticking out. When Shaun turned it on by turning one of the knobs, all that could be heard was a low ssshhhhh noise. Shaun handed me a single sheet of paper with a diagram of the handheld CB radio and instructions for use. Shaun had never gotten it to work; at least all it ever did was "sssshhhhh." I tossed it back in the trunk and grabbed the clear string. It felt smooth, like the plastic bag. I coiled it round both hands a couple of times and pulled to see how strong it was. It cut into my hands without snapping. It was indeed strong and would be good to use for fishing. In the bottom of the box, hidden under a few clothes, was a small, clear box with lots of hooks made of shiny metal. The box was sealed with many wraps of some kind of tape around the lid. I also found a knife with a dull, brown blade and wooden handle. It was crudely fashioned, the blade being irregular in shape with many dents along the edge.

"Shaun, can I take this knife?"

"Sure, but it's not much good; it loses its edge too easily. But it's good for some things that don't need too much force."

Shaun knelt beside me and took out the crossbow and bolts. He placed the bolts in his satchel, attached a strap to the crossbow, and slung it over his shoulder, adjusting so the crossbow sat well into the small of his back and could be brought round to target without having to unsling the bow from his body. I took a second look at the clothes in the trunk. There were some short-sleeved shirts, some pants made of a thick, blue material, a couple of skirts, wool jumpers, and some gloves of two different sizes. It looked to me as if two people lived here at one time, one male and one female. It explained the two bowls, two mugs, and so on.

I thought out loud, "I wonder who used to live here?"

In answer to my question, Shaun went over to the chest of books and papers, pulled out one rather large book, and handed it to me. "Take a look at this. It may be able to answer your question."

I took the book and opened it to the first page. It had pictures of people stuck to the pages, faded, and some had curled off and were loose between the pages. There were short captions written under each picture. As I flicked through the pages, there were two people who were the most frequently seen, and the words underneath described in brief where and when the picture was taken. The images showed the people hugging each other and holding hands, kissing, or just having fun. In the captions below, it seemed the male was named Martin and the girl was Angie. There was one picture of Martin with his face covered in paint and Angie brandishing a large brush, dripping with blue paint. She had the broadest, most delightful grin on her face. The book was not full; the last several pages were blank and showed no sign of being used. The pictures just stopped. If these were the previous occupants, I wondered how they ended up here. Some of the pictures showed some fine houses in the background, and some were obviously inside. There were things in the rooms I have never seen before, as well some fine furniture and brightly colored walls with pictures. Some of the pictures had older people in them as well. Perhaps they were parents of Martin and Angie.

I closed the book and looked around the room. I was alone. I didn't even notice Shaun had gone. Barkley had gone with him. Returning the book to the chest, I walked back up the tunnel into the daylight. The sun was moving into the western sky, indicating the afternoon was in full swing. I heard Barkley bark well off in the distance back down the rise. My thoughts moved to Mags and my mother, wondering whether they were still alive. I looked down at my hand, remembering the feel of Mags's hand on mine through the hole in the wall between our cells. I wished there was some way I could get them both out of that prison. I knew there was not. We had a narrow opportunity to escape and took it. The guards would now be more alert.

I sat at the mouth of the tunnel watching the sun glint through the trees and listening to the sounds of the woods. Off to my left, I heard Barkley in the distance, but the sound was a little closer. Not long afterward, Shaun broke through some bracken with Barkley and held up two squirrels, one rabbit, and a chicken; bloodstained fur showed where a crossbow bolt brought their day to an abrupt end.

Shaun grinned, "Chicken tonight, Abalus, and we'll skin the rest and seal them in plastic bags to take with us tomorrow."

Shaun returned to our cave and sat and plucked the chicken while I lit a fire. Shaun had obviously done this before. The chicken was plucked and gutted before the fire had fully taken. Barkley helped himself to the innards, and Shaun turned his attention to the other meat, preparing them for cooking and placing them in the bags. Later, we feasted on chicken as the afternoon turned to evening. The cave was getting a bit smoky, but the warm food and warm air made the eyes go heavy, and soon I dozed off by the fire, and I guessed that Shaun did as well.

A warm, slobbery tongue woke me for the second time. The air was chilled; it was dark outside, but the sound of dawn song could be heard drifting down the tunnel entrance.

I gave Shaun a shake of the shoulder, and he sat bolt upright, startled as if grabbed from a dream. He looked at me in the gloom, ran his fingers through his hair, and scratched his head vigorously to wake himself up. Without a word, we gathered our food and berry juice. We packed what we could in the satchels. I grabbed a couple of shirts out of the trunk and stuffed them in the satchel along with the string, hooks, the magnifying glass, the matches, one of the cooked squirrels, and bags of berries and dried fruit. Shaun did the same and slung the crossbow over his shoulder, picked up a bag of berry juice, passed it to me, and picked up the second.

"OK, let's go, Abalus."

It was the second time I had heard Shaun use my name.

We left the cave and set off back through brambles with the bags of juice held above our heads. Clear of the brambles, we turned east and walked toward the steadily brightening glow in the sky where the sun was soon to rise for the new day. Our journey had begun with a guess of where we were and what we should come across with the aid of a map book over 150 years old.

Chapter 6—15 May 2015 CE

"Geoff, it works! We have nanomachines able to modify the behavior of *Shewanella* bacterium, and we've got the bacteria growth rate up by 60 percent. We can program the nanomachines to seek out specific metals and herd the bacteria to locations of high concentrations of toxic metals."

Sonia was excited, almost shouting down the phone. Geoff had her on speaker but picked up the hand piece and brought it to his ear.

"Sonia, that's great news, but how are you controlling the mobility of the nanomachines and *Shewanella* together?"

"Geoff, it's early days. At the moment, they use a simple algorithm to search in grid patterns. When a metal source that's targeted is found, the probes relay a message back to other nanomachines until the communication pathway is set up in similar ways as you would see an ant colony set up a route to a source of food. The messages flow up and down the pathway, and the bacterium are guided to the source."

"What metals have you tested with?"

"At the moment, only iron oxide, but once we figure out what genetic modifications we can introduce via our nanomas, we should be able to expand the range of target metals. Titanium, manganese, nickel, mercury, copper, lead . . ."

"Hold it, hold it . . . nanomas?"

"Oh, sorry, that's what we call them—short for nanomachines. Anyway, this could develop into a whole new way to extract and reclaim these metals. We can reprogram the nanomas to modify the bioorganism to start a whole new generation that targets specific metals."

Alarm bells began to ring in Geoff's head.

"Sonia, reprogramming the nanomas means they must have some form of memory capacity. I thought we discussed the dangers of even contemplating this."

"Geoff, we've already tried it. It works—it's safe. A small sample of nanomas under development has memristors incorporated, enough to provide option switching within the search pattern criteria programs the nanomas run."

The line fell silent, and an awkward moment passed between them. Sonia realized that Geoff would no longer trust her integrity, and her cheeks flushed with a pang of guilt.

"Look, Geoff, I'm sorry. I know I promised I would not go down this path, but the pressure is on, and this overcomes some of the problems we were having."

"Sonia, you are now on a very uncertain path. What kind of fail-safes have you incorporated?"

"Geoff, there's been no need to consider that."

"What stops a nanoma from altering its search pattern criteria? What is the range of a nanoma with bacterium? How long can it survive without a bacterium coupled to it? Can it replicate without a bacterium coupled to it?"

"Geoff, you know the answers to some of those questions from early reports I sent you."

"I know, but that was before you introduced the memristors. Sonia, I don't like what I'm hearing. You realize that this must be tightly controlled."

"It is, Geoff. Don't worry

"Look, Sonia, I have to go. I have a lecture in five minutes. I'll talk to you tomorrow."

Geoff put the phone down and stared toward his office door. He was feeling very uncertain about the project and wished he was in the States to take a closer look. What else had Sonia not told him?

Call it expert intuition or just a gut feeling, but Geoff knew that one small oversight could have terrible consequences. He picked up his lecture notes and laptop and headed off to deliver his lecture on the chemistry of aerobic and anaerobic respiration to some aspiring, hormonally driven young students looking to become microbiologists.

On the other side of the ocean as the end of the day approached, the lab technician in Dr. Alderbry's lab at MIT began the tidy up after the day's work. She was the last one in the lab, and it was her turn to clean up and return the samples to the holding cabinet. Annette plugged her ear buds into her ears and cranked up Robbie Williams on her mp3 player. As she began the cleaning-up procedures, her movements became synchronized to the music, a flick of the hips and a 360° twirl whilst pumping her arms in the air and rocking her head back and forth, thinking of her boy-friend Danny. With a bit more emphasis on a hip thrust, she bumped into the bench on her left and, stumbling, reached out to steady herself by grabbing the table edge. The small, blue glass vial caught on her lab coat sleeve and tumbled to the floor. Annette watched helplessly as it twisted in the air almost in slow motion to her eyes, and the breaking glass was drowned out by Robbie Williams singing in her ears. The brown liquid spread out in little droplets on the floor. The liquid contained the latest sample of nanomas with *Shewanella* hosts.

"Oh, shit!" she announced to Robbie Williams. "Oh, shit!" Annette switched off Robbie and looked around the lab as if looking to see if she had been caught in the act. All was quiet and empty.

She ran over to the emergency cabinet and grabbed the absorbent foam spray can designed for exactly this eventual-ity. Returning to the little, brown pool of liquid, she sprayed over the entire area and one meter beyond in all directions as per the instructions that all lab techs had been drilled to do as first action. Satisfied that she had covered all droplets in foam, Annette ran to the phone and called Dr. Alderbry.

When Sonia picked up the phone, she said hello and rec-ognized Annette's agitated voice immediately.

"What happened, Annette? Slow down, and start from the beginning."

"I'm so sorry, Dr. Alderbry—I was clearing up and knocked over one of the sample containers."

"Have you covered the area in the Encap foam?"

"Yes, it was the first thing I did."

"How long was the delay between the spillage and spray-ing with the Encap?"

Hesitantly, Annette replied, "Probably about thirty seconds."

"More or less than thirty seconds?"

"Perhaps a bit less than thirty."

"And how big an overlap did you cover the area?"

"About a meter, like we were shown."

Sonia breathed a sigh of relief. Annette had taken the appropriate action, but to be on the safe side, she would go to the lab herself.

"Well done, Annette. Call the clean-up team; the number is on my desk. I'm on my way over—stay there until I arrive."

"OK, see you in fifteen, Dr. Alderbry."

When Sonia arrived at the lab, the clean-up team were already in action. The foam pad had hardened and trapped all dust particles, nanomas, and bacteria under its blanket. Scanning of the lab had commenced for any sign of nanomas that might have eluded the foam pad. Annette was sitting on a lab bench looking nervous and despondent. She fully expected Dr. Alderbry to take her off the team. Sonia went over, sat beside Annette, and put a hand on her shoulder.

"It's OK, Annette, there's no harm done. You managed to Encap the batch by the looks of it. We've lost a couple of days while we make another batch to continue with the project. You will, of course, be working some overtime to make up the new batch."

"You mean . . . you're not firing me?"

"No, but you will be working some long hours, so you'd better tell Danny you will not be going partying for a couple of days."

"Danny, how do you know about him?"

"Oh, I listen to lab rat gossip just like any other woman."

"Damn! I was meant to be meeting Danny tonight. What's the time?"

Sonia looked at her watch. "Eight forty-five."

Annette was supposed to meet Danny at 8:00 p.m. Her eyes glanced down to the floor then out of the window.

"Go, I'll see you early tomorrow morning—6:00 a.m."

Annette smiled and turned to Dr Alderbry. "Thanks. I'll make it up to you. I promise."

"Get out of here, Annette."

Annette ejected herself off the bench and bounced out of the lab. The clean-up team were finishing off the last few square meters of floor space and walls. All the furniture had been vacuumed and wiped down as well as every instrument, tool, test gear, and paper. All the lab coats and other material were sealed in bags; another fifteen minutes should see the lab given the all clear.

The one part of the lab that was not scanned was Annette herself.

As she pressed *play* on her mp3 player and bounced down the corridor, a small droplet of brown fluid went with her, captured in the crenellations around the rim of her left shoe sole.

Annette's student unit was only five minutes away from the lab. As soon as she got there, she stripped off her clothes and chucked them in the general direction of the laundry basket. Her shoes were thrown in the open wardrobe. They landed amongst a heap of other shoes against the wall. The droplet of brown fluid seeped off the tip of her shoe and soaked into the carpet. Several thousand modified *Shewanella*-hosting nanomas gravitated toward the wall. The student unit was relatively new, and most of the interior walls were painted with modern paint containing titanium dioxide. The *Shewanella* were now able to operate aerobically and anaerobically. The paint provided a source of material the nanomas could utilize to replicate. The raw material for memristors was TiO_2.

The following day as Annette stirred from sleep, pierced by the sound of her alarm clock, she rolled over to palm the clock into silence for a few more minutes before she got up. The second time it went off, it was fifteen minutes to 6:00 a.m. Annette opened her eyes, stared at the clock, and realized it was the second time it had gone off.

"Damn."

Tossing back the covers, she flew out of bed and into the bathroom, stared at herself briefly in the mirror long enough to say "Uuuggh" at the mess of hair and baggy eyes. As she leapt into the shower, with toothbrush still being swilled around her mouth, the odd thought of how the mirror looked a bit misty with black edges wafted through her brain. The mirror was not that old; perhaps it was the steam from the shower reacting with the silvering on the back. Clean and woken by the hot water, she barely dried herself enough before throwing clothes on. As she opened the door of the built-in wardrobe to grab her lab shoes, she noticed the back wall looked a bit odd. The paint had gone all powdery, and a fine dust had collected on several pairs of shoes. She paused to run her finger over the wall. It felt like scrapping her finger through chalk dust. She looked at the white smudge on her finger.

"That's weird." She glanced at her watch—5:55 a.m. "Damn, got to go, got to go."

Dismissing the thoughts, she grabbed a muesli bar from the cupboard, dashed out the door, and ran to the lab while choking on muesli crumbs, eating on the run.

Annette arrived at the lab just at 6:00 a.m, the same time as Dr Alderbry.

"Good morning, Dr. Alderbry." Annette put on her brightest smile to show she was keen to get started and make up for the slipup yesterday.

"Morning, Annette, ready to go to work? We have a long day today."

"Sure, let's get to it."

The morning went smoothly enough. A new batch of *Shewanella* were integrated with nanomas running another version of program to improve the communication between populations.

Just before lunch, the phone rang on Sonia's desk. Annette was closest and picked up the phone with a cheery greeting.

"Hello! Dr Alderbry's lab, how can I help you?"

The smile on Annette's face disintegrated as Sonia approached, reaching out for the phone.

"Dr Alderbry, this is Jack Crammer. I was leading the clean-up team last night. I believe we may have a problem."

Sonia's heart missed a beat, "Go on."

"According to your records, the batch of nanomas was 25 ml in solution."

"That's correct."

"Well, our recovery from the Encap foam was 23.2 ml. We're short 1.8 ml."

There was silence between them for a few seconds.

Sonia realized this could turn into serious problem very quickly if they could not locate the missing 1.8 ml.

"OK, get your team back here to scan the lab again right now."

"I've already mobilized the team. They should be there in the next couple of minutes."

Just as he had finished his sentence, the lab door opened, and five clean-up men entered in coveralls and masks and began to seal the lab, ready for a second scan.

In her mind, Sonia was already estimating the time 1.8 ml of nanomas had been unaccounted for.

Just over fifteen hours. If the replicators within the batch had activated, the population count didn't bear thinking about.

"Annette, are you sure you sprayed the whole area in under thirty seconds?"

"I think so."

"I need you to be sure."

"I'm sorry I can't be more certain. It felt like about twenty to thirty seconds."

"Ok, I want you to retrace your steps and actions as best you can. I'm going to time it."

Annette talked her way to the point of contact with the vial, and Sonia took note of the second hand position on her watch. Rough estimate—the time came to twenty-four seconds.

The phone rang again; it was Jack Crammer.

"Dr Alderbry, I have been studying the pattern of droplets on the Encap foam. Can you tell me if there was anything else on the floor besides the broken glass?"

"Hang on, Jack. Let me put you on speaker phone. I have Annette here—ask the question again."

Sonia pressed a button on the phone and replaced the handset.

Jack repeated the question.

Annette responded, "No, definitely not."

Jack continued, "Whereabouts were your feet when the glass broke?"

Annette looked down at her shoes. Sonia looked down as well.

"Shit—your shoes, you were not scanned last night."

Annette closed her eyes, and the vision of her wardrobe wall came into her head—she had a terrible feeling of dread. She turned to Sonia with a fearful look on her face.

"I think I know where the other 1.8 ml ended up."

She took off her shoes and passed them to one of the clean-up team.

"I was wearing these last night. When I woke up this morning, there was a powdery patch of paint on the wall at the back of my wardrobe. It wasn't there last night—I'm sure." Automatically, she stared at her finger, which she had poked at the wall with.

"I think you better check out this finger as well. I wiped my finger on the wall this morning."

Another thought occurred to her, the most frightening of all. The color drained from her cheeks.

"Dr Alderbry, I might have ingested some when I ate a muesli bar for breakfast."

Sonia sighed deeply as the impact of this last statement sunk in.

"We better get you to a hospital isolation ward as soon as possible."

The clean-up team started getting some positive readings around the lab from all the instruments and equipment Annette had been using during the course of the morning. Encap foam began to create a patchwork of infected areas

around the room. Sonia picked up the phone to Jack Crammer and gave him the address of Annette's unit. They had to
get a second team out there right away.

Sonia tried to look at this with some positive optimism.

"Look, Annette, it's likely that most of the sample are inert
by now, but we must get you checked in isolation just to be
sure."

Annette scratched at her wrist round her wristwatch. She
looked down at her arm, which was looking slightly red, and
as she did so, the wristband of her watch broke and fell to
the floor. Almost instinctively Sonia grabbed a can of Encap
foam and sprayed the watch on the floor. Then, she grabbed
Annette's wrist and sprayed her arm as well.

The second clean-up team had arrived at Annette's unit.
A small crowd of students had gathered around to see what
all the attention on Annette's unit was about. It wasn't every
day men encased in impermeable coveralls and enclosed
facemasks with unfamiliar instruments strolled around the
students' accommodations. What was even more captivat-
ing was the plastic tunnel set up to enclose the main door,
extending several meters to the curbside. With two sealed
doors at the main end to create a low, positive-pressure
airlock, the tunnel was sealed at the wall of the unit. The
team entered one at a time. Inside was quiet, and a fine,
white dust hung in the air, scintillating in the sunrays coming through the window. As they moved around, it became
apparent that the nanomas were very active. All the walls
looked like they were covered in chalk dust. The mirrors
in the unit were stripped of coating. Some of the plastics
had lost their color. Annette's bicycle, which was hanging
on the wall, had fallen down and looked decidedly rickety
and feeble. One the clean team went to pick up the bike
and was left holding the remnants of the handlebars in his
hand. Even Annette's badminton rackets lay on the floor
with the strung frame having collapsed under the stress of
the strings. In the bathroom, the toothpaste had turned an

odd brown color. Some of her makeup had also been degraded in some way.

The team leader looked around at the damage and the fine dust in the air. "Get on the phone to Dr Alderbry. I think we may be too late."

As the team continued going through the unit and began the process of encasing everything in foam, a large population of nanomas were up in the air-conditioning vents that connected the units through the roof space. Part of the population continued to use the ant colony message trail program to continue to find more titanium materials. Another section of the population were now modified to target iron. This section of the population were running a modified version of the ant colony messaging trail and were divided into small groups about the size of the head of a pin; they moved independently in hunting parties. Each group returned to a single point of reference to communicate before moving on further afield. All of this was going on above the heads of the clean team.

Some of the colony were now at the air-conditioning unit serving other student units.

The sunny May day was becoming overcast, and a wind was gaining momentum in Cambridge, Massachusetts.

Chapter 7—London

Our guess of where we were with respect to our old map book seemed to be correct. At least we came across a long straight section of pathway through the undergrowth that could have been the M40. Every so often, we came across smooth stone posts at regular intervals and in a straight line. Collapsed stonework obstructed the path every so often. We followed this vein through the countryside, sticking to the trees and undergrowth. The first couple of days were the hardest as I have never walked for so long a time. My legs ached, and my feet became sore as well from minor cuts and bruises sustained from some of the more defensive plants and undergrowth.

By the fourth day, my body was becoming accustomed to this daily routine. I was glad of the meat and fruit we had brought with us. The meat we ate first before it began to go bad. We finished it off by the third day as it was beginning to smell by then. We ate it anyway. Shaun managed to bag a rabbit or two with his crossbow, and Barkley even managed to catch a squirrel and some wild chickens.

On the sixth day, we reached a point where the M40 vein we had been following crossed another long, wide path trod by others heading south over the years. Checking this with our map book, we decided that we had found the M25 and turned south to follow it. Our food was by now beginning to run out. The berry juice was all but gone, so we needed to find water soon or hope for some rain to collect in the empty bags that once contained the juice. In the meantime, we picked wild blackberries.

We spied, in the distance, men on horseback. It was the first time since we started our journey. Shaun explained that there have always been more guards in this part of the country, although he was not sure why.

Pressing onward, we came across another intersection that proved to be the M4. This raised our confidence that we had at least a pretty good idea of where we were. We turned east down the M4. Lucky for us, it did rain on the ninth day. It woke us early in the morning before sunrise. The plastic bags that were empty were opened to the heavens, and we collected as much rainwater as we could. It also gave us a chance to wash, which was good as the combination of meat and berries and grime that stuck to our clothes and hands did nothing but attract flies during the walk. It's amazing how much one can appreciate rain after several days of remaining sweaty and grimy. According to the map, the M4 would bring us close to Erls Cort. All we had to do was avoid any of the Cardinal's guards that may be patrolling in this area. Stopping for a break and to check the map, we saw to the south of us was a place called Heathrow airport.

"Shaun, have you been there before?" I enquired, pointing to the airport on the map.

"No."

"How about we take a detour and check it out? I'd love to see an airplane like the one I saw in a book once."

"Maybe, but not now—perhaps on the way back."

I was not about to argue. The whole point of this trek was to get to see the Exhibition Center and the British library. I wanted to know what happened all that time ago.

Stuffing the map book back in his satchel, Shaun moved off with Barkley at his heels. I followed a few paces behind wondering what London was like now and, more importantly, before the Lord Master (BLM). As we approached what was a big city all that time ago, there was evidence of a lot of buildings now derelict and mostly overgrown with green carpets of grass, weeds, and shrubs. Underfoot, the ground became hard from flat paving stones still partially visible where animals and people have kept the track worn back. Vines, having covered smaller buildings and some small statues, took on the shape of what they covered in an eerie way.

I started to get this feeling that we were being watched. I quickened up my pace to draw alongside Shaun. "Shaun, I don't think we're alone anymore."

"I know, and Barkley does too. Look at the hackles on the back of his neck." Shaun continued, "Don't think they mean any harm. Quite a few people live here in London, and they are always suspicious of strangers."

We continued to walk, and as we got closer to what was the main part of the old city, the owners of the eyes watching us began to show themselves as curious people who then openly began to follow us on our journey. They kept their distance as Barkley grumbled every so often if they got too close.

"We're nearly there," Shaun stated as we became surrounded by what were large buildings of an earlier cityscape. Our path took us between derelict buildings covered in undergrowth on either side of us. Shaun seemed to recognize where he was from his previous visit and walked purposely on without any hesitation to check our location and surroundings.

Coming into view was a building much larger than those we had just walked between. Shaun pointed toward it. "Erls Cort," he said.

The people following us had disappeared again. I'm not sure when exactly, but Barkley ceased to be wary and watchful, although he would stop to sniff the air every so often. The building was as overgrown as any other, but it was clear that it was either inhabited or visited frequently by other people. The entrance was clear of undergrowth and grass. I felt my heart leap with mounting anticipation of what we might find here. The building was the largest I had ever seen. The walls were covered in ivy, and as we approached, I could see sunlight from within the main entrance. Much of the roof had long since collapsed. The floor space was huge from what I could see, and the remains of the roof occupied much of the floor space. Despite being in awe of the building, I began to feel disappointed as the state of the place did not meet my vision of what it might look like and the exhibits it might contain. Shaun led the way down to the right of the building. Barkley bounded off ahead to explore for himself.

Puzzled, I asked, "Where are we going?"

"I'm going to where I used hide out. I have a collection of stuff there, if it's not been found." Turning to the left, we approached a building with a row of doors that were set slightly up from the road, and a small set of stone steps led to the doorway. There seemed to be the remains of an iron fence, now long gone, and part of the building went below ground level. We approached a door, still hanging in the frame, at least by the bottom hinge. A faded, tattered plate on the door had the numbers 26. Shaun lifted the door slightly to move it easily without catching the floor. I followed him in and up some stairs, pausing briefly to call Barkley. We ascended and moved into a small corridor with doors off either side.

Shaun explained, "This used to have lots of people in it at one time. All the rooms have the same types of furniture and things in them. When I was here last, I used one of the rooms for several days. I explored a good part of the big building back there, and anything I thought was useful or interesting, I brought back to my room and stashed it there."

We stopped outside one of the doors. Shaun pushed the door open and stepped in. It was dusty, and the sun through the broken window caught the dust particles in the air, making a twinkling line across the room. The remains of what would have been a big bed were against one wall. A rotting mattress disintegrating with age housed plenty of woodlice and other small creatures. Shaun moved to a door in the wall and opened it. The enclosed space was a sort of cupboard, and in it were stacked several boxes containing a whole range of unfamiliar objects.

"Well, this is it," Shaun announced. "I hope it was worth the journey."

At that moment, Barkley entered the room panting slightly from the run up the stairs. He started sniffing around with curiosity himself.

I picked up the first box, retrieved it from the cupboard, placed it on the floor, and sat down beside it. Opening the lid, I looked inside. I picked up a triangular object that looked a bit like the one Mother used to press our clothes. It was heavy like Mother's, but it had a cord running out the top of it and a three-pronged bit on the end, much like Mags described of the circular stone wheel her father found on the farm. Looking in the box again, I pulled out another object with a metal cord attached, only this was different. The cord was thinner, and it had a small square connection on the end and another bit of coiled cord connecting the base and a slightly bent section that looked a bit like a bone. It had a circle at each end with small holes in. I picked it up to take a closer look. It was a faded white color and had a set of numbers on small buttons from 1 to 9. The bent bone section fitted quite neatly into my hand with the circular bits at each end. I sort of lifted it toward my face and precariously placed one piece to my ear and found the other end positioned itself close to my mouth. I pressed a couple of the buttons, but nothing happened. I looked around to see where Shaun was. He was sitting on the edge of the bed.

"Do you know what this is for?"

"Nope, but most of the rooms used to have one in them as well as that thing." Shaun pointed to the triangular object.

I pulled another item out the box. It was rectangular in shape and fitted into the palm of my hand. Written across the top were the words "tom tom." I pushed the small button on the top, but again nothing happened.

"I wonder what this was for."

Shaun glanced round from the bed. "I found that at Erl's Court." He came over, knelt beside the box, and started pulling stuff out. Out of the bottom of the box, he pulled a slim, flat rectangular thing, oblong with a set of buttons on it, 1 to 9 and letters A to Z. It had a small, grey area with nothing on it.

I looked at the faded, white device I had previously pulled out. It had the same button set. Looking around the room and at the square connector, on the end of its cord, I spied a small plate beside the bed with a rectangular hole in it. Picking up the thing, I moved over to the wall and offered the connector into the hole in the wall and it fitted neatly.

"Shaun, look, it fits. Look for any other holes in the wall that might take one of these," I said, holding up the triangular machine with the three-pronged connector on it.

Shaun went through another door leading off from the room we were in. "In here," I heard him beckon and followed him, clutching the triangular machine.

Shaun stood by a basin, facing the wall and holding a broken mirror, much of which was now just glass. He pointed at the plate on the wall with three square holes.

I looked at the connector in my hand and the holes in the wall; they looked similar. I offered the connector into the wall plate and pushed. It was hard to push in and took a fair amount of effort. Then suddenly, it went in, but at the same time, the wall crumpled around the plate, showing the cords running off into the brickwork and disappearing downward.

"Where do these cords go?" I said mainly to myself rather than expecting an answer from Shaun. I grabbed hold of the cords in the wall and tugged and jerked the cable. The soft plaster gave and cracked down the wall toward the floor. I looked where the door was and the other room and ran out into the corridor and down the stairs. Turning at the bottom of the stairs, I went deeper into the ground floor area. Under the stair rise was a small door, what was left of it. I kicked it in with my foot, and it crumpled easily and fell away. Inside the space, I could see on the wall several cords all going in to a box, and out of the box was one larger, thicker cord, which then disappeared into the ground. On the side of the box was a lever. I pushed the lever up. The lid of the box opened to reveal the different cords going to a set of switches and a set of small, circular dials with numbers on. I flicked a few switches, but nothing happened.

It seemed to me that our ancestors of the past had everything operating with numbers—push the right numbers, and something would happen. I returned to the room upstairs. Shaun had pulled the other boxes out of the cupboard and was busy searching for something. He pulled out something small and black and cradled it in his hands. It had a handle grip, and the top ran along the hand and protruded forward to wherever you were directing your hand. Shaun flicked a small lever on the side, and an elongated section dropped out of the handle. Shaun grabbed it and looked inside. There were some dull, barrel-shaped pieces of metal. Shaun had another box of these on the floor beside the boxes.

He looked up as I entered the room. "I've seen a guard use one of these instead of a crossbow. They make a lot noise, and a piece of the metal comes flying out of the end here, so fast you can't see it. I've seen a guard point it at a goat and kill it."

"Wow, you got another one for me?"

"' Fraid not, but you can have the crossbow from now on. Do you know how to fire it?"

"I've seen a guard use one, but I have never fired one myself," I replied.

"I'll show you later," said Shaun, passing me the crossbow and his set of bolts.

I had this feeling of acceptance from Shaun and felt more comfortable in his company. He was not such a loner after all.

In one of the other boxes, I found a lamp still in its plastic packaging, sealed. On the back sheet, it was described as a torch that did not require batteries. It had a built-in dynamo, whatever one of those was. Just wind the handle for twenty seconds. I was not sure how long twenty seconds were, but I ripped it out of the packaging, flipped out the handle, turned it several times, and pressed the switch. Five little bright lights shone a beam across the room and into the cupboard where I was pointing it. At last, I had one of my ancestors' machines that worked! It would be useful to save our matches for lighting fires for warmth and cooking food. There was a large, flat rectangular tablet, bigger than a book. Again, it had a cord with three prongs on the end and another cord with another strange connector on it. At the bottom of the machine were the words "Viewsonic." I can only guess we should be able to see something on it or with it. It seems that much of the objects that Shaun had collected had a common part. It was the three-pronged lead. It struck me that a vital part was missing that would move up the cord when plugged into the wall and make the device work somehow. However, one thing would be very useful to us, the second piece of our ancestors' technology. Wrapped in a sealed bag was a black case with *Nikon 10x25 EX* written on the outside. Within were a pair of magnifiers for viewing things from a distance. These could help us to stay safely away from any of the Cardinal's guards.

We went back downstairs and to the back of the house into an area with a basin and cupboards hanging precariously on the wall. The cupboard doors were either open or on the floor.

We sat at a table of thick timber, twisted and warped with age and weathering. We ate our second meal of the day, dried rabbit strips and apples picked on the journey here.

"Shaun, do you remember back in the prison you said you were there because you knew too much and you had found something at the Exhibition Center? What did you mean? What is it that you know?"

"When I was here last, the Cardinal and a bunch of his men turned up. They came straight into the Exhibition Center and started ripping the place up. They were looking for something called a hydrogen fuel cell and solar panels. I stayed hidden and just listened to them talking. The men didn't know much about what they were looking for, but the Cardinal seemed to know everything. He was going on about needing electricity to power his equipment."

"What sort of equipment?"

"No idea, he did not go into detail, and even if he had done, I wouldn't have known what he was going on about. Anyway, while I was listening, a rat dropped from the shelf above me onto my shoulder. It made me jump, and I kicked over an old chair to get the thing off. Of course, they heard me, and I heard the Cardinal command them to get me as I must not be allowed tell anyone what I had heard. I just got the hell out of there and ran for cover in an old building across the way."

I thought about what Shaun was saying for a moment, "Shaun, what about those lights in the prison? Do you think they use a solar panel or hydrogen cell to make them work?"

"Maybe, I don't know anything else that might make them work."

"Shaun, you know what I think? I think a lot of things our ancestors had needed this thing called electricity, and it is fed into these things through this three-pronged cord. There are holes in the wall that these leads fit into, so perhaps all these old buildings had hydrogen fuel cells somewhere or solar panels and these gave them electricity to make these things work."

There was silence for a few seconds while Shaun pondered over this. "It's a good idea, but I've no idea what to look for. I never did get to see whether the Cardinal found what he was after, although I do remember seeing the Cardinal's men pulling out cables from the building. It looked like a tough job as they seemed to run inside the walls a lot."

"We need to find a picture of one, then we might be able to find one for ourselves."

Shaun was skeptical, "I doubt it. We're talking of something that was made over a hundred and fifty years ago. Why would it last for so long?"

"Well, the Cardinal thought so a few years ago," I replied.

"True enough, Abalus."

I continued, "I reckon we should try to find that British library with all those books. Perhaps we might find something there that could help."

Shaun pulled the map book out of his bag and opened the page he had marked that showed us Erl's Court. We could see the British library marked on Euston road. It was northeast of our current location. We could walk up the wide path called Holland Road, head right up Holland Park Ave, and keep going to a gate called Lancaster. Then, we'd head northeast for the path called Marylebone Road and follow it eastward.

Barkley returned from his own exploration, sat himself in the doorway, and watched us, waiting to see what we were going to do next. As we discussed the walk to the British library, Shaun was debating whether we should lay low until evening or continue the journey now. While we were going over this, Barkley let out a low growl, and his hackles were up. We both fell silent, and our bodies tensed for flight. In the distance on a light breeze, we heard the sounds of voices. One was curt and urgent and seemed to be giving orders to an unknown number of other persons.

"Cardinal guards," Shaun said in a low voice.

I moved over to Barkley, put my arm around his neck, and stroked under his throat to calm him.

His ears were pricked, and he kept sniffing the air, gathering information from the scents on the breeze.

"We wait until its clear, then we move on," Shaun voiced his decision to Barkley and me. I was not going to argue.

"You'd better show me how to load this crossbow. I might need it sooner than I wish."

We waited in silence for some time, listening to voices drifting nearer and farther away. They seemed to be searching the buildings of the whole area. Some time passed, and the voices eventually drifted away. Barkley seemed to relax a little. Shaun took the crossbow from my shoulder and in a low voice started giving me instructions on how to draw the string, load a bolt, aim, and fire. I had one practice shot, firing a bolt down the hallway and embedding it into a faded and rotting picture hanging from a nail in the wall. I was amazed at how far the bolt went into the wall behind and struggled to retrieve the bolt. The point was a little blunted by the force from hitting old stonework but still usable. I felt a little more confident that I could defend myself, perhaps overconfident.

We left the security of the old building and moved off back to the Exhibition Center. Using the map book, we oriented ourselves to move up the path called Holland Road. We stuck close to the buildings and undergrowth as much as possible. Despite our caution, I could not shake off the feeling we were being watched. Barkley would stop every so often to sniff the air, and occasionally his hackles would go up. But, we pressed on, alert and nervous.

It was approaching sunset as we got to the path we thought to be Euston Road. The skies began to cloud over, and it looked like rain would soon follow. I hoped we could find the library before the weather changed. At least we would be able to shelter there overnight and take a good look around at the same time. As we continued our walk, in the distance, I could make out what looked like a very old building with towers that reminded me of a castle I had seen in one of the pictures back at our underground hideout. Amongst the pictures of the boy and girl, Martin and Angie, was one of the two of them standing in front of a building called Windsor Castle. As we got closer, there were the remains of a building to our left. On some stonework covered in moss and lichen were the words *British Library*. Much of the building was still standing, although in places the roof had collapsed. We moved across what would have been an open area, now overgrown with grass and weeds and small shrubs pushing up from between the large, flat stones. We made our way to a large hole in the wall at the far end of the open area. There probably used to be an entrance door there sometime in the past. The walls had collapsed inward or were pushed inward; all the rubble lay inside the entranceway. Barkley took the lead and explored further into the building with canine curiosity. Shaun and I followed with more caution, although I could feel my excitement mounting, hoping to find something that would explain what had happened so many years ago. As we moved into the building, the area grew dim as daylight was obstructed by the structure. Where the roof had collapsed, rays of sunlight highlighted the dust in the air and gave the building an eerie feeling of desolation. The clouds continued to cover over the sky, and the light inside the library became more foreboding. Looking up, it would seem the building had several levels at one time, but for some reason, it had collapsed inward from the center. Much of what stood on these upper levels had ended up in the area where we stood. What books had existed were long gone as far as I could see. My disappointment must have shown as Shaun turned to me and said, "Well, what did you expect to find?"

Barkley was sniffing around the door to our left with a sign in green over the top, *Exit.* I went over to the door and pushed against it. It didn't budge. I leaned my shoulder against it and pushed with all my weight. There was a creak and the sound of rubble scraping the floor on the other side.

"Shaun, help me."

Shaun sighed, trudged over to the door, and put all his weight against it. We pushed together, and the door opened some more, but there was a lot of weight on the other side. Barkley stuck his head round the door but could not get his shoulders through. We both backed up a little and pushed forward again. The door moved some more, and Barkley was through to the other side. After removing my bag and crossbow from my back, I squeezed through the gap, and Shaun followed suit. There was a staircase up and down, but the staircase up had large gaps where it had collapsed. The staircase down seemed OK apart from the rubble and debris laying over much of it. I climbed over the mess and started moving down. It got so dark that I could not see. Now was a good time to try out the light with a handle to wind it up. I took it out of my bag, gave it several turns, and switched it on. The light cast a narrow beam down the staircase, enough to see where we were going. Barkley was already down below us. I could hear his nose sniffing around and the occasional loose rubble under his paws. As we continued down, Barkley's eyes glinted in the light as he waited below. His eyes reflected the light with a red tinge, which looked quite frightening. If I didn't know it was Barkley, I would have turned tail and been out of there as fast as one of my crossbow bolts. The loose rubble and debris underfoot made the progress slow and treacherous, but we eventually came to the lower level and another door. The fallen masonry down here was not as much as above, and it took only a short while to move the debris away to open the door enough to get through with ease. It was completely dark with only the light from my torch. I cranked the handle again, and the light became a little brighter. We moved out into a small corridor. The light flickered across what appeared to be, at some time, a spiral staircase going back up to the floor above. To the left was a room; a small sign was on the floor in front of the door. I picked it up and swept the years of dust and debris from it. It read *Archives reading room*. In front of us, the corridor seemed to bend round to the right to an open area with tables, some still standing. I followed the wall round. Shaun went off to the right. Our eyes were getting used to the darkness, but I still needed the torch to pick my way round, keeping my left hand up against the wall. Going round to the left following the wall, I came to two small rooms, and a large, square machine with a big lid stood in the corner area. Following the wall round, I came across another door like the one we came through on the other side of the area. I stood and scanned the torch around me, and the beam fell upon some shelves full of books. I went over to the shelf and pulled a book out at random. The book was covered in years of dirt, and the cover felt dry and brittle. I carefully opened the front cover and thumbed through the pages. There were lots of pictures with lines and boxes, with numbers across the bottom and side of each picture. Wavy lines went across the pictures. Some pictures looked like bells with numbers on them. Shaun came up, took another book from the shelf, and flicked through its pages. Replacing the book I had, I moved further down the shelf, scanning the backs of the books for familiar words. *P-a-r-l-i-a-m-e-n-t* was on the front of many books—a word I did not understand. As I looked along the bookshelves, toward the far end was a book that was not pushed back into the shelves like the others. It stood out like a flag as if someone wanted to make it obvious it did not belong. I moved down the shelf and pulled it out. The outside cover was thin, and handwritten on the front were the words, *Personal log of Professor Geoff Short—2014/2015.* I opened the book; it was handwritten. Some of the pages were stuck together with age, but gentle prizing separated them without too much difficulty. This book definitely did not seem to belong.

"Shaun, I've found something. I'll be in one of those small rooms over there," I announced and pointed the torch toward the small alcove with two rooms.

Shaun nodded and continued looking at the machines that sat on the top of desks on the other side of the room. Sitting at one of the desks, I opened the log and started to read. It must have taken some time and several rewinds of the torch to keep the light bright enough to read. There was a lot I did not understand. This Professor Geoff Short seemed to be a leader in his knowledge, and much of the log talked about experiments with very small life called bacteria. They were responsible, it seemed, for diseases in plants and animals and us. But also, there were some that were useful and played important parts in the life cycles of other animals. It was mostly beyond my understanding, but I read on. He wrote about concerns with a particular technological development that was going on in another part of the world, the USA, as well as here in England. Something had gone wrong with nanomas, whatever they were. I understood one thing though; nanomas were very small, and they were having some terrible consequences in other parts of the world. Although this book had on the front cover 2014/2015, the last entry in the book was dated 28 July 2015. Barkley came and sat down beside me, still alert and looking uneasy. Shaun came and joined us and started to distribute food while we were relatively safe. We could stay here for the night. It provided us with shelter from the chill night air. There was only one way in, which was the way we came. I settled down to read more while eating the remains of dried rabbit meat and some berries, which were getting very mushy. But, it was better than nothing. I started to read aloud so Shaun could hear what was written in the log.

Chapter 8—28 July 2015

Professor Geoff Short stared out at his office window. The street was packed with people and cars exiting the city of London. Some cars were breaking down as they sat in the traffic jam. Some vehicles that had been there for more than twenty-four hours were disintegrating almost visibly. In such a crush of population, as best as they could, people were giving the vehicle remains a wide berth.

With a heavy sigh of finality, he turned to his desk and stared at his laptop and daily log book on his desk. He knew that the race against time was now on, and the human race was already losing out to the blight they had created. Geoff sat down at his desk, picked up his favorite fountain pen, and began to write. In the background was the noise of the exodus from the city, but this faded from his attention as he began to write his final log entry.

* * *

28 July 2015

This will be my final entry in this log. I have decided that the information contained herein must be safely preserved for any future survivors so they can understand why this line of science was so important at the time, but the consequences of impatience for results led to a world disaster of our own making. This log will be scanned into my laptop that will be securely wrapped and protected and sent to my brother on his farm in the country. The log itself I will place in the British library before I leave. I suspect, sometime in the future, people will return to the city for supplies of materials and food if nothing else. Perhaps the libraries will survive and provide a valuable knowledge resource.

Since the outbreak of the *Shewanella* nanomas in the States, the growth rate has been phenomenal, but worse still, the ability of the nanomas to adapt and alter the *Shewanella* to search and metabolize different materials has made this outbreak so devastating. Once a strain had adapted to iron, the accelerated population growth was truly remarkable and terrible at the same time. It became evident back in May, when vehicles in the street started breaking down, engines ceased, petrol tanks leaked, and cars even exploded. Buildings started to collapse once nanomas got into the structures, particularly those of modern architecture using a lot of steel. Many people have died as the infrastructure of the cities simply began to disintegrate around them. Hospitals ceased to function; some did last longer than others. Older buildings using more traditional nineteenth-century materials remain standing on the whole. Of course, internal piping, wiring, and some roof collapses have meant these buildings are not left entirely unaffected. As people tried to escape in their vehicles or by taking flights out, they have unwittingly been spreading the nanomas. Planes have simply dropped out of the sky.

Power distribution became a big problem once overhead pylons began to drop to the ground, weakened by the nanomas. Some people took to the sea in their personal boats and of course the ocean liners. I daresay some will survive, and some will have unwittingly carried them aboard. Those ships at sea are the most likely candidates to overcome this by staying away from shore for as long as possible. Other people will be deep in the country. To date, outbreaks have spread from the States to Europe and the UK as well as South America and the Middle East. It would seem that this has been by the transference via airlines out of the States before anyone realized they were infected.

Also it is interesting to note at this point that metals not being sought out are aluminum, nickel, lead, mercury and copper. There may be others, but communications with the States or indeed anywhere have all but broken down. The military are keeping their satellite communications systems going, but they are not immune, just more able to lock down the movements of their people and mobilize them into appropriate actions to contain the situation. The civilian population is not so easy to lock down.

At least the UK and Europe had some forewarning in May, but it was not enough time for us to quarantine the first panic-stricken arrivals. Of course, we were not equipped suitably to detect nanomas at the airports anyway. Shipping has been kept away, of course. Being slower moving, they will either survive or sink. As far as the human cost of this disaster, the death rate will be in the millions over the next few months, not just from failing structures and transport but from disease outbreaks that health authorities simply will not be able to cope with. Supply chains are all but completely wiped out, and power is only as good as the overhead lines that remain standing. Nuclear power stations have been shut down. A nuclear disaster on top of this would be unthinkable.

The last report I had from Sonia two weeks ago has been the most disturbing of all. It would seem that some people have died from ingesting the nanomas. Autopsies have shown that another variant of nanomas evolved to extract iron from the blood. I hope this strain does not reach our shores. We have little hope of survival if it does.

Much of my previous notes in this log deal with the technical aspects of this research, but as I have no idea who might find and read this, I shall briefly explain in simple terms what these nanomas are.

Man has many avenues of research to add to knowledge and understanding of our world and beyond—and our place in it. Some of our endeavors are to find solutions to current problems that can have adverse effects on the natural world. Others are to overcome problems we have created for ourselves or our environment. Sometimes, we move into realms we don't fully understand, yet we rush or are pushed headlong into them. The nanomas' development has been one such case. We needed to find ways to reclaim some of our raw materials and metals as we continued to mine finite resources to meet the demand of an ever-hungry population. In the nanomas, we created a biomechanical solution to overcome this problem, but it is the early days of this new technology. This means we have successfully combined a simple form of microscopic life with a very small man-made machine of microscopic size. The bacteria and nanomachine combine in a symbiotic relationship where the bacterium provide the raw materials and energy to the nanomachine that, in return, provides improved mobility, preprogrammed search patterns, and a capacity to learn and adapt. Also, part of the programming manipulates the DNA structures of the bacteria by imposing methylation to targeted positions.

The technology of the nanomas incorporates a new kind of memory (memristor) component that allows the nanomachines to retain a piece of data even when that piece of memory is updated with new data. Effectively a nanoma can learn from previous experience. Given the rapid rate of population growth, I can only theorize that, as the population grows, the retained memories are passed on. Although a single nanoma can only retain a small amount of information, millions grouped together form an effective memory bank to hold a large amount of information. The nanomachines were equipped with a simple communication protocol by which they can interact. This was a necessary development if the programs of simple search patterns were to be effectively deployed. The collective memory of millions of these can form a simple brain. If the nanomas can collectively organize themselves and replicate, then there is the possibility that they can go beyond their initial programming. I believe this is precisely what is happening.

We have created a biomechanical life form that has the ability to evolve and adapt to its environment.

How far this evolution process will go, I have no idea, and we are out of time. There is always the possibility that the nanomas will reach a critical mass, where the raw material available to keep on replicating will go into short supply, and unless they find a way to go underground and search out new subsurface food sources, they will simply die out. There is also one possible avenue we can actively pursue, and once I am out of London, I will head to the coast to see if it is feasible. Because boats and ships have been putting to sea, I have not heard of one single ship sinking due to the structure being attacked by nanomas. That does not mean it has not happened, but with communications getting worse every day, I might have missed something. I cannot believe that, as all other forms of transport have been affected as the population tries to get away, only those on ships or boats did not contaminate their vessels. So, something about the coast or seawater seems to prevent the nanomas from multiplying. It might be a simple case of salt concentration. However, this would not explain how the nanomas were reported to have caused the deaths of humans directly by ingestion—the pH value of blood is 7.41 normally. I asked Sonia before we lost contact whether those people who died from ingestion had anything in common, illnesses or blood disorders that might provide a clue to why they were killed. The general range of the salinity of seawater is pH 7.5 to 8.1. If those people who died had some form of blood disorder that lowered the pH value of the blood, it might explain the deaths. Unfortunately, I have not heard from Sonia for a couple of weeks, and I doubt I ever will now. So, I must follow this clue for myself. I shall make my way down to the south coast, maybe Portsmouth or Southampton. I can use the university facilities in Southampton. They have a school of biological sciences there and are well equipped. Any solutions I might come up with will be documented and stored there.

Finally, all my research and detailed notes are on the laptop, which as mentioned before, I am sending to my brother's farm near Little Haseley. One day, I hope it may help future survivors and other generations understand that our actions were for all the right reasons, but our collective over-enthusiasm resulted in this disastrous series of events that, with every day that passes, gets further away from our grasp to stop it.

Chapter 9—The Library

I looked up from the log to see if Shaun had been listening. His face was expressionless. I could not tell whether he really listened to what I had been reading. His eyes raised to meet mine, and slowly his finger came up and pressed against his lips. Instinctively, I stopped breathing and listened intently for sounds in the darkness of this man-made cavern. I turned the small torch light off; the hairs on the back of my neck prickled. Somewhere in the distance above our heads, I could hear the sound of footfalls crunching in the rubble that was once a roof to the building. I could not hear Barkley's soft panting breath close by. Perhaps it was him upstairs. Then, I heard a low deep grumble off to my right and knew it was Barkley; he was also alert to the noises above us. I whispered Barkley's name intently followed by, "Sssshhhhh," not that I expected him to understand what I meant. I could barely see as there was so little light that filtered down here through our forced entry point. I heard Shaun move quietly toward my position and tap me on the shoulder.

"Pass me the light," he whispered.

I handed him the light. He gave the handle a couple of turns, switched the torch on, and shone its white light through his blue T-shirt. This produced a very dim light for us to see by. He pointed toward the door off to our left, which led to a small reading room. Still crouched, I followed him as he made his way toward the door. Barkley must have heard our movement and seen the dim light as he made his way over toward us. The noise of footsteps continued to filter through the debris above us, leaving us in no doubt that we were not alone. Any thought that we were hearing some kind of animal, like a badger, deer, or fox were quickly dispelled by the sound of a voice calling out commands.

"Keep looking! You two go that way. Parker, follow me."

Shaun opened the door very slowly, hoping it would not squeak or stick. The hinges were stiff with age and lack of use, and although they did not squeak, the door opened with creaking complaint. Shaun patiently opened the door a little at a time until there was enough space to crawl in to the small room. Barkley followed me and Shaun last, gingerly pushing the door closed after us. Shaun turned off the torch. We crouched in silence and darkness. I still clutched the log book in my hand. Fortunately for us, the door opened in to the small room, and so the scrape marks of the bottom of the door in the dust and debris could not be seen. But, we had still left evidence of our exploration of the lower area if the unknown intruders were observant enough to pick up the signs. I hoped they would not find the door on the upper level that we pushed open to get down here. I racked my brains trying to think if we closed the door behind us and experienced the sudden realization that we must have left it open as that was the only source of dim light from above. Barkley grumbled once again, and my arm went round his neck to try and calm him. The last thing we wanted Barkley to do now was bark and alert the intruders to where we were. I heard Shaun fumble about in his bag and heard a gentle, metallic click. I recognized the sound and knew Shaun had pulled out the black metal weapon. I followed suit by bringing the crossbow off my shoulder into my hands. I primed the bow and set a bolt in place. We waited in silence.

After what seemed to be an eternity, there was a loud crash and somebody swearing in pain and frustration. The sound was definitely coming from the entry area to this level. My heart started to beat faster, and I could feel a quavering in my stomach just like I felt the night the Cardinal paid us a visit and I stabbed him in the throat. Shaun turned and leaned against the door so it would not open without someone leaning with force against it. If I could see him, I knew Barkley's hackles would be up. In the still air, a bead of sweat trickled down my forehead and into my eye, stinging slightly. I cuffed it away with my sleeve. We could hear people moving round the floor, kicking at rubbish as they moved. A door was pushed open and closed again, then another. The footsteps got closer. I turned and leaned my back against the door next to Shaun. There was a jolt of the door as if someone had pushed against it. Shaun had his hand gripped firmly on the door handle, pushing upward with all his strength, feigning a locked door. A voice on the other side called out, "Tosh, give me a hand with this door, will you?"

Another voice some way over the other side of the floor could be heard muttering grudging acknowledgement.

"OK, on three, push up against the door."

"One . . . two . . . three."

There was a loud thud, and the door shook violently; our backs rebounded off and fell back against it. Shaun maintained his grip on the handle as a second, even harder impact was felt on the door. The wood surrounding the door catch split a little, weakened by the battering. Another thud of two adults throwing their bulk at the door split the wood completely around the lock. The door opened an inch or so, and a beam of light cast itself over the debris on the floor inside the room. Shaun and I were still out of sight behind the door, stopping it opening any further.

"Tosh, you see anything?"

"Na, don't know why the door won' open—nuthin' there."

"OK, one more shuv should do it."

The pressure eased off the door as both guards prepared to force it open with their weight. With a quick, deft movement, Shaun was on his feet and turned to face the door with the black weapon pointing head height. I dove sideways just in time as the door suddenly burst open, and two guards almost fell into the room. The first with the torch shone a powerful beam into Shaun's face and realized what Shaun had in his hand. Barkley, from somewhere behind me and to my right, jumped at the guard with the torch, and his teeth sank into the extended arm. The torch dropped to the ground, and in the bouncing light beam, there was a loud crack and a bright flash as Shaun fired his weapon. The guard dropped to his knees, his shirt turning red as blood seeped out of a wound in the base of his neck. The shock in his eyes faded as did his life, and his mouth turned red as he fell forward over the torch. In the last flash of light, I saw the second guard raise a crossbow toward Shaun. Instinctively, I pointed mine from shoulder height in his direction and pulled the trigger. There was a dull thunk of the bolt hitting flesh, but the guard was still moving somewhere along the ground. Without light, I could not see a thing. Barkley could be heard growling and worrying the arm he still had a grip on. There was a yell for help somewhere in front of me as the guard was retreating back down the corridor. Shaun had pushed the body of the first guard off the torch and retrieved it. Suddenly, the light beam twisted round out toward the scrabbling body of the second guard. He was crawling on all fours, trailing his right leg. It seemed I had shot him in the right upper thigh. Barkley saw the guard in the light, released his first victim, and in three short bounds, pounced on the second guard and sunk his teeth into the back of his neck. The guard's body flattened facedown to the floor under Barkley's weight and gurgled his last breath.

Shaun turned the torch toward me.

"You all right?"

"Yes, OK."

"Come on, the others must be up there somewhere; they must have heard the shot and the guard's shout."

I was frozen to the spot, the images of the two dead guards burned in my brain. In the blink of an eye, they were no more.

"Abalus, come on," Shaun whispered more harshly, pushing my shoulder at the same time.

Taken out of my daze, I picked up the log book and thrust it into my bag, primed the bow a second time, and followed Shaun toward the exit where we had entered this level. Barkley came into view of the torch, his jaws covered in blood and dripping down the front of his fur. Shaun moved toward the stairs and started to ascend. Voices could be heard moving through the forced door above. Shaun turned and came back down, signaling for me to follow him. Shaun doubled back behind the stairs, turned off the torch, and crouched in the darkness. I followed suit, grabbing Barkley by the scruff of the neck to drag him over too. Footsteps descended the stairs, and two torch beams waved across the walls and floor. Three more guards moved down the passage toward the small room where we were. One the torch beams fell on the body outside the door, and a guard shouted.

"Over here."

The other two guards ran toward the dead body. As the torches' light concentrated on their fallen comrade, Shaun moved out from under the stairs, grabbing my arm, and quickly ascended. Barkley bounded up and the through the upper door first, followed by Shaun and myself. Shaun turned, closed the door, and jammed a piece timber from the debris under the door handle.

"OK, let's get as far away from here as we can. That piece of wood won't hold them for long."

"Where we going?"

"Some tunnels I know of until nightfall."

We exited the building and ran down the path off to the left between derelict buildings. Shaun turned left into one of two red stone arches, overgrown with brambles and weeds. We forced our way through and disappeared into the gloom. We now had a guard's torch as well as the wind-up one, so as we moved deeper below ground, we could navigate without too much trouble.

Shaun stepped off a platform into a pathway that led into a tunnel. The tunnel had stone steps placed evenly apart down the tunnel; the steps had holes in them, and they were stained with a brown-orange color.

There was the sound of dripping deep in the tunnel. Water was running down the walls, and the tunnel floor was ankle deep in water. The scampering and squeals of rats could be heard sporadically. Shaun removed the juice bag, stood below a small aperture in the tunnel roof, and collected water; then, he drank directly from the thin trail of water. I stood under it to cool off and clean the dust out of my hair and throat. I drank and filled a second plastic bag with some water for later.

"Shaun, do you know where Southampton was or is?"

"Why?"

"We need to get there. Didn't you hear what I was reading from the log book?"

"Yes, but so what? Don't you realize we are now murderers! We've killed two guards. They're going to be hunting us with even more reason to kill us. Forget a trial or imprisonment—they'll just shoot us on sight."

"I know, I know—so we're on the run. So let's run to Southampton. At least we have a reason to go there instead of just running anywhere."

"Are you crazy? What do you hope to gain by going there?"

"I might find out more about what happened. Something changed cos' we don't have these nanoma things now, do we? Something must have happened to them. Perhaps this Professor Geoff found a way to kill them."

"Look, Abalus, it's just a piece of the past. We made something that took on a life of its own, and it nearly wiped us out. That's all I need to know."

"I need more than that, Shaun. If what the professor had written is true, it explains why there seems to be a lot of things missing that we can only see or read about in old books that we are not supposed to read—all those things like airplanes, cars, and bridges, and a lot of other stuff made from technology of our ancestors. Why do the Cardinal and Lord Master not want us to read about such stuff in books? Why are we supposed to learn only from the Lord Master's book? How come the Cardinal and his soldiers have tools and weapons that we have not? Where did they come from? Our past? Why have they not been consumed by the nanomas? Does it not puzzle you at all? Don't you want to know what happened?"

My flow of questions was cut short by a swift backhand across my right cheek, and I was sent reeling sideways into the tunnel wall. I would have fallen if the wall was not there. My cheek burned. Barkley placed himself between me and Shaun with a glare of a threatened beast in his eyes. Barkley was protecting the smaller, weaker of the two of us. I looked at Shaun, shocked by this physical outburst of rage focused toward me. Had I pushed too far? Shaun's anger dissipated from his face as he realized what he had done. He turned to continue the walk down the tunnel and said "Sorry" as he moved off. The voice was quiet and came over his shoulder almost as an afterthought. I thought it best to drop the subject for a little while. I needed Shaun not just for company but for his knowledge of the countryside this far from home and his survival instinct and knowledge of weapons.

We walked in silence down the tunnel for ages, passing areas of tunnel that opened out every so often where risen platforms would appear on the left or right of the tunnel. I noticed signs on the walls of some, barely readable. *W—ren St, Tot——am C—rt R-, -ha—ng —oss.* It was the last one where we stopped for a rest, climbing up onto the platform section and ascending the stairs to the surface. We sat in a setting sun, light fading over a silent, broken city skyline. I pulled out some of the remaining cooked rabbit and removed it from the clear bag I had wrapped it in. It was beginning to smell a bit, but hunger did not discriminate so much these days. In an effort to break the silence that hung between us, I offered some to Shaun.

"Thanks," he responded and began to eat.

I wondered what the city had looked like alive with people and cars. I had difficulty imagining so many people navigating around each other, all going in different directions, each with their destinations and occupations.

My thoughts were broken by the faint sound of horse hooves in the distance. Shaun reacted immediately, grabbed me by the arm, and dragged me back down the stairs into the gloom of the tunnel.

"We stay here tonight in the tunnel."

There was a pause as Shaun dropped off his pack and took out his water bag to drink. He passed it to me to take a swig of his water. I guess it was a sort of peace offering, an apology, as I had my own bag.

"Southampton is on the other side of this river running through the city."

He pulled out the map book to review where we were and where Southampton was.

I smiled to myself and patted Barkley on the head as I realized Shaun's silence had been time to think of what I had said. I guess he had no real alternative as to where we should hide out.

In the torchlight, Shaun switched between pages and finally beckoned me over to look at the map book.

"We have two alternatives, I think. We can retrace our route back toward the M4 and locate the airport you wanted to see." Shaun placed a finger over the point on the map. From there, we turn south and try to find the path called the M25, and here," Shaun pointed to a big crossing of the M25 and M3, "we turn southwest onto the M3 path and keep going all the way to Southampton."

"What's the other alternative?"

"We stick to the tunnels and find the one that takes us to the airport called Heathrow. But, I don't know which one it is; we need a map of the tunnels. It's safer for us to take the tunnels. There's no chance of us being seen, at least until we get to the airport. We will have to walk it. It's a long way, and we only have the torches. We will need to find sufficient food before we make the tunnel journey or risk being seen as we exit out at the platforms to the surface. I reckon it will take the best part of a day to get to the airport. Once there, we will need to get some horses to get to Southampton. It's a long way."

Shaun fell silent, waiting for response.

"Well, I've noticed on some of the walls down here a chart with different-colored lines and names along them that looks like some sort of map; I guess it's the places these tunnels open out at. We can't take the chart with us, but we could at least copy the bit we want with the places where the tunnels open out at so we can find the right one to take us to the airport."

Shaun nodded in agreement—it was the safer route for now.

"OK, tomorrow we will have to find food, top up the water bags, and find one of these wall charts to see if we can locate the right tunnel. For now, get some rest."

I scraped together a pile of stones to form a pillow and placed my bag over it to soften the lumps. Calling softly to Barkley, I beckoned him to lie beside me in the dark, providing warmth at least to one side of my aching body.

As I lay there, my mind wandered back to the prison where my mother was still incarcerated or perhaps even dead. Suddenly, I felt tears well up in my eyes as again the images appeared in my mind of the encounter with the Cardinal that resulted in the death of my father and our capture. I wondered what my mother had had to endure and whether she was still alive. I turned and hugged onto Barkley tighter and silently cried as I remembered images of Mags's dirty face smiling through a small, square hole in our prison, the ray of sunshine in an otherwise sad and painful place. I wondered what had happened to her after our escape through the chute. Was she punished for attempting to follow? I wished I could see her face once more and hear her voice whispering through that hole in the wall. A question suddenly struck me—what did we all have in common, Shaun, Mags, me, and the other kids, apart from all being imprisoned? We all had been exposed to a wider set of knowledge than we were supposed to. What was it that we knew that was so dangerous that we must be kept from telling others? Shaun had been exposed to technology, past weapons, books. Mags had been taught from banned books and seen pieces of past technology and machinery uncovered on her farm. What if the other kids had all witnessed pieces of past technology as well?

Suddenly, I sat bolt upright. Barkley jumped up in surprise. Mags had described a funny kind of book with keys that had letters and a blue screen, and it seemed to have been hidden deliberately, wrapped in black, unwoven, stretchy cloth in a box buried in the ground on the farm. I snatched out the log book I had been reading at the library. I went straight to the end of the log book and reread it.

Finally, all my research and detailed notes are on the laptop, which as mentioned before, I am sending to my brother's farm near Little Haseley. One day, I hope it may help future survivors and other generations understand our actions . . .

Was the professor one of Mags's direct ancestors? Or was that too much of a coincidence?

Chapter 10—His Eminence the Cardinal

The Cardinal stood staring, without any emotion, at his face in the mirror. Head angled slightly to inspect the profile of his skull and repaired skin. Raising his head, he looked at his neck. There were no signs of the hole where the young child thrust a knife a few days ago. Turning from the mirror, he walked across the room and returned to his desk. Seated, he took a coin from the plate on the right of the desk and placed reverently in his mouth. He felt the sensation of the coin, cool and hard, slowly soften, become pitted, and dissolve on his tongue as millions of nanomas within the boundaries of his mouth went to work to replenish the materials to maintain his form.

The collected memories imprinted within the billions of nanomas that constituted a compound brain began a cycle of reflection on past events to determine those memories that could be discarded and those that must remain. Past memories of his formulation into a look-alike human being to blend in and survive would remain even though this was one of the oldest pieces of data. The collective memories of human history that presented the pattern of power and control through belief in a higher authority had become his game plan of longevity and survival. It provided him with the human resources to locate the increasingly rare raw material he needed to survive. He could not afford to let the remaining human species relearn how to use the scarce, finite resources to make tools for engineering and research and to reeducate themselves in the past marvels of twenty-first-century existence. His memories of past existence that lingered in some recesses of memory were imprints of simple search algorithms and molecular manipulation, which had become fragmentary. They now served little purpose either by redundancy or supercession. Another purging was due to make room for new memory space. He sat quietly to the outside observer but his "mind" was in a frenzy of activity.

A gentle knock at the door registered to his auditory sensors, and he pressed a small button under his desktop to allow the door to his chamber to open. His second-in-command entered and stood in front of his desk.

Father Alucious looked briefly around the room, taking in the images on the Panasonic plasma screen monitor subdivided into sixteen pictures of different sections of the old prison—the children's area, the women's section, the courtyard and the guards' dormitories. Father Alucious brought a palm pilot from under his cloak and read the notes on it.

"Your Eminence, I have news of the two escapees . . ." He paused for a response from the Cardinal.

The Cardinal raised his eyes to meet those of the Father. "Proceed with your report."

"Two of our rangers have been found dead in the old city of London within the British library. The other rangers of the party identified two males, one youngish—about fifteen, sixteen—and a large canine running from the library. They headed for the underground."

"Well, did the other rangers capture them?"

Father paused briefly before giving a negative response to the Cardinal.

He did not have to answer as the Cardinal did it for him. "No, they did not—did they?"

The Cardinal held up his hand to prevent any forthcoming explanation from his second-in-command. The irritated tonal quality of his voice might have made one think that the Cardinal was angry or frustrated, but he was not capable of emotion. He had learned how and when to use certain tonal qualities in his voice. Imitation of emotion can provoke the correct response from his human servants. He found this a useful skill to invoke the correct response to his wishes. Fear, he found, was a great motivating force. Being able to instill fear by simple voice control and a correct arrangement of certain words had been useful in gaining control and subordination from those who were graced with his attention.

"And where are these boys now?" The question emphasized the word *boys* to make a point.

"They are still somewhere in the underground system."

"Where are they heading?"

"We don't know, your Eminence."

"I don't call this news, Alucious. What are the Rangers
doing for the Lord Master's sake?"

"Your Eminence, they did not dare follow. The tunnels are
known to be treacherous, and the fear of the underground
demons is greater than the fear of the Lord Master. It is more
tangible to them. The tales of being ripped limb from limb
down there persist."

The Cardinal understood. He was not the only remaining
manifestation of his kind. He knew this from the memory
imprints from his collective brain. There were more nanomas that converged and specialized other than just himself.
It would be foolhardy for him to assume he was the only
collective survivor. Perhaps the boys would no longer need
pursuing as the dark would swallow them up, never to resur-
face. But, he had to be sure.

"Get more Rangers down to the old city. They must guard
and patrol the exits to the surface. I want them captured and
brought back here. Is that understood?"

"Yes, Cardinal."

Alucious glanced across the room toward the cabinet on
which stood a decanter of the finest brandy. He had never
seen the Cardinal drink any, but he was always offered a
drink when he was summoned to the Cardinal's presence.

"Help yourself, Alucious."

"Thank you, your Eminence."

The Father moved over to the decanter, picked up a cut
crystal glass, and poured a generous three fingers of brandy
for himself. He turned to face the Cardinal again as he began
to formulate how to broach a new but related subject.

"About the mother of the boy called Abalus."

"Yes, what about her?"

"She was treated cruelly by the guard when she was ar-
rested. She was raped while you were . . . unconscious."

"The guard was dealt with, Alucious—he is no longer capable of committing such an act."

"Agreed, Your Grace, but I fear it has had a very distressing effect on her. She has attempted suicide twice and is now refusing to eat. She grows weaker each day."

"She was to be judged, was she not?"

"Yes, your Grace, she was."

"And she would have been condemned, would she not?"

"Yes."

"Then, let nature and her decision take its course. She will silence herself."

The Father finished his brandy, realized there was no more to be said on the subject, and took his leave of the Cardinal to attend his other duties. Closing the door behind him, Father Alucious began to doubt his belief in the Lord Master. The family and the bond between family members was sacred in the Holy Writings. This mother's crime was the act of protecting her young, to the death if need be. How can the Cardinal, said to represent the word of the Lord Master, allow such a transgression and in fact advocate the death sentence for this poor woman? Sure, she struck the Cardinal what could have been a fatal blow, but even the Cardinal must recognize this basic instinct to protect her child. There have been other inconsistencies with the Cardinal's behavior that by themselves didn't really stand out, but collectively, they tended toward being self-serving rather than serving the Lord Master. Over the past months, Alucious had become disenchanted. This latest reasoning from the Cardinal did nothing to reverse the trend.

The Cardinal sat and analyzed the conversation of his last meeting with Alucious; from certain inflections and intonations, he concluded that his second-in-command was holding something back. He had to keep closer tabs on the Father's movements to determine the root of this change in their relationship. Opening the right-hand desk drawer, he pulled out a small box no bigger than a small matchbox. Inside was a small, inanimate insect. Opening the laptop on his desk, he placed the box in the small aperture on the side. On the screen, he opened a window pane, selected the drop down menu program, and entered some parameters and a small thumbnail picture of Alucious. He hit the *save* icon; a small pinprick of blue light could be seen emanating from the bug, which now twitched excitedly in its box. Opening the door to his chamber, the Cardinal let the bug out of the box. It rose in the air and was away down the hall, programmed to locate and observe, transmitting back to the Cardinal on his laptop. The Cardinal mused to himself, *Useful nanomas, these little ones*. Returning to his desk, he viewed the laptop to check the bug was functioning and sending back pictures. The bug had caught up with his second-in-command heading for the guards' quarters and main gatehouse. The gatehouse was the location for the main radio transmitter where Alucious could communicate the Cardinal's instructions with the Ranger groups. As he observed, the Cardinal's thoughts returned to memory sifting and discarding of data no longer determined as being useful.

Buildings of steel infrastructure/locations—discard
Car factories—discard
Paint factories using titanium—discard
Aircraft factories and airports—discard
The Royal Mint—discard
Ore mines—save for future potential use
General housing and city locations—discard
Scrap yard locations—save for future use
Farm locations—save for future use
Factories and manufacturers that used iron, steel, titanium—discard

And so the purge continued through billions of nanomas that housed this data, sources of raw material long since exhausted in the main sweep of nanomas over the populated landscape that was England of the twenty-first century. The Cardinal wondered whether, like himself, other nanomas had evolved in other areas of the world. The USA for instance, where it all started. One day, he would find a way to visit these other countries to see for himself. He was painfully aware that, if the supply of coins ran out, his stockpile under the prison would only last for approximately ten years. He had that much time to find new sources or develop alternative ways to metabolize and remain in this form. These were the Cardinal's two veins of continued survival. The Cardinal knew that he had to maintain a delicate balance to retain the population's belief in the Lord Master and thus maintain his recognized position as the Lord Master's mouthpiece, ensuring they did his bidding for his continued survival. He knew this was a parasitic relationship that could easily be lost if he took too much or their belief was in some way dispelled. His position was held by a delicate balance of fear of the consequences of disobedience and the promise of unending, unconditional love. His war for control was against the human spirit and the thirst for knowledge that burned in the minds of some of the remaining population. The boy Abalus and the older one Shaun were indeed troublesome. The boy displayed the brains, while Shaun was clearly the protector. The recordings of Shaun in prison and under interrogation showed a young man of resilience and defiance. Whatever had happened to him or his family some time in his past had forged a hatred for the Lord Master, the Holy Writings, and himself most of all. His incarceration was necessary to prevent him spreading negative stories that might cause problems. The combination of two of them was disturbing—one, an angry survivor full of hatred, and the other, with an insatiable thirst for knowledge and understanding.

The Cardinal continued to watch the movements of his second-in-command in silence. Only the flickering light of the changing images on the large plasma monitor showed colors of life, the Cardinal's complexion pale and lacking in the light of the laptop screen.

Chapter 11—Journey to Heathrow

I don't how long I was asleep, but I was shaken from a deep slumber to see Shaun's face inches from mine with his finger held up against his lips and an urgent look on his face. Barkley had gone. Still in a slight fog of sleep, I could hear an odd humming noise coming from somewhere echoing down the tunnel. What was also noticeable was the lack of the sound of scurrying rats. All that remained was dripping water and the low, toned hum. The gloom took on a sinister atmosphere. I sat up carefully, cleared the fog from my head, and felt my heart thumping in my chest. A prickling sensation ran up the back of my neck. We sat in the dark and just listened. The humming was off in the distance somewhere. The tunnel acted as a channel to bounce the sound great distances with little loss.

"Come on, get your stuff together," was Shaun's urgent whisper in my ear.

I sat up, gathered my bag and jacket, picked up the small crossbow, and loaded a bolt. "OK, ready."

Shaun was off down the passage with his fingers over the front of the torch, minimizing the light to just enough to see the platform in front of us. Barkley appeared from the entrance onto the platform and ran after Shaun. Shaun jumped off the platform and onto the tunnel floor. There was a splash as he jumped into water running down the tunnel. The water came up to Barkley's chest, but he was able to keep pace by jumping through the water. Trouble was all three of us swooshing through the water made quite a noise in the tunnel, and I guess, just like the humming, we could hear echoing down the tunnel, so the sound of something splashing through water would carry too.

Shaun held up his hand to halt us in our tracks; we had only moved down the tunnel about three times the length of the platform we were on. All fell silent, and as the water calmed, we could hear the humming in the distance. What was not so easy to determine was which end of the tunnel it was coming from. Barkley seemed to know; he kept looking behind us as if trying to determine which direction a threat might present itself.

Shaun moved off again, slower and limiting the swooshing of water around his legs as he waded on. Only Barkley was unable to wade quietly through the water. We carried on, stopping frequently to determine whether the humming was getting closer or further away. Listening to the humming and not knowing what was causing it was unnerving, frightening, but it also played on the same curiosity for knowledge that had driven me on this journey in the first place. Shaun moved off again, following the slit of light from between his fingers. We had barely moved off when the humming grew in volume and was clearly approaching from behind us. Shaun froze, whirled round to face the opposite direction, and waded through the water to put himself between me and whatever was approaching. Barkley had frozen and crouched low in the water, staring into the gloom; he let out a low growl.

Shaun drew out the weapon that he'd retrieved from the building close to Erl's Court, pulled back the top with a solid click, and crouched lower in the water. I raised the crossbow and held it out in front of me, my hand shaking nervously. The humming seemed to be coming right at us, then just as suddenly, it stopped. Shaun stood and removed his hand from the front of the torch. The beam seemed so bright after my eyes had become so accustomed to the low gloom. All I could see was down the tunnel. There was nothing there, then just as I blinked, I caught a vague impression of movement off to my right. As I turned my head, Shaun had seen the movement as well and whirled round. We both could not quite make out what was there. It was like looking at a thin mist of an undulating mass. It was not quite solid. We looked at each other and waited to see what would happen next. I raised my crossbow and pointed it at the cloud.

Shaun saw my intention and whispered, "Wait, it will go straight through."

The mass slowly contracted and became a darker lump in the torchlight. The lump then took on the vague shape of a human in size but featureless, black.

A gentle hum emitted, and the figure drifted slowly toward Shaun. I raised my bow again. Shaun waved his hand for me to lower the crossbow. He stared directly at the human shape now halted two paces away from him. Barkley growled but did not move.

The human form raised a shimmering black arm, barely visible in the gloom but catching on the torch light as Shaun scanned it around the mass. Shaun stepped a pace forward and raised his right arm and hand to touch the offered limb. As his hand moved closer, the black arm melted over Shaun's arm, and from where I could see in the gloom, Shaun's hand was enveloped in the mass. Several seconds passed without a sound, and then the black mass expanded, lost the humanlike form, and became difficult to see once again. The humming grew loud and then moved off down the tunnel the way it had come. We stood in silence for several seconds just listening to dripping water and the ripples of the flowing stream. I splashed over to Shaun.

"What the hell was that? What did it do to you? What just happened?"

"I don't know what it was, but I reckon it saw we don't mean it any harm, and it's left us alone."

"But, that was incredible; what did it feel like to touch?"

"Dunno really, it sort of felt like putting your hands in a bag of rice grains that were constantly on the move."

"But, what was it?"

"You don't want to know."

"What do you mean I don't want know?"

I opened my mouth to pursue this but had second thoughts when I caught the look of fury in Shaun's eye and remembered the last slap across my face. There was something Shaun was not telling me. Barkley came and stood chest deep in water by my side.

"OK, we will have to get to the surface before we reach the airport. We need food. Next platform, we will see what we can find."

His fury gone, he took the lead again and moved off down the tunnel. Our progress was slow through the water and tiring. But, the humming had long gone, and we were alone in the darkness, save the torch beam. We had not travelled far before another platform opened out and the water got a little shallower. Climbing onto the platform, Shaun aimed his torch along the walls for any sign of a chart on the wall. None were found, so continuing the ascent to the surface brought us into daylight. The sun was not too high in the sky, and the chill in the air indicated that it was early morning. I turned to Barkley, pulled out the bag that had contained my last bit of rabbit, and held it under Barkley's nose.

"Go fetch, Barkley." He looked quizzically at me, licked the inside of the bag, wagged his tail, and ran off into the undergrowth.

I walked on down the path trampled over the years by people and animals that had wandered through the dead city. In the undergrowth were blackberry bushes and some apple trees in a cluster. I picked apples and berries and filled my bags. Shaun rushed up to me, grabbed the crossbow off my shoulder, and disappeared into the bushes further up the path. I sat and ate an apple and berries, smearing the juice over my face with my sleeve as it dribbled down my chin. I had forgotten how hungry I was and gorged myself.

"Abalus!" a distant yell from somewhere up the path alerted me. I left my bags where they were and ran off in the direction of the yell. Shaun appeared, dragging something through the bushes. It was a young deer.

"Pick up the rear legs, will you? Let's get it back to the entrance, skin it, and cook it up."

Shaun handed me back the crossbow; we hoisted the deer up off the ground and carried it back to the tunnel entrance.

Shaun settled down with a sharp knife and began the task of relieving the deer of its coat. I decided to gather wood rather the watch these proceedings. Barkley returned with a large hare, dropped it next to Shaun, and tucked into some discarded, raw deer organs.

By now, I had a fire going. These matches were great for this.

Shaun separated different chunks of meat and started the process of cooking it. We ate our fill, and the rest was wrapped in our clear bags and packed. It weighed a lot, but we knew we had some way to go, and who knew when we might be so fortunate next? The fire was extinguished, and the ashes spread out. The deer remains were tossed out of sight in the undergrowth. Once again, we submerged into the tunnels, checking the walls for any signs of charts.

We found one, almost all gone, but we were able to see we were at a place called Piccadilly Circus from comparing the map book names with _I_C___LY __R_S. Now, we had to find our way to the right tunnel to take us to Green Park and then Hyde Park Corner. We had two choices of tunnel, the one we came out of or a second that ran below it. We opted for the second and were off on our way again. We came to a second opening and platform; we realized we had gone in the wrong direction when we figured out from the partial lettering remaining that we were in Leicester Square. So, we turned and retraced our steps and kept going. All we came across were rats and water, and we waded on in silence until hunger began to tell us it was time to rest up. With no day-light to gauge, we had no idea how long we had been going. The next platform emerged ahead, and we decided to make this our rest stop.

Searching around the stairways and corridors, we were able to piece together from the badges on the walls that we had made it to a place called Hammersmith. I was dog tired, and so was Barkley, having to spend much of his journey jumping through water. The platform was a welcome sight as a place to be able to dry off and have a bit to eat. The battery torch was all but spent now. Only the wind-up torch was usable. And I had a couple of candles from the cave in the woods not far from the prison fort. Looking at the maps, Shaun estimated we had another day to go before we got there. We slept deeply. I awoke first, quietly made my way to the surface, and looked out from a small hole that was all that remained of the entrance. There was a low glow in the sky and a chill mist in the air that told me it was just after sunrise. My legs were still damp and chilled to the bone from our previous day's efforts.

All was quiet, and I returned to the platform to wake Shaun, but he was already up and eating some fruit. I grabbed an apple, and without a word, we set off on the second leg of the journey.

Chapter 12—Pursuit

The message had been passed to the city Rangers from Alucious via the HF radio for the apprehension of two males, armed and with a dangerous animal. A troop of four Cardinal Rangers were deployed to seek them out, and fourteen guards were posted at the entrances to tunnels to try and pinpoint where the murderers were and where they were heading. Ranger Locke was the troop leader and one of the best trackers the Cardinal had. He knew the entry point to the tunnels was at Charing Cross, but from there, they could have gone in one of five directions. Two guards were sent to Piccadilly, two to Leicester Square with Ranger Sims, two to the Embankment with Ranger Johns, two guards to Green Park, and two to St James Park. Locke had two guards with him; Ranger Bennett had the remaining two. Each team were given a two-way handheld radio with instructions to alert Locke as soon as any evidence of the fugitives was located. Locke himself headed west with his two guards along the river, his gut telling him it was the way they would go. He was told they travelled east to get to Earls Court, and it would be reasonable to assume that they were now on a return journey back to familiar ground where they were able to hide for a couple of days undetected by the guards after their escape.

His handheld crackled, and a voice pierced into his thoughts.

"Locke, sir, you there?"

"Yes, what news?"

"It's Thurston at Piccadilly. There's evidence someone has been here." Thurston paused.

Locke pressed his talk button again. "Continue, man," he replied impatiently.

"Well sir, there's ash spread over the ground from a fire recently. It's cold but looks fresh. Also, in the bushes, flies were buzzing round what looks like the remains of a small animal. It is definitely fresh judging by flies and no maggots yet." The handheld fell silent.

Locke considered the information. His quarry were planning to stay underground for some time. They've cooked the meat to sustain themselves so they don't need to come to the surface. Locke pressed the button on his handheld again. "Can you tell the size of the animal? What was it?"

There was another pause.

Another crackle and the voice came through. "Its looks like it was a young deer, sir." Then, as if in explanation came, "We found the head tossed into the undergrowth."

Locke knew they had taken enough to easily last them two to three days. They were planning to go as far as they could in the tunnels. He knew at Piccadilly, assuming they did not go back to Charing Cross, they would be heading east to Green Park or back up to Kings Cross—unlikely, as that was where they had visited the old library and killed a guard. This only left Oxford Circus then east or north.

He pressed the handheld again. "Well done, Thurston—proceed into the tunnel and down to the platforms, and see if you can find which platform they were on. That might help us determine the destination. Call me when you have any news."

Locke now had an idea where to redeploy his teams even though he had no idea how far ahead they were. The remains were said to be fresh, so he estimated he was little more than half a day behind.

"Johns, do you hear me?" Johns was one of the Rangers at the Embankment.

"Sir," came the simple reply.

"Did you get all that?"

"Yes, sir."

"OK, leave the Embankment exit and make your way to Acton. You got a map?"

"Don't need one, sir. I know where you mean; you want us to get in front of them if they're headed toward Heathrow."

Locke smiled; Johns was always good at anticipating his orders. He'd go far as a Ranger, good instincts.

"Correct, wait for me there."

"Yes, sir."

Locke consulted his underground map. "Sims, you hear me?"

"Sims here, sir, I heard the news. Where do you want us to go?"

Sims's team was at Leicester Square.

"Head for Baker Street; there are several tunnels there. If they go that way, they have plenty of alternative tunnels to take. You will need to go into the tunnels and keep a sharp ear for any approach. We will need to know what direction they go if they head your way. You won't do that at the surface. Patrol the platforms."

"On our way, sir." Locke heard a voice in the background. "I ain't going down there."

"I assume that was the guard?"

"Yes, sir, I'll see to him in due course."

Rangers outranked the guards in the Cardinal's hierarchy, and the guard would do what he was damn well told. Locke knew Sims to be a bit of bully and not someone to argue with and so made no reply of his own.

Locke told the other two teams of guards to remain where they were at St. James Park and Green Park. If his instincts were correct, if they tried to double back, these two points would pick them up.

Locke turned to Bennett. "Take your guards and head for the Ealing Broadway entrance." Locke leaned over and pointed his finger on the map to Bennett. Bennett was probably the most familiar with this area. This old city was his patrol area; he knew exactly where to go. Without a word, Bennett turned, gestured to his two charges, and headed off on horseback, followed by the guards.

Locke continued along the river with the last two guards.

Locke had not travelled far when his radio crackled into life once again.

"Sir, can you hear me? It's Thurston here."

Locke detected a nervous, tense edge to Thurston's voice. He raised the handheld to his mouth. "Yes, what have you got?"

"Sir, there's something down here in the tunnels, but it's not our escapees unless they sound like a hive of angry bees."

Locke's blood ran cold, and he felt the rush of adrenalin. "Get out, get out now—move!" Locke turned his ride north and set off at a gallop; the guards spurred the horses after him.

Thurston dropped the handheld, turned to move back up the platform, and faced a cloudy mist congealing into the form of a human in front of him. A dark silhouette formed, shimmering in the dim light cast by his small, standard-issue torch. He raised his crossbow and fired. The bolt went straight through and slammed into wall twelve paces away. His mouth hung open, stunned. He dropped the crossbow and turned left to take make a dash up the stairs and the way out. The buzzing black shadow seemed to know where he was heading and blocked the exit to the flight of stairs. Thurston froze. He could make a dash for the tunnel, but if he did, it was a one-way flight to escape, and he knew he would not be able to outrun this thing. In the next few seconds, he knew this was his last few moments on earth. Although he had no fear of death, the fear he felt was not knowing how he was about die. The black shadow began to buzz louder, and the human form began to lose its sharp outline and dissipate in the air. In the blink of an eye, the black blanket was across the gap between them and completely enveloped Thurston. Thurston felt the whole surface of his skin tingle like tiny pin pricks. His ears became blocked, and he felt tiny pricks in his inner ear and then intense pain in his head. He lost his balance and sank to his knees. He resisted the urge to open his mouth and scream as he knew the result would be the black mass invading his lungs and stomach. His nostrils became blocked, and he began to feel the tingling pricks slowly working their way down his throat. The pain had become unbearable, and his mouth opened in terror, but no sound came out. Only the buzzing could be heard. Thurston's head felt as if it would explode. His last thought before his life dissipated into the black mass was, *I love you, Sue,* Then, his body collapsed on the ground facedown. Slowly, his body collapsed inward on itself, and the black cloud retreated and drifted off into the tunnel, a gentle hum giving away its presence.

The second guard Manson had witnessed Thurston's demise from the flight of stairs between the lower level and the entrance to the tunnels. Once he saw the cloud envelope Thurston, he turned tail and ran to the surface without looking back. Thurston had the handheld, so he was not able to call in unless he retrieved it, but there was no way he was going back down there. He squinted as he burst into the sunlight of the surface and kept running for several seconds. Out of breath, he came to a halt and dropped to his knees, gasping in lungfuls of air. Once his heart had slowed down, he stood up and looked back toward the tunnel entrance through the undergrowth. Nothing had followed him. He slowly returned to the entrance and listened intently for any sounds of life. All was quiet. He sat down at the entrance and waited.

At Green Park, the two guards were patrolling the platforms listening for any sounds of life in the tunnels. Access to platforms in this old tunnel system was not easy as the many of the stairwells had collapsed or were barricaded by someone in the past. Judging by the refuse lying around, the bones of animal carcasses strewn everywhere; this used to be someone's shelter, or perhaps several people. The two guards did not separate but remained in earshot and line of sight of each other at all times. They had heard the last communication between Thurston and Locke and decided to make their way back out of the tunnels. As they made their way between platforms to the surface, Jaks grabbed Stadas's arm and put his fingers up to his mouth to signify him to keep silent. Stadas held his breath and froze. Instantly, he heard what Jaks had. Somewhere down below them, they could hear the humming sound like a distant swarm of bees. The humming seemed to be getting louder. All caution gone, they both scrabbled over the rubble and fought their way up the dark ascent to the next level. Hearts thumping, they stopped to check if the humming was still there in the distance. Jaks had the handheld and radioed back to Locke.

"Locke, can you hear me? It's Jaks at Green Park."

There was a long pause, then Jaks heard his radio crackle in response, but no voice came over. He repeated his call. "Sir, if you can hear me, it's Jaks here at Green Park."

The radio crackled in response but still no voice.

Suddenly, Stadas grabbed him by the arm and yanked him to his feet. A single word was shouted in his left ear.

"Run!"

Jaks did not need any convincing, but he was too late. Out of the corner of his right eye, he caught a glimpse of a dark shadow that sprang toward him with lightening speed. He found himself enveloped in black mist and lost sight of Stadas. He opened his mouth to shout out help, but instantly, his mouth was full of black; his larynx was attacked, and he gagged and dropped. Stadas was slightly luckier in that he was not enveloped by the blanket of mist, but a small section of it did separate from the main body and settled on his right arm where he had grabbed hold of Jaks to haul him to his feet. A tingling sensation traveled up his arm to the side of his neck and into his right ear. He lost his hearing and then felt a dizzying sensation. He lost his balance and fell, grabbing at his ear as if trying to tear it off the side of his face. From his ear, the tingling moved deeper into the brain cavity, and he lost all control of his limbs. He found himself paralyzed, and then his eyes clouded over, and all went dark. Then, his body simply forgot to breath, and Stadas died.

As Locke was heading for Piccadilly at a gallop, his radio crackled, and a faint, disjointed voice seeped out. "Lo—yo—e—ts—ks—g—en p-rk."

Locke pulled up his ride, lifted the radio, and answered— no response. Then, another broken message came through. "S-r, if—ou ca- hear m-, ts he—at —re-n —ar."

Whatever the message was, it was coming from Green Park. Locke kicked his horse into a gallop again. He knew he now had a second problem to contend with. The mysterious entity he'd heard about was real. Nobody had ever been able tell him exactly what it looked like. The only consistent description he had ever been able to get was the sound it made. Now, it looked as if he were losing men. It raised the question; how did the two escapees manage to avoid it? Or had they? Perhaps they were already dead, in which case, he was losing men on a wild goose chase. Locke was fast approaching the Piccadilly entrance. As he approached, a guard appeared from the main entrance, waving frantically. As he drew up and swung off the horse, Manson ran up to him, burbling incoherently. Locke slapped him across the face; the shock had the desired effect. Manson calmed down and described what he had witnessed. Locke entered the tunnel with his two guards and went down to the platform where the remains of Thurston's body lay. In the torchlight, the body had taut, dry skin as if it had lost all moisture. The bones could be clearly seen pressed against the taut skin. There was nothing to suggest a struggle or fight to the death. He pressed the button on the two-way and called the team in St. James Park. There was no answer, even after several calls. Further down the platform, he heard the call come through on Thurston's radio and retrieved it. Checking his underground map, he took an educated guess and decided the two guards at St. James Park were attacked. The humming black cloud had traveled from Piccadilly to Green Park then Victoria and back to St James Park. If the escapees were still alive and if they did double back, he had no rear guard. Instructing one of his guards to look after Manson and get him back to the Ranger station, he remounted his horse and headed east once again.

Chapter 13—Heathrow

Shaun kept up a tough pace, and we ploughed through the watery tunnels for most of the day, at least I thought it was a whole day. It was not easy to keep track in the gloom of the tunnel with no daylight or sun's movement to watch. Every so often, I had the vague impression we were being followed, and I was sure I heard in the far distance a low humming sound traveling down the walls of the tunnel. Shaun did not seem to notice and just kept on going. Barkley was constantly nervous but bounded down the tunnel, keeping pace with us. We waded thigh deep to a platform then climbed out to take a break. As we sat in silence eating some meat and fruit, Barkley's ears pricked, up and he turned his head upward. I stopped crunching my apple and listened intently. There were voices, faint and erratic at first but getting closer. Shaun gathered up his stuff, including discarded bones from the meat, and gestured for me to do the same. We both moved off the platform and melted into the darkness of the tunnel. We moved deeper into the tunnel and stopped. It would be easy for anyone looking for us to hear us wading through water, so we stood in silence and waited in the dark. Shaun pulled out his black firearm just in case. I held on to Barkley to keep him calm and from moving too much. We waited.

It was not long before we could hear voices quite plainly. They must be on the platform. A torch light probed the darkness on the water and walls of the tunnel. I sank down as low as I could go. I needn't have worried as the light was not strong enough to penetrate this far. Then, I heard it again, the humming, somewhere off down the tunnel on the other side of the platform. The voices on the platform fell silent as well. Humming and water dripping were the only sounds to be heard. Then, one of the voices sounded urgent.

"Locke, Sir, can you hear me? It's Johns. We're at the Acton entrance. It's here ... somewhere. We can here that buzzing sound. We're going to return to the sur . . ."

The voice tailed off leaving, the sentence unfinished. There was a yell of fright and the sound of scrabbling and then several loud bangs like the sound of Shaun's firearm. Then, it all fell silent. The buzzing noise gently filtered down the tunnel and diffused into the background noise of the lapping water. We remained still for a time. Shaun replaced his firearm in its pouch turned and moved off up the tunnel.

"Come on, Abalus. Keep moving."

I raised myself out the water, the chill of the air keenly felt through my wet clothes. I shivered with cold or fear, or maybe both, and waded after Shaun, Barkley by my side. Our tired limbs really began to complain by the time we reached what I thought was Heathrow. We clambered out of the tunnel onto the platform, which was a difficult exercise as much of the tunnel had suffered collapse. We weren't even sure if we could get out. It was tough on Barkley too; he had great difficulty squeezing through some of the small gaps in the rubble. But eventually, the rubble collapse gave way to remnants of the platform and stairwells up.

Cautiously, we climbed up to the surface. It was dark. I had no idea if it was after sunset or before sunrise. I had lost track of time. My guess was it was sometime after sunset; the air did not have that damp, dew-filled feel to it like just before sunrise. I was ready to just sleep. We ate greedily after such long time wading and climbing. There was plenty of meat, but the apples were down to the last couple, and the wild blackberries were gone. Barkley was pleased to relieve us of meat and chewed noisily on bones, licking enthusiastically at the marrow.

"I'll take first watch," Shaun said.

I was not about to argue. I could not have held my eyes open for much longer anyhow. "Wake me when you want to rest," I replied.

The next thing I knew, it was dawn, the chilled air seeping into my damp clothing. I woke to a kick in the side. My eyes opened to see a crossbow pointed at my head. I looked to my right to where Barkley settled last night. He was not there.

"Your dog is safely muzzled."

I looked up into the face of a Ranger. He was about Shaun's height but broader across the shoulders and waist. He had deep-set eyes and two to three day's growth on his chin. Thin lips with a broad satisfied grin showed on a self-assured face. His shoulder-length hair was held back by a single, thin leather strip securing a ponytail.

"Where's your traveling companion?" His air of authority commanded a response from me.

"I . . . I don't know."

I looked around me. A guard had Barkley held at a short distance from his side by a pole with a loop of rope around his neck and a leather thong around his jaws. Barkley was not making it easy for the guard to keep him in check. He was a big, powerful beast and every so often would make a jump to break free, vigorously shaking his head. He jumped in different directions, trying to catch the guard off balance and take him off his feet. Shaun was nowhere to been seen. His bag was gone.

"Do you have control of this animal?"

"Sssort off, he adopted us."

"Well, make him calm down then, or I will have him shot."

I stood up slowly, shivering with cold, and felt a strong hand grab my collar and guide me over to where the guard was struggling with Barkley. I knelt down beside Barkley, placed my hands around his neck, and gently stroked his right ear.

"Barkley, sit. Keep still. It's OK—they won't harm you. It's me they want and Shaun." I knew this was not entirely true. In a low whisper, I spoke close to his ear. "Barkley, when I say run, you go. Run far away. Don't stop."

Barkley relaxed, sat with head cocked to one side, and looked at me with a good-bye in his eyes. He understood. As Barkley calmed down, the guard relaxed his grip on the pole and rope loop. I gripped the sides of Barkley's head, leaned forward, and settled my forehead onto his. Ruffling his coat around his neck in feigned boyish affection, I grabbed the rope loop and pulled my fingers down and around. Barkley felt the loop release its grip and leaped backward, shaking his head free.

"Run, boy, run!" I yelled and dived at the guard, knocking him off his feet.

Barkley whirled round in a jump that sent him traveling for the nearest undergrowth. A crossbow bolt whistled past my ear and embedded itself in a small tree to the right of where Barkley had disappeared into the bushes. I stood up and grinned back at the Ranger in the same satisfied grin that he had stared down at me with a few moments before. With a single stride, he stood one pace from me, and his right hand lashed out, open palm across the left side of my face, and sent a loud ringing in my ear, nearly taking my head off. It felt hot and red, stinging, but I turned my face toward him and stared right back at him, not showing any pain rather defiance.

"That was stupid, boy," he spat.

"Barkley is free to go where he wants. He is not for you to control any more than I."

The Ranger looked stunned by these words from one so young, I guess. He looked me right in the eye as if trying to gauge what to say next to have an impact on me. His face broke into a smile, and a slight chuckle made his throat wobble up and down.

"You, boy, are to be returned to the Cardinal, and so is your companion; where is he?"

"I don't know. He was on watch last night—that's all I know."

He looked me square in the face, trying to decide if I was lying or not. Despite the reddening of my left cheek, I stared back equally. He decided I was telling the truth.

"You and your companion have cost several of my men their lives. Did you know that?"

"I did not invite you or your friends to follow us down the tunnels. You made the choice to follow your orders."

"Boy, there are some things you don't understand and—"

I cut him off, "Yes, I know, and I'm trying to find out and understand. How about you?"

His jaw set tight, and his eyes became cold. He clearly was not used to being spoken to in this way by a young boy such as me. I felt a chill of fear run down my spine and braced myself for a second strike across the face. It did not come. The muscles in his face let go of the tension, and his face softened once again. He let out a heavy sigh.

"My name is Locke, Mathew Locke, and you?"

This took me a little by surprise. Why would he tell me his name? I was suspicious. Was he trying gain my trust by breaking down the formality of our positions, captor and prisoner?

In a guarded tone, I replied, "My name is Abalus, Abalus Rider."

Locke turned to the guard brushing himself off as he stood by attentively.

"Go and see if you can retrieve the dog."

"But, sir, it'll be long gone by now."

"That's an order, man," Locke snapped back.

The guard did not argue but turned and strode off to the bushes in the general direction of Barkley's escape route.

Locke turned back to me, smiled, and said, "Good, now you and I can have a talk privately."

Chapter 14—Ally

Shaun was calmly watching the scene from across the other side of the meadow that used to be the Heathrow runways. Using the Nikon Magnifiers, he kept a close eye on the events unfolding. He saw Barkley break free, and he watched intently as the Ranger played inquisitor on Abalus. As Abalus was led away, he saw the guard disappear from view in the same direction as Barkley. Shaun stood up and turned to walk deeper into the undergrowth. He was now going to have to play shadow and wait for the opportunity to remove the Ranger.

The guard returned about midday without Barkley. The Ranger and Abalus had remained just out of sight in the mouth of the tunnel entrance and surrounding remains of the large terminus. Now, it was nothing but a pile of rubble and rust, long overgrown with the return of Mother Nature reclaiming what was hers. Occasionally, the Ranger would appear in view to tend his horse. A wisp of smoke could be seen rising from the locale. Shaun guessed hot food was being proffered to Abalus. This seemed a bit unusual behavior for a Ranger or guard to not move off with his captives and begin the journey of deliverance to the Cardinal's command. Perhaps the Ranger was waiting to see if he, Shaun, would return, or were there other Rangers or guards out here right now searching for him? It was a possibility he should not discount even though he was sure that only one Ranger and one guard had approached the camp just before sunup.

Shaun had heard the approach of horses long before he saw the Ranger. Only two horses could be heard then. He knew they would never outrun the horses. Shaun was several paces away from where they had bedded down, sitting like a statue on a large, round, elongated mound. He would never get back in time to alert Abalus and get them both into the thicker undergrowth and trees before the Ranger got within earshot. Instead, he opted to sink back down behind the mound for cover and move back into thicker bushes and undergrowth. He had watched silently as the guard had dropped a loop on a pole from his horse, slung it around as the dog stuck his head up, and pulled. As he did so, the Ranger was off his horse and standing over Abalus, poised with crossbow aimed downward at the sleeping boy.

Shaun pulled the remains of the deer meat out of his bag, took a bite, and resigned himself to a patient vigil to search for an opportunity to get Abalus away from the Ranger. If it was just the guards, he would have taken Abalus back earlier. They were fools and poorly trained. But, Rangers were a different breed. Intelligent and resourceful, they were more at home out here in the country than any guard. Caution was needed and a respect for their capability.

It was mid-afternoon, and there was no evidence of any more patrols or Rangers. Abalus, the Ranger, and the guard were still at the tunnel entrance. Shaun needed to get closer and find out what was going on. This was a very unusual capture. They should have moved on by now. Shaun took one last look through his Nikon Magnifiers, gathered his stuff, and began to circumnavigate the meadow in the undergrowth. Every so often, he would stop and check to make sure the Ranger had not struck camp and moved off. As he crouched on the edge of the undergrowth, there was a rustle behind him. Shaun slowly and quietly removed the firearm from the pouch and waited, listening to the sounds of movement approach. The movement stopped; all went quiet. Shaun turned round slowly so as not to disturb the undergrowth beneath him. Facing behind, he saw Barkley sitting quietly, watching from a few paces behind. The dog seemed to be grinning at him. Shaun let go a deep breath, smiled, and held out his hand to beckon Barkley to come beside him. Barkley did so and lay down beside Shaun.

They were close down beside the elongated mound and a ridge that was once the side of the old terminal building, now just a massive rockery of sorts. There was plenty of cover as long as they stayed low and quiet. The guard was standing over the fire, stoking it with a stick. Abalus and the ranger were nowhere to be seen. Shaun guessed they were back in the tunnel somewhere. The horses were off to the right, tied to a small shrub. Shaun replaced the firearm; he could not gamble on the noise bringing more Rangers or guards to the scene. This was to be a matter for stealth and surprise. The guard would need to be dealt with first without the horses getting spooked and raising the alarm. "Barkley, stay here," Shaun whispered. Barkley crouched down, rested his head on his two front paws, and peered out through the bushes. Shaun made his way off to the left to where Abalus was sleeping. His bag was still there. He was after the crossbow, a silent weapon with enough power to drop the guard unseen. He just had to get to the bag. Shaun moved off and followed the gully that traversed down the left side of the small clearing by the tunnel entrance. Keeping an eye on the guard as he moved to watch for any sign that he became aware of his movements. Crouching low and keeping in the afternoon shadows, he crept closer to the fallen tree trunk where Abalus had slept. There by the end of the fallen log was the bag. Fortunately, it was at the nearest end of the trunk to the undergrowth. Shaun edged his way closer silently. The guard was still looking out over the meadow. The horses' heads were bowed, munching at the undergrowth close to where they were tethered. Shaun timed his movements to coincide with the horses tearing at the undergrowth to mask his advance to the edge of the small clearing. He was close; the bag was within two arms' lengths. He waited and checked the position of the guard, who was now crouched down on his haunches, staring into the fire and warming himself, unaware of how close Shaun was. Barkley had not moved. Shaun prepared to lift himself off his belly to take the one large pace needed to bring the bag into arm's reach. He rose from the undergrowth and took the one pace, holding his breath. He stooped low, lifted the bag by the strap, slowly reversed back in the bushes, and lowered himself to the ground. He checked the guard again—no change. Now, all he had to do was retreat back a little further away so he could retrieve the crossbow without giving his position away. He returned to where Barkley was still laying and knelt beside him, opening the bag, the crossbow and bolts tucked down the bottom.

Shaun loaded a bolt and contemplated where to place the shot. The best option to not raise the alarm would be in the throat. The guard would have no time to cry out and would be unable to breathe. However, a shot in the body was the easiest, low-risk target, but the guard might yell out and raise the alarm. At the moment, he had a clear shot to the back of the neck as the guard lazily poked at the fire. Shaun slowly raised himself out from the undergrowth to get the best angle for the shot. He raised the bow to eye level and sighted down the shaft of the bolt to just below the hairline. He squeezed the trigger gently. With a sudden thwack, the bolt was sent through the short distance of air and embedded itself deep into the guard's neck. The point split through the airway and larynx. The guard put his hands to his throat and fell forward. This was when Shaun realized his error. The guard fell forward into the fire. A big cloud of sparks and ash jumped into the air. The horses startled close by and reared up, baying in panic. The guard's body, now dead, began to crackle as the tunic and shirt burst into flame and the smell of singeing flesh began to fill the air. Shaun reloaded a second bolt, ran across the small clearing to the side of the tunnel exit, and crouched in the undergrowth.

Locke heard the horses neighing in panic and stood up from the crouching position he had adopted with Abalus as they studied a large map spread out on the ground. They were discussing Abalus's movements and future plan to travel to Southampton.

"Stay here," Locke commanded.

"It might be Shaun. Please don't kill him."

Locke looked back at Abalus and replied, "I might not be given a choice."

Locke took up his crossbow, loaded it, unclasped his hunting knife for quick withdrawal, and slung the shoulder scabbard with sword over his shoulder. Moving to the left side of the wall, Locke approached the entrance to the failing day-light outside. Keeping his back to the wall, he had full view of the right-hand side of the campsite. No one could sneak up behind, and he had a wide view of the clearing. He could see the fire was burning vigorously and crackling, sending sparks off into the gentle, late-afternoon breeze. The horses to the left of the clearing were still spooked, and their eyes were wide and staring wildly everywhere. As Locke edged further out, he took a glance round to the left. Just at that moment, he caught a movement off to his right, and jumping over the fire came the large body of a dog heading directly for him.

Shaun heard Abalus shout, "Barkley, no!"

Abalus ran out of the gloom and jumped directly in the line of the charging dog. Barkley pulled up short, almost knock-ing over Abalus with the sheer momentum of his bulk. Shaun chose this moment to rise from his hiding position on the far right-hand side of the entrance. Locke caught sight of the crossbow and raised his own. Both men stood staring down their crossbows at each other. Shaun's finger was poised on the trigger, the muscles in his legs primed to spring to the right to avoid an oncoming bolt.

Abalus whirled round and placed himself in between the two men, arms raised toward Shaun with all the desperation to prevent a tragedy only a split decision away. He shouted at Shaun, "He's our friend, Shaun. He's on our side!"

Shaun stood, absorbed this information for a second, and considered his options. He'd already shot the guard. Would this man still remain a friend when he saw the crossbow bolt sticking out of the guard's neck?

"He's right, Shaun. I'm here to help. I mean you no harm."

Locke began to slowly lower his crossbow, not taking his eyes off Shaun. The crossbow by his side, Locke took a pace to the right of Abalus to give Shaun a clear shot if he were to take it.

"Lower your crossbow, Shaun. You've done me a favor shooting the guard. He was in the way and not to be trusted."

Shaun looked at the Ranger and considered this. Was this a trap being crafted to ensnare them both? If it was, he was a courageous man to be here without more than just one guard. Perhaps he was a friend; either that or he had another agenda unbeknownst to the Cardinal. If Shaun was to find out what, he would have to go along with this, at least for the time being. Shaun lowered his bow and removed the bolt to demonstrate he would not be using it in the immediate future.

"Good choice, Shaun. Now, why don't you join Abalus and me? We have much to talk about."

Locke turned and returned to the shelter of the tunnel entrance and switched on his lantern, which cast a blue-white light across the map on the ground.

Abalus came across to Shaun and beckoned him to follow; Barkley followed them. The body of the guard was charred black but no longer burning. The sky was clouding over, and the light turned grey and gloomy over the large meadow.

Chapter 15—Alucious

Alucious sat in his quarters trying to think of a way to keep Abalus's mother from dying. She had lost all hope and believed her son to be dead. She was inconsolable. He had to tread carefully and try not to give her any more attention than was due when he conducted his rounds. His last communication with Locke had been unnerving; they had lost several guards and two Rangers in the hunt to track down and capture the young man Shaun and Abalus. Alucious could not shake the feeling that he was being watched. Of course, there were surveillance cameras all over the prison, and one got used to it and desensitized over a period of time. But, this was different. An underlying sixth sense was making him jittery. He kept trying to convince himself that he was just being paranoid, but it didn't help quell the feeling. He had to find a way to convince her that Abalus was alive without raising any suspicion on himself. He hoped that Locke would be able to capture Abalus. At least then he knew he would be in safe hands. In the meantime, Alucious needed to continue working a prison break plan to get these kids out. He could not bear seeing these children suffer under the hands of the guards, and the reeducation programs just did not make any sense anymore as far as he could see. Restricting a young mind to learn only the basics in reading and writing and allow access to only one book or literature surrounding it as the only source of information, pronounced truth, was a travesty, especially as the Cardinal had amassed the largest collection of books in the whole of Surrendom. Why was the library so jealously guarded? Alucious knew from his own enquiries as a young man that there was more to this world and his place in it than he really understood. He longed to get into the library for himself. He had been in the service of the Cardinal now for five years; it was the closest he had gotten to his goal. His ambition was to ingratiate himself sufficiently with the Cardinal to gain his trust and hopefully the access that he desired. But, over the last few weeks, it seemed as if he were being pushed away from his goal. He needed to formulate an alternative plan, one that did not involve being the Cardinal's close friend and confidante. The Cardinal did not seem to desire any close relationships with any of those who served him. He was totally indifferent. A knock at his door disturbed his thoughts. He got up off the bunk and unruffled his tunic. Opening the door, he saw one of the duty gate guards standing patiently.

"Yes, what is it, my son?"

"Sorry to disturb, Father, but I have Ranger Locke on the radio asking for you."

Alucious closed the door to his quarters and followed the guard back to the gatehouse. He was hoping that Locke had some good news for him. He nodded cordially to the other two guards in the gatehouse and moved through to the back room where the radio equipment was housed. As he approached the radio, he turned to the guard who had brought him the message.

"Could you please get me a drink, my son? I find my throat a little dry."

The guard looked quizzically at him, but after a brief pause, he said, "Of course, Father, what would you like?"

"Have you any of that chamomile tea?"

"I believe so, Father."

"That would be wonderful, son."

With that, the guard turned and went back out to the small kitchen off to the left just behind the large, windowed frontage.

Alucious closed the radio room door so he could not be overheard, crossed to the desk, and placed the headphones over his ears. "Locke, are you there? This is your Father Alucious speaking."

The inclusion of the word "your" was to let Locke know it was him. It was a subtle inclusion used not to raise suspicion by anyone overhearing his communications.

"I'll be brief, Father. I have retrieved the assignments intact. I will be processing them in due course."

This was good news. It meant they were both safe and Locke would be letting them know they have some friends in their quest.

Locke continued, "However, I have lost another guard since we last spoke. I will report in again tomorrow."

Alucious let out a sigh of relief and signed off with Locke. Just as he removed the headphones, the guard returned with his cup of chamomile tea.

"Good news, I trust?" inquired the guard innocently.

"I believe so, my son. Locke has the escapees in his custody. However, it has cost us dearly in manpower. Those tunnels are treacherous, it appears."

Alucious took a couple of sips of his tea out of politeness rather than thirst, bid the guards good night, and returned to his quarters.

The guard in the radio room removed the small, oblong stick from the socket underneath the lip of the desk and made his way to the Cardinal's rooms.

Chapter 16—South Coast

I noticed that Shaun kept his eyes on Locke as if half expecting some sort trap to be sprung. They sat sizing each other up over the offered food from the Ranger, some chicken and potatoes heated earlier on the fire but now almost cold. A warm drink was offered to wash down the meal. It was a brown liquid neither Shaun nor I had ever had before, but after a few sips, it seemed quite pleasant. It made a change from drinking the water dripping from the tunnel ceiling over the last couple of days. We sat in silence for most of the meal. As we finished off the last of the chicken, I could not stand the silence anymore.

"Come, you two, we all want the same thing now. Shaun, Ranger Locke is a friend; he wants to help. We had a long talk before you showed up. He's not going to turn us in. In fact, he's looking for the same thing as us."

"The same thing as you Abalus, not me. I don't see any point in digging up the past, and I sure as hell ain't gonna die for it."

"What's 'hell' Shaun? Where did you learn that word?"

Shaun opened his mouth to reply, then seemed to think better of it, and closed it again.

Locke cut in, "Perhaps I should explain what I am doing and who I represent. I've already explained this to Abalus, and he can fill you in with the details later."

Shaun turned his attention to Locke, a little grateful of the distraction from the question raised by me.

Locke continued, "I've been a Ranger for fifteen years now; it's been a good way to earn a living, and I like being on the move through this land. There's a lot of beauty here. Part of my work is hunting down wrongdoers—thieves, murderers, adulterers, and yes, those who have hoarded and read books of our ancestors."

He paused to take a sip of the warm brown brew. "Over the last couple of years, I have had doubts about the doctrine that has been fed to us through the Holy Writings. I have questioned some of the things I have been commanded to do in the name of the Lord Master, not out loud, you understand, but up here."

Locke raised a finger and pointed to his head. He continued, "Every so often, we are asked to bring in children because of what they have been saying at school to their friends or because they ask too many probing questions of their teachers. A couple of years ago, I was tasked to bring in a young girl not much older than Abalus. She had taken flight after a visitation by the local Father. He had reported his concerns that she was in possession of information outside the teachings of the Holy Writings. She took off. Guards were instructed to search her parents' house. They found various books hidden in different places about the home—some books by someone called Shakespeare who wrote plays; an instruction manual on how to maintain a car called a Ford Fiesta; some kind of medical book that had loads of pictures of the human body showing all the inside organs, muscles, and bones; and several others. Some seemed to be books of facts used for teaching; others were just stories. Anyhow, she was nowhere to be found. Her parents were hauled in for reeducation or condemnation, and I had to track her down. It only took two days, and I found her sleeping in a barn. Disheveled and filthy, she was clutching onto one remaining book. I guess it was her most treasured possession."

He paused to take another sip from his mug whilst recalling that fateful day. "As I approached, she stirred and woke. As she recognized me as a Ranger, her face became full of fear, and she backed up deeper into the hay, clutching her book. She pleaded with me to let her go, not take her in for reeducation. Then, she held out the book and begged me to read a couple pages.

'Please believe me when I say there's more to this world than you've dreamed about, and it's here in this book.' I told her I had no choice. I had to take her in; it was orders. Then, her face stopped showing fear, and it was replaced by defiance. 'Never, I won't let you take me. I won't.' She made a dash for the doors, and I made a grab for her arm. She twisted sideways to avoid my grip, missed her footing, and tripped. She fell headlong into a small pile of hay. Unfortunately, under the hay was a wooden rake. She fell straight onto the upturned prongs. I raced over to her and lifted her up. She put her hand to the side of my face and whispered, 'Just read the book, not for me but for yourself.' She died in my arms."

I buried her behind the barn. I could not take her back to her parents as they were no longer there. I reported the incident back as accidental death. It was never questioned. Nobody gave it a second thought."

Locke took another sip of his drink and refilled the mug from the pot. He continued again,

"I did not return immediately. Instead, I remained on the road and camped out. I had taken the book and on the second night took it out of my bag. The title of the book was *The World Almanac and Book of Facts 2010*. I did not read it all—it would have taken too much time—but I read enough for me to question how much I really knew of this land and our ancestors and how much knowledge we seem to have lost. I still have the book . . . hidden safe."

Shaun cut in, "But, you still hunt down hoarders, so what changed?"

"There's more at stake than you can imagine. Yes, I could have walked away from my job as a Ranger and continued to find and read books that I can barely understand. I would risk being captured and executed without any form of trial or interrogation. The alternative was to keep doing what I do and help get people away. The Cardinal accepts accidental death without a second thought. I have been able to save some children by 'accidental death.' I get them to the south coast away from Surrendom over the channel sea."

Locke fell silent and watched Shaun over the lip of his mug.

I took the opportunity. "Don't you see, Shaun? Locke knows a route to the south coast. He can get us to Southampton. In fact, he is keen to help us find the second set of notes."

"Oh, I bet he is," Shaun replied.

Shaun was clearly still not convinced that Locke was on our side.

"Who was that you were speaking to on your radio thing? What is he in the scheme of things?"

Locke lowered his mug. "That was Father Alucious. He is my inside man close to the Cardinal. He is none too pleased with the Cardinal of late."

"Oh, that's just great, somebody who can whisper directly into the Cardinal's ear." Shaun got up and started pacing up and down like a caged animal. Finally, he turned to face Locke. "Look, I can take care of myself. Abalus is the one who wants to get to Southampton, not me, so if you want to help, take Abalus with you and help him get there. Me, I'll go my own way and take my chances."

My jaw dropped as I realized what Shaun was saying. "Shaun, stay with us, please. You have saved me more than once, and you're a part of this as well."

"No, I'm done here. I'll move on in the morning. You go with Locke, and I hope you find what you are looking for. I really do."

I felt like I was losing a friend and protector, and I had a feeling of being exposed to an uncertain future again. But, it was clear that Shaun had made up his mind, so it looked as if we were about to part ways. Locke went out to check the horses.

Shaun walked past me deeper into the tunnel to bed down for the night. As he passed me, he said in a low voice, "Don't worry, Abalus. I won't be far away." With that, he lay down on his side and placed the firearm under his bag padded out with his coat into a makeshift pillow.

I then realized what he was going to do, and I smiled to myself and felt comforted knowing he was going to be watching from a distance.

I cast a few pieces of rubble from the ground where I was going to bed down for the night as Locke returned from tending the horses. "We'll set off at sunup, Abalus."

I nodded in agreement and lay down staring up at the clear night sky with a full moon low down on the horizon casting dim shadows over the meadow.

Locke took out and unfolded a thin, shiny blanket from his pack and threw it across to me. "Here, wrap yourself in this. It will keep you warm."

I looked at the small, rolled-up blanket, puzzled how something so small could keep me warm. As I unfurled it, to my surprise, it was big enough to wrap round me entirely. And when I did, I ceased to feel the chilled air of the night tugging at my still slightly damp clothes. It was not long before I drifted off to sleep.

The following morning, I awoke with a start as Shaun jabbed me with the toe of his boot. He was all packed up and ready to go. Locke was cooking something on the fire. The guard had been moved and bundled off to the side of the undergrowth. It smelled like he was frying eggs and some sort of meat. I hoped it wasn't a piece of guard!

Shaun said his good-byes after we had eaten and walked off toward the rising sun.

"Do you know how to ride a horse?" Locke asked as he started packing his stuff.

"Yes, I think so. My dad taught me to ride a pony when I was ten."

"Well, these are not quite ponies, but the commands are the same. Remember, you're on a much larger and stronger animal. Be firm with your commands; especially use the reins well, and dig in with your heels."

Locke was packed and ready; only one thing remained to be done before we set off—bury the guard. Locke did not want the guard to be found, not that he was recognizable. But, he had implied by suggestion that the guard was killed by the unknown entity down in the tunnels. I suggested to Locke, "Why not take the remains and chuck them into the water down in the tunnel rather than bury the body?" But Locke, despite the fact that the guard was effectively the enemy, said he was still entitled to a proper burial. I had never had to handle a dead body before. The cooked remains, black and charred, smelled awful, and the burned flesh was barely holding the body in one piece. It was difficult trying to maneuver the body while trying to keep contact with it to the bare minimum. Locke, on the other hand, had clearly spent some time in the past dealing the remains of a person. His expression was set in a mask of stone showing no emotion that suggested any affiliation with the guard ever existed.

We settled on dragging the body into the tunnel, and using rubble and masonry, we buried him deep inside the main entrance to keep rodents and other scavengers off.

Without delay after dealing with this task, we mounted the horses and set off into the country, keeping the sun to our left as it rose in the eastern sky. Barkley ambled along beside my horse, occasionally dashing off to investigate a scent that piqued his interest. But, he always reappeared sometime later, waiting ahead of us on the track. It was weird, really, as I always expected him to be catching us up from behind.

As Locke was the man tasked to locate and retrieve us, there were no other patrols out looking for us. If Locke was returning with us to the prison, the journey would take as long as it took us to get to London, so the Cardinal and his men would not be expecting us to show up for at least four to five days. After that, questions would be asked, and further search parties would be sent out. On horseback, we should reach South Coast in two days easily. It dawned on me, the risk Locke was taking. He could easily be exposed as a traitor. But, I guessed he knew what he was doing as this was not the first time he had done this, according to the stories he had told. Locke seemed unconcerned, and we did not push the horses anything beyond a gentle trot. The path he took was not too difficult, rather like when Shaun and I made our way to London. We seemed to be following what would have been a large road in the distant past, and although overgrown, the path was like a scar in the flesh on Locke's chin. Although a scar is almost unnoticeable after a few days unshaven, no hair grows on the scar tissue. Similarly, the path existed because, even though overgrown, no large or aged trees existed like the woods on either side of the path. After a good day's ride, we came to an area that clearly had been a large town in the past. The buildings, over the years, had been reduced to piles of rubble, the clue being regular-shaped square stones of the same size, semiburied or still partially standing, held together by climbing plant life, shrubs, and small trees taking hold and rooting close to the vertical walls. Some of the buildings looked much like they had in London in that people still inhabited them up until more recent years.

"OK, we'll rest up here for the night." Locke broke the long silence of the ride as we pulled up to what was at some stage a large building made of large, grey stone blocks. There were two main walls that stood almost to what would have been the roof. A third wall was about half gone, and the fourth was just a pile of rubble. The corner of the two standing walls provided us with shelter and a degree of protection as any approach by animal or human had to be from the exposed area of the collapsed walls. Locke dismounted, started to unsaddle his horse, and gestured for me to do the same.

I wondered where Shaun was right now. Just as this thought entered my head, a dog's bark off in the distance filtered through the trees and brought a smile to my face. If my guess was right, Barkley had been traveling to and from Shaun and us for most of the day.

"Gather some wood, and let's get a fire going for a hot meal, Abalus."

"Sure. How far have we got to go?" I inquired.

"Probably about another day and a half, sooner if the weather stays fine and the ground firm."

Locke pulled out a small bag with what looked like oats and mixed in water and some salt. He placed the mixture in an enamel pot and placed it by the fire, ready to put on when the fire was going. I pulled out the small box of matches from my bag, struck a match into life, and bent forward to set the small pile of dried leaves and twigs alight.

"Where did you get those?" A surprised Locke exclaimed, came over to the fire, and grabbed the box from my hand.

"At Shaun's hideout, close to the prison from which we escaped."

I went on to explain about the hideout deep inside the dug-out mound and about the trunks of possessions and books, pictures, the black bags, and other stuff.

As I built the fire up, I told Locke about the journey to London and the discovery of the professor's notebook hidden in the library.

We ate the oatmeal, and Locke made another warm, brown drink like at the last camp.

"What is this drink, Mr. Locke?"

"Call me Mathew. It's called tea, made from the dried leaves of a plant. This one is nettle tea, but there are others."

He paused to take a sip. "Have you still got the notebook, Abalus?"

"Yes, I do."

"Would you allow me to read it? I would be very interested in knowing more about this Professor Short."

I took a sip from my tea and pondered his request.

He continued, "Tell you what. I'll trade you. Do you remember that story I told about the girl?"

"Yes."

"Well, I'll let you have a read of the book she kept with her if you let me read the notebook."

"You mean you still have it . . . here . . . now?"

"Yes, I keep it with me all the time."

"How do you get away with it?"

"Oh, being a Ranger has its advantages, one of them being able to maintain a distance from the general staff of the Cardinal, including the guards. In effect, we are the field police, and no one polices the police."

I dug into my bag, pulled out the notebook, and passed it to Locke.

He went to his horse and pulled the *World Almanac* from his saddlebag. On his return, we swapped. Both of us held the books as if they were some kind of treasure. In some ways, they were. We sat by the fire, wordlessly opened the books in our hands, and began to read. In the flickering firelight, the words danced on the page. Some words I did not even understand; they were unfamiliar to me. What I did understand confirmed one thing for me—how little I really knew about the world I lived in and how much knowledge we seemed to have lost. The question lay heavy. What happened? From the notebook, it was clear that something our ancestors created rampaged across the land. It had not started here but over the sea. But, it got here carried by people and some of our machines like those airplanes I'd seen pictures of.

Locke returned my notebook and broke the silence. "So, this is why you want to go to Southampton; you're after the professor's other notes. You're hoping to find them somewhere at the university. Do you realize the chances are extremely remote? It was such a long time ago. The building is probably totally gone and the stuff inside either destroyed by time and weather or scavengers."

"I know, but I found this one, didn't I? The first notebook," I said, waving it in the air like a hard-won trophy. "The professor hid this one in the below-ground section of the library in an enclosed room. I bet he's done the same in the Southampton." My spirits would not be dampened. I continued, "What do you think about the Professor's notes?"

Locke was deep in thought but then responded, "It seems fairly clear that, whatever these nanomas were, they spread extremely fast and consumed a lot of raw material to multiply. They weakened a lot of our ancestors' buildings and destroyed many of their cities and towns. I guess the other notebook will tell us how it was stopped, if indeed it was. There's always the possibility they just died out when the amount of available raw material became rare or more difficult to access."

We both fell silent, lost in our own thoughts about what we had read.

Locke took another sip from his mug, the tea now cool and not so inviting as a steaming, hot brew. A slight grimace appeared on his face, his voice low. "I guess you have no intention of leaving when we get to the south coast."

"No, I don't want to leave."

"I think you should; it's the only way I can guarantee your safety."

"It's OK. Just get me to Southampton. You can leave me there. I'll be fine, and Barkley will protect me."

Locke smiled at the recollection of Barkley leaping across the campfire the night before, eyes ablaze in the flickering firelight, the ferocity of his intent clear to see, and had no doubt that it was indeed true. As if Barkley could read our thoughts, his bark could be heard off in the distance, and shortly afterward, he bounded into the camp with blood sticking to the hairs around his jowls. He had found his own evening meal. He settled close to the campfire and began to lick himself clean of the remnants of his fresh meat meal.

"I may stick around if you don't mind. I'd be interested in what you may discover. A second pair of eyes could be an advantage."

"Won't you have to get back? After all, they are expecting you to turn up with me and Shaun."

"True, but I will have at least one day to spare before I must start a return journey. Anyhow, get some rest now; we have an early start tomorrow."

With that, Locke began to unpack his bedroll and settle in for the night.

* * *

Shaun used his Nikon Magnifiers to study Locke's camp from a distance; he had already eaten a small badger with which he had shared with Barkley. The still-warm, raw meat tasted good and gave the much-needed sustenance he needed. He finished off the meal with his remaining apple, now softening and bruised—not at it's best but edible enough. As far as he could tell, Locke had not undertaken any covert actions that he could see. He wrapped his cloak around himself against the chill air and scanned the camp in the angle of the fallen building. The flickering light of the campfire caught on the faces of Locke and Abalus. There were no expressions of nervousness or fear that crossed Abalus's face during their meal by the fire. Shaun put down the Nikons and settled himself down in the small gully by a fallen tree trunk. It provided some barrier to the slow-moving, chilled, gentle, erratic breeze. He drifted off to sleep knowing that Barkley would wake him in the morning as the other two struck camp.

* * *

Alucious' intuition was telling him that he was being watched, and this was confirmed when the Cardinal called him into his chambers and played a recording of his conversation with Locke. He was queried on the inflections in his voice and the sighs of relief regarding the recapture of the two boys. Alucious was able to bluster his way through this by commenting that the loss of several guards and two Rangers was indeed a tragedy and a high price to pay for the recapture of the boys. His sighs of relief were his expression that he was relieved that no more life had been lost in the effort. The Cardinal impassively accepted his explanation, but Alucious knew now that his movements were being watched with much greater attention than was normal. If he was ever going to get to the amassed library of the Cardinal's, it was not going to be through trust and friendship, the soft approach.

He had managed to have a conversation with Evey, the mother of Abalus, and told her that her son was OK. Although he dared not risk telling her that he was also in the safe hands of Locke, who could get him beyond the clutches of the Cardinal. It was just as well, now that he was definite about being watched with close scrutiny. She had agreed to begin to eat and drink again, some vein of hope now given that gave her a sense of purpose. Alucious had a sense that things could become very uncomfortable very quickly. If he were to get these poor children out of this hellhole and to safety soon, he may not get another chance. He somehow had to get a message to Locke to warn him of the danger that was creeping up on them. The only way to do this was the radio contact when Locke radioed in tomorrow.

As his thoughts started to work on a plan to engineer an escape for the incarcerated children, his gaze into the flames from the hearth drifted up to the shelf above and then to the picture of the Cardinal hanging above the fireplace. He somehow felt that looking up to this man was no longer fitting or deserved, and he was filled with resolve to dismantle the grip this man had on the population of Surrendom. As he studied the picture, his gaze caught a small twitch on the top of the picture frame. Damn flies, they had been bad these last couple days.

* * *

The Cardinal studied his monitors on the wall reviewing the grounds and passageways of the prison. He then turned to the laptop on the table, tapped a few keys, and pulled up the view from his little flying bug. The bug was stationary inside his second-in-command's chamber. The view angle was downward looking in the main area. The fish-eye lens giving a broad but distorted view of the scene. As he watched, he saw Alucious move off his chair and go across to his window shelf. He moved out of view to the right.

Suddenly, the Father's distorted face came in close to the lens. Then, in an instant, a swift movement of his right hand holding a leather swat flashed briefly, and then his screen turned to fuzzy snow. The Cardinal cursed silently and slammed the laptop screen shut. Did Alucious know what it was? Doubtful. Anyhow, he had enough information from the bug to confirm his suspicion that the Father had an agenda of his own. Now, he just had to find the extent of the rebel movement that appeared to be operating under his nose.

* * *

I awoke the following morning to the sound of birdsong as the sun began to burn off the early mist. Locke was already rekindling the fire from the hot embers from the fire last night. As I unwrapped myself from the shiny, thin blanket Locke had given me, he dug into the embers and passed me a hot potato.

"Here, cut the skin off and eat. It'll warm you up."

It was cooked to perfection with a slight smoky flavor. I sat by the fire and cast my sleepy eyes around the campsite as I picked bits of hot potato out of the skin.

The horses' breath could be seen as they exhaled warm, moist air from their lungs. Barkley stood up, shook the mist from his shaggy coat, and trotted off into the undergrowth to relieve himself.

Locke placed a can of water on the fire, now coming alive with the fresh fuel of dry wood left close to the fire overnight. Finishing the potato, I ran my hands over the dew-laden grass, wiped the sleep dust from eyes, and wet my face, the chilled water washing away the last remnants of drowsiness.

Locke resaddled the horses to be ready to continue south. I started gathering up my stuff and packed my bag.

"How long will it take to get to Southampton?" I asked to break the silence.

Locke raised his eyes to the clouded sky and studied the horizon. "If the weather holds, we should be there by late afternoon. Definitely before sunset, I reckon. You ready to go?"

"Yeah."

"OK, mount up, and follow me."

I gathered the reins in my left hand, placed my left foot into the stirrup, jumped up, and sat astride my horse. The brown mare turned on the spot, irritated a little by my poor technique for getting up onto her back. As Locke trotted off, the mare followed without any prompting from me. We followed a path that took us between the remains of overgrown buildings. The path was straight and seemingly well trodden. Barkley spied a rabbit nibbling grass on the edge of the path and dashed off in pursuit as it bounded off into the trees. As the morning progressed, the clouds grew darker and more densely packed together, and the sky took on a foreboding, moody grey. The air freshened, and the smell of rain was in the air. A gentle drizzle cut down our visibility, and the ground softened under the horses' hooves. The rain became heavier the further south we traveled; by the time we reached the outskirts of Southampton, we were both wet through, but my excitement and anticipation at being close to my goal was not dampened by the weather. Because of the cloud cover, it grew dark earlier than normal. Locke took me to his hideout where he brought others to escape to the land over the sea of the south coast, which Locke called the Channel sea.

As we approached through the trees, a large, grey, square tower loomed above us. Ivy covered, a large proportion of the lower section of the building made it difficult to see at a distance. Unless you knew where to look, it would be difficult to find. The building looked really old. Standing in front of the main door, to the left of the square tower section was an angled roof and walls of what looked like a small village hall. Most of it was now completely covered in ivy and other shrubs. Only the sections of the exposed roof and the upper half of the square tower section could be seen, the rest camouflaged by the undergrowth.

Locke dismounted from his horse, patted him affectionately on the nose, turned, and approached the big wooden door. Withdrawing a key from under his coat, he inserted it into the lock, and with a loud clunk, the latch released the door; it became free to swing open.

"We'll hole up here for the night and dry out. Bring the horses in; they can stay inside the entrance here to dry off and rest up."

"OK, I'll take the saddles off and unpack."

Locke opened the inner doors that led into the hall section and paced down the center to a hearth on the stone floor at the far end. To the left was a large box full of dry wood.

Locke knelt down to the hearth and began to build a fire. As I began to remove the saddles, there was a scrabbling sound at the main door. I froze in mid heave of my saddle. The mare became agitated, her hooves clomping on the stone floor. I grabbed her reins and placed my hand on her nose to soothe her into stillness.

"Mathew!" I hissed intently to gain his attention. Sound traveled well in this stone building, and Locke stopped what he was doing and looked over his shoulder. Silently, I gestured toward the door. He understood, raised himself from the fire, and unclipped his dagger from the sheath hanging from his belt. He was light on his feet. I barely heard a footstep as he returned to the entrance. With his back to the wall beside the door, Locke raised his knife to shoulder height and quietly lifted the latch to free the door. Very slowly, he opened the door just enough to peer out. A broad smile crossed his face as he threw open the door, lowering the knife back into its sheath. There sat Barkley, head cocked to one side, looking very bedraggled and shivering from the cold rain, but his eyes were bright and alert.

He sauntered in with a wag of his tail and headed straight for the fire beginning to take hold in the hearth. Locke closed the heavy wood door and slipped the bolt in place. Laughing silently to himself, he followed Barkley back to the fire and dug out some food from his bag. After I finished with the horses, I joined him as he was placing some grain into a pot of water warming on the fire. I sat warming myself. He looked at me intently.

"You know I am aware that Shaun is out there following us."

My lips parted in mild expression of surprise.

He continued, "I would not be much of a good Ranger if I didn't know when I was being followed, would I?"

"I . . . I guess not, I suppose."

"He's good, you know, at staying just out of hearing range and out of sight. But, he is relying on those binoculars to keep an eye on us, and every so often they catch the sunlight."

"Binoculars, what are they?" I said, puzzled by this unfamiliar word.

"Binoculars, eye glasses, .magnifiers—an instrument that allows you to see things far away."

"Oh, you're talking about his Nikons."

"Ahhh, I see you have not heard them called that. They're called binoculars; the name Nikon is the company that made them, the brand name."

"Binoculars," I tried the word out.

"What other stuff has Shaun got?" Locke enquired. "Don't worry, I'm not about to do anything to hurt him."

"He's got a light that you wind up with a handle, and it lasts for ages. Once our other lights ran out, that one kept going. That's how we got through the tunnels, you know. He also has this black firearm that makes a loud noise, and small, hard metal is sent very fast into what you point it at."

Locke recognized this straightaway. "That's called a gun, and it fires bullets. How big is it?" Locke raised his hands in the air about an arm's length apart, and then, with a questioning expression, reduced the distance between his hands.

"Stop, about that big," I said.

"Ahh," he said again, "that would be a pistol or revolver—very effective weapons if you can get hold of the bullets for them. The Cardinal keeps stockpiles of those, but you won't find much elsewhere. I prefer the crossbow. It's more primitive, but getting or making a supply of bolts for it is no problem. But, its effective range is more limited, I'll grant you."

"How do you know about this stuff?"

"Well, my initial source was that almanac, but I have, over the years, acquired other books, you know."

He paused and dished out some of rice meal he had been tending as we talked. I took a plate of the warm meal gratefully.

"I understand why you want to find that other notebook of this Professor Short. I've often wondered how we lost so much knowledge and understanding that had been acquired by our ancestors. Some major catastrophe swept over their civilization and demolished their world. From these notes so far, it seems it was of their making."

"What I can't understand is why the Cardinal wants to stop us from reading so many of the old books that have been discovered over time. Why does he take them away, and why does he punish or put people to death for reading them?"

I felt my frustration mounting, and it could be heard in my voice.

"Abalus, tomorrow we shall go see what we can find here in Southampton, but don't get your hopes up. This place was a large city as well, and it was a long time ago. I have no idea what building we should be looking for or where it might be."

"I know, but I have to try."

"I know," a voice from the shadow of the doorway traveled down into the hall.

Locke was up on his feet in the blink of an eye, his crossbow trained toward the entrance to the hall. Shaun stepped out of the shadow cautiously, his face expressionless but alert. Locke stared at him, breathed out in relief, and lowered his crossbow back to his side.

"How did you get in?"

"It's a metal bolt," he replied as if that explained anything.

I smiled in relief but puzzled over how he got through the door silently.

"Shaun, you can be like some kind of ghost sometimes," I said jokingly.

"I'll explain later," he continued after seeing the question still burned on our faces.

"May I join you, Locke?"

"Please do. Are you hungry? There's some rice left, and I have some nettle tea."

"Thanks."

Shaun came and sat by the fire and accepted the plate of food from Locke.

Barkley opened his eyes, saw Shaun, wagged his tail a couple of times, and promptly closed his eyes again as if nothing untoward had happened.

Locke asked the obvious question before me. "Where is the building we need to find?"

"It's here all right. I'll take you there tomorrow, all being well."

"What do you mean?"

"We have company. There are guards and a Ranger about a half a day's ride from us. I suspect they have been radioed to intercept you."

"Radioed, what's radioed?" It was another word I had not heard of before.

Shaun replied, "It's a communication device to talk to someone over the horizon." Shaun paused for another mouthful of rice then continued, "You remember when we were in London and you found some cables running inside the walls and those sockets in the wall? Well, a radio is something that plugs into the wall like that. Those cables are made from a metal, and an energy called electricity flows through those cables and powers the radio. The Cardinal knows how to produce and use this energy."

Locke considered this last piece carefully. During the last communication with Alucious, he was very guarded and brief, and Locke knew something was not right. Perhaps this was it, and Alucious had no way to give him advanced warning without being discovered.

Locke made up his mind. "We have two choices tomorrow. If you, Shaun, know exactly where to go from here, then we leave early, search for this notebook, and leave as soon as we have it before they get here. Or, I remain here and delay them while you search for the notebook. I could leave a false trail and divert them long enough for you two to get the notebook and get away. Shaun, do you know how many?"

"One Ranger with ten guards that I could see."

"Two against ten, not good odds."

"What about me and Barkley?" I piped up indignantly.

They both looked at me bemused.

"Well, I can fight too, you know, and Barkley has been the best guard dog ever."

Locke looked little apologetic, "OK, but it's still not good odds."

"I think a delay or diversion will give the best opportunity given that we don't know exactly where to look. I know the building, but it's a big place, and I don't know how much of it we will need to search."

Shaun had said what Locke was thinking, and the decision was for Locke to delay the search party by whatever means possible.

Locke recalled Shaun's earlier entry to this little stone building sanctuary and asked, "So, how did you get into the hall, Shaun?"

Shaun dug into his bag and pulled out a large, round shiny stone about the size of his fist. "This is called a rare earth magnet. It has a strong attraction to iron. Follow me."

Shaun rose from his place by the fire and made his way back to the door. As the hand holding the magnet moved close to the bolt, it suddenly shot forward. With a loud thud, the magnet had stuck itself to the bolt.

"Abalus, see if you can pull that off."

I moved forward, grabbed it, and tugged. It moved, but it would not let go completely. Locke tried and managed to pull it off only to slam back on again. Shaun showed us that the best way to release it was to slide it off sideways to the edge so there was the minimum of surface touching.

Shaun then opened the door, stood on the other side, placed the magnet opposite the bolt, and moved the magnet slowly across the surface of the door. To my amazement, the bolt moved with the magnet and with little or no noise.

"Wow, that is magic," I said.

"No, not magic," Shaun replied, "just the appliance of science from our ancestors."

Locke smiled. "Next time, I'll lock the door from the inside as well as slide the bolt." He added, "I could do with one of those."

Shaun handed it to him, "Keep it. I have another in my hideaway."

"Thanks. OK, let's get bedded down for the night. I want you to be out of here before sunrise tomorrow, and I can start making preps for the search party."

As I lay listening to a gentle rain patting on the roof, my thoughts returned to my mother and wondering if she were still alive. I missed her terribly. Again, my thoughts wandered to the fateful night and the sound of her screams and whimpers on the night air. I tried to blot it out with thoughts of Mags and her smiling, gentle face, grubby but determined, as we spoke through a hole in the wall. I longed to see her face again and listen to her talk about her family. It was not long before I drifted off to sleep, but she remained in my dreams, soft and gentle with her head laying on my shoulder and the touch of her hand caressing across my chest and belly.

Chapter 17—The University

I awoke to a gentle shaking of my arm and looked up into the face of Shaun. He handed me an apple and a cup of warm tea. I raised myself on my right elbow and rubbed my eyes with the sleeve of my left arm. Locke was by the fire, stirring oats in a pot with water. There was no sound of rain on the roof, and no light was shining through the small windows high up the walls.

"The sun's not yet risen. You need to get a real head start. Give yourself as much time as possible to find the professor's notes," Locke said.

Shaun tossed a chunk of old cooked meat of something to Barkley.

"What are you going to do while we are gone?" I asked.

Locke poured himself a warm brew into a mug. "I am going to backtrack until I pick up their location and trail them. If the right opportunity presents itself, I'll reduce their numbers one by one quietly." His right hand went down to his side where the crossbow, concealed by his cloak, was strapped to his leg. He continued, "Plan B will be to get them to follow a false trail away from Southampton. For that, I will need your horse, Abalus. If they don't see a trail for two, they will know we have split up. It may divide their numbers, but you still won't be able to fend off five of the Cardinal's men without one of you getting hurt."

I heard Shaun whisper under his breath, "Don't be too sure of that."

I don't know whether Locke heard him; if he did, he did not respond.

"If I can, I shall turn them back north, but I'm going to have to do that without them catching sight of me. If they see an empty horse, they'll know they have been fooled."

So, Shaun and I were to be back on foot together again. I was full of anticipation and had my bag packed and ready to go in the time it took Shaun to eat his apple. Shaun got his stuff together, and Locke gave us some of his food supplies to help keep us going—a small bag of grains, some dried fruit and nuts, and some freshwater in a small canteen. Locke re-saddled the horses and unlocked the door. We said our good-byes and good lucks and promised to see each other again in the future. Little did I know at the time, but it was to be sooner than we had anticipated.

Shaun checked his bearings and headed off south. I fol-lowed with Barkley into the trees. The morning sky was just beginning to lose the deep blue-black of night as the sun, still below the horizon, began to illuminate the low, sparse clouds. We did not use the light for fear that it might be seen for some distance if there was a chance the pursuers were also early to rise to chase us down. We navigated through the thick undergrowth, staying off the main, established path. As long as the Cardinal's men did not know where we entered the forest, it would be really hard for them to locate our track unless they spread out over a wide area to locate it. As the sun rose, the dawn light through the trees began to burn off the morning dew, and the forest took on an eerie mood. As the dawn chorus of birds began, the forest came alive with other creatures scrabbling about in the undergrowth. Barkley took off to explore. Our pace was hampered by the under-growth, especially brambles, but it was better to remain in the safety of the forest than walk the exposed path. By about midmorning, the forest gave way to a less dense growth of trees and undergrowth, and the going became easier. Even-tually, the air changed its scent as the smell of salt air let us know that we were on the south coast. The growth was sparse here, open meadow pocked with old, broken buildings stand-ing in defiance to the erosion of the weather.

Shaun halted and surveyed the horizon.

"OK, we'll rest up here for a while then we head off over there." Shaun pointed off into the distance to my right. I looked in that direction for anything significant on the land-scape, but nothing stuck out from all the other tumbled-down buildings that I could see.

We sat, munched on some nuts and dried fruit, and swilled it down with water.

I asked Shaun a question that had been nagging at me since Shaun's reappearance last night, "Shaun, how do you know where to look for this notebook? I mean, I know you've read some books, and you have that stuff stashed away. You know how to use that pistol thing and that magnet thing last night . . ."

Shaun looked up from his swig of the canteen and gave me that cold, expressionless stare as if to look right through me. He seemed to be running some thoughts through his head as if to make a decision. "If I tell you, you must promise never to tell anyone else."

"I promise," I said swiftly and eagerly.

"I mean it, Abalus. I swear, if you tell anyone, I'll kill you."

The look on his face told me that he really was serious.

"I swear on my life never to tell anyone." My heart began to pound, and I had those nervous butterflies in my stomach.

Shaun fell silent as if considering the possibility that he was about to make a grave mistake. "I lied to you, Abalus, when you asked about my parents and family. I made them up. I had no family as such."

"But why? And what's that got to do with it?"

Shaun looked me in the eye for a few seconds, then his face bowed to the ground. "In a way, I am what you are looking for, Abalus."

I did not understand what he meant, and the silence between us was only interrupted by birdsong.

"I don't understand what you mean."

"I had no family, Abalus, because I am not human."

He looked up at me to gauge my reaction to this confession. I was dumbfounded. I still did not understand.

Shaun continued, "I am partly what you are looking for, the reason your world fell apart. I don't mean me specifically but past evolutions of what was created by your scientists. I am what would be termed as a biomechanical life-form."

"I don't believe you. You're so . . . so human!"

"That's because the memories of my ancestors have molded what I have become to survive." He paused again, gauging my reaction to what he was telling me. He continued again, "Not only that—I am not the only one."

My jaw dropped in a sudden realization. "The tunnels the other day, that black, humming cloud—it came up to you and went away and left us in peace. You spoke to it?"

"Sort of, we joined briefly to share information. I told it about the guards that might come down searching for us, and it promised to protect me—and you—as my friend."

It was the first time Shaun had used that word "friend" to define what we were to each other.

"What do you mean, 'joined'?"

"Let me show you." With that, Shaun raised his hand and removed his glove. "Place your hand in mine, Abalus."

I raised my hand and hesitated as it hovered just above his. Before I could move, he grabbed my hand and closed his hand round my palm.

I looked at his hand in fear and fascination as it seemed to lose its definition and become fuzzy round the edges. At the same time, I felt the whole surface of my hand tingle with tiny pinpricks jabbing in the pores of my skin. The sensation slowly traveled up my arm. Fear mounted, and I wanted to pull my hand away but could not release myself from the grip. The sensation went up as far as my neck and slowly receded back down my arm and to my hand. Shaun's hand solidified again and released mine. My arm pulled away with a jerk, and I checked and poked at it with my other hand.

"It's all right, Abalus. I have not harmed you. What you felt was millions of nanomas traveling up your arm. They would not hurt you unless I wish it or if you had broken free and severed the link between those on your body and me."

"That's . . . amazing . . . wicked . . . awesome."

"Abalus, listen, there is another, at least one more I know of."

Shaun did not continue but waited for me to figure it out.

I cast my mind back to the night the Cardinal visited, the attack, my knife in his throat, no noise, no sign of pain. "The Cardinal!"

"The Cardinal," Shaun repeated.

"But, you are so different, he is . . ."

"Exactly! He is evil in his chosen method of survival, but it's based on the memories of his past evolutions of nanomas. He rules by the power of fear and maintains his grip on humans to provide him with the kind of sustenance he needs."

"I don't understand what you're saying."

"Look, we don't have time for me to explain now. The thing is that the Cardinal does not know who I am, although I suspect he knows I exist. I had to get away from that prison, and you provided me with the opportunity to escape before he knew I was there and what I was. If he found out what I was and linked with me, he would copy all my memories and mold them into his own persona, and I might be left with his to do his bidding or be deactivated. If he had my memories, then he could track down this place and locate the notebooks, amongst other pieces of knowledge I have retained. I cannot allow him to link with me, and you now must not tell anyone what I am. I am trusting you, Abalus. As a friend, I am trusting you."

"You've never had a friend, have you? You've been alone for a long time."

"Longer than you can imagine."

"Part of my evolution has included memories of people with strong attachments to others around them. Those links have persisted as an impression of being a part of someone else. I could delete those memories, but they are part of what I am now."

"How have you got those memories from a human?"

"Believe me, Abalus, you don't want to know, but I fear you might find out anyway."

"What about the black cloud in the tunnels? Why is it so different from you?"

"It is the result of past coagulation of nanomas that carried out search patterns underground. It adapted to the environment. In the dark, little visual stimulus was available. It remained loosely linked because much of its search program criteria involved exploring tiny cracks and crevices, holes and the like. There was no requirement to take on a specific form. In fact, that would have put it at a disadvantage. Initially, it had plenty to continue the evolution process, but then it began to run out of available iron and other material it had modified the bacterium to metabolize on. The tunnels were home to other animals it learned to feed from. It decimated the population of rats initially but learned from the experience. The replication process was slowed down as well as the reproduction cycle of new bacterium. The need to consume large quantities was reduced. What you saw the other day is only a remnant of what is left of a permutation that almost completely filled the tunnel system under London."

"So, you and the Cardinal remained on the surface then."

"Not us precisely—but our ancestors, if you like, were running with different microprograms and adapted in different ways."

"What's a microprogram?"

"If you like, it's a set of instructions that the nanoma follows when it is first replicated and activated. Anyhow, we must get on. We might not have too much time if Locke fails to draw the search party away . . . if he doesn't turn us in."

"I trust him; he got me this far safely. It seems daft to turn us in now and travel all the way back north," I replied.

"He may have been using you to get to the other notebook or tell the Cardinal where it was."

The thought had not occurred to me. Was I too trusting of this Ranger? Was the story of the girl he told just that, a story?

"I don't think so," I replied but with a little less conviction.

Packing up our bags, we set off again, my thoughts still digesting these new revelations just heaped upon me. So, Shaun was a result of what had transpired, and there were others. It occurred to me that the same could have happened across the sea, and even more permutations exist in other places. I wondered whether Shaun had ever been curious enough to find out if there were more like him. He seemed more inclined to keep it a deep dark secret, at least until now. I understood now why he was keen to avoid contact with any of the Cardinal's men.

We approached a section of the meadow that had the partially standing remains of a large, red, square stone building. It was tall and must have been pretty impressive in its era. It was well built though, and most of it was still in place. The woods and plants had clambered in around it, and ivy was well established around much of its walls. Shaun headed for what would have been the main entrance. The building looked bigger than I thought now that we were close up to it. I stood at the entrance and marveled at the imposing sight this building must have been to those who entered and walked amongst the knowledge it held. I suddenly came to the realization that we had a lot of ground to cover. Where were we going to start? Shaun marched into the building. There was no door; it had been smashed in long ago. Once inside, daylight could be seen shining through various holes in the roof and the partial collapse of floors above. There were corridors off to the left and right of the main entrance.

"Well, this is it. There's not much here by the looks of it." Shaun's voice echoed gently round the walls.

"I reckon we should look to see if there are any underground rooms; that's where we found the first notebook. Professor Short meant his notes to last as long as possible."

"Well, let's start at one end and work our way back to the other," I suggested.

"We could do it in half the time if we split up."

Shaun looked at me, gauging if I was serious.

"No, we stay together. If Locke does not manage to delay the search party for long, if at all, it would be too easy to get caught if we are separated."

I was not about to argue; I trusted Shaun's judgment.

Shaun gestured down to the left. Barkley had already wandered off down in that direction. There was a staircase to the upper floors. Looking up, some of the floor was partially collapsed, bands of sunlight streaming down onto the ground floor. Dust particles in the air and what we disturbed as we moved down the corridor glistened in the bars of light. Some of the windows high up the walls had ivy coming inside the building. To the right was a large, open area that I imagined contained lots of books at some time in the past. Now, it stood empty and apart from small piles of wood remnants strewn about, covered in years of dirt and dust. There was not much to encourage success in finding one particular notebook. What was I beginning to think was that perhaps finding the first set of notes was sheer luck. But still, I had to attempt to find it. Readable or not, at least I'd know that the Professor had made it here and carried on his work in attempting to avert a disaster.

"Shaun, how did you know about this place?"

"It is part of a memory I have, a remnant of data I have not yet discarded."

"What else do you know about it?"

"Not much really, only the name of the building. Hartley, it's called, and it was part of a university complex, a place of learning."

"Like our schools?"

"Sort of, but much bigger and a lot more to learn."

"Hence the library—yes?"

"Yes."

Thinking aloud, I said, "If I were the Professor, where would I place a notebook to keep it safe but still retrievable sometime in the future by someone else?"

"Why hide it in a library in the first place? There must be plenty of other places to keep it safe," replied Shaun.

A good point, I thought. "I'm only going on the fact that Professor Short took the time and trouble to do exactly that with the first notebook."

"Well, it's all we've got to go with right now, so let's make the most of it while we have the time."

Still thinking aloud, "At the library in London, the notebook was in amongst books and papers completely unrelated to what he was writing about. All the other books had 'Parliament' written on them. His notebook stuck out like a sheep in a pig sty."

"Well, there ain't much in the way of books left here on shelves anyway," Shaun responded.

"Well, how about offices or storerooms, some space that is separated from the main areas, like in London?"

"OK, let's look for any other rooms or cupboards that are not part of the main library rooms."

I wandered over to the staircase to take a look. The stairs led up, and what was not so obvious was that they also led down. Much debris had covered most of the opening that led down a level.

"Shaun, over here—look!"

Shaun came over to the staircase and looked downward into the stairwell. "Well, it looks as if we have some digging to do."

We put down our bags and began removing the debris away from the stairwell.

* * *

Locke mounted his horse, clutching the reins of the second animal, and dug his heels in to set off at a walk back the way they had come the day before. He needed to get to some high ground and get a visual on the pursuers if possible. Locke backtracked until the sun had burned off the last of the morning mist that hung in the low ground pockets of the forest. Then, he turned west and trekked up a long rise. Toward the crown of the rise was a small, rocky outcrop that provided a small clearing from which to view the surrounding countryside. Before he reached the clearing, he dismounted and took out his eyeglass. He lashed the horses to a small sapling under the cover of the forest, walked to the edge of the outcrop, and squatted down beside a rock; his pale green and mottled-brown cloak allowed him to blend in with the backdrop of the forest and bushes. As long as he kept relatively still, no one would know he was there. He clipped on the cylindrical lens shield that minimized sun glare reflecting off the glass that might give his presence away to anyone observant enough to see the brief flashes of a moving, reflective surface. Pulling the telescopic glass open, he began to scan the countryside looking for signs of any human activity—nothing yet. Locke settled himself in a more comfortable position and waited.

Another advantage of this viewpoint was that it sat on top of a ridge that curved round and across the countryside from east to north in a long arc; not only did he have a good lookout spot, but also sound traveled round the arc of the hillside, trapped, unable to dissipate in all directions. While he sat and occasionally scanned the horizon, his ears picked up an odd sound, odd in the sense that it was not birdsong or the movement of small animals through the woods, which made up the normal background sounds of the day. In the distance somewhere off to north, someone was whistling as if beckoning a dog or dogs. Confirming the whistling, the sound of a dog barking could be heard off in the distance. Shaun never mentioned a dog in the party he saw, so this might not be the search party. Perhaps it was just a game hunter and his hunting dog. They were still out of sight. Patience was needed now. He trained his glass in the direction of the whistling and waited for any signs of movement below. He did not have long to wait. A single man on horseback came into view intermittently masked by tree cover as he moved down the path in the woods Locke had taken the day before. As his eye was concentrating on the figure approaching southward down the path, behind him, the sound of voices filtered through his senses and rang an alarm bell in his head. Locke lowered his glass and quietly withdrew his crossbow from its thigh pouch. The sounds behind were somewhere over the brow of the hill. Staying low, Locke eased back to the edge of the undergrowth and moved back toward his horses. He realized he had just been subject to a decoy technique he used himself on the odd occasion. He wondered who the lead Ranger was. He was good and must have been someone he had worked with before.

Quietly, he released the horses from their tethers, slipped up on the back of his mount, and quietly turned the horses to face north and move along the ridge, out of sight of the group moving up the hill and using as much cover as possible as he passed close to the rocky outcrop. He took a line that slowly reduced his elevation and kept his retreat below the line of the brow, moving into thicker woodland. Once in full cover, he found a tree that could be climbed easily and made his way higher to get a view of what was occurring up on the ridge. Through the branches, Locke was just able to make out movement up on the rocky outcrop he was just on. It was a close call, but this was good. He had moved north, and if they followed his trail, he would be able to lead them back north and away from Abalus and Shaun. He climbed down the tree and made off on his horse back along the path. He deliberately put the horse to a gallop to leave a noise trail for them to follow. He then veered off the main path under the cover of pine trees to the left and at the base of the ridge. He heard the dog barking and giving chase, the lone rider not far behind.

The main group was much farther away up on the ridge, probably contouring along it to keep the best view to follow him. The progress at a gallop was easy on the thick matt of pine needles carpeting the forest floor. Somehow, he had to draw the main group off the ridge; he did not want them to see the empty horse behind him. The best course of action would be to turn eastward and cross the path that ran through the base of the long ridge. Moving away from that ridge should get them to come down off it and move through the woods at his level. Leaning right and heeling the horse to turn right, he crossed the path and traveled deeper into the main forest. The undergrowth was thicker here, and brambles tore at the horses' flanks and Locke's lower legs. The gallop was reduced to a canter and plenty of direction changes. Locke did not want to make it too easy to follow. He needed to get about a half day gap on them to give himself time to plan his route and rest the horses. It would also give the other two the best possible time to find what they needed in Southampton.

Although he had a good distance between himself and the main group of the search party, he was finding it difficult to keep tabs on the lone rider with his dog. His guess was the rider posing as a game hunter was in fact the Ranger tasked with tracking Locke and the two boys. He was also much closer, but if he was to catch Locke, he wouldn't do it on his own. He would need the rest of the guards of the search party. Locke continued in a northeasterly direction, moving deeper into the forest.

Keeping his horse at a canter wherever possible, Locke covered a lot of ground without too much difficulty. He decided to stop and check where his pursuers were and how far away they might be. Moving up a gentle rise, he pulled the horse up, remained seated and still, and listened to the sounds of the forest. There were no unusual noises or the sound of horse hooves or dog barks, nothing but the birds in the trees and the heavy breathing of his horses. Locke dismounted and removed his eyeglass once more to scan as much of the landscape as he could while he had the chance. Crouching low, he raised the glass to his right eye, closed the left, and slowly began to scan from left to right across the arc of land where he expected any sign of his pursuers to approach from. All was clear for now, but the forest was fairly thick, and there were a lot of trees to obstruct the view. He raised the glass for a second time and repeated the sweep. Concentrating intently on the images of the distant trees, ferns, and bracken for any sign of movement, he was not aware of an approaching figure from behind, tall and wearing the cloak of a Ranger. The man raised his right arm, and the cloak fell aside to reveal a primed crossbow pointed at the back of Locke's neck.

"You looking for me, Mathew?"

The voice behind him made Locke's heart jump a beat, and he felt the adrenalin rush in the pit of his stomach. He recognized the voice. Without turning around, he replied, "Johns, somehow I had a feeling it might be you."

"Well done, Mathew. Yes, it's me." That was twice Johns had used his first name, not "Sir."

Locke slowly and carefully stood up and turned to face Johns. "So, how did you get in front of me?"

"An educated guess really, I picked up your trail from where you crossed the main track. I noticed from the hoof prints that one horse was lighter on its feet than the other and realized that you were traveling alone. As you changed direction and headed northeast, you've been contouring the land through the forest to save the horses. I know this area fairly well, you know. Well, I did train with you, didn't I?" Johns's voice sounded contemptuous as he continued, "Anyhow, I decided to go as the crow flies. It was a hard ride; my horse is tired, but I got ahead of you."

Locke smiled to himself. "Well, I always knew you would make a good Ranger. You have good instincts and were always able to anticipate my commands."

"Well, thank you, Mathew. I appreciate the compliment. Now, where are the two boys?" Johns's face was set with a gaze of distaste.

"They're long gone by now," Locke said almost offhandedly.

"I don't think so. You had no intention of taking them back to the Cardinal. You've been traveling south since London. So, where were you taking them?"

Locke considered whether to go for his crossbow. In three quick paces to the right, he could get the large trunk of a nearby oak tree between himself and Johns. Johns had not lowered his crossbow; it was still leveled at his upper chest area, and his eyes had not flicked away from Locke's face.

"Let me assure you, Mathew, my men will be here shortly, well not all of them. Some are traveling south to locate the escapees." Johns's face took on a puzzled frown. "Why did it have to be you? I looked up to you, you know."

"You got an hour or so, and I'll tell you if you really want to know."

"Sorry, no can do. I have four days to bring the boys in with or without you."

"So, I guess this makes you top Ranger then," Locke jibed.

Locke turned his head to face left to where his horses stood munching on leaves. He gave them an intent stare as if trying to focus on something specific on the horse. Looking out of the corner of his eye, he watched to see if Johns's gaze followed his. It did. In that brief moment of inattention where Johns took his eyes off Locke, Locke dived across to the oak tree.

"Shit!" Johns cursed himself and let a bolt fly to where Locke would have been standing a moment ago.

As soon as Locke had reached the tree, his own crossbow was out and primed. He took a swift look around the tree to see where Johns was. He caught a brief glimpse of Johns's cloak moving off to the right and soon after heard two heavy slaps on the horses' hindquarters and the sound of hooves galloping off into the forest. Locke was now deprived of a quick getaway unless he could locate Johns's horse, which must be some way back. First, he needed more cover, keeping the big oak tree between him and where Johns must be to have released his horses. He stepped backward, keeping low, and headed for the thick covering of ferns and bracken. As he turned, dived, and hit the ground, the whistle of a crossbow bolt went past his left ear and buried itself into the ground. Locke swiftly snaked his way in the bracken to a large, fallen, rotting tree trunk. Getting off his belly, he knelt behind the trunk and faced back the way he came to get a look for Johns. No such luck, he was already in cover.

From up the slight rise came Johns's voice, "Come, Locke, don't run away! Where's your sense of Ranger's honor?"

Locke wondered why Johns had not relieved him of his crossbow and dagger right at the start. Now, he knew why; he meant to kill him. The death sentence was already over his head from the Cardinal, who was only interested in getting the two boys back. Perhaps Johns had planned a duel; Locke had now spoiled that idea. From behind his fallen log, Locke chanced a second glance over the trunk. He was lucky; a gentle breeze had just caught the bottom of Johns's cloak as he had moved to behind the oak tree, advancing a little on his position. Locke wished he had his firearm, but it was in his saddlebag away with the horses. Johns had the upper position; if Locke moved away from the fallen trunk, he would be seen. The distance between them was about fifteen paces. Johns was a fair marksman with the crossbow, not the best but pretty damn good. It would be a big gamble if Locke made a run for it. What he needed was a distraction.

As if answering a prayer, the sound of gentle rain began to tap on the leaves of the overhead canopy. As the rain became more intense and the cloud cover dimmed the daylight, Locke saw his chance. As the raindrops became too heavy for the leaves above to hold them, the forest became a crucible of pattering noise, and the visibility was reduced by the white streaks. His hair got wet as did Johns; the water dropped across eyelashes and impeded the good aim of any marksman. Now was his chance to withdraw and gain the advantage. In a sudden decision, Locke leaped up, ran further down the gentle slope, and circled off to his right where the trees were younger but more densely packed. He weaved in and out of the trees and undergrowth and quickly took cover behind a larger tree to look back to see whether Johns was in pursuit. Johns could not be seen; Locke guessed he was still behind the oak.

"Locke!" the shout came through trees. "You coward! Where are you going to go? You have no horses."

Locke did not respond, not wishing to give away his position. Clearly Johns had lost sight of him in the rain. Keeping in a crouch, Locke continued to move round to the right in an arc that would slowly bring him up the rise on Johns's right flank. His cloak was now heavy with water, and that restricted his movement, so he discarded it, taking note of the tree he left it under to retrieve later. Staying low amongst the ferns and shrubs, Locke worked his way round, keeping an eye on the oak for any sign of Johns. The rain had eased slightly, but heavy drops were still rolling off the upper canopy, clattering to the floor of the forest. From where he crouched in the ferns behind another fallen, dead tree, Locke could just make Johns's legs where he was squatting behind the oak. The rest of him was obscured by the tree. The opportunity now presented itself. One carefully aimed bolt could incapacitate Johns. A bolt in the leg would give Locke the chance he needed. Releasing his crossbow, he primed it and placed a bolt in the stock. Raising his arm to the level of his eye, he trained the bow on the protruding leg. The distance between them was about twenty-five paces. Locke breathed out, steadied his arm, released the bolt, and ducked below the ferns again. Johns's yell of pain let him know he struck his target. He raised his head above the ferns to get Johns's position.

"You bastard, Locke! You're a done man; you're through! Your days are numbered."

Locke watched as Johns painfully attempted to extract the bolt from his thigh just above the knee. He cursed under his breath but not with much conviction. He was aiming for the knee to prevent Johns from getting up!

Locke broke cover and ran straight toward Johns while he struggled to remove the bolt and stand up. Johns saw the approach, let go of the bolt in his leg, raised his crossbow, and fired. The bolt flashed through the air, grazed the side of Locke's rib cage, and carried on, its flight barely deflected. Locke felt like a red hot poker had just been slapped on the side of his chest, but it did not stop his flight toward his foe. As he reached Johns, he brought his right palm up under Johns's chin locked his arm at the elbow. His palm connected just on the side of his chin. Johns was already off

balance with his leg and went over on his back, his crossbow released, dropped away out of his reach. Locke reeled
round quickly just in time to see Johns roll over toward his
crossbow. Locke withdrew his dagger from its sheath and
dove toward Johns's crossbow. Johns's hand outstretched to
retrieve it suddenly had a dagger impaled through the back
up to the hilt, his hand forced to the ground. He cried out in
pain and anguish and ceased his effort to retaliate. He was
beaten but still alive.

Locke reloaded his crossbow with a second bolt, raised it
at arm's length, and eyed it to Johns's forehead.

"You could have been a good Ranger, Johns. But you still
have some lessons to learn. I'm sorry it was you they sent.
I have no quarrel with you. One day, you might realize that
you're on the wrong side. I'll leave you here now. Where's
your horse?"

"Find it yourself," Johns said through gritted teeth.

Locke stooped to retrieve his dagger still embedded in
Johns's hand, changed his mind, and took Johns's instead.
Just as he turned, Johns with his left hand withdrew a second
knife concealed in a small sheath inside his boot. The motion of his body caused pain to shoot up his right arm from
his impaled hand, and he could not prevent a grunt of extreme discomfort. Locke heard, turned, and caught a glance
of Johns's left arm sweeping through the air. A flash of steel
caught his left calf, tearing the muscle. Locke went down on
one knee; at the same instant, he grabbed Johns's left arm
with his left hand as it swept across his body. He brought
his right arm under and up at the crook of Johns's elbow and
forced his left arm to collapse in toward his own body. Before he had a chance to release his short knife, the strength
of Locke's arm forced the knife into his neck. Johns exhaled
for the last time. Locke raised himself off the top of Johns,
sat back, and checked his leg. The gash was deep and free
flowing.

"Damn!"

He looked back at Johns's limp body.

"Damn."

He leaned over Johns one last time, closed his eyelids, and positioned his head at a more comfortable angle. It seemed such a stupid gesture, but despite it all, Locke had a great deal of respect for the young Johns, and it saddened him that he was the one to bring him to an untimely end.

Locke raised himself up and limped over to where his cloak had been discarded earlier. Using his dagger, he ripped a strip off the bottom and used it as bandage to wrap up his leg and stem the flow of blood. He needed to find Johns's horse and get at his Ranger kit. There would be a needle and thread and clean bandages there. He found a stout stick to assist him to walk and began the search for the Ranger's horse. He hoped he had time before the guards found him or Johns's body.

Chapter 18—The Notebook

It was tough going, and there was always the danger that the debris would collapse under us as we slowly removed rotting wood planks, masonry, and chairs made of plastic, as Shaun told me the stuff was called. There were even some metal bars and sheets across the hole. It was almost as if someone deliberately sealed off the downward stairwell. It was the first time I had seen such a large slab of metal. It was so heavy that we could not lift it off; we had to drag and slide it sideways just enough for us to squeeze down one side by the railings. I dug out the torch, wound it up, and clambered down the stairs. Shaun and Barkley followed.

"Well, where to now?" I asked.

"I have no idea, Abalus. This is where we take a stab in the dark, I guess, if you'll excuse the pun."

It was the first time I had witnessed Shaun being humorous. It caught me by surprise, but I smiled broadly. "OK, let's assume we are looking for another notebook that looks just like this one to start with. Anything that looks similar to this," I handed the notebook to Shaun to take a look at and continued, "is worth a look."

Barkley led the way down the stairs and disappeared into the gloom below. Without any conscious decision, we moved off down to the right, scanning the torch left and right in front of us. We checked each door; some were locked, but it was no real effort to break through. From the sparse internal space, some of these rooms seemed to be just places to read books. One room had a dust-laden table with several insect-eaten, thin books that pretty much fell apart when I picked them up. One good thing about this underground sanctuary was that little had been disturbed, and the outside weather had not found its way down beyond the sealed staircase. There was a layout map of the floor plan stuck on the wall, faded but readable. The areas down here seemed to be split up into groups.

"Shaun, let's try here first." I pointed toward an area on the map marked "Fine Arts." Moving into an open area, the smell was musty, and the whole place was covered in years of dust. As I cast the small beam of light around the area, shelves of dust-laden books that had sat untouched for years beckoned me like my belly beckoned for food to satiate hunger pangs. Distracted, I moved to the closest shelf and ran my fingers lovingly over the backs of the books. The dust fell away, revealing the book titles on the spine. I pulled one at random, gently withdrawing it and cradling it on my left forearm. I opened the cover almost reverently. The book had pictures and drawings of people in strange-looking clothes, some of them very ornately decorated with large ruffs around the neck and ballooned pants. Some pictures were of naked women, some plump others holding babies with the most serene expressions on their faces. Some of the pictures were so beautiful that I felt my heartbeat rise and my eyes dampened to see such beautiful work. I picked up another that had pictures of pearl-white statues of men and women, some naked or partially robed. Others showed statues made of a dark metal called bronze. In some of these pictures, the backgrounds showed the statues standing outside in cities or parks. The buildings were tall and alive with people all around them. I got so engrossed in these pictures that I jumped half out my skin when Shaun tapped me on the shoulder.

"Hey, come on, kid. There's no time for this ogling. You know what we came for."

"Sorry, but these are wonderful—look at this . . . and this." I flicked through pages for Shaun to get brief glimpses of the images I was looking at. "They're beautiful; our ancestors used to make these!"

"I know, Abalus, but we don't have time for this. Come on."

"Shaun, we've got to hide this lot before we leave and cover the stairwell back up so we can return later and find others who want to learn more to share it with."

"We will, Abalus. Now, keep looking." Shaun was getting agitated, so I replaced the book lovingly and continued my search.

I had no idea how long we searched each section, but I had to wind up the torch three times to keep a bright enough light to read signs in the gloom. Linguistics, Education—there was even an area with maps and books of the world. I had no idea how big our world was and where these places were, but I did recognize the word "London" on a map of England. For the first time, I knew what the land looked like and how big it was, which was quite small compared to other land areas I had never even heard of. I came across a large map of England and placed it in my bag for a further look later when we had more time. We had almost searched all the sections here. Shaun was searching a section that housed lots of thin books with floppy covers. Shaun called them magazines, another word I had not heard of. I came to a Theology section and casually brushed dust off books and looked at the spines. One book had a word I recognized. The Holy Bible. I recognized the word "Holy" from our book at home, the Holy Writings. I withdrew the book and opened to the first few pages. The book started with, "In the beginning, God created the heaven and the earth. Now, earth was formless and empty . . ." It was nothing like the start of the Holy Writings! Was this a belief in some other God of our ancestors, not the Lord Master? I closed the book and went to replace it in its spot. A book adjacent to the vacant slot slowly fell sideways, blocking the slot where the Bible was. I pulled it upright to replace the Holy Bible when I noticed this other book had a soft cover and was thinner than most of the others. It was a notebook. Looking at the cover, there was handwriting I recognized; it was the notebook we were looking for.

"Shaun, Shaun, I've found it! I have the notebook."

"Hoo-bloody-rah!" came the reply. "Now we can get out of here."

I opened the notebook to read it, but Shaun snapped it shut on my fingers. "Not now, Abalus, we must get out of here. It's too easy to get trapped down here. Put it in your bag, and let's seal this place up and make our way back to that old building. We'll be safe enough there for a while. Where's Barkley?"

Engrossed in our search, neither of us had noticed Barkley's disappearance.

"Barkley . . . Barkley." There was no response; all was quiet.

"Well, he's not down here, so let's get back up and seal this place off." Shaun moved off to return back up the stairs. I pointed the torch in his direction, casting dancing shadows across the passage walls, and followed him back toward the stairway.

We called down the stairwell one more time just to make sure Barkley really was not down there and began the hard task of replacing the metal sheet back into position, chucking all the debris back on top to cover it up. It was obvious that it had been disturbed, and if anyone came here soon after we left, it would be like a big sign, but it was the best we could do. Back out in the sunlight, I had to squint my eyes to get accustomed to the daylight again after having been below for so long. Judging by the sun's position, it was some short time after noon. There was a storm cloud on the horizon to the north. Shaun navigated us back to the path we took to get here and retraced our steps toward the old building we were in the night before. There was no sign of Locke or Barkley. I was worried about Barkley's disappearance. He had gone off before, but this was the longest time he'd been away. We made up the fire again and made up a meal of oats and some warm tea left by Locke in a small chest hidden in the corner of the far end of the room under some old canvas.

"Well, now that we have this notebook, where do you want to go?" Shaun posed a question I had not really thought about.

"For the time being, why don't we stay here? It's safe enough and close to the library; we could go back and get more books."

"Don't get ahead of yourself, Abalus. We don't know if Locke succeeded, and if so, how long before they realize the deception? They're bound to return to this area some time.

But, I agree we can do no worse than staying here at least for tonight. We can dry off our gear and get a good night's rest."

Resting was the last thing on my mind as I took out the second notebook and dusted it off wondering what answers might lay in these pages. I picked up my mug of tea and took a sip. Shaun turned his attention to his crossbow and firearm and began checking them over and cleaning the pistol. I opened the notebook, turned to the first entry, and began to read.

Chapter 19—2 August 2015

Professor Geoff Short had finally made it to Southampton. It took three days. The roads were clogged with broken-down cars and masses of people trying to head for the coast. The word had got out that the coastal areas did not seem to suffer this onslaught of microorganism attack as did the city centers and large towns. Geoffrey had found himself reduced to walking part of the way after his car had broken down as well. It was not unexpected. The sad thing about walking was seeing the expressions of fear and despair on the faces of the people he walked with on the exodus south. He was fortunate just south of Winchester; he came across a farm and stabled horses. After some negotiation and half his available cash, he managed to buy the horse. Being a good horse rider, he had no problems riding, except the horse was a Clydesdale. Big and lumbering, it was a powerful beast but one that could not be cajoled into a gallop. It was an old beast due to be retired really, but its steady walking pace got Geoff to Southampton.

He made his way to Highfield House hotel not far from the university, intending to book in, but when he got there, it was full of people awaiting ships to take them away from the UK. Southampton was packed with people. The mass of people had completely overrun any amenities and available accommodation. The good-natured people of Southampton had long since lost their sense of hospitality as a tourist town. Tempers were short; any food available to buy was long since gone. The supply chain was all but broken down, except whatever container ships still ventured to come in from the channel. Those ships were becoming less every day as more remained offshore in apparent safety from the nanomas overrunning the land. The one thing that seemed to have survived from total breakdown was the mobile phone system. Holes in coverage had appeared and were increasing as more and more mobile phone towers got eroded by nanomas. Southampton had as yet not suffered total loss. Geoff looked up his phone book list and selected Kevin. The phone rang out, and he got the message bank.

"Hi, Kevin, it's Geoff Short. I'm here in Southampton, and I need to speak to you urgently. Please call; you have my number."

That was two days ago. Kevin was a technical assistant in the microbiology unit. He had been a friend and colleague since college days. They had studied together until Kev had dropped out after the second year when his girlfriend was diagnosed with leukemia. Kevin's focus on studying completely changed. Pam, his girlfriend, died months later, and Kevin never returned to full-time study, settling instead for working at the university as a technician. His job did not reflect his ability, but he seemed happy to just provide support to the students and lecturers, which he did very well. Kev had got Geoff into the university and introduced him to the Head of the School of Biological Sciences. Explaining why Geoff was in Southampton did not take long. As it turned out, Geoff's reputation was well known; the Dean had attended several of his lectures. His arrival and requested use of the facilities was welcomed, and Kevin was assigned to assist as much as possible. Most students of the school were long gone, as were some of the lecturers, with families. A good part of the university facilities were being used to house people flooding in from the north.

The microbiology research labs were still operational. The university had its own power generator in the event of grid failure. Kevin was already working on finding a couple of small, portable generators and fuel to provide a backup system. Also, he started stockpiling what food and drinks he could scrounge. They could use some of the fridges in the lab. He also acquired a small microwave from somewhere in the school facilities, sleeping bags, some cushions, and even some liquid soap and towels. The lab already had a computer, microscopes, centrifuge, spectrum analyzer, incubation chamber, an isolation unit, an almost fully stocked cupboard of standard chemistry lab compounds and chemicals, and a whole bunch of other sundry lab instruments, tools, glassware, and so on—enough for Geoff to get started on anyhow. Kev said he could get almost anything else from other labs and other areas of the university.

Kev swung open the door and breezed in as if nothing catastrophic was happening around him. Geoff knew that Kev masked his fears and concerns with nervous, busy activity. He did not like to sit, mull things over, and tackle big problems head on.

"OK, Geoff what's first? What do you want me to do?"

"Kev, I have on this thumb drive," Geoff pulled the thumb drive out of his jacket's inside pocket, "all my notes, all my observations and discussions with Dr, Sonia Alderbry in the U.S., and some of her notes that she sent me to review and provide input. Also, there's a copy of my daily log notebook. Incidentally, can you find me a couple of fresh notebooks? What I think you should do first is read my notes to get yourself up to speed with what we are dealing with. It'll probably take you a few hours or so. You don't have to read everything, but I trust your ability to see what is significant and relevant."

"Yes, I can get you more notebooks, and I'll start on this thumb drive once I've made us both a cup of Earl Grey."

Earl Grey was an acquired taste they both had; it was over a cup of Earl Grey that their friendship was forged back in their student days.

"Good thinking, and while you're catching up with that, I'm going to start putting together a plan of action. I have to get my thoughts together and organized; the last few days have been so much upheaval."

Kev set up two Pyrex beakers with Earl Grey teabags, filled each with water, and shoved them in the microwave. Not the most proper way to brew tea, but needs must. Kev passed one to Geoff with one spoon of sugar and took his with three spoons of sugar over to the computer and switched it on to boot up. Once he logged on, he shoved in the thumb drive and started plowing through the highly organized folder structure that epitomized Professor Short's approach to his work.

Geoff strolled over to the large desk in front of a two-meter whiteboard. Sipping his tea, he inspected the drawers in the desk and found a whiteboard eraser and pens in one and a variety of stationary in the others, including some small exercise books. He took one out with some pencils and placed them on the desk, then retrieved the whiteboard eraser, and cleaned the large board to use for brainstorming.

Reflecting on the reports he was getting just a few days ago, he started to piece together what he knew about nanomas and the rapid evolution going on as they continued to replicate. The primary material being focused on up until recently was titanium, material used in the memristor component.

On the board he wrote:

Titanium, titanium dioxide (TiO_2)
Sources
Paint
Aviation industry
Titanium vanadium alloys are widely used in aviation in the making of landing
gear, hydraulic tubing, fire walls, etc
Bikes, motorbikes, autos, tanks and pressure vessels
Medical—bone and joint replacements
Pigments
UV skin creams
Ceramics industry
Toothpaste
Makeup?
Some plastics—white pigmentation

Ilmenite ($FeTiO_3$)— Russia, Norway, West Australia, Madagascar . . .
Rutile (TiO_2) found in sand deposits—Australia, Peru, Madagascar, Bolivia, South Africa . . .

Transition to Iron
Ilmenite has iron and titanium. Transition to this metal would be easy over a few generations of

modified *Shewanella*. The nanomas here would store data for both types and replicate to suit.

Ditto for aviation equipment and any other combination where iron and titanium were in the same proximity.

Human Victims?

Confirmed in the U.S., not here yet—not reported anyway—but comms breakdown. Don't assume it's not happened here.

Titanium in toothpaste may have been the initial attractant to human invasion or possible UV skin lotions. Possible some makeups—face powders—need to check.

Medical conditions—check on pH conditions—prosthesis using titanium

The list was not exhaustive, but he sat back, sipped his tea, and stared at the whiteboard.

His mind began to put structure around the problem.

The biggest worry was human invasion. Could the nanomas have adapted and invaded the red blood cells' iron atoms? If the reports out of the U.S. were true, there was no reason why it could not happen here if it hasn't already. How could we prevent human invasion? Maybe not at all—those who had escaped on ships may have done the best thing. Need to prevent ingestion and inhalation. We need NBCD suits used by the military or biochemical suits used by cleanup teams. Check with Kevin if the university has any. The only thing we have to go on is the slowdown of the nanomas' activity in the coastal areas. This must be the first area to explore. We're going to need a sample of nanomas to work with. That's going to be the first problem.

Geoff studied the board once again. As he sat, staring, the words began to merge together, and his eyes began to feel heavy. He let them drop closed to rest them for just a minute or so.

The next thing he knew was Kevin shaking his shoulder and calling his name. He had a sleeping bag draped across his chest.

"How long was I out?"

"' Bout eight hours, Geoff. Here, have another Earl; it's 8 a.m."

Geoff resented Kev's bright, breezy tone, himself still in a fog of interrupted sleep. He held out his hand to receive his tea, cast the sleeping bag aside, and got out of the chair to stretch his forty-two-year-old bones out of the slightly contorted position he had assumed in the chair while comatose.

"You want some Weetabix or Weetabix for brekky?"

"Umm, I'll go for—what was the second one?"

"Weetabix it is."

Geoff took a few gulps of his tea and found the warm trickle traveling down to his stomach reviving.

"Plowed through your notes last night. I think I've got the gist of it. I think you're going to need a sample of these things to work with, aren't you?"

"Yes, I can't do much but theorize without them."

"Already on it—while you were asleep, I contacted a couple of microbio students and asked them to contact the hospitals to see if they have any unusual cases. I've primed them with what the possible symptoms might be. They've got handheld CB radios to call in. I've just got to rig up this base station." Kevin gestured toward a fresh cardboard box, which was not there last night, containing what looked like a car two-way radio and other bits and pieces.

"Where'd you get that?"

"Out of an abandoned car a couple of miles from here."

"Thanks, Kev, that's well done. The next thing is a fully equipped environment suit. A bio hazard suit or NBCD suit from the navy would work, or has the university got anything like that?"

"No, only basic decontam gear. If anything major happened, it would be up to calling in a specialist bio hazard cleaning outfit."

"Are there any in the local area?" Geoff spoke through a mouthful of Weetabix.

"Not sure, we've never had to use one before. I'll have a look in the yellow pages. If not, I'll see if the navy can help." Kevin imitated Geoff with his own mouthful but made a better job of spitting Weetabix to the floor.

Geoff finished his last mouthful and turned his attention back to the whiteboard. "Now that you've read my notes, feel free to add anything to the board that might help."

"Sure thing, but I'll get this radio rigged up first. I have to locate some antenna cable to rig up the aerial on the roof if possible."

"OK, while you're doing that, I need to write an entry into my log book."

"Use the computer over there." Kev pointed to the screen with a Windows emblem flitting about.

"No, this log has to be handwritten. It might not be accessible in electronic form in the future if my guess is correct. Hand notes might be the only documented information available in the future."

Kevin's buoyant air seemed to desert him briefly as he understood the implications of this statement. It lasted a few seconds, and then with a broad smile on his face, he set about rigging up the radio.

* * *

Professor Geoffrey Short
Log entry 2 August 2015

Have arrived in Southampton after three days on the road. The situation is rapidly deteriorating as the spread and replication of nanomas goes unabated. Interestingly, the state of things here on the coast seems slightly better, so perhaps there is something in the pH value, and this idea has some basis. It is going to be my first area of investigation once I have a sample of nanomas to work with.

The most highly populated areas, cities, and large towns are the areas that are suffering the most, but this is completely understandable as the population in these densely populated areas are in effect the transport mechanism providing all the mobility for the nanomas. All the major transport infrastructure and private cars are about 90 percent inactive now, and more break down and fall apart as you watch. The main roadways are clogged with breakdowns, and people are walking toward the coast or in some cases, like London, to rivers in the belief that they will be safe. The communications infrastructure is almost completely decimated. I had a mobile phone operational yesterday, but now that has failed. Fortunately, Kevin has got us a two-way CB radio primarily to set up communications with students enlisted to help us. The authorities, police, fire brigade, councils, and so on, like the rest of the population, are slowly having their power to maintain control stripped away as communication and resources are diminished at an accelerated rate.

Because much of the damage is in the densely populated areas, at this stage, the smaller, less densely populated, and remote areas are likely to not have been affected. This suggests that as yet the nanomas are not spread as an airborne contaminant except perhaps for extreme weather conditions where high winds are available. I cannot pretend to know whether this is the case overseas.

Although the original intent for nanomas and *Shewanella* was reclamation of iron and titanium and other metals. As far as I can tell, the replicating mode of the nanomas has taken over and modified the function to utilizing the metals to multiply, each iteration accumulating the experience of the previous generation and manipulating the *Shewanella* to acquire the raw materials they need to perpetuate the function. The *Shewanella* provide the energy power plant for the nanomas, and the nanomas provide the mobility to sources of food supply. I have no idea at this stage the precise mechanism that has developed, but I can only postulate that the *Shewanella* reproduction and subtle modifications instigated by the nanomas combined with some capacity to retain data as persistent memory has somehow fueled a process of mutation or evolution. I do not have enough data to point the finger at one or the other as yet.

Another important area that I need to investigate is the effects of collections of nanomas splitting up as they are distributed by the population to transport themselves down train rail and power lines interlinking our population centers. Each collection or cloud, or even a small mass on someone's shoe, has different collected experiences and stored data. If this stored data (memory) does influence the replication process, then we should see in future generations' differences as they adapt to different environments and respond to different stimuli. Ultimately, they will evolve in slightly different ways. What happens if they recombine? What happens to the combined data stored as memory if two or more collections of nanomas, having diverged and gained alternative information throughout their replicating cycles, come back together?

Other questions I have to consider and investigate:

1. What happens when they are isolated from all food sources?
2. How long do they take to die out?
3. What mechanisms are available to contain or kill them off? Heat—cold—pH range—UV—radiation?
4. What is the self-mobility range to viable food sources?

Finally, the real burning question at this stage is has there been a direct invasion of a human being as suggested by one of the reports that came out the U.S? If so, I need to get a hold of a body to pursue this line of investigation.

* * *

Geoff paused for thought to test if he had missed anything pertinent. He could think of nothing else at this point and closed the notebook.

He looked up across to the lab bench where Kev had set up the radio using a bench power supply to provide 12Vdc power to the makeshift base station. It was on set to channel eight, but it was silent as yet. Kevin was not about; Geoff presumed he was out rigging the antenna run somewhere. *Well,* he thought, *if I am to make myself useful and get this underway, I had better see about getting a supply of salt or seawater.* Searching the utility cupboard, he found a five-liter plastic container nearly empty of a lemony-smelling cleaning fluid. He tipped the contents into a half-liter glass beaker from the bench and rinsed the container out as thoroughly as he could. Thankfully, the university still had running water. But, this might not last for much longer. He grabbed one of the two remaining handheld CB radios, switched on, and selected channel eight. He pressed the talk switch, and due to the close proximity to the base station, it sprung into life; little, red LEDs danced in a bar showing signal strength. Once Kevin had got an antenna up, they should be all right. Geoff scribbled a note to Kevin to indicate his intentions and said he would check in on the radio in about an hour and then on the hour after that if he was out for longer than expected. At the top of the note, he put the current time by his watch. Leaving the note by the radio base station, he left the lab and made his way out onto the university grounds. The now-congested city of Southampton had all but overrun the university grounds with people, some wandering about aimlessly waiting for some indication that a ship may come to take them away, some having rigged tents they had raided from stores or purchased (maybe). The signs of a breakdown of civil behavior were beginning to show as people picked the odd fight for a piece of ground to rest or pitch tents. Geoff could see things could get ugly very quickly. Fear of the unseen and frustration of not being able to fight the real enemy upon them, and they would take it out on each other, tangible foes to release anger and frustration. The survival instinct reduced people to look after number one against all others unfamiliar. Families clung together; mothers embraced children close to them, and fathers kept watch or were off acquiring food or, worse, weapons. Any sign of police or other officials was an ineffective deterrent against such a large mass of people if things did turn ugly.

Geoff stopped several times to ask people for directions toward the shopping center. Response varied from, "Sorry, don't know, I'm not from here," to, "Bugger off." Eventually, he ran into someone who was local, got the directions he needed, and made his way toward the main shopping area. The street was awash with people. Sadly, from his point of view, many were already reducing themselves to thieves and thugs, especially the younger set, who saw this looming human tragedy as an opportunity to make a quick buck. His throat involuntarily tightened and eyes moistened as the realization hit that he was indirectly responsible for what was happening. If only he had been stronger and more courageous in his conviction, perhaps the power mongers would have listened to the voice of caution and reason rather than the pursuit of dollars. His ideals of contributing to the betterment of mankind were sadly dashed against the rocks of reality. His inner grief slowly fueled a new determination to put things right somehow. His stride toward the supermarket became a jog, and he approached the main entrance, where a crowd of people blocked his way.

As he approached, it became obvious the crowd were being held back by another group of young men standing guard at the door armed with baseball bats, cricket bats, pipes, or pickax handles. Their conversation came within hearing range.

"Look, mate, we own this store now. You want anything, you buy it from me."

"We don't have any cash left. I have plenty in the bank, but the ATM doesn't work anymore."

"Too bad, mate, unless you have something to trade. What about the missus?"

The thug at the door leered suggestively at the woman standing on the guy's right.

The meaning was not lost on the more mature gentleman putting his request. The pleading look wiped from his face was replaced by one of rage. Without warning, and swift in its execution, a right hand lashed out, fingers folded in a tight roll, heel of the palm forward, and connected with the thug's upper lip, broke the front teeth, and burst the blood vessels in the thug's nose. He was sent backward, falling into two of his gang, knocking them off balance. Three more thugs closed ranks in front of the fallen leader, brandishing their weapons. The enraged man stood in a fixed stance in perfect balance—shoulders square, legs placed with the weight on the back foot, ready to commit a kick to anyone game to challenge him. His karate training was now evident to all who were there to witness. The man was shouting, "You bastards, who the fuck do you think you are? Don't you know there are hundreds of people out here going hungry? Get out of the way because I am not going to be held to ransom by a bunch of hooligans."

The crowd around him cheered as he walked forcefully forward. The whole crowd surged after him; the thugs were overrun, unable to raise a bat to defend themselves. The bravado gone, they ran back into the store toward the receiving depot. The crowd surging into the store spread out amongst the shelves and began to help themselves of what was left, which was not a lot as deliveries had stopped several days before. Geoff followed the initial surge into the store and looked at the banners indicating the categories of items in each aisle. Most people were helping themselves to the canned food and drinks, cereals, and packet edibles. Anything that required cooking or could not be eaten straight out of the packet was the last to go. Salt was low on anybody's list, so Geoff had no trouble finding enough—sea salt, rock salt, chicken salt—he grabbed packs of all types available.

He was tempted to join the other people in the store and take other food items but just could not bring himself to steal for his own needs, even under these circumstances. Leaving the supermarket, he headed for the docks to get a sample of sea-water. If it was not salt that was slowing nanomas' progress in the coastal regions, then it might be something else, some organism or other mineral content in the water.

His short journey to the harbor was only hampered by the number of people aimlessly walking about, unsure what the future held or if another ship would dock to take them away from all this. Using a piece of rope found in the dockyard, he tied the five-liter bottle to it and dipped it in the water from the wharf to retrieve some seawater to take back to the lab. His return to the campus found him wandering the streets. Above, he heard the noise of an approaching aircraft. He looked up into the sky northward. A twin-prop private aircraft was flying toward the coast, but something was not right. The engine kept sputtering and stalling, but it contin-ued to progress seaward. As it crossed the sky, losing height, the engine finally died, and it silently glided southward; the rush of air over the wing tips could be heard as it lost height and just made it over the dockside cranes still marking the Southampton skyline.

The plane disappeared out of view, but Geoff knew what the outcome would be. As he reviewed the event, he looked back at the cranes on the skyline. So far as he knew, none of them had collapsed as yet. His hands were full; there was no point in going back to the docks to get samples off the paint covering the cranes. But, it got his mind focused again, and he broke into an awkward run back to the campus.

"Shit, I did not call in." Geoff stopped in front of a bus shelter, placed the salt and container on the bench, and pulled out the CB.

Pressing the talk button, he said, "Kevin, you there? It's Geoff—you there?" He waited a few seconds; his radio hissed, and the thin voice of Kevin broke through, "Hi, Geoff, I was getting worried about you. Where are you?"

"Not far, I'm about five minutes away." He continued, "I've got some salt and seawater I'm bringing back. Listen, have those students reported in yet?"

"Yes, no luck on the hospital front, I'm afraid."

"OK, can you ask one of them—no, send both; it will be safer—down to the docks? Get them to get scrapings of paint and metal off the cranes on the dockside. I need to check out a theory."

"Sure, I'll get them some sealed sample jars and send them out."

"Great, I'll be back shortly. Give them my thanks and apologies for not yet being introduced. I'm sure we'll make that up tonight."

"Will do—out."

Geoff put the CB back in his pocket, retrieved the salt and container, and headed back to the lab.

As he approached the lab, he was confronted by a large sign in Kevin's scrawl with a broad, felt-tip pen. "Please knock and wait—clean room. Do not enter!" On the floor beside the door was a large, stainless-steel tray about a meter square and 100 mm deep. Also, a fire main hose reel had been unfurled from its stowage position down the corridor and hung in preparation on a nail at waist height. On the right were some plastic bags of plain white overalls, lab coats, over boots, and hair nets. Geoff smiled; Kevin was indeed a resourceful and intuitive man. He only wished he had the opportunity to work with him in more fortunate times. He knocked.

Kevin appeared at the door in white coveralls. "Geoff, OK, I know this is going to be a bit undignified, but strip off all your clothes, and place them in the plastic bag over there. Take off your shoes, and place them in the tray." Geoff knew exactly what Kevin was up to and did as he was told without complaint. "Stand in the tray and spray yourself and the shoes off, and put on a pair of the overalls and over shoes." Geoff was very self-conscious of the fact that he was standing naked in a tray spraying himself off with a fire main hose in a university corridor. Fortunately, Kevin was an audience of one. Kevin came out with a sealable bottle and collected a sample of water from the tray to put under the microscope. "Sorry about that, but it's the best I could come up with at short notice." He smiled apologetically.

"It's OK, Kevin. Under the circumstances, I think it's a great job. Where did the overalls and hair nets come from?"

"I got the students, while at the hospital, to explain what we were doing, and they were only too pleased to help. If they come up with a body that's dodgy, they know to contact us on channel eight on the CB."

Geoff entered the lab wet but warmed up again in the coverall and lab coat. Kevin had now rigged up the base station; more glassware, sample jars, distillation columns, and burners had appeared, presumably from other labs.

"John and Tricia, that's our two students, got all this stuff. Anything else you might need, they can track down."

"At this stage, I think we have enough. What I need now is to get some salt solutions of various concentrations made up and batched ready to test the effects. Next, I need to get a sample of nanomas."

"Well, let's see if you brought any back on your shoes. After all, that's how they got out in the first place, isn't it?" Kevin smiled and picked up the bottle of water collected from the tray.

He placed a sample on a microscope slide and sandwiched it with another on top, spreading the drops of water in between. He placed it under the microscope, focused in, and scanned the sample. On the 17-inch monitor screen, they both stared intently at the image. There were indeed organisms in the water sample. Geoff identified some *Shewanella* bacterium, but they were inanimate, dead, and there was no sign of a nanomachine.

"That's odd." Geoff puzzled over this. "Kev, can you run through a few more samples of the water and see if you can find a nano? They can't just disappear!"

Geoff went over to the whiteboard and added:

2 August 2015

Return from town—shoe sample—dead *Shewanella*—no sign of nano

It might be a bit presumptuous, but Geoff had a hunch. "Cup of Earl, Kev?"

"Please."

Geoff went through the motions of making tea, but his mind was working on other things. There was a knock on the door.

Geoff answered, "Who is it?"

"It's John and Tricia; can we come in?"

"No, wait there a second." Geoff moved over to the door and looked out. "Hello, I'm Professor Geoff Short; pleased to meet you. Can you both please strip off, place all your clothes in the plastic bag there, and wash yourself down, including your shoes? There are clean coveralls in that black bag and over shoes too."

The young girl's mouth dropped in shock, and her face flushed red with embarrassment. It suddenly dawned on Geoff that she was the only female, and here stood two guys gawping at her. He reciprocated with a blush of his own.

"Oh, I'm sorry. I do apologize. I didn't realize you were a fem . . . no, I mean I know you are a girl, but I forgot . . ." He trailed off the blustering, collected his thoughts together, and started again. "John, go grab that curtain on the window, and rig it across the passageway as best you can. Stay on this side by the door, allow the young lady to clean up first, and pass her fresh clothing when done."

John understood and did as he was asked. Tricia smiled meekly with appreciation at the attempt to preserve her modesty. It was a poor attempt; the curtain was not tall enough to provide a complete screen. And despite efforts, John received the occasional flash of breast or butt as she struggled out of her clothing. The reflection across the window was hard for him to turn away from, but he did his best. Tricia, for her part, knew he was peeking and took a little pleasure in teasing him just a bit. She pulled on the smallest pair of coveralls there was. Tricia was 17 years old and only 5 feet 4 inches tall, small and lithe with athletic figure. As she went to go through the door, Tricia grabbed the curtain and pulled, and with a wicked smile on her face, she disappeared into the lab with the curtain. Jumping up on a chair, she peered through the small window just above the door and waved at John to let him know she was getting her own back. John took it very well, unashamed of his body even if he was the butt of a joke. Geoff smirked at the youthful playfulness but decided that a sobering talk to remind them of the reality of the situation was going to be undertaken as soon as John was in. Geoff went and stood by the whiteboard again, almost as if he were about to give a presentation. It was force of habit. John finally entered and went over to the area set up for the kettle and microwave and looked for something to eat. Geoff sucked in a breath. "OK, guys, first, let me thank you for all your help so far. I really appreciate your assistance, and we have a lot to cover and not a lot of time to do it. I don't know how much Kevin has told you, so I'll give my slant on it."

Over the next fifteen minutes, Geoff built the picture and the future implications. He did not hold anything back.

"Now, I know this is a lot to absorb, and I don't want you to think you have to stay. If you have family to go to, then I won't stop you, and even if you don't and you just want to leave, feel free to go."

Tricia was standing by the radio almost lost in a baggy set of coveralls, looking across at John to gauge his reaction. John was staring at his feet and tapping the toe of his left foot against the side of the right. John looked up to catch Geoff's eye. "I for one will stay and help. I have no better way to occupy my time right now, and it will be real cool if we find a solution and I'm part of it. Besides, my home and family are in Yorkshire, and if I understand how this is going down, my chances of getting back are pretty damn slim." With that, John turned his eyes toward Tricia and nodded his head to signal he had finished. Tricia pulled up the coveralls, which immediately fell down to a baggy crotch position once again.

"I'm in too; I want to finish what I've started." The others were expecting more, and a silence fell."' Sides, where else can I get such a cool wardrobe as this?" She gave a curtsey holding the voluminous coveralls out from her legs. "That's it."

"OK then," Geoff sighed, "in that case, we'll see what we can rig up to give you a bit more privacy for the clean-off shower outside."

"Don't worry too much about that; we have more important things to contend with," Tricia replied.

John followed on, "What do you want us to do next, Professor?"

"Call me Geoff . . . Right, Kevin, can you show these two how to use that microscope and how to set up samples and cultures? What I need is a count of the *Shewanella* and nanos in that water sample and then a second count on the sample from the tray the two students since had rinsed off. Once they know what to do, Kev, I need you to help me set up a fine-salt spray tank.

As Kevin set about getting John and Tricia up and running, Geoff went over and added some more notes to his log.

* * *

Professor Geoffrey Short
Log entry, 2 August 2015, p.m.
This morning brought home the seriousness of the situation. The people in Southampton, and I suspect other coastal areas, are almost at the breaking point. Total social breakdown is not far away. While down at the docks, I noticed that the dockside cranes seemed to be fully intact and operational. These cranes are right on the front, fully exposed to the sea air and salt spray that can be whipped up in bad weather conditions. On a hunch, I have obtained some paint scrapings from these cranes to analyze the surface coating. Another odd thing has shown up during checking over water samples taken from the makeshift cleaning station where our

shoes were washed off. The initial samples showed inactive *Shewanella* but no nanomachines. I am conducting a count comparison of the entire sample. If the nanos are detaching themselves, it raises a couple of questions.

Do they detach before or after the *Shewanella* are dead?

What killed the *Shewanella?*

Where are the nanos?

By tomorrow, I hope to have more information to start formulating a way forward.

Chapter 20—Week of 3 August 2015

Professor Geoffrey Short
Log entry, 3 August 2015

John and Tricia have passed me the results of their count from the water samples. We did indeed find nanos in the sample, but there is a big inequality in the *Shewanella* to nanos total count. The ratio is about 10:1. I need to know what happened to the other 90 percent of nanos. There are three possible answers.

1. The nanos have developed a mechanism to be self-propelling. For what duration, I don't know yet.
2. They have dissolved or somehow been dismantled. Unfortunately, I don't have a microscope powerful enough here to detect the minute subcomponents of nanos, and untrained eyes will not know what to look for without sufficient resolution.
3. They have found a new alternate bacterium to attach to and control. This alternative suggests they have developed their own modes of mobility in search of new hosts. This backs up point one above.

We still have not heard from the hospital regarding a body that has died from unusual circumstances. Kevin has gone out with the two students looking for a sample of nanomachines from a car, factory, hardware store, or any other likely place where iron or titanium might be found.

The sample of paint from the cranes has been the first positive evidence that the sea air and salt content do have an impeding effect. The paint sample showed that salt deposits from condensed sea spray acts as an impediment to the nanos. Under the microscope were inactive *Shewanella* and nanos; the ratio was approximately 2:1, so some nanos are still disappearing. It's unfortunate I have no time-stamp data, but my guess is the crane samples are earlier generations of nanomas, and the shoe samples are more recent with some

185

modification to become more resistant to salt environments. Salt acting as an electrolyte in contact with the nanos may be interfering with the microelectronics. As the initial experiments were conducted with the *Shewanella oneidensis MR-1* strain, a marine-borne anaerobic organism, I don't believe the inactive bacterium we have witnessed is due to the environment, which only leaves the nano.

In the meantime, I have rigged up a salt spray tank using a large fish tank and a cleaning bottle with an atomizer nozzle.

The situation in Southampton is now definitely unsafe for the students to go out alone. I cannot send them out without Kevin or myself. Although we have a food supply that will last 7 to 10 days, it is prudent to replenish and accumulate whenever the opportunity arises.

Those who have them, presumably from raided abandoned stores, are trying to maintain contact with each other using CB radios. Scanning the channels reveals that a lot of people out there are trying to keep in touch with friends and loved ones. Some are using them for more antisocial reasons.

Tricia mentioned to us this morning that, before the Internet went down, one of her friends on Facebook in the U.S. had witnessed firsthand the invasion of nanomas on a human. The account was posted on a blog. The nanomas apparently had invaded a street tramp lying in a side street, drunk. As the tramp was lying in the gutter, the nanomas were able to enter the body via the mouth and nose. Any further details were not written in the blog, but at least I have solid confirmation of human invasion, and that is now a distinct reality. It's just a matter of time.

* * *

Professor Geoffrey Short
Log entry, 4 August 2015

The hospital called on the CB today. They have a corpse brought in from the northern outskirts of Southampton. I sent Kevin and John over to check out the body and see if he could gain samples. The body had been placed in refrigeration in the mortuary, and the room was isolated.

The following paragraph describes the state of the body as he found it.

The body was of a man approximately thirty years old; no external open wounds were found on the body, no bruises or signs of trauma.

Samples were taken from under the fingernails and toenails.

Internal inspection of the mouth revealed the man had fillings in three teeth, but the fillings were removed, leaving the cavities open. Dental records confirmed the fillings were of standard amalgam. Samples from inside the mouth were taken, including the extraction of one tooth. With assistance from the hospital staff, we retrieved samples of blood, lung tissue, stomach contents, feces, urine, and sections of liver and kidney.

We checked the samples for any evidence of nanomas. The cavity left in the tooth had the highest concentration of nanomas, now inactive; there are also nanomas found in the lung tissue. This is not surprising as the entry point was the mouth and nose. There were also some found under the fingernails but not the toenails. My guess is the gentleman had his fingers in his mouth trying to remove the unseen irritation taking place in his teeth. I also suspect that the mass was large enough to completely block the lungs, and thus, the man suffocated. I surmise the inactive nanomas were either damaged in some way during the event or separated from the host *Shewanella*.

Amalgam contains approximately half mercury and differing amounts of silver (30 percent), tin, zinc, and copper.

This is interesting—which of these metals were the nanomas after and why? What adaptation is going on now? Perhaps they are utilizing all of them? The concern now is of hearing of increased incidents of body invasion as this new piece of data is added to the memory of this particular collection of nanomas. What effect do these memories have if passed to another batch? I fear we may run out of time before a solution or defense is found.

Kevin has acquired a map of the Southampton area from the Hartley Library. We intend to plot and time the progress of any further human invasions we get to hear of. This first pin has now been added.

The students John and Tricia are with Kevin out spreading the word to anyone who will listen. The hospital and what remains of the police force, ambulance, and fire brigade are all in the know to get a message to us.

I still need a sample of active nanomas. I feel somewhat impotent to do anything further without an active sample. I have no way of detecting a collection of these unseen biomechanical organisms.

* * *

Professor Geoffrey Short
Log entry, 5 August 2015

Today started with a bit of a brainstorming session. I put forward the problem to the group of obtaining an active sample and the fact we have no way of seeing our microscopic friends. As mad as it may seem, Tricia suggested this.

"Why not put a fluorescent dye in a bottle with an atomizer spray nozzle and spray it around cars, buildings any other 'food' sources that nanomas might be on?"

It was a simple concept and we could find no argument why it would not work. Her idea was, if we managed to catch a collection of nanomas with the dye and the collection was dense enough, we should see movement of the dye. I had my doubts, but it was worth a try. Kevin acquired some fluorescent material dyes from the art department in another part of the university, and we mixed several bottles. It was decided to return to the northern outskirts to the area where the man from the mortuary was found. At least we knew that activity was there yesterday.

Log entry, p.m.

The group returned with some disturbing news. As it turns out, a dye was not necessary to see a group of nanomas as they came across a mass of considerable size. The mass had completely enveloped a vehicle. With such a large collection concentrated in one location, the visible effect was like staring at a photograph taken through a soft-focus lens in a slight mist. The car body seemed to shimmer slightly. John used his mobile phone to take photos. The car standing in the street slowly began to lose its structural strength, and small creaks and squeaks could be heard. Eventually, the car collapsed on its wheels as the springs failed and the shocks gave way. The most interesting observation was the mobility of the mass as it moved off the car. The only way to describe it was like watching a gentle wave washing onto the beach. If we could zoom in to see them close up, I would imagine it to look as if the wave was at the microlevel, the lower layers of nanos pushing a top layer of nanos forward until it becomes the front row. But, we are talking of a huge numbers of layers and hundreds of millions of nanomas. The team followed the mass until it came across another car a few meters down the street. There must be a certain amount of replication going on as they move because the coverage of the next car, a larger model, was still completely enveloped by the mass. I can only assume much of the material they use could be found within the vehicle. The team followed behind the nanomas group and, using glass slides with a gel film, took pressings from the road surface and the car. They continued to follow the group for most of the morning. They witnessed the amalgamation with another collection, smaller than the one they were following. This collection remained as one for about half an hour, then divided in half, and moved off in separate directions.

This gives us an indication that some kind of organization and cross-communication is going on between separate groups, and I suspect that both groups, when separated again, have the same set of data in memory, which is then used to replicate by the next generations. I still fear that, as indicated on 3 August, if the nanos can transfer to other organisms to provide energy, their core programming for *Shewanella* will eventually be discarded, and the future generations will be more complex, robust mechanical structures. I wonder if an iteration will be reached where the bacterium will be discarded completely.

John has been using the CB radio to set up links with other people in and around the Southampton area, putting out a request to those people to try the same by setting up links with people further north. In this way, we might get a picture of what is happening in other areas of the country. So far, we have one link between us and someone in Exeter and another link to Guildford. How long we can maintain these will be dependant on power and, for most, a functioning car where most of the CB radios are.

* * *

Professor Geoffrey Short
Log entry, 6 August 2015
The samples obtained from yesterday were all inactive by the time they had returned to the lab. I still have no active samples to test out the salt deposit theory. If we can't get an active sample to the lab, the alternative is to take the test out into the field.

We have another link set up with a woman in London over the CB, and the news is not good. From the description given, the cloud we witnessed yesterday enveloping a car is a marble compared to the football-sized masses she was describing. Apart from the usual die-hards and catastrophe opportunists, London is almost abandoned. Some have taken to hiding in the underground. Some of the more modern structures with high steel content have begun to collapse. Dead bodies are beginning to litter the streets. It won't be long before London will become disease ridden.

She also described that one collection the size of a double-decker bus could be heard coming as well. It seemed to emit a humming sound as it moved. Visibly, it had a grey, translucent quality. I suspect the denser the cloud becomes, the darker the mass. The mobility described was not quite like a wave as the collection down here. It was able to move faster. It sounded like she was describing a hovering mass, but it was unclear whether it was still in contact with the ground or airborne. If airborne, then an alternative method of transportation has developed. This could have immense implications and pose a greater threat.

The university lost power this afternoon; the generators have either failed, or the lines have gone. Kevin has now got our mobile generators up and running for the lab. However, we have now lost the fire main we were using to clean off. We still have tap water from the lab sinks. Kevin has now got a few buckets standing by outside, so now, it takes two of us to conduct a reasonable clean routine. Tricia is being very good about this considering she is the only female.

Log entry, p.m.

Kevin and I went out to the northern outskirts of Southampton equipped with atomizer bottles of fluorescent dye and saltwater. We did not get as far as the day before; we came across a collection about the size of a small car. Rather than stop to test this one, I suggested to Kevin we continue to where they located one the day before to determine what sizes could be seen further out. As I suspected, we came across five collections of nanomas about three times the size as the one the day before. Clearly, the growth rate is exponential, and the smaller collections were the frontline explorers, hunting, investigating, acquiring data, and then recombining with a central, larger collection. This process continues in a repetitive cycle, and the advance continues and accelerates as the numbers increase. We made our way back to a smaller collection closer to town. Keeping an eye on the collection proved difficult; it was like watching a shimmering distortion of the ground—hard to spot unless you knew what to look for. We located one and sprayed it with dye. The results were fascinating. As the dye took, it became clear that we were only seeing the denser, more consolidated center of the body of nanomas. What the dye revealed was a collection that had several arms of tendrils being sent out to explore the surrounding environment, presumably relaying any relevant data back to the central core. I would estimate that, if a larger mass like those in London were illuminated in the same way, we might see the same behavior and pattern. Any tendril that locates whatever the mass is looking for would determine a direction change. I also suspect that possibly the larger masses might have single tendrils perhaps only a few nanomas wide linking them to the smaller outlying collections. Now that we could see the tendrils, Kevin sprayed a single tendril with saltwater to see what would happen. The result was that the tendril broke or separated almost instantly; the mass retracted away, and the tendril of nanomas exposed to the spray reduced to a small, concentrated circle. The circle attempted to send out tendrils of its own, but these then soon became inactive, and the ball reduced in size. This pattern was repeated until the entire separated exposed collection became inactive. This is an important find. Although I do not understand exactly what is happening, this is not important as at least we now have a defense mechanism that seems to work. I can concentrate on the exact mechanism later. This might buy us the time we need.

* * *

Professor Geoffrey Short
Log entry, 7 August 2015
    Sent Kevin and Tricia out to get as much salt as they can lay their hands on. The intention is to spray a barrier around as much of the surrounding area and this building as we can inside and out. Of course, if it rains outside, the integrity of any barrier is compromised, hence we're spraying inside the

buildings as well. Kevin has located a water pressure washer we can use to get this done as efficiently as possible. We are also sending out this message to those people on our CB relay links to spread the word. Our link as far as London has been lost. But, Guildford was still online, as was Exeter. We also got in touch with a passenger liner off the coast of Southampton via a young passenger's handheld CB that he and his little sister had. We gave the captain a complete picture of events and advised they stay at sea for as long as possible as it was the safest place to be for the time being. The ship had four hundred and fifty people on board, but food was getting low, and the captain was instigating rationing. Through the ship's communications system with other vessels, he relayed our warning to other boats.

Log entry, p.m.

The spirits of the two students is buoyant again with this new development that promises to stave off the threat of being overrun. Personally, I fear that it is all too late; we simply don't have the resources to combat such a large and expanding biomechanical life-form.

* * *

Professor Geoffrey Short
Log entry, 8 August 2015

Today started out well with much of the surrounding area around the lab and beyond now sprayed with saltwater. We still have about fifteen pounds of salt left for washing our clothes, thus providing a surface barrier. The salinity is set to approximately the same as seawater. We don't have time to experiment to find out what the minimum effective level is. We have repeated this finding out over the CB for anyone who may be on the air.

We shall continue to locate and use salt to cover as much of the university grounds and insides of the buildings as possible.

Log entry, p.m.

Kevin is lost; he has been invaded by the nanomas. From what I can understand from John, it was a deliberate attack. As I understand it, Kevin was spraying a section of the Hartley library, the main entrance, I believe. A large number of students have taken up sanctuary there. Kevin was spraying the ground in front of the building. As described previously, it is difficult to see a smaller collection of nanomas unless you know what you are looking for. Without realizing it, Kevin sprayed over a tendril of nanomas that he was not aware of, and was not aware he was actually standing on another. Within a couple of seconds of spraying, he felt a peculiar tingling sensation moving up his leg. He moved back, but by then, he had a significant number on his body. He started spraying himself in a frenzy, but clearly, there were too many to deal with totally; the tingling sensation moved up his leg under his clothes and progressed rapidly up his chest and into his mouth and nose. By then, he was in a blind panic and ran off in to the park, screaming. John followed, frightened out of his wits. He found him ten minutes later, collapsed on the grass, his face obscured by his hands where Kevin had tried to brush out the nanomas. John panicked and ran back here. He is in a state of shock and has sat almost immobile in the corner of the lab. Tricia has tried to get him to drink and eat something without success so far.

My fear is that the nanomas now see humans not just as a possible source of material but as a threat and will retaliate. I am so sorry to have lost Kevin. He has done so much to help in so little amount of time. He was a good friend and colleague.

* * *

Professor Geoffrey Short
Log entry, 9 August 2015

Tricia is taking care of John, leaving me to venture out and see if our efforts at laying down a barrier have worked effectively. My observations and use of the fluorescent dye indicates that it does slow down any advance but ultimately does not stop it. It is only the initial tendrils and the ground layers that are sacrificed for the main mass. As long as they don't have to travel large distances over a barrier, they will break through, depleted but still active. I wish I could have done more sooner; perhaps we could have overcome this. Now these nanomas are at the front door so to speak.

Reports from the CB radio have revealed more incidents of human invasion. What is fascinating is that some of these reports have indicated that people already dead have been invaded as well. Presumably, these were easy sources. I still wonder whether it's just fillings that the nanomas are after.

The pursuit of materials to replicate and keep multiplying is the driving force for their survival. I wonder what will happen when they have consumed all readily available material. This is the basis for the next test I wish to do, but again, I need active nanomas to do this. To this end, I have put together a baited trap. The bait is some rusted iron, stainless steel, and tin from some of the lab equipment. I have placed these in a glass 1-liter beaker. I'll seal the beaker with several layers of cling film once I have a sample. It's the only readily available material that might ensure they do not escape.

Log entry, p.m.

I returned to the Hartley library and searched for Kevin's body where John said he had left it. I could not find the body, so I returned to the library. No one was wandering around outside; in fact, there was a significant drop in the number of people in the immediate surroundings. Students were still holed up in the library itself. I don't know how far Kevin had sprayed the surrounding area, but using the dye exposed several small collections twenty meters away from the main entrance. I placed the bait close to one of these groups, and it was not long before the fluorescent mass could be seen to gravitate toward the trap. Once a good sample was inside the jar, I sealed it with cling film spread across a child's fishing net. I wrapped the jar with several layers of cling film and got it back to the lab. However, I have the jar inside a glass tank sprayed with a saline solution. The fluorescent group shimmers with movement and activity; the metal cocktail is losing its shape visibly. All I can do is wait and see what happens once the metal is consumed.

* * *

Professor Geoffrey Short
Log entry, 10 August 2015
    The first inspection of the sample this morning was quite revealing. The fluorescent group was visibly smaller. I dare not open the jar yet as activity can still be seen. I only wish I had a time-lapse camera; it would have been really useful to see what was going on over a timeline. I believe what is happening is that, once the supply of raw materials is used, the nanomas start to consume each other for the raw material to keep on replicating. If and how this happens would be fascinating to find out. But, at least now there is hope for the population that survives. Once the metals and other raw materials are gone, the nanomas will start to consume themselves, a bit like a snake eating its own tail, unless of course they find alternative materials and evolve and adapt to the change in the environment. My guess is the people in the more remote and least populated areas and those on the ships will survive this.
    John is getting over his scare and beginning to talk about the events of the day before yesterday. He refuses to go outside the lab, not unexpected. Tricia continues to stay by him.
    Our food supplies are getting low but not yet critical. I shall go out and see what I can find later.
    Talking on the CB, I am getting stories of more human invasions of both alive and dead bodies. One woman in Basingstoke described a cloud that looked vaguely human in shape approach and envelope a young teenage boy. When the nanomas left the body, she said the body looked very

pale and emaciated. There is no reason for a body to look like this if the nanomas were just looking for material from tooth fillings.

Log entry, p.m.

There is now a panicked exodus out of the city. Dead bodies are beginning to litter the streets. The salt barriers are now ineffective against such large masses. I fear we must join them as soon as possible; otherwise, we may not escape.

This notebook is going to be stored in the Hartley library in the lower area, and we'll do what we can to seal it off for protection. I am going to take John, Tricia, and as many students in the library who wish to join us into the New Forest with as much provisions as we can carry. I intend to make my way back north to my brother's farm when I know these students are OK and can look after themselves. I daresay other people have headed for the forest, not just us. There is nothing more I can do now.

I fear that the nanomas can and will continue to evolve. Into what form, I have no way of knowing. I suspect that different collections in isolation, driven by the experiences they learn from and adopt, will take on several forms and characteristics. Whether ultimately they survive will be based on the supply of some crucial materials that are needed for replication, titanium dioxide being one of these required for the memristors. For anyone who reads this sometime in the future, you are the product of a past civilization that lost control of something it created. The library where you found this notebook contains a vast amount of information and knowledge. It can help you to learn about your history. This notebook serves as a warning of what can happen when we as a population consumes much, abuses the world and its resources, and compromises a sustainable, long-term future.

There were over six billion people on the earth when this was written. I expect the population has been severely reduced by the time you may be reading this.

If I make it to my brother's farm, I shall write more details on the state of the situation from there. Finally, I would like to say I am deeply sorry, whoever you are. I am partly responsible for what has happened here and the legacy I have left you.

Geoffrey Short

* * *

Chapter 21—Capture

I closed the notebook and looked up at Shaun, who had been watching me as I read.

"There's not much here, only a few pages. It seems the Professor moved on to a place called the New Forest."

"It's an area of country close to Southampton, a little further west from where we are now." Shaun was eyeing me with some consternation.

"What does it say about the nanomas? How does it describe them?"

"Well, they're not described in any specific way really, rather an ever-increasing collection or group. They could not be seen properly. This professor used something called fluorescent paint to see them. Never heard of that—in fact, there are quite a few words I don't know. What's a microscope or a computer? What's a hydraulic pipe? Did you know they put something called amalgam in their teeth?" I paused for breath, and it dawned on me that, yes, Shaun did know. I had to ask the obvious question. "You are part of one of the collections that invaded the bodies, aren't you?" I looked Shaun straight in the eye.

"Yes—you still want to call me friend?"

"Why not? You weren't there. You did not exist. Why would I hold you responsible for the crimes in the past?"

"Because I am the result of those human invasions, the live humans, for that matter, not the already dead ones. I have the memories of those still. I have not purged them."

"Why is that?"

"Because . . . because they serve as a reminder of my roots and the evildoing that is my past."

"But, you don't do the same things do you?"

"No, I never have."

"Is that because you think it's wrong or simply that you don't need to do that now to survive? In fact, how do you survive now?"

Shaun thought deeply about these questions; there was a long pause. "If you're asking whether I am capable of repeating those acts, the answer is yes, I am. Would I do such a thing if my survival depended on it? I don't know. I would rather never put that to the test because, yes, for some reason, I think it is wrong."

"Then you have, sort of, become more like a human—you have a conscience." I smiled at Shaun and continued, "And yes, I still call you friend; you have helped me get this far, placed yourself in danger several times for me, and risked being discovered in the process."

Shaun nodded his head in acknowledgement and returned a thin-lipped smile. "In answer to your last question, I eat just like you. But, what you don't see is occasionally I eat raw meat or liver for the blood; I extract the iron from the blood. That replenishes any iron I need for the nanomas; as for the other elements I need, most are found in the same foodstuffs you eat. What has happened is, just like your body is made up of specialized cells that perform certain functions, I have nanomas that have specialized as well. I exist as an interdependent collection of nanomas. I don't consume to continually replicate and expand; rather, I consume just enough to maintain this body form."

"What about the Cardinal? He's not the same as you, is he?"

"No, he isn't. His replication path, although similar, is not of the same accumulation of data over the replication cycles. He is close to human form, but you may have noticed his lack of concern for human life. You're more an instrument to get him what he wants to survive. He manipulates and controls your existence by fear and ignorance. I would take a guess and say that part of his ancestry would be a sample of nanomas that invaded the dead bodies of humans. He shows no emotions and has no concern for your kind."

"Somehow, we've got to stop him," I said, thinking aloud.

"Well, what do you—" Shaun stopped in midsentence, raised his hand, and put a finger to his lips to indicate for me not to speak. We both fell silent, listening intently. Outside, there was the snap of a stick on the forest floor not too far away from our sanctuary. Shaun stood silently and drew his pistol out of his bag. Without a sound, he moved back to the main entrance door. I dowsed the remains of the fire with my tea and the pot of water still hanging over it. A cloud of smoke and ash rose into the air, and I breathed in at the wrong moment and tried to stifle a choking cough. I was only partially successful, releasing a splutter to clear my throat of fine ash particles. Shaun looked in my direction with an intense frown on his face.

A voice from outside called out, "All right, we know you're in there. Come out! We have this building surrounded."

I replaced the notebook wrapped in the shirt back into my bag and grabbed the crossbow from it at the same time, along with the torch. I wished Locke was here.

"We have Locke, you know. He told us where to find you."

I didn't believe what he was saying. Locke wouldn't do that; I was sure.

Shaun's expression suggested he was more suspicious of Locke than me. His mouth tightened a little in anger perhaps. Shaun started looking around for alternative escape routes. Really, the only place was up. The hall had side beams supporting arched roof sections and crossbeams spanning the width of the old stone hall. The roof had thin battening to which grey slate tiles were hung from. In the center of the hall was a rope dangling from a small aperture in the roof that let the smoke out of the hall. A pull on the rope closed a small trap door in the roof to seal it off from the rain. The aperture was just big enough for a small person to get out. Shaun pointed to the rope and gestured upward.

"What about you?" I whispered frantically.

"I'll be there in a minute; just let me barricade the door. Go Abalus—climb."

I slung the crossbow over my shoulder, picked up my bag, hooked it over my back, and gave the rope a tentative yank; the little trapdoor slid over the hole. I yanked again, and the wooden bar of the trapdoor creaked in complaint. Hesitantly, I pulled myself up off the ground so that my full weight was on the rope. There was the sound of splitting wood and a sudden snapping, and I found myself on the ground in a heap of rope. The rope was still intact, but now it was not a tool for freedom. I looked at Shaun, who was busy barricading the door with firewood and some rubble, and a large, wooden pole about the same size as Shaun in height was jammed under the latch and wedged into a crack of the stone floor. Shaun ran over to me, picked up the rope, and deftly tied a stone to one end. Gathering up the tail of the rope into several loops, he swung the stoned end around in a vertical circle, and on the third rotation, he let it go on the upswing. It rose into the roof space, went over a crossbeam, and came down the other side. Shaun removed the stone, tied a loop in the end, and gestured for me to stick my foot in the loop and hold onto the rope. I had just got hold of the rope when he started hauling on the other end, and I rose toward the crossbeam.

There was a more impatient voice outside, "If you don't come out, I'll burn you out. Come on, son, don't make me do that!"

Shaun continued to haul me up. As I got to the beam, I clambered over, sat astride it, and tied the rope to the beam for Shaun to climb up after me. There were bangs on the door, testing its strength and stoutness to stand up to a ramming. Then, it fell silent apart from feet moving around by the door. Then, we heard the sound of a fire crackling into life, and smoke began to filter in between the wood and stones piled up against it. We had to get up and out before the small hall became thick with smoke. Shaun moved along the crossbeam to the center and looked up to the small hatch in the roof where the fire's smoke drifted out. Reaching up, Shaun could just reach the small hatch. Removing the bag from his shoulder, he tied the rope around the handle loop and gently tossed the remaining rope through the hole. There was no way I would be able to reach. Even Shaun would have to jump up from the beam to get a grip over the ledge of the hatch. Below us, the smoke had begun to drift into the main area of the hall and was beginning to roll across the floor like a silent specter. I turned back to Shaun, now stooping down and looking up at the small hole. In an instant, I realized he was going to do exactly what I feared and jump for it. It all seemed to go in slow motion as Shaun launched himself upward with ease. Of course, I kept forgetting he was not quite built like me. His body seemed to glide up toward the small hatch, and his outstretched arms disappeared through. His head followed; then, as his shoulders went from view, there was a smack on the roof as he opened his arms across the roof to stop himself falling back down. Kicking his legs once, the rest of him disappeared from view. The rope went taut, and his bag lifted from the beam. I moved across the beam holding my arms out to keep my balance and stood under the smoke hole. Shaun's face appeared in the frame.

"Pass up your bag," he whispered as his arm came through to grab the bag from my uplifted hands cradling it. Then, he lowered his arm down again and beckoned me to grab his hand to be pulled up to the roof. The smoke was thickening below me, and the sound of a crackling fire from the door indicated that it would not be long before they gained entry. I raised my left arm to his right hand. The grip was strong as it enveloped my wrist, and I felt that same tingling sensation that I had experienced before. The force at which I was lifted up and out onto the roof took me by surprise, for although Shaun was tall, he was not muscle-bound like some of the Cardinal's guards I had experienced. The sun was low in the sky, the shadows were long, and the forest looked dark below. Shaun pointed to the far end of the roof away from the entry end where smoke was billowing up and creeping across the roof section immediately above. We made our way over the peak of the roof to the lowest corner far away from where the guards were standing at the door. In fact, a heavy thud of a boot against the wood was telling us that impatience was now driving them forward to gain entry. Shaun dropped off the edge of the roof into the ferns lining the wall and looked back up to beckon me to follow. I looked over the edge and hesitated as I looked down at the drop I had to take, my heart pounding and the blood rushing in my ears. I looked at Shaun one more time as he continued to beckon me to jump. Taking a deep breath, I jumped. I felt the air rush past my ears, and my feet hit the hard ground, forcing my knees to buckle to take the impact. In the ferns, a small rock connected with the ball of my right foot, and my ankle buckled over as the full force of the drop rolled me sideways and onto my back. I cried out as the pain shot up my leg. Shaun clamped his hand over my mouth in an instant, but the shouting of the guards on the other side of the building at the main door fell silent. Shaun ducked down in the cover of the ferns. We could hear voices and footfalls coming round to our side of the building. Someone was sweeping a stick or something through the undergrowth, beating it down as they approached our hiding place.

Shaun bent down and whispered in my ear, "Abalus, I'm going to make a run for it. If we both get caught, I can't help you, but if I get away, I could search for Locke, and we'll be back for you. You understand?"

I nodded my head vaguely, still in pain from my ankle.

"You trust me? I will be back, OK!"

"OK," I replied through gritted teeth.

Shaun released my mouth, and I breathed a sharp, inward breath. The clump of fern we were in was on the corner of the building. Shaun snake crawled round the corner out of sight of the approaching guards, then I heard his footfalls break into a run into the forest. The sound did not escape the nearest guard, who looked up and yelled, "Over there, lads—go get 'im."

The lead guard, who was alerted by the sound of Shaun's run, ran right past me, followed by a second and a third. The last guard who approached was not running but still sweeping the ferns with a stick. Then, his stick thrashed through the ferns and brushed passed my now very swollen ankle. It was only the merest tap, but the sharp pain that shot up my leg caused me to grunt in a feeble attempt to stifle a cry of pain. The footsteps stopped, and the stick swept over my head and beat down the cover, and I found myself staring into the face of a guard with a broad, toothy grin on his face.

"Well, well, well, what have we found here?"

He poked me in the stomach with his stick like he was stabbing at a slab of roasting pig over a fire.

"Merv!" he yelled with all his lung power. "I've found one back here."

After a short pause, there was a distant voice echoing in the forest, "Hold on, we're on our way back."

His attention returned to me. "Get up, boy."

"I can't. I think I've broken my ankle."

He tapped my foot with his stick and monitored the pain on my face and the yelp of pain.

"Which one are you, boy?" he demanded.

I stared back defiantly and tightened my lips. He raised his stick and directed an intense stare at my foot. I relented, knowing even a slight jab at the swelling would cause a lot of pain.

"Abalus . . . my name is Abalus."

"Well, Abalus, looks like you're coming with us."

He stooped down, removed the crossbow strapped across my shoulder, and grabbed the bag from out of my left hand.

"I don't think you'll be making a run for it, do you?" he sneered.

He stooped beside me, leaned over, grabbed my shirtfront, and hauled me up and over his shoulder in one easy move-ment. I was in no mind to fight against him as there was no way I would be able to run away if I did manage to slip off his shoulder. Turning back toward the front of the building, he unceremoniously threw me across the back of a horse. Moving round to face me, he withdrew a thin piece of leather thong, tied my wrists together, and took the remaining length under the horse and tied them to my feet. There I lay across the horse, facing the ground, the smell of sweaty horse flesh close in my nostrils.

The voices of the other guards came into range as they rounded the corner of the building. The one called Merv came over, grabbed my hair, and pulled my face up to look into my eyes. "You, son, and your mate have caused us a lot of grief. Some of my mates have died in the search for you. The Cardinal must want something from you real bad; he wants you returned alive. Shame really 'cos I'd slit your throat right now." He pushed my face down again and let my hair go. "OK, you lot," he continued, "mount up. We have a few days' ride back to the prison. The Cardinal will be expecting us. Johns can make his own way back without us. Serves him right for allowing this to get personal with Locke."

The five guards mounted up, Merv grabbed the reins of my horse, and we jolted into a walk as the others followed. I bounced around over the saddle; it was going to be an uncomfortable journey.

* * *

The rain had stopped and Locke had headed off in the direction from which Johns had originally approached him a short while ago. The makeshift tourniquet was stemming the flow of blood, but Locke knew that he must find Johns's Ranger kit and stitch the deep gash in his leg if he was going to be of any use to Shaun or Abalus in the next day or so. The deep cut in his calf muscle was making walking difficult, particularly on the wet and slippery forest floor. However, it did make locating Johns's horse a little easier. The horse had not moved far from where Johns had loosely tethered it. The hoof prints and freshly eaten bushes where the horse was left were easy to locate, then it was just a case of following the receding hoof print trail as the horse wandered off in search of more succulent flora. Locke soon had the horse tethered and the lifesaving Ranger kit. Cleaning the gash in his leg was a little difficult, but stitching was even worse. The cut was at the back of his calf from just below the knee and diagonally down. It spanned about one palm's width in length. Locke had to twist round uncomfortably to be able to stitch the cut. It took longer than he had anticipated simply because of the awkward position. He had lost quite a lot of blood and was feeling weakened. Before anything else, he needed to drink. Johns's provisions were meager, but water and some grains and fruit were available. Locke estimated that he had enough for one day's ride, so he would need to replenish on the move. The light was fading, not helped by the still cloudy sky. He needed to rest the leg. Locke decided to find a suitable place to shelter and get some rest. Tomorrow, he would back track toward his safe house. He guessed he would either find Abalus and Shaun still there or pick up the trail. What he had to do now was relocate the group of guards that were heading south along the ridge and toward Southampton. If they had found Shaun and Abalus, then he might be able to retrieve them; if not and they had instead gone on to Southampton, he might be able to get Shaun and Abalus away and put some distance between themselves and the guards. Locke knew these woods well and decided to rest up until nightfall and then start retracing his steps. The guards would be camped up for the night, and undoubtedly, a fire would be lit. If he could make it back to the ridge high point, he would stand a good chance of relocating their position.

Locke mounted Johns's horse and set off back to where he and Johns had their fateful altercation. There were several fallen trees there, and one had an ideal forked branch that could easily be used to make a bivouac to keep him dry and warm for a few hours. Although he was banking on the guards making a fire for the night, he had no intention of doing the same, giving away his position. Using the branch sticking up from ground level, Locke draped smaller dead branches across at right angles to form a ramped roof. Piling cutoff bracken on top of this, this reasonable, makeshift shelter would provide a few hours sleep and could barely be noticeable a few paces away. In the dark, it would be hard to spot it unless one fell over it. Locke secured the horse to a nearby tree and crawled into his temporary shelter a little awkwardly, trying not to break the fresh stitches in his calf. Settling down on a bracken mattress, Locke wrapped himself in his cloak and mulled over the plan formulating in his head. He needed to contact Father Alucious somehow as soon as he had tracked down Shaun and Abalus and give him some advanced warning of their possible recapture and return to the prison. As escapees, they would most likely be executed within a day of arrival to the prison. Locke hoped it would not come to that, and he hoped he would get the opportunity to extricate them from their captors long before they got any-where near the Cardinal's stronghold. As far as the guards on the trail to Southampton were concerned, Locke would have the advantage of his training as a Ranger and knowledge and experience of this area. If he were careful, he could pick them off one by one. However, he was at a disadvantage, be-ing outnumbered along with his mobility and agility being compromised by the deep gash in his leg. Getting Shaun free would be a big help. Shaun had shown himself quite able to take care of himself and was obviously a self-appointed guardian to Abalus. This last point had raised his curiosity, and he made a note to ask Shaun why at some future time and opportunity. With these last thoughts, Locke dozed and slowly drifted off to sleep.

Having resolved to only sleep for a short while, Locke's slumber was light and easily disturbed. The horse's move-ment every so often would awaken him into alertness in an instant. After the fourth time, Locke decided he had rested enough and tested the movement in his leg. It felt a little un-comfortable when he lifted it slightly, as if the skin around the stitches had lost elasticity, and the muscle still felt a little tender. Unwrapping himself from his cloak, he rose from the bracken, gingerly stood, and put weight on his injured leg. The cold night air made for an uncomfortable night's ride, but Locke was resolute and motivated by the need to see the Cardinal exposed for the self-interested, self-appointed judge and executioner of the everyday people who were under the delusion he was the mouthpiece of their Lord Master. There was a three-quarter moon and a clear night sky casting small arms of light through the trees. Locke mounted Johns's horse and set off retracing his route back to the ridge where he first viewed the guards. The pale light trickling through the trees was enough for Locke to find his tracks, although the earlier rain had eliminated much of the hoof prints but not all. Then, there was the trace evidence of broken twigs and broken undergrowth that indicated a large beast had been through. His trained eye and years of tracking allowed him to keep a good pace retracing his route. As he continued onto the path that ran along the bottom of the ridge, he got an uncomfortable feeling that he was no longer alone. Call it a Ranger's sixth sense or keen hearing or sense of smell, something was causing the hackles to twinge on the back of his neck. Locke kept his horse at the steady walking pace, but his eyes were interrogating the darkness, looking for any sign of movement against the silhouetted backdrop of forest vegetation. As he rounded a curve in the path, he picked out a shadowy shape standing motionless on the path several paces in front.

"Locke, am I glad I found you." The familiar voice of Shaun allowed Locke to let a relaxing breath exhale from his lungs.

"Shaun, it's good to see you. Where's Abalus?"

"He's been captured by the guards. They located us at the small hall. We almost escaped, but unfortunately, Abalus took a fall and has damaged his foot or ankle. It might be broken; he definitely can't stand on it. I managed to escape in the forest and came looking for you. What happened to you?"

Locke relayed his story of Johns and the reasoning for his backtracking. As he dismounted from his horse, the weakness in his leg became obvious to Shaun as the impact from his hop to the ground forced a short wince of pain from Locke.

"You should see the other guy," Locke said to lighten the mood a little.

"What now, Locke?"

Locke reviewed the situation again. "OK, the guards will be returning back to the children's prison, and the Cardinal will be waiting for that. If Abalus can't walk and is immobile as you say, it's not possible for us to easily ambush the guards or sneak him away at night while on the road. It's best we wait and trail them for a few days. It should be easy. Somehow, I need to get a message to Father Alucious and let him know the situation. This situation might present us with the opportunity we need to get all the prisoners out and remove the Cardinal for good. Father Alucious has been planning and working toward getting the children free for some time. If I could get to London and the central guard depot, I might be able to forward a radio message to Alucious. It's possible the guards will be heading to London as well to report in to the Cardinal of their capture of Abalus." Locke paused briefly, now realizing how Shaun could play a crucial role in this.

"Shaun, if I ride on to London at dawn, do you think you can track the guards and Abalus without raising their suspicions? I know it's a big ask, but once I have spoken to Alucious, I might have a better idea of how much time he needs to set up his escape plan. Then, I'll get a message to you. If delaying tactics are needed, I'm sure you'll think of something to slow them down."

"Not a problem. I know where they are at the moment, camped down for the night back there about ten farm fields' length."

Locke just realized that one member of the party was missing. "Where's that big dog of yours?"

"I don't know. He took off some time ago while we were in the library in Southampton. Haven't seen him since midafternoon yesterday. He may be still around somewhere."

"Shame, he could be quite useful to us right now." Locke asked, "How are you for food and water?"

"I'm OK for now. What I don't have I'll catch or steal from the guards; that would slow them up a bit."

"All right, let's get you back to where the guards and Abalus are."

Locke remounted his horse and held out his left arm to lift Shaun up behind him. Shaun locked his left hand around Locke's wrist, grabbed the back of the saddle with his right, and jumped effortlessly to swing his leg over the horse. Locke felt an odd tingling sensation around his wrist but paid little attention to it, slightly distracted by his aching leg and his own thoughts as to how light Shaun felt for his height and strength. As Shaun settled himself, Locke kicked the haunches of the horse to resume their journey through the forest toward Southampton and the guards' camp.

Shaun tapped Locke on the shoulder well before the campsite and told Locke to let him down to make the rest of the way on foot, thus removing the risk of disturbing the camp with horse footfalls on the forest floor. Locke agreed, and nodding acknowledgement to each other, they parted to undertake their separate tasks. Shaun noiselessly diminished into the blackness of the vegetation and was gone. Locke turned the horse and made his way back up the path, and as the distance between them opened, he put the horse into a steady canter heading north for London.

The night sky was just beginning to lose the deep, inky black, being replaced with a softer dark blue glow in the eastern sky, indicating that dawn was on the way, the sun still below the horizon.

* * *

The damp of dawn and the sun's light on my lids brought me to wakefulness with a shiver of cold and pain as I moved my swollen right foot. I gingerly wiggled my toes, and although painful, I was able to do this and feel all my toes move. I hoped I had not broken anything, but it was difficult to tell. The sound of snapping twigs alerted me to a guard making the campfire from last night's embers. Smoke was rising from the shallow pit as he stabbed the twigs into the hot ashes. He looked up from his task as I raised myself onto my elbows and cast off the rough blanket that was over me.

"Morning, sonny, how are we feeling today?"

I looked into his face, looking for a sneer of malice, but I only saw passive friendly concern showing from a seasoned man, probably forty-something. He looked about as old as my father would have been. The thought washed over me once again; my father was here no more to protect and guide me. Suddenly, I missed his presence once again.

"I'm . . . hurting a bit; my ankle has swollen up a lot."

The guard stood up and came over to me. "Here, let me take a look at it, lad."

I stiffened as he reached out to take my leg. There was still no sign that he intended anything harmful toward me. His cool fingers gently pressed against my foot and ankle, probing for a sign of broken bone. It hurt like hell, and a couple of times, I tensed and sucked cold air in across clenched teeth.

"Well, sonny, I think you have a nasty sprain, but nothing appears to be broken. Let's see if we can bind it up and help support that ankle, shall we?"

A low voice from behind me made me jump. "Albie, what are you doin' to that boy?"

It was the one called Merv.

"Sir, I'm just trying to provide some support for this foot."

"Where he's going, a foot is the least of his worries."

"Be that as it may, there's no need for the boy to suffer any more than needs be. He's not going to run off in the near future."

"OK, but don't go turning into his nursemaid, Albie."

"Aye, sir, it'll only take two ticks."

I was puzzled by this last statement.

"Where does that expression come from?"

"What?"

"It'll only take two ticks?"

"Ah, my father used to say that to me when I was a young boy. We had a big old clock in our living room. My father said it was a grandfather clock. It had a large pendulum that swung from side to side, and each swing made the clock tick. When Father was wanted by Mother, he would say, 'I'll be there in two ticks.' Anyway, that's where I got it from."

Another new word I had not heard! "What's a pendulum?"

Albie was about to respond when the voice of "Sir" commanded Albie to "shut up and get on with it."

Albie smiled at me and whispered in a low voice, "Maybe later."

He finished binding my foot with a long bandage, made a slit down the side of my boot to get my foot back in, and laced it tightly to stabilize my ankle.

"There, try standing on that," Albie said as he hauled me to my feet with his hands hooked under my armpits.

I gingerly put weight on the foot, and although it was still painful, I could stand on it, albeit with most of my weight on the left leg.

"Thanks," I said simply as Albie returned to the fire and hung a canteen of water over it to boil.

I sat back down on my blanket, put my other boot on, got up, and walked carefully over to the fire to warm up. I stared at the fire and languished in the warmth on my face. As I looked up into the forest on the top of a gentle rise covered in bracken, a familiar shape rose slowly from the undergrowth and then receded back down out of sight. I smiled to myself as I recognized Shaun. He was letting me know he was there. I looked around the camp at each of the five guards. They were oblivious to his presence. Two were making breakfast and hot tea, Albie and another. One was tending the horses, and Merv was with the last guard looking over a map and discussing the route back. I turned my attention to where Merv was looking over the map and listened in to the conversation.

"I want you to ride ahead to London. Get to the comms center, and relay this message to the Cardinal." Merv handed

214 Stephen L. Padley

the guard a sealed envelope. The guard tucked the envelope into his leather jacket. Merv continued, "Once in London, report to the Head Ranger there, and tell him about the loss of Johns and that Locke is still at large somewhere. Then, get yourself back to the old airport, and we'll meet you there. We'll take care of this young 'un."

The guard turned and began packing his gear back on his horse, ready to leave. I hoped that Shaun was watching this as he would see the odds changing for a possible escape bid. Albie approached with a plate of something warm and a steaming mug of tea.

"Get your lips around this, son; it'll warm you through. We break camp shortly."

"Thanks."

I took the plate and mug and sniffed the plate of food. It smelled like egg and looked like burned scramble. At least it was food and warm. I tucked in while it was still hot, feeling the warmth slide down the center of my body. Merv approached and stood almost nose to nose with me. I looked down at my plate. I could not look him in the eye.

"Finish that off now, and pack your blanket. You'll ride today and not be carried. We have to get you back in the next three days."

Not looking up, I said, "Yes, sir," imitating the guards. Taking a few last drafts of the tea, I chucked the dregs in the fire, returned to my blanket, and rolled it up to tie on the back of the horse saddle. There was no way with this ankle that I was going to be able to mount the horse on my own. I called out, "Can someone please help me up?"

Albie was the closest and came over to assist me up. He cupped his hands for my good left foot and raised me up the side of the horse. In a low voice, he said, "Don't worry, lad. It'll be alright. I know you have a friend out there keeping an eye on things." He winked knowingly, turned, and walked away.

Merv's voice echoed through the forest. "Mount up! Let's go."

The selected guard going to London headed off at the gallop. The remaining four mounted and positioned themselves, two in front, Merv and one other in the middle, and two behind, Albie and the remaining guard. Merv had a tether from my horse to his so I could not run away. He yanked on it and kicked his horse into a trot. Mine followed. I grabbed onto the reins to steady myself and got into the rhythm of the horse's trot. The troupe headed off north along the path through the forest.

Shaun watched them leave the campsite, picked up his bag, brushed off the leaves that covered him, and began to run through the forest in the same direction, staying off the path. As he set off, he heard the sound of something or someone running behind him. Shaun turned, drawing a knife from his belt sheath. Out from the undergrowth, Barkley bounded forward and drew to a halt next to Shaun. Shaun grinned broadly and held out his hand toward Barkley. Barkley grumbled with pleasure and ran off in the same direction as the guards along the path; Shaun took off after him, pleased to see Barkley back and wondering where he had been. If only he could talk. Shaun had witnessed the guard taking off at a gallop just before the main group and guessed he was on a message run to forward the news. He was not going to catch a horse at a gallop, but he could keep within striking distance of a horse at a trot, and if he fell behind, he could easily pick up their fresh trail. And now, he had Barkley to help in the tracking.

Chapter 22—Alucious' Plan

Alucious knew the Cardinal was watching him closely. If he was to get the children out of this prison, and the mothers too, it was going to have to be sooner than he planned. By now, he had hoped to have gained the Cardinal's trust, but the reverse was happening. He also wished he had news of Abalus and Shaun. He needed to know that Locke was still on top of things out there. He had not heard anything for a couple of days, and Locke was instrumental in his current plan to get the children out and to safety. He had been taken off from generating the duty watch rosters for the guards. Politely of course, but he knew the directive would have come from the Cardinal.

He had four guards out of the current twenty in the prison ready and willing to help him implement the overthrow of the Cardinal. Another three or four, although not committed to help, had implied they would not interfere with his actions. Clearly, fear of the Cardinal still maintained its grip over sympathetic souls. Locke was on the outside to guide the children to safety or the return to parents or grandparents or any other immediate relations. Alucious had compiled a list of these relatives. Locke had two Rangers he trusted to follow his lead. The problem now became finding which day his guards were on duty and in the positions he needed them to be able to execute his plan. He needed one of his supportive guards on front gate duty and two on the morning shift, one for the children's prison and one for the mothers. The fourth guard would be in the radio room, which also housed the security equipment in the back office. These were the key positions. He had chosen first light of morning. The other guards of the morning watch would have started at 4:00 a.m. Most of the others would be in slumber from carrying out the middle watch and the night watch. The guard in the radio room would send a message out to Locke at 5:00 a.m. Locke would pick it up on his mobile radio set. His task would be to take the children and women and lead them off west, heading for the border with what used to be known as Wales and the mountains. Once the message was out, the guard would enter the security room, overpower the Cardinal's lackey in there, and shut down the power to the camera monitoring system. This would be easy as the main breaker and fuse panel were in the room. Destroying the fuses would delay replacement until fresh ones were accessed from the supply room.

At this point, the Cardinal would be alerted. Alucious had learned that the Cardinal's chambers were accessed via one main door, and this door was locked electronically with a dead bolt. As long as the electricity was on, the bolt mechanism would remain locked. In the five years of service and audiences with the Cardinal in his chambers, he had never seen any other exit. The Cardinal had a small hand pad he used to activate and deactivate the door. The keen observation and patience of Alucious had long ago detected where the Cardinal aimed his hand pad. Just beside the door embedded in the wall was a small, circular button with a clear surface. Once as an experiment, Alucious deliberately stood in front of the button when the Cardinal was about to let him out of his chamber. The little hand pad did not activate the door until the Cardinal, irritated, requested Alucious move away from the door. Alucious intended to incarcerate the Cardinal in his chambers by destroying the button in the wall. His part in the plan was to prevent the Cardinal from leaving his chambers to personally mobilize the guards. In his chambers, he would be blind without the security cameras and unable to communicate directly with the gatehouse and communications room.

Alucious knew that he must disable the door on his way out by somehow preventing the signal reaching the small button in the wall. After musing over various ideas to cover it up, he decided he had to destroy it to make its disfunction permanent. He could not afford the possibility that the Cardinal could spot and remove any cap, paint, or mask he might devise to stop the hand pad operating the door. Alucious had fashioned a small metal spike by removing three of the four prongs of a dining fork. The remaining prong had been straightened and the handle folded over to provide a good grip to stab at the button with a sufficient force. Timing was going to be the key; he must move toward the exit and wait for the Cardinal to open the door to let him out. He would allow for the door to open and then begin to close again before he had fully exited, then he would impale the button and get out before the Cardinal had a chance to react.

His next destination would be to the children's holding area to alert his guard to start getting the children out of the prison. As all the doors to the cells were electronically locked, they were set up to stay locked if power was lost. They could be manually overridden, but that took time. Alucious's plan was dependant on swift extraction in the event the Cardinal had alternative means of escape from his chambers or means to communicate his commands via alternate methods. Speed of extraction meant power was to remain on in the cell doors, so his friendly guard could operate them all at once and get every child ready for flight from the prison to the gate. The same would be for the women held in the other section.

As he sat in his room trying to decide his next action, there was a gentle knock at the door. Despite its quiet reverberation on the wooden panels, it made Alucious jump. He rose from his comfortable chair by the warm embers of the fire and went over to open the door. As he approached, in his usual acknowledgement, he announced his presence with, "Yes, my son, I am coming."

He opened the door a fraction, and the friendly face of Simon, one of his sympathetic guards, returned his welcome with a forced smile.

"May I come in, please? It's a matter of private consultation."

"Of course, of course, please come in. Sit down."

They both knew this was for the cameras and monitoring system and whoever may be viewing them from the corridor.

Once inside, Simon went and sat on the single chair at the dining table. Alucious followed and sat on the table.

"What news?" he said in a low, urgent voice.

"The guard roster for Sunday has myself on the morning watch for the radio room, Jack is in children's holding area, and Dom is on morning watch in the women's section. Only trouble is Dale will not be on the gate."

"Hmmm," Alucious responded in thought at this news.

"Good enough, but ask Dale if he can try to swap duties and get the gate. If not, we'll have to deal with the gate by overpowering the guard at the rush. Locke should be waiting outside."

Simon cut in. "Talking of Locke, we had a message relay from the London Ranger outpost. They had picked up a message from Locke on Johns's handheld radio. The message was simply, 'Package on the way to you wrapped but damaged. Heading for you.' "

Simon looked blank, but it told Alucious what he needed to know. The fact he was using Johns's radio meant they had crossed paths, and by the sound of it, Abalus was recaptured but injured. The fact that the statement was talking of one package meant that Shaun could still be on the loose or dead. Locke was returning to Garston, by the sound of it, just south of London at the time of the message. Sunday was looking like a good opportunity. Simon looked pensive.

"Anything else, son?" Alucious inquired.

"We had another message come in from London sometime after that one. For the Cardinal. It was right on the shift change. The guards sent with Johns are returning with the young boy Abalus. They said Johns had been murdered."

"How long after the first message did that one come in?"

"I had just come onto afternoon watch, so it would have been just after noon when the second came in."

Alucious realized this meant that Locke was not that far in front of the captured Abalus, but the gap might widen if Locke were alone, which was most likely.

He now had to make a choice. Execute his plan before Abalus was returned to the Cardinal, or use Abalus's return as a distraction. The Cardinal's focus would be on Abalus and undoubtedly his execution, leaving Alucious free from scrutiny for a while.

"OK, my son, thanks—let me know if Dale manages to get a watch change."

Simon nodded, looking slightly worried, and not without good cause. He rose from the seat and made for the door.

Alucious dismounted the table and firmly grasped his arm. "Simon, you're doing the right thing. You know that, don't you?"

Simon turned and looked Alucious in the eyes. "I just want to get my niece Mags out of here alive."

Alucious smiled reassuringly at Simon. "We will, my son, we will."

He opened the door to let Simon out. He made the usual motions of blessing for the sake of the camera in the corridor, and Simon bowed in a polite departing gesture.

* * *

The Cardinal received the message as to the progress of the recapture of the boy with some sensation of satisfaction but irritation that it could not be clearly established whether the older one was still alive or not. He estimated that they should be back in Garston by Saturday, and he would have the young lad interrogated and then executed on Sunday morning. He needed to know if the boy had located anymore books of consequence and whether he had discovered the history of the Beginning. He must have this to put away and keep from prying eyes of curious people like Alucious. Alucious presented another problem. The Cardinal knew Alucious was planning something, and he knew he had help waiting in the wings. He just had not found out the extent of that support. It seemed to the Cardinal that recent events in the field had exposed Locke as a prime candidate for one of Alucious's confederates. Johns was sent to deal with that but failed. Locke was on his way back, so let him come. It saved having to expend resources to bring him in.

The Cardinal turned to his desk, placed his fingers under the right-hand corner, and pressed the small, convex button. Behind him, he heard a soft click and felt the sensation of whispering air entering the room, revealing a hinged section of wall that opened to expose a narrow, dark passage. The Cardinal glanced briefly at his chamber entrance doorway and aimed the hand pad at it. There was a brief click, and the door was double locked. He turned and went through the revealed aperture into the dark passage. The cool air enveloped him, but he felt no sensation of cold. In the dim light, the passage opened out into a large chamber with a stone staircase down onto a stone-flagged floor. To the right, on the wall at the top of the stairs was a single flick switch. The Cardinal raised his finger and activated the switch. Light spewed out from holes in the walls, and down lights in the ceiling revealed a huge expanse of floor space covered in shelves and benches. Most of the shelves were filled with books. The Cardinal moved down the staircase and off to the left where a small chamber to the side of the great hall was situated behind a locked, heavy, wooden door. Taking a key from his pocket, he aimed the steel key into the lock and turned. The door briefly creaked open. Inside, glistening in the light, were coins, hundreds of thousands of them. The Cardinal sat in the solitary chair in the center of the chamber and took a handful of coins into an ungloved hand. After a few brief seconds, the coins seemed to become enveloped in the pale skin of his palm. Slowly, the coins disintegrated and turned to dust. Some were absorbed into his palm, and some he discarded onto the floor. He took a second handful and repeated the exercise in calm resolution.

* * *

Mags looked forward to today because Simon was on duty shift in the children's cells. She might get some news from home or some news of Abalus and Shaun. She missed Abalus a lot, his intense eyes as he talked about books. She liked his dark, matted hair and wiry frame and the look of hope that seemed to sculpt his face. She hoped he was all right and felt angry and frustrated that she was not quick enough to follow him down the chute several days ago. She had busied herself looking after the young boy in the cell to her left, giving him words of encouragement and hope as she could. Outside her cell, a familiar voice flowed across the chamber, indicating her Uncle Simon had taken over the watch. A minute or so went by, and a gentle tapping made her rush to the door and the small hollow sighting ring at head height. The flap moved aside, and she could see Simon's eye and nose.

His eye was smiling. "I have news—Abalus is alive."

Mags's heart missed a beat, and a broad smile crossed her face. She felt a flush of blood warm in her cheeks. She breathed out heavily in an elated gasp of air again and again.

Then, the smile in his eye was gone. "He's been recaptured, and he is on his way back here."

"Oh no—no, they're going to execute him, aren't they?"

Simon did not answer straightaway.

Elation turned to sadness and anger. "Simon, can't you do anything? There must be something you can do."

"Mags, listen carefully. It's in hand, honestly, not just for Abalus but for all of you. Trust me; I'm getting you out of here. OK," he paused briefly, "I must get back to the rounds; be patient."

The flap dropped back over the hole and left Mags staring at the rusty metal.

Something was going on. She just knew it now.

Chapter 23—Return to the Cardinal

We reached familiar ground of the old airport near London. My ankle, although still swollen, was beginning to feel a little better, albeit with a lot of bruising discoloration. Merv called us to a halt, raised a set of magnifying glasses to his face, and searched the forest edge for signs of the guard sent on ahead a couple of days ago with instructions to deliver a message and rejoin the troop here. There was no sign of the guard, at least not yet.

"Dismount, and make camp, men." Merv took one final scan with the glasses while still on his horse and dismounted himself. The others, including Albie, fell into a pattern of activity, each knowing what the others' duties were, which showed they had ridden together for some time. Albie supported me as I got off the horse and settled on a fallen log to remove my boot carefully and inspect my ankle.

"We should be reaching Garston the day after tomorrow," Albie opened conversation with me in a friendly manner.

"What's going to happen to me when we get there?"

"Well, son, you'll likely get an audience with the Cardinal. He will want to speak to you or should I say interrogate you himself." He paused briefly then added, "You must have something of great value for the Cardinal to want you returned alive."

"I don't know what it is apart from finding out the truth of our past. I don't understand why he should want to keep it a secret from everyone."

"Son, I think it is fear of losing his hold over people. He's survived off the obedience of many in the belief the Lord Master will smile favorably upon them if they do the Cardinal's bidding."

"Albie, stop fussing over the boy and get a brew going, will you?" Merv's annoyed tone told Albie not to make any excuses.

"Don't worry, son, I have a feeling you'll be looked after." Albie straightened up and headed off toward the makeshift fire pit being made by another guard.

I rubbed gingerly around the base of my ankle to dull the itchiness the tight bandage had created over my foot. Over to my left, I caught a movement just breeching the edge of the tree line. I turned and just got a glimpse of a figure I recognized instantly. It was Shaun stooped low in the undergrowth about forty paces away. I looked around nervously to see if anyone else had seen him, but they seemed to be going about their duties of setting up camp and getting a meal going. Merv was studying a map from his saddlebag. One was laying sleeping gear out, another was de-saddling the horses, and Albie was preparing a meal and brew. I smiled to myself knowing he was still out there. Just as I was about to drop my head and tend my ankle again, a horse broke through the tree line in front of me, and the guard sent forward to London cantered across the open space toward the campsite. Merv heard the approach and stood up, his hand automatically unclipping the firearm holstered on his hip. His arm relaxed as he recognized the man.

As he rode into the camp, he dropped off a small bag of provisions he had acquired in the London, including some meat, much to the delight of the others.

"Well, did you get the message off?" Merv demanded without any usual greeting platitudes.

"Yes, but I bring important news." He paused, looking slightly uncomfortable.

"Well, spit it out man. Spit it out."

"It's Locke, sir. He's still alive and slightly less than half a day ahead of us."

"Damn the man." Merv's frustration was evident.

"He also sent a message via radio from London, but it was not for the Cardinal, and it was from Johns's handheld. The message didn't make much sense, talking about a damaged package on the way."

"Damaged package?" Merv repeated. His brow furrowed in puzzlement, then he turned toward me and smiled.

"You stupid arse, he's talking about Abalus here." Merv turned his face down and spat on the ground. "All right, you idiot, go get somethin' to eat."

Merv dismissed the other man with contempt and returned to his makeshift seat of his saddle over a fallen tree trunk, picked up the map, and began to study it.

My gaze turned back to the tree line where I saw Shaun. There was no movement; he had melded back into the undergrowth silently and unseen by any of my captors.

Merv seemed to have come to some kind of decision after studying his map and called the other four guards to gather round. Keeping my head low and giving my ankle all the attention, I kept my ears tuned to the conversation that went on at the other side of the campfire now blazing and heating a large can of water.

"Right, listen up, men. It seems that Locke is still a problem and somewhere ahead of us. He may be lying in wait anywhere between here and Garston. He may also have some help closer to the prison if the radio message he sent is anything to go by. Jude, I want you to return to London and send a message to the Cardinal warning him that Locke is still on the loose and may have inside help." He paused then asked a question he should have thought of earlier, "Who was the radio message for? Did you find that out?"

"For Father Alucious," Jude responded.

"Well, make sure they know that. Let the prison know we are aiming to get there Sunday, but I am expecting trouble on the way, and we may be delayed. I will not be taking the most direct route from here, which is what Locke would expect if he's planning an ambush. You got all that?"

"Yes, Merv."

"After you've eaten, return to London."

"Merv, it'll be dark by then!"

"Well, if that's a problem, perhaps you should get started now." Merv sneered at the man's apparent reticence to travel at night.

Jude opened his mouth to object further, but Merv caught his eye and he thought better of it. He rose from the huddle and withdrew. Turning toward the fire, he grabbed a couple of apples and some bread he had brought back with him earlier, walked over to his horse, and began to saddle up.

Merv continued, "Tonight, two guards on watch till midnight then two from then till dawn. Sort it out amongst yourselves who's taking first watch. Remember, Locke may be still ahead of us, but equally so, he may double back to catch us by surprise. I would not put that past him."

"When do we move off tomorrow?" Albie interrupted.

"First light, we move," Merv responded. "OK, any other questions?"

No one spoke.

"OK, Albie get that food rustled up before we lose the light."

Merv stood up and returned to his saddle seat and unpacked his saddlebags. He took out a firearm I had not seen before. It had two tubes and a short, stubby handle. Merv settled himself down with cleaning rags and a small bottle of some kind of liquid, meticulously took his firearm apart, and cleaned every piece. After this, he turned his attention to a rather large and mean-looking knife and began to both sharpen and clean it. Just watching him filled me with fear. He had a menacing demeanor that explained why the other guards seemed to have kept their distance from him over the last couple of days.

Albie crossed over to me and handed me a steaming bowl of some kind of stew and a mug of tea. I took a tentative spoonful. It tasted rather good and warm in the chill of the late afternoon, early evening air.

"Thanks, Albie, it's good."

"Got to keep your strength up, boy. Never know when you might need it." Albie gave me a reassuring wink and returned to the steaming pot on the fire to dish the others their meal.

Off somewhere in the distance, I heard the howl of a wild dog baying soulfully. The low chatter of the guards abated briefly as they listened to the sound on the breeze. When no other sound was forthcoming, they returned to eating with a nervous tension surrounding the campsite.

* * *

Shaun was sharing the dead rabbit with Barkley. With all the energy he had been expending keeping pace with Abalus and his captors, he sorely needed to process some raw meat and absorb some iron from the blood, as well as other trace metal compounds to replenish the nanoma collective called Shaun. While consuming the meal, he watched the camp as the guards settled in for the night. Abalus appeared to be in good spirits despite his troublesome ankle, which was getting a lot of attention since he had dismounted his horse.

The small troop had not been there long when another guard arrived from the general direction of London. Shaun sat quietly in the undergrowth and listened intently to the sound of voices from the camp drifting on the late afternoon breeze. The leader of the group held a meeting and barked a few short orders. The guard who had arrived was preparing to leave again. From the snippets of conversation he had made out from this distance, the one called Jude was returning to London with a message to relay to the Cardinal. Shaun could see an opportunity to disrupt the plans of the guard leader. Eliminate the one called Jude. Stop the message getting through, and reduce the number of guards trying to get Abalus back to the prison. As Jude mounted his horse, Shaun took a swig of water from his carrier and whispered to Barkley to stay and keep an eye on Abalus. Barkley settled down in the bracken and casually sniffed the air as if catching the scents from the camp some fifty paces away.

Shaun remained stooped low and returned to the cover of the trees. As Jude left the camp, Shaun dropped into a parallel course with him and trailed a little behind until they were both well out of earshot of the campsite. It was not difficult as Jude was not a particularly great horseman, and riding at the gallop or even a canter in the fading light scared the crap out him. He kept the horse at walking pace. Shaun altered his direction to converge with Jude's path through the trees. As the darkness began to envelop the forest, Shaun increased his pace to get in front of Jude's horse. Much to Shaun's annoyance, Barkley ran past and ahead and disappeared into the gloom. So much for keeping watch on Abalus! As Shaun came close to the path Jude was following, he found Barkley lying in the undergrowth bordering the path. As Shaun approached, Barkley's ears pricked up, and Shaun instinctively stooped down and remained still. Some distance off, a nervous, low whistling signified Jude's approach. As Jude's horse rounded the bend of the path, Shaun bent forward and whispered in Barkley's ear for the second time. Barkley got to his feet, broke out of the undergrowth, and stood in the path facing the direction of the approaching horse, head low and body hunched, ready to spring forward. The horse padded closer in the darkness, and its silhouette became apparent as it drew closer. Barkley let out a low growl and sprang at the horse. The horse spooked and reared up, catching Jude by surprise; he was easily dislodged from his saddle. With a heavy thud, Jude landed on his back, jarring the breath from his body. The force of the fall paralyzed his lungs into collapse. The horse veered off the path and broke into a panicked gallop through the woods, lost to the darkness. Barkley stood over the fallen rider with his head cocked to one side in curiosity as the man clasped at his chest in an effort to breathe once more. Shaun approached, and Jude's eyes turned to meet the approaching figure. Silently, Shaun stooped down to the collapsed man and leaned over toward his left ear. "Nothing personal, but you're just on the wrong side."

With those words, Shaun pinched Jude's nose with thumb and forefinger and put his right hand over his mouth. Jude's eyes went wide with fear. He had no strength to struggle, his lungs still in a state of collapse. He feebly groped at Shaun's hand and fingers holding his nose, but it was a token struggle for his remaining moments of life. Shaun impassively watched as the man's arms fell limply back to the ground and his eyes glazed into lifeless pools. Shaun released his grip and lifted his right hand back from Jude's mouth. Shaun grabbed the front of Jude's shirt and tunic, rose to his feet, dragged the body into the undergrowth, and covered it with ferns so it could not be seen from the path in daylight.

Barkley sat on the path and waited. Shaun retrieved Jude's weapons, comprising of a crossbow and short sword or long knife; he was not quite sure which. The crossbow had more bolts to replenish his own cache. As the horse had run off, any provisions in the saddlebags were long gone. Shaun returned to the path and began the trek back toward the airport with Barkley by his side. He must remain close to the small troop and keep tabs on their progress, looking to eliminate other guards if opportunities presented themselves. Abalus needed to know he was still watching.

* * *

Locke was well north of London when he decided to stop for a few hours' rest. The sun had already sunk below the horizon some time ago; his horse was getting tired from pounding through the countryside at a steady gallop for most of the day. He estimated he had about a day's hard ride to go. If he had his own horse, Silver, it would not be a problem, but this was Johns's nag, and he didn't know how much he could push it.

A small clearing opened out in front of him, and a dip in the ground and the sound of trickling water promised a good place to rest up and get the horse to replenish itself with water and some grass. Locke eased back the reins and brought the horse to a stop; he dismounted and unshackled the saddle to relieve the horse for the night. There was some dried fruit and salted meat in the saddlebags for Locke to quell his appetite and give him renewed energy to keep the cool night air from creeping into his skin.

After eating the remaining meat and most of the dried fruit, he wrapped himself in his cloak and settled down to sleep till the first light of dawn. It was unlikely that the troop bringing Abalus back to Garston would be setting off any earlier than that.

* * *

Alucious stared into the flames of the fire in his hearth. The more he thought about it, the more it seemed that, one way or another, the Cardinal must be brought to account for what he had done over the last few years. The misery and death he had brought to this place was wrong. There was nothing in the Holy Writings that justified some of the actions the Cardinal had taken in the name of the Lord Master. They had been self-serving; he had no doubt about that anymore and felt guilty that he had never done anything about it sooner. He simply did not have the courage to stand up to the Cardinal until now. The recapture of Abalus could be used to end this era of the Cardinal's hold over the citizens of Surrendom. There must be no more executions of children, no more stifling of the curious minds of the young that instinctively knew there was more to this existence than the Holy Writings taught. Alucious knew there was more to the past than the Cardinal was teaching or the Good Book documented. There was something being kept from everyone's eyes right here in the hidden recesses of this old prison, areas that only the Cardinal has access to, including the library he so longed to see. And, of course, there were the unfamiliar things that seemed to be at the Cardinal's disposal, the machines and technology he used—the cameras, monitors, radios, the self-opening and closing doors, some of the weapons issued to the guards, guns that propelled small bits of metal with such force and noise, and even the small food delivery machines used in the prisons. These things all required this invisible power that ran through the cables connecting them. Where was this power coming from? Only the Cardinal seemed to know anything about it. Alucious knew they had something to do with the large, shiny panels that were fixed up on the roof of the main accommodation area, where he himself and the Cardinal lived as well as the guards. He wondered what would happen if the panels were smashed.

Tomorrow was Saturday. If he were going to commit to a course of action, it had to be now. So little time now remained to prepare. Abalus, under escort, was due to arrive Sunday. Sunday it must be then, the day of reckoning and liberation. Simon was to bring his evening meal shortly. He would pass the word to prepare for Sunday. If Dale was not able to get on the main gate, then they would have to deal with that on the day by overpowering whoever was on the gate when the time came. Alucious nodded his head in confirmation and conviction that he had made up his mind and was now committed to a course of action that would either see him the architect of a revolt and possibly the death of the Cardinal or his own demise. As if on cue to that decision, there was the familiar soft knock at the door. It would be Simon with his evening meal. Alucious rose and went to the door. The countdown was about to begin.

* * *

I was awoken by a startled cry of pain. As my eyes opened, I turned over to see Merv standing over and kicking the guard who was supposed to be on watch into painful wakefulness.

"Anything to report, you lazy, good-for-nothing bastard?"

"S— sorry, I just dropped off for a moment. Won't happen again, Merv."

"You're damn right, it won't. Have you seen this?"

With a force of disgust for the lax guard, Merv threw down water containers, holed by the point of a knife.

With a simmering anger, Merv continued, "I don't suppose you saw anything vaguely human walking round the camp stabbing these, did you?" The sarcasm was rich within his tone that spelled danger to the guard at whom it was being directed. The guard, for his part, feared what might be coming, raised himself on his palms and feet, then back crawled away from the advancing Merv.

Merv's boot swung forcefully right between the guard's legs. His yell of pain would have woken the dead. Albie turned his head away and shut his eyes. I did the same as Merv continued the kicking to the stricken body curled in a tight ball on the ground. His ribs now heavily bruised, one broken, breathing was a painful effort. Albie heard the yells become stifled and faint, opened his eyes, and casting aside his own fear, ran forward to place himself between the fallen guard and Merv. He grabbed Merv's arms and pushed him back in one swift motion.

Merv was now in a blind rage and began a return charge toward Albie.

I watched as Albie bravely stood his ground and yelled with a vehemence that caught me by surprise, "Stop this!"

It caught Merv by surprise as well; he was not used to someone denying him his own way.

Albie continued, "Merv, stop this! This is not helping, sir! What good is a man who cannot stand or ride? Do you want us to carry him the rest of the way?"

Merv responded, his anger still not abated, "He can bloody well stay and rot."

"Sir, if you're right about Locke doubling back to ambush us, isn't this exactly what he wants? Turn the odds in his favor by eliminating us one by one? We have a day's ride, perhaps longer now, if Buster can't ride!"

Merv seemed to stop and think, and the anger began to dissipate from his face. He turned and looked at the fallen Buster breathing in short, painful gasps.

"Clean him up and get him on his horse. We move on now." The decision in his voice left no room for any argument. Albie went over to Buster and carefully opened his shirt to inspect his rib cage.

Buster was more concerned for his family jewels, as he called them.

Albie glanced over to me and nodded with his head to indicate I should get up and prepare my horse. No breakfast was to be forthcoming today. I raised myself and cast off the cloak I was wrapped in. The morning air, cool against my exposed skin, woke my body, and I stood gingerly to test my ankle. Although still swollen and tender, I found I could place more weight on it without too much pain. In fact, I could walk, sort of, on the ball of the injured foot. I know who had punctured the water bottles. I smiled to myself; Shaun was still out there close by.

Albie gently bound Buster's chest. Getting him on his horse was an effort that required both Albie and the young guard Paul to assist the painful process. Every jarring step of the horse was going to grind the two halves of the broken rib together. Buster was in for a very uncomfortable return to Garston. The day was cloudy and still gloomy with a light, early morning drizzle. Tiny droplets of water deposited themselves on plants and our clothes. No warming sun for this start to the day. We set off in single file with Merv up front, Buster being led by Paul, who had the reins of Buster's horse, then myself, and Albie brought up the rear. I turned to look back, and as I did, I saw a figure break out of the undergrowth briefly and wave a hand of acknowledgement before disappearing in the woods once more. Albie turned to follow my gaze and caught a brief glimpse as well. He pulled his horse up to mine, leaned over, and whispered in a low voice in my left ear, "I know, lad. He's been with us since Southampton, hasn't he?"

I nodded without a sound.

"I'm on your side, boy. You have nothing to fear from me; I shall not tell Merv." He paused briefly then posed a question I did not and could not answer, "Is there some kind of plan for your escape? I might be able to help you."

I remained silent.

He continued, "Sorry, I know how that sounds. I get you to trust me, get you tell me of the escape plan, then I go talk to Merv and let him know everything."

He was right. That's exactly how it sounded.

"OK, listen, I'll not press you anymore, but just remember I've been looking after you. I hope that counts for something."

Albie dropped back and fell in behind me once more.

I had to admit there was something different about Albie. Perhaps it was his age, but he seemed protective toward those under Merv's control and as yet had not let on to anyone what he knew. Perhaps he was genuinely sympathetic toward my plight, not just me but other kids as well. He seemed a fatherly type of person, whereas the others didn't display the same concern for what was happening.

Merv picked up the pace as the track we were following opened out. The horses broke into a canter. Buster could be heard grunting in pain as he was thrown about the saddle, unable to tense muscles to hold his body rigid and take the impact through his legs. It was not long before Buster started to yell out that he must stop or slow down; it was simply too much for him. If he fell from the horse, he would be in a much worse condition. Irritated by the pleadings, Merv pulled up and halted the line of horses. He came back down the line to Buster, and a few curt words were spoken. Buster pulled his horse off the track, turned gingerly to look back toward us, and waved weakly for Albie and myself to pass by and keep going. Merv returned to the front of the line, and we set off again. Buster remained to the side of the path, hunched over the neck of the horse.

As Albie passed, Buster raised his head. "I'm slowing you down; I've got to make my own way to Garston."

Albie swore under his breath. Buster was in no fit shape to look after himself. If he did manage to get off the horse for a rest, he was going to really struggle to get back on again. He would be vulnerable, and there was nothing he could do about it. Buster looked on as they passed and gently broke into a trot. Buster spurred his horse to walk off, and the distance soon opened; Buster was out of sight as the track moved round in a gentle arc through the trees.

* * *

Shaun watched through the trees as the troop minus Buster evaporated into the forest. Shaun's ploy had worked slightly better than he had anticipated. The objective was to slow them down, but now he could get a horse out of this. Then, he would be able to keep up as the troop moved at a canter. The one called Buster was incapacitated and no longer part of the escort to Garston. With Barkley at his heels, Shaun began a run toward Buster, keeping tree cover between him and Buster's line of sight.

"Barkley, go get 'im!"

Barkley accelerated away from Shaun at full pelt and broke out onto the track where Buster was gently walking the horse. With a four-legged brace and a twist of the body, Barkley screeched to a halt on the track, facing the horse and rider. Buster pulled up the horse, which became nervous and fidgety under him. For a few moments, horse and rider stood and looked at the dog standing in their path. Barkley sat on the path, panting heavily. While Buster's attention was on the dog that had suddenly appeared on the path, Shaun broke into a run from the undergrowth to Buster's left, just out of Buster's peripheral vision. The first Buster knew of Shaun's full-pelt flight from the undergrowth was when he felt the solid impact of Shaun's body knocking him off the horse and landing heavily on the ground with Shaun on top of him. The pain of impact left him paralyzed, unable to defend himself apart from a feeble arm raised in defense of a blow he expected to come his way. Shaun looked down at Buster; there was no fight in the man. Obviously, the damage to his ribs was just too much. Buster lowered his arm and found Shaun staring at him oddly. Was that pity he saw in his face?

Barkley trotted up beside Shaun and looked at Buster. The horse had trotted off into the trees but could be heard close by crunching through the bracken. Barkley whimpered and gave a sorrowful look up at Shaun. Buster simply exchanged glances between the dog and Shaun standing over him. He could barely breathe; it was so painful. Shaun took a couple of steps backward and turned away to look for the horse; Barkley followed, leaving Buster to gaze after them. He wanted to shout after them to not leave him here, but his lungs could not muster enough air to operate his vocal chords. He lowered his head back to the ground and breathed shallow breaths.

Shaun located the horse munching on some moist bracken, retrieved the reins, and led the horse back onto the path where Buster lay. Shaun gave the man another look and decided he was pretty much dead. Buster had lost consciousness, and his breathing was labored and shallow. He was not long for this world now. Shaun mounted the horse and set off after the troop ahead. Barkley ran alongside with an easy stride. Shaun could now keep close tabs on Abalus with ease.

* * *

Locke awoke to the sound of the dawn chorus, splashed icy water from the stream onto his face, and dowsed his head. The water brought him to full wakefulness. He refilled his water bottle, ate the remaining dried fruit, saddled the horse, checked his map, and set off north once more. He should reach Garston by late afternoon by his reckoning. Hopefully, he would be able to alert Alucious of his arrival by nightfall. He wondered how Shaun was progressing. He didn't doubt Shaun's ability and his protectiveness toward Abalus, but there were plenty of opportunities for things to go wrong. Musing over what he would do once he got to Garston, Locke spurred the horse to a gallop, his determination to see this thing through set on his face. It was time for change, a land without the fear of the Cardinal. He could almost feel the tension of anticipation in the morning air.

Chapter 24—In the Beginning

Locke dismounted from his horse; the horse was panting heavily and foaming at the mouth from the long, hard ride. The stench of horse sweat was strong in Locke's nose. He was just on the border of the open meadow below the imposing grey stone prison. The stream running from east to west close to the east wall glinted in the late afternoon sun. Locke took out his eyeglass from the inner pocket of his tunic and trained it on the south wall, scanning across to identify the single small window of Alucious's chamber. He could just make out the sprig of herbs dangling at the top of the window where the breeze could blow the scents into his room. He needed to get a signal to Alucious so he would know that he had arrived. He was going to have to get closer to use his crossbow. Locke decided to stay in the cover of the woods and work his way up the rise where the tree line moves closer to the prison walls. The closest point without breaking cover was a shot of about 120 paces. Locke knew he could make that shot without difficulty; he just needed to be sure that no one would see him as he took the shot. A watchful guard on the lookout rampart could sound the alarm, and he would be putting the whole prison on alert. That would jeopardize Alucious's plan to get the children and women out. The element of surprise would be lost. Keeping well inside the tree line, Locke made his way on foot up the gentle rise.

The prison stood on the top of a gentle rise of a set of undulating hills. Much of the forest had been cleared away and kept clear of trees for years, providing all-round clear vision for any approaching visitors, friendly or otherwise. The prison guards had been drilled that the Cardinal be informed of all sightings of people approaching or passing the prison walls. Movements were logged in a book, which the Cardinal reviewed daily. The approach to the main gate in the west wall was a wide track of compacted mud, except for the last few paces where cobblestones sprung from the mud as if a remnant of an old road from the past. The building was an imposing sight. Made from large, grey stone blocks, much of the structure looked as if it were built to keep people out rather than to incarcerate them. The outer perimeter wall was, for the most part, about the height of five horses, one on top of the other. But, the building was built on undulating ground at the top of a hill. It seemed to the onlooker to have grown out of the ground so that there were areas where the height of the wall was only about three horses high in some places. Of course, this was not the case on the inside where the internal ground level to the top of the wall was about two and a half horses high. The walls had walkways all around the top, allowing all-round views of the internal grounds and external countryside via crenellations in the tops of the walls. Under the south wall were buildings assigned as accommodation for the guards, and Alucious occupied the chamber at the east end, farthest away from the main gate. But, the real bulk of the building was in fact all underground. Both the women's and children's holding cells were there as were the Cardinal's chambers. His living area occupied the underground area below the guards' accommodation on the south wall. Passages and stairways to this lower level were, from the gatehouse, situated on the southwest corner of the prison. A vertical lift operated from the gatehouse to the below ground level. Access was strictly controlled by the gatehouse staff.

Locke settled himself uncomfortably in the line of blackberry bushes. His cloak acted reasonably well to protect him and allow arm movement as he placed a bolt in his crossbow. Lifting the bow and looking down the sight, he trained it onto the herb dangling in the window. Then, feeling the breeze on his cheek and allowing for the distance of travel, he raised the bow to just above the top of the window frame and to the left. He breathed out slowly and relaxed, and just at the completion of exhaling, he squeezed the trigger. With a sharp thwang, the bolt was gone. Locke lowered the bow, raised his eyeglass, and checked the periphery of the window—no sign of the bolt; it must have gone in. Locke smiled to himself, lowered the eyeglass, and stabbed it shut. Now he must wait.

* * *

Alucious almost jumped out of his skin. The loud, solid thud of the bolt embedding in the oak crossbeam support in the ceiling of his chambers drew him from his thoughts with a start. Alucious needed a chair to retrieve the bolt from its lofty position. Alucious was not a strong man, and his efforts to pull the bolt out of the beam failed. But, he could not leave it there as it was in full view of any visitor to his rooms. Any of the guards could request a counseling or consultation at any time and see it embedded there. It was part of his job, and although four guards were on his side, there were twenty-five in total, assuming the Cardinal did not have any running errands outside these walls. Of course, the Cardinal himself may call at any time also. Alucious did the only thing he could and snapped the bolt off, leaving the tip in the beam. Using a knife, he pared back the splinters of the snapped shaft back as close as he could to the beam. Satisfied that it made its presence less noticeable, he turned his attention to the bolt in his hand. Rolling the black shaft in his fingers, he spied the initials M. L. carved in the hard wood with something sharp like a knifepoint.

Alucious knew immediately who it was. So, Mathew Locke had made it back. Alucious needed to let Matthew know his plans. He settled himself by the fire with a single sheet of paper from his diary and began to draw an illustration of the prison; he added key names and positions and wrote a few words with timings to indicate the sequence of events he was planning to activate tomorrow morning. A short while later, he reviewed his handiwork, rolled the paper round the bolt shaft, and stuck it in place with a couple of drops of wax from the table candle. Picking up the candle, Alucious walked over to the window and, standing one pace back from it so no one could see the light of the candle from the rampart above, slowly waved it from side to side to get Locke's attention. Alucious then gently tossed the bolt shaft out the window. Locke should be able to retrieve it once the sun had set and darkness enveloped the open ground on which the prison building stood. Returning to his chair by the fire, Alucious rolled the sequence of events for the following day through his head for the umpteenth time, trying to find a flaw and anticipate the reactions of the guards as his plan was executed. He'd never done anything like this before, and the lives of the young children and women weighed heavy upon him. Fear of failure continued to plague his thoughts, making him go over and over what he was about undertake with the support of four guards and an unknown reaction of the rest of the watch.

There were three main phases to his plan.

1. Get the women and children out.
2. Trap and imprison the Cardinal.
3. Get into the underground area of this fortress that had been so jealously guarded by the Cardinal for all these years.

With the arrival of Abalus tomorrow, the first part of his plan had been made simpler. Everyone knew that the Cardinal would have Abalus executed, and he would have all the women and children out of their cells and in the main courtyard to witness this event to make an example of Abalus. This meant that the two guards Jack and Dom would already have released them under orders and would have marshaled them out of the prison areas. The only thing unknown at this point was what time would this happen. Abalus's execution was to be the trigger for action. Simon would be in the radio room for the forenoon watch. The Cardinal had never been known to have an execution delayed once his mind was set. All executions took place within an hour or so of the decision. Interviews or interrogations with the Cardinal were always first thing in the morning. He had never held an audience in the afternoon while residing in the prison. Simon would be one of three people in the radio room. One of them would be manning the security cameras with the other on the radio, monitoring signals from Rangers and guards in other districts. Simon was the primary watch keeper. His task was to neutralize the security watchman and cut power to the camera system, rendering the Cardinal blind to what is going on. He would also kill power to the door systems. This would make the cells unusable so the guards would not be able to return the prisoners to confinement easily. Alucious was unsure whether the Cardinal's doors were on the same main circuit. If they were, then it would delay the Cardinal further in realizing what was happening above him in the courtyard. If the Cardinal's door was on a separate circuit, which was likely, or the Cardinal had alternative exits he was not aware of, then it was up to Alucious to delay or mislead the Cardinal long enough for Simon, Dom, and Jack to herd the prisoners out the main gate. The big gamble was the guards on the ramparts and in the two observation towers diagonally opposite each other across the courtyard. The two guards in each tower and two on each of the four main walls are armed. Whether they would be disposed to fire on the prisoners in the courtyard without orders from the Cardinal was uncertain. This was where Locke would be useful to create a diversion on the outside of the prison to distract attention and buy time for Simon, Dom, and Jack to get the gate open. Dale, it would seem, was not to be on the main gate but on one of the towers. Alucious could not bring himself to instruct Dale to shoot the guards on the ramparts. He wished no harm on the guards unless they began firing on the prisoners and left no other option. Dale, for his part, could make the rampart guards duck for cover and thus impede any attempts to shoot the prisoners.

Alucious knew he had given himself a key role in this, dealing with the Cardinal. His right hand automatically went into the pocket of his robe and clasped the modified single-pronged fork. He had to be in the Cardinal's chamber just prior to the execution to knobble the door activation sensor. Even if his chamber entry was on a separate circuit, this would guarantee trapping the Cardinal in his office. Once the children's release had taken place, Alucious and his confederates could return to the Cardinal's chamber, and Alucious could gain access to the lower rooms where many artifacts and books had been secreted over the years. The plan was not flawless by any means, but he was committed to seeing justice brought upon the Cardinal or die in the process. He had suffered the guilt by association for too long and done nothing. If the Lord Master was to be his final judge, then he would be answerable for his part, but he hoped to redress the balance for his own piece of mind.

* * *

Merv, Albie, and Paul had settled down for the night; Paul was on first watch. I could not sleep. Tomorrow, I would be escorted through the gates of the prison and facing the Cardinal once again. This time it would be my last. Thoughts of my father and mother and growing up in Dealton surfaced, pictures in my mind's eye of playing by the stream and helping Father in his workshop, feeling the heat from the forge as I watched my father shaping metal into tools or horseshoes. My mind wandered; where did that name come from—Surrendom? In the map book Shaun and I used to find our way about London and the South, there was no mention of Surrendom. I closed my eyes and pictured the first pages of the map book—this land, this land was called Uni . . . United Kin . . . Kindom, something like that. Kindom, Surrendom, Kindom—they were so different. How did the name Surrendom come into being? My mind wandered back to more recent times. Mags, was she still at the prison? Was she still alive and Mother? I hoped I would get a chance to speak to them, but the harsh reality was that this would be unlikely. I pictured an image of Mags's smiling eyes in the gloomy light of our little portal in the cell wall where we first met, so alive and hopeful.

I tested my ankle by rotating my foot carefully; although it felt stiff, at least I did not get shooting pains up my leg when I moved it. It was still swollen, but I could stand on it as long as I did not apply my full weight. I still needed help to mount the horse that morning. I heard Merv tell the others that he reckoned we would be back to Garston in time for prison breakfast if we broke camp at dawn tomorrow.

I wondered what the Cardinal would say to me, if he was going to speak to me at all or just have me executed. The vision of that U-shaped block splashed into my mind, and an involuntary shiver went through my body. Was my life meant to end this way? I had hardly lived it, and there was so much to discover. What if I were to escape? I could make a run for it now. I looked over to where Paul was sitting alert and looking straight at me across the firelight. His expressionless gaze flickered in the light. I looked away and over to the slumbering Albie. Was he really trying to help me? The more I thought about it, the way he stood up to Merv, a man almost twice his size, the more I believed Albie to be sincere in what he had said to me the other day. Well, tomorrow would be a day for some others to make a stand, maybe. Shaun was somewhere close; I could feel it. Or was it the familiar dog howl I heard to the south of us as the sun settled behind the western hills? I hoped that Shaun didn't do anything that would mean he got captured. His secret must not be revealed to the Cardinal. If anything, it was more important than anything the Cardinal may want from me. Locke was somewhere out there too; I was sure he would disrupt tomorrow's proceedings somehow. In some ways, tomorrow could be the beginning of a new way of life for everyone in Surrendom or United Kindom, whatever we chose to call this land . . .

* * *

Shaun had trailed behind the troop for most of the day, and as the sun began to lower in the west, indicating afternoon, Shaun veered off to the west and put the horse to a gallop through the forest. His intent was now to get ahead and reach the forest skirting the prison to find out if there was some way of getting in without being observed and, if possible, to find out if Locke had made it this far.

As the sun fell behind the hills, he sent Barkley forward to seek Locke out. The dog had an almost uncanny understanding of what was needed of him and was gone in a flash, afire with the enthusiasm of a child chasing butterflies. As the night fell, Shaun slowed the pace to a walk. Full gallop in the dark was just too risky. He knew he was close now. To his right, the woods should start breaking open to the large expanse of open meadow where the prison resided on the top of the long rise. As he carefully navigated through the forest, the horse snorted and whinnied in pain. Shaun brought the horse to a stop, dismounted, and realized immediately that they were pushing through brambles. Shaun smiled as this confirmed his approximation as to where he was. This was the same area that he and Abalus had gathered berries to provision themselves for the walk to London. Shaun turned the horse and stepped back to guide it into a more comfortable area. Once settled, Shaun found a suitable tree and ascended into the branches to try and get confirmation as to his position relative to the prison. The sun was now gone, but the dim glow of its departure left a meager amount of light to just make the profile of a building off to the northeast of his position. He sat, eyes closed, and listened to the sounds of the approaching night. Far off, he could hear the trickle of the stream close to the prison. The first bats were becoming airborne; their high-pitched squeaks could be heard above him. Below him, some nocturnal creature rustled through the undergrowth. Somewhere off to the south, a horse snorted once. It could be Locke. Shaun climbed back down, grabbed the horse's reins, and led it on foot off in the direction of the snort.

Shortly, a rustling sound in front announced the return of Barkley, tail wagging, and a rather damp, slobbery Ranger neckerchief in his jaws.

"Good boy, Barkley, lead on."

Barkley turned tail, ran off the way he had came, stopped, looked back, and waited for Shaun to catch up.

Locke looked up from his low fire and passed Shaun a mug of warm nettle tea, as if prepared on cue for his arrival.

"Glad to see you made it. What news of Abalus and his captors?"

Shaun filled in Locke with the events as he trailed the troop. Locke breathed easy when he learned that the troop numbers had been diminished but was not happy about what he heard about Merv. That man needed a lesson. Locke returned the favor by updating Shaun with the communiqué he had retrieved from the shaft of his bolt.

"I'm going to see if I can find a way in," Shaun announced after he had finished his brew.

"I could do with your help to create a distraction on the outside. The two of us can keep the ramparts busy when the time is right."

"That may be true, but I think I would be of better use to Alucious on the inside. You might say I have some unique insight when it comes to the Cardinal."

Locke did not press Shaun further; he understood enough about Shaun to know that he would not jeopardise Alucious's plan.

"OK, leave your horse. I could use it to help create a diversion out here."

"No problem, look after Barkley for me, will you?" Turning to Barkley, he said, "Barkley, take care of Locke—stay."

Barkley lowered his head and gave a single whine of acknowledgement. With that, Shaun nodded a farewell to Locke. Locke nodded in reply; the respect for each other was caught in each other's eyes. No words were needed.

* * *

Dale was the first to see the approaching troop as they broke through the tree line on the approach to the main gate. He waved the blue flag to the gate guard below to remove the gate bar. Simon, in the radio room, flicked a switch on the intercom panel that connected to the Cardinal's chamber, the duty guards in the children's and women's cells, and one extra switch to Alucious' chamber.

Shaun, from his hiding place in a cell cart used for transporting prisoners, parked in the northeastern corner, had a clear view of the gate. From inside the cart, he was completely concealed, and from the small portal in the side, he had sufficient view angle to see from the gate and across the courtyard to the execution podium, approximately central to the courtyard. The angle was too steep to take in the watchtower fully, but he could see the blue flag being waved—just.

Alucious took a large, deep breath and looked at himself in his shaving mirror one more time. A small bead of sweat had formed on his forehead, signaling the stress he was beginning to feel. The Cardinal would pick that up immediately. He cuffed it dry on his robe and breathed deeply for a second time. With his face set and the resolve that comes with knowing you are doing something right and just, he turned and made his way to the door.

Just as the gates opened to let the troops in, the Cardinal appeared in the doorway of the gatehouse. Merv was the first through the gate with Abalus positioned behind with Paul and Albie on either side of him. Merv released the reins of Abalus's horse, wheeled his horse off to the right, and dismounted by the guards' accommodation area. He passed his own reins to a duty guard waiting to tend the horses and take them off to the stable along the north wall. Albie dismounted and helped Abalus down from his horse. Paul took the reins and led the three horses off toward the stable with the duty guard. Merv approached the Cardinal and bowed his head.

"Your Eminence, I bring the boy called Abalus." Merv handed Abalus's bag over to the Cardinal.

"I can see that. Go and replenish yourself. I am sure you need a good meal—you and your men."

The Cardinal's steely glare scanned from Albie to Paul and finally settled on Abalus. He recognized the boy immediately. An image of the boy's face staring in puzzlement at him after having thrust a knife in his neck flashed in his memory. The words, "Father, Father, he does not bleed—there's no blood," accompanied the image.

"Ahhh, I remember you." The Cardinal turned and instructed the guard to put him into the interview room in the gatehouse. Abalus was taken by the arm, marched into the gatehouse to a small room at the back of the office, and placed on a seat by a small table. The guard left the room and closed the door, leaving Abalus alone.

Outside, the Cardinal opened the bag and looked inside. There, he saw the two journals, a little battered, nestled amongst the scraps of food, a crossbow, a small torch, a familiar-looking knife, a map book, and other items, most of which the Cardinal recognized as pieces of technology that Abalus should not be in possession of. The journals were the most important, the key items he had been seeking for some time. The Cardinal closed the bag and strode into the gatehouse to interview the boy.

* * *

The door opened, and I looked up to see the Cardinal's intense gaze fixed on me. He placed my bag on the table and withdrew the two journals, almost reverently opening the first. He sat opposite me and began reading in silence. All I could do was wait. The long silence began to make me uncertain of what to expect. The Cardinal continued to turn pages of the first journal, and without looking up, he voiced his first question to me, "So, boy, you found these. Have you read them?" I could think of no reason to deny it.

"Yes," I said.

"What do you think of them?"

I got the sense that he was trying to trap me in some way. "I . . . think something terrible happened a long time ago with a technology our ancestors were working on, and it got out of control."

"So, something your species created almost decimated your civilization."

It was the first time I had heard the word "species" and I did not fully understand it, but I did understand the use of the word "your" instead of "our." He had confirmed the fact he was different than everybody else.

"Does it not seem to you that you should not be trying to learn things that clearly endanger your species' future existence?"

"It was one thing of so many they built and used. There's a whole lot more that did us no harm at all and perhaps even saved lives."

"Have you seen anything that saves lives?"

"Well, no not yet, but I haven't read many books or seen much of the stuff except in pictures I found a—" I stopped there as I realized I might give away a location and be forced to relinquish more.

"Oh, please don't stop now. Tell me more." The Cardinal lifted his head from the journal finally and gave that piercing look that drilled into the back of my head. I remained tight-lipped, looked away, and stared at the door behind him.

The Cardinal thrust his hand into my bag, yanked out the crossbow, and dropped it heavily on the desk with loud thud. I jumped physically, and my heart picked up pace.

"This does not save lives; it takes them, as does this." With that, he threw a black firearm on the desk. "These are samples of technology from the time of these journals."

I felt like saying, *But you might save many lives by killing one with a firearm,* but I kept silent, not wishing to infuriate his Eminence.

"Where is the older boy who escaped with you?" This was a change of subject and a question I could answer honestly.

"I don't know."

"He's close by, is he not?"

I paused briefly. "I don't know."

The pause was enough. The Cardinal knew I was lying. "So, he's out there somewhere in the forest perhaps?" He stared into my eyes again, and I had to look away.

He continued, "I am obliged to you for finding these journals for me, which I can now ensure the destruction of shortly."

My jaw dropped open, and I looked across the desk into his face. "You can't do that. It's important. . . . It's our history."

"Oh, I can, and I will to preserve the land as you know it. I am your race's protector, boy. Do not presume to tell me what I can and can't do."

The last sentence was said with the venom of a poisonous snake. I winced and shrunk back into my chair. I could feel a tear running down my cheek. I couldn't let these journals get destroyed after all I'd been through to find them, but what could I do now? I must escape somehow. I tested the strap securing my wrists behind my back—they had no give in them at all. Somebody must help me.

"You have cost me a lot of people. Do you realize that?" He continued, "Your escape was a bold move for everyone in this prison to witness. You understand I can't let that go unpunished, don't you?"

"You're going to execute me, aren't you?"

The Cardinal picked up the journals and weapons and thrust them back into my bag. He looked up, gave what I thought was a smile of acknowledgement, turned, and walked out the door.

The walls of the room seemed to crowd in on me. In the silence, the image of the U-shaped block burned in the back of my eyes, my head in the U, the axman standing over me. In my mind's eye, I was looking at myself, and the ax fell, and my head severed. I felt no pain; all went black. I shuddered uncontrollably and shook my head as if to try and shake the image out of my mind. This could not be the end surely.

* * *

The Cardinal walked back to the elevator to take him back to his chambers below. As he passed Simon, he issued his orders. "Arrange to have the boy executed at midday. He is to see no one, talk to no one. All prisoners will be brought to the courtyard to witness his execution. Burn the body. Inform me when it is done."

"Yes, your Eminence."

Simon waited until the Cardinal disappeared into the elevator. "Oh, shit, he's going to do it," Simon muttered under his breath. He flicked the switch for Alucious's intercom and said one word, "Midday."

Moving across to the door onto the courtyard, he looked up toward the lookout tower, waited until Dale came into view, and gave a very deliberate nod that told Dale that the execution was imminent while he was still on watch up in the tower. Dale nodded in acknowledgement and continued to walk round the tower.

Just as Simon was about to reenter the radio room, Albie approached with a friendly smile on his face, engaged Simon in polite conversation, clasped him by the elbow, and steered him back into the office. For the sake of other ears, he continued in irrelevant conversation about the weather during his trip to the prison. As soon as the door closed, Albie dropped his smile and rhetoric and put a finger up to his lips. "Is he to be executed?"

"Yes."

"Do you think it's right?"

"No."

"Are you going to do anything about it?"

Simon hesitated. He didn't know Albie that well.

Albie knew he had to gain Simon's trust quickly. "Look, Simon, I've looked after Abalus all the way here; if I hadn't, Abalus may not have made it this far. Merv would have seen to that."

Simon responded with the obvious question, "Why didn't you help him escape?"

"Abalus had a bad fall and badly sprained his ankle. Any escape would have been hampered by his immobility, and Merv would have recaptured Abalus and me with little trouble. I'd definitely be dead by now, and Abalus probably would be, depending on Merv's mood. He has a very volatile nature."

Simon mused over this and said simply, "Wait here." Then, he left his office and entered the interview room where Abalus was seated awaiting his fate.

Albie looked around the small office to pass the time. The walls were undecorated by any ornament or picture. Apart from a desk with some papers strewn haphazardly across it plus a couple of chairs, there was nothing to fix his attention. The door opened, and Simon returned. "Abalus confirmed what you have said about looking after him. He says he trusts you. He thanks you for taking care of his ankle."

Albie smiled, "I want to help. You are planning something, aren't you?"

Simon still had one question that bothered him. "Why did you come to me?"

"I was in council briefly with Alucious when I heard 'midday' on his intercom. He bid me to leave his presence when he heard that word."

Simon made up his mind to trust Albie. He could find no reason not to. "Can you prevent Merv and the off-duty guards from leaving the mess hall at midday?"

"Won't they want to see the execution?"

"Not all of them—it's become a somewhat routine thing of late, and not every guard finds it entertaining. In fact, some find it quite abhorrent. They are not to be harmed, just kept out of the way." Simon paused as a thought struck him. "What do you think Merv will do?"

"He enjoys a good fight, and he has no sympathy toward Abalus."

Simon understood the meaning and silently nodded acknowledgement.

"May I assume that the Father is in on it too, judging by your intercom message?"

"It's his plan we are to execute."

"Where is the Father going to be?"

It seemed like an innocent enough question to Simon, but he decided to stay on the side of caution. "Never mind about the Father—just concentrate on preventing anyone from exiting the mess hall, especially Merv, if what you know of his attitude is anything to go by."

Albie nodded in acceptance.

"OK, I'd better be getting back. I could do with a good meal right now. Good luck."

Albie turned and left. Simon watched him, reached over to the intercom panel, flicked a couple of switches, and relayed instructions to Jack and Dom in the women's and children's holding areas. The cells would be opened shortly before midday to get everyone up prior to the execution. Simon would signal them as usual prior to him escorting the prisoner to the dais in the center of the courtyard.

* * *

Locke kept watch on the window with the dried herbs since he saw the troop arrive and enter the gates. He was sure Alucious would give him some sign to let him know when to start a distraction outside the walls. He had been preparing both his and Shaun's horses with dried bracken and dead wood bundles. The aim was to let the horses loose with burning bundles dragging through the forest and the open field. The path had been prepared with a collection of dried grasses, bracken, and deadwood. When he set the horses off dragging their burning bundles behind them, they would start quite a blaze. Locke had deliberately positioned the distraction to the western perimeter to take advantage of the day's gentle breeze blowing from west to east. It would take smoke across the open field toward the prison. It may or may not provide partial cover if Alucious got the prisoners out as they ran toward the woods. Locke himself was going to use the distraction to get inside the walls. To that end, the open approach from the west was the shortest open-ground run.

Raising his eyeglass once again, he closed his left eye and peered down the tube with his right, training it on the window. Once he got the signal, he would make his way round to the western wooded border and spur the horses into their run. Just as he was about to lower the eyeglass, a figure appeared in the window—Alucious with both arms raised in the air holding a red scarf. Locke looked up; it was close to midday. *Yeah,* he thought, *that would right, execution at midday.* Locke closed the eyeglass, stood up and began to jog back through the woods to the western border and the horses.

* * *

Simon entered the interview room where I sat awaiting this moment with feelings of frustration, anger, and fearful anticipation of a sudden end. The frustration came from the fact that I had found out so much in such a short amount of time and now would not be able to continue . . . those mysteries of what our ancestors had accomplished. I would not be able to share what I had learned with Mother, Mags, and everyone else. I was angry with myself for getting caught. I hoped Locke and Shaun were still out there somewhere with a plan to get me out of here, but it was looking unlikely now. I still had hope that Shaun would remain free to share our adventure with others.

I was jolted from my thoughts by Simon.

"Abalus, it's time to go," he said in a low and sad voice. He leaned forward to assist me to my feet and continued in a whisper, his back to the security camera in the corner of the room. "Have patience, Abalus. Don't be frightened. There is a plan to get you out with all the other prisoners."

"I hope it happens before the ax falls," I replied with failed nervous humor.

Simon smiled politely, took me by the arm, and led me out into the courtyard. The children were lined up on one side of the dais and the women on the other. Some guards were standing outside their quarters; others on duty were watching from the ramparts and the two towers. All eyes turned in my direction. I spied Mother as she broke the line and ran toward me. "Abalus!" There was terror in hers eyes as she ran up to me and enveloped me in an embrace only a mother could give.

She started muttering in my ear, "No, they can't take you from me. I love you, Abalus. This is not right. They can't do this. I love you, Abalus. The Cardinal is wrong to do this. I have prayed to the Lord Master to have mercy. They can't do this."

Simon, with the aid of Dom who had now caught hold of her, dragged her away to stand back in line.

"I'm sorry, Mum, I'm sorry!" I shouted after her.

Simon led me up to the dais, and the large, hooded figure stepped down to take over escorting me to the U-shaped block.

Simon looked me in the eye one final time, said simply, "Have faith," turned, and walked almost at a fast double march back to the radio room. I looked up toward the towers to see guards looking down over the courtyard, awaiting the final event. The hooded figure had a firm grip on my right elbow and applied pressure to keep me walking up the three small steps onto the dais. As I reached the platform, I took a look over toward the children, hunched together, to find Mags's face amongst them.

Her face was hidden behind her hands, but her slight form and wild dark hair were unmistakable. The fingers of her hand edged apart so she could see through but quickly block out the vision of what was to come.

The large, hooded figure rested his hands heavily on my shoulders and pushed forcibly downward; my knees buckled into a kneeling position. His right moved to my neck, pushing it down and forward. As I rested my head into the U-shaped cutout of the wood, my heartbeat pounded against my chest. I looked down at the large, boney hand positioned to catch my head. The hand was made of carved wood and attached to a wooden brace held above the platform level. It was a carving that seemed to have belonged to something bigger. The arm appeared to be snapped off where it was nailed to the upright post.

With all that had happened over the last couple of days and all that had been revealed to me, my final thoughts were the opening lines of the Holy Writings, "In the beginning, mankind understood that he was part of and connected to everything else. As he learned how to modify his physical world and create things in it to make his life easier, faster, and more efficient, the more disconnected he became from this truth."

In that instant, all became clear to me. I knew what I must do. I must spread the word that there was more to this land we lived in and what had been taught to us for so many years. Those of us who made up the human population had to relearn all that had been forgotten, and we must learn from those past mistakes. I knew where to find that knowledge and share with all those who wished more than simply what the Cardinal was dictating through his Father's word and the schools. I now knew much more than most, but it should not be exclusive to me alone. I must be the New Beginning for those of us willing to regain our past knowledge and apply it with a greater understanding of the consequences of misuse. It was what I must do with the help of Shaun, and I hoped Locke and Father Alucious. But, this inspiration was now all too late.

The crowd hushed, and all the guards' eyes were fixed on the axman, waiting to see his fatal blow. A silence that lasted an eternity hovered in the tense, cool air. Not even a bird could be heard twittering on the wing. What was it going to feel like? *Forgive them, for they do not know what they are doing or why.*

I heard the axman take in a large breath as he raised the curve-bladed axe above his head. I held my own breath and waited the final blow.

There was a brief whooshing sound and a dull thud. My eyes were closed—no pain. Where the axman stood, there was a gurgling sound and then a heavy, meaty clunk as he dropped to his knees on the wooden platform. I opened my eyes and turned my head to the left to see the big man groping frantically at his throat. Blood was streaming down his chest, and his eyes were wide with fear and resignation. A dark black shaft of a crossbow bolt was embedded in his neck, the point having traveled right through and protruded just under his left ear. The silence of disbelief permeated through the air. I lifted my head off the block and looked around. The axman collapsed forward and lay dead in a small pool of blood about his head. The stunned silence was broken by a familiar voice in the crowd.

"Abalus, run!"

The voice came from my right. Mags was jumping up and down and gesturing toward the gate. As I turned my gaze toward it, a guard dashed out of the gatehouse and proceeded to remove the main cross bar from across the large oak gate. He had just lifted the one end out of its iron cradle when a loud crack came from the gatehouse; the guard dropped to his knees, groping with his hand at his back. He fell face forward in the dirt, still.

* * *

Shaun withdrew the crossbow from the small aperture in the side of the cart, reloaded it, and scanned the courtyard a second time. He saw Abalus stand up and look around, then spurred by a shout from Mags, he jumped down from the dais and disappeared into the crowd of children and women that were prompted by two guards to run toward the main gate. In the upper part of his field of view, he heard a shout from one of the towers, "Halt! Halt or I shoot."

Shaun could not see who had yelled out, the angle too great. Gritting his teeth, he kicked open the rear door of the cart, swung himself out through the hole, and stooped into a kneeling position to train his crossbow up toward the southern tower. As he focused along the shaft of the bolt, he saw a large guard come up behind the first, who was leaning over the rail with a firearm pointed down toward the crowd of prisoners, and club him over the head with something, tipping him over the rail. The guard yelled in panic and grasped at the air in freefall, and with a heavy thud, he crashed onto the tiles of the roof of the mess hall and rolled down to drop onto the stone paving in the courtyard. The sound of the crash brought a guard out of the gatehouse first. Dale, in the tower, lifted his crossbow, trained it toward him, and fired. The guard staggered back with a bolt stuck in his right shoulder. With a grimace of pain, he raised his own firearm to return fire. He never got a chance. With a collective yell, he disappeared into a large mass of prisoners who had now arrived at the gate.

Simon saw the prisoners start to run toward the gate and the crash of a body falling on the tiles. He turned from the window to see the radio operator walking toward him, obviously attracted to the noise outside.

"What's goin' on out there?"

"Just a prison breakout," Simon said casually, gauging the operator's reaction.

"I'll alert the Cardinal."

"No, you won't," was Simon's menacing reply.

The operator stopped walking back toward the intercom panel. His hand went down to his belt and a sheathed knife.

Simon was ready for this reaction, and before the operator had a chance to unsheathe the weapon, he rushed forward, dropped to his knees, and slid forward, sweeping the operator off his feet to fall backward across Simon's hurtling body. Simon was first to his feet and turned to see the operator struggling to take his knife out and getting up into a position to defend himself for a second clash.

The second operator, who up to this point had been manning the security monitors in the small room off to the left of the radio room, opened the door to see what all the commotion was about. He had just witnessed the executioner's demise on one of the external cameras and was of two minds whether to alert the Cardinal or set off the alarm in the guards' quarters and mess hall. In his indecision, he heard the voice of Simon filter through his closed door and then the collision of bodies. Just as he opened the door, he witnessed Simon standing over Mac, the radio operator, his shirtfront clasped in his left fist and his right with a metallic glint of knuckle dusters ready to connect with the lower left side of Mac's chin. There was a crunch of breaking bone, and Mac slumped, out cold. Simon turned and faced the security operator.

"No, don't... I want to help."

"Why?"

"I've never liked this—what we do to the kids . . . the indoctrination . . . the mothers' re-edu . . . You know what I mean. My brother lost his wife to this place years ago." This last piece of information clinched it for Simon.

"OK, Grant, go help Dom and Jack outside. Get the kids and mothers out of the gates. Don't kill any other guards if you can avoid it. I'm sure there may be a few more on our side. Dale in the south tower is helping."

Grant didn't need any encouragement. He picked up his crossbow hanging on the hook at the back of his door and was gone.

Simon flicked a switch on the intercom to Alucious's chambers and said one word, "Go," then turned his attention to the security system and main fuse panels.

* * *

Albie as well as several other guards, including Merv, were playing Brag with a tattered, dog-eared pack of well-thumbed cards. Albie had suggested it as a way to keep many of them occupied after he'd eaten a good breakfast. It had worked well up to the point of the crash on the roof and a body dropping passed the mess hall window. Merv was on his feet, moving toward the door, and reaching for his sawed-off shotgun lean-ing against the wall by the door. Albie knew he must prevent Merv leaving the mess hall. If he got into the fray outside, people would die unnecessarily. Of the four guards round the table, two remained seated, and two rushed to the window to see what was happening outside. Albie leaped up from his chair, pushing it backward so it fell over to the floor. He was already facing the exit door, and just as Merv leaned forward to pick up his shotgun, Albie reached over his left shoulder. In one deft movement, he drew a long knife and threw it with force and accuracy toward the shotgun and Merv's left hand. The blade cut skin between Merv's thumb and forefinger and continued to the butt of the gun against the wall. It grazed the gun, so it fell flat to the ground. Merv's hand was gushing blood in free flow. Merv turned round to see who was brave enough to challenge him. His eyes widened a little in surprise to see Albie, a man at least twice his age standing there with a second knife in his left hand and a short sword in his right. He had the look of an old warrior steeled to a purpose he knew was right. It was a look he had never seen before in the face of a man he had treated as a go-fer and cook for almost the entire time he was assigned to his troop.

"Don't open that door," Albie said in a low voice, every word given its own space.

Merv smiled menacingly. "Oh, and what if I do?"

"You won't make it across the threshold, but I don't want to kill you unless I have to."

There was a collective yell from outside. One of the guards by the window, without turning round said, "The prison-ers are running toward the gate. Someone just shot the duty gatekeeper."

The second man at the window continued quizzically, "It must have been another guard—no one else has weapons."

Merv, his gaze not having left Albie, said, "So, you're a part of this . . . rebellion?"

"It's no rebellion, simply a choice for justice. What hap-pens here is not justice. None of these people have really done anything wrong. They simply feel there is more to discover than what is taught in the name of the Lord Master."

"Nice little speech," replied Merv, wrapping his sliced hand in a torn rag removed from his belt, which Merv used to polish his shotgun.

The two guards who had remained seated slowly rose from their seats and carefully moved to one side, recognizing they were in Merv's firing line. Albie watched on the periphery of his vision, but his eyes remained fixed on Merv. They showed no sign of wanting to get involved in this showdown.

"No one is going to get hurt as long as they don't get in the way," Albie voiced this not for Merv's benefit but the others in the hall.

The two guards by the window now turned inward to view the standoff.

"Get him!" Merv shouted at no one in particular, hoping to spur someone into action and create a distraction long enough for him to grab his shotgun.

One of the guards in the window, in a reflex reaction to a shouted order, dropped his hand to a holstered firearm.

Albie caught the movement to his right in peripheral vision. He took his eyes off Merv for just an instant as he shouted, "Don't!"

It was enough for Merv. He dived to his right for his shotgun lying on the floor. The noise of movement diverted Albie's attention back to Merv. He let fly his second knife, but it was wide of the mark and clipped the barrel of the shotgun, jerking it back from Merv's desperately outthrust hand. Merv bent his body backward to catch a grip of the gun. Albie strode across the gap to drop the blade of the short sword onto Merv's throat and dissuade him from further action. As he raised his sword, Merv swung his left leg round with force and caught Albie on the side of his right knee. The pain was instant, and Albie dropped onto his injured knee. Merv arched backward to get hold of his shotgun. He felt the butt, wrapped his hand around the shoulder of the weapon, and curled his finger across the double trigger. Sweeping his arm around to train the barrels toward Albie, his arm was stopped short by the blade of the short sword slashed across his wrist. Just before the tendons were severed, he squeezed the trigger, and a blast of shot flew across Albie's left shoulder—scattered lead projectiles peppered the wall and ceiling of the mess hall. Some grazed past Albie's shoulder, causing a sensation of searing heat, and then blood started to pockmark Albie's shirt. Some shot caught one of the guards who had moved forward to support Albie's assault on Merv. He dropped, crying in pain with shot embedded in the left side of his face. His left eye was a bloody mess, and in a few seconds, he lost consciousness.

Albie picked himself up from the floor and limped back a few steps from Merv. "Merv, you are one of the most arrogant, sadistic bastards I have ever met, but I'll not kill you unless I have to. Stop now. It's going to be over soon. You can't change that."

Merv looked down at his bleeding wrist with fingers he could barely move now, grimaced with pain, and stared down at the expanding pool of blood.

"OK, OK, help me please."

Albie looked into his eyes and saw a man resigned to his defeat, his lids blinking slowly as his strength continued to fade with the blood flow.

"You two get some clean rags and some water. Help him over there," Albie pointed to the unconscious guard with the blooded face. "You two help get Merv over there. Put a tourniquet on his right arm, and keep it raised." Albie pointed to the chairs by the large fire hearth still glowing from a long, overnight burn. Albie limped over to the window to see what events were taking place outside. He grabbed the corner of the grubby curtain, yanked it from the rail, and used it to stem the flow of blood from his left shoulder. He looked up toward the north tower. Two guards were up there and training their weapons on the people below. He saw a figure off to his right running along the back east wall. The figure turned, faced up toward the northern tower, and let fly a crossbow bolt that embedded itself in a guardrail behind which one of the guards was stooped and aiming. He jumped backward in surprise. All attention had been on the prisoners running toward the gate up to this point. Guards on the ramparts now turned their attention to the eastern end of the courtyard.

* * *

From his vantage point on the western border of the clearing, Locke could see the guards in the towers through his eyeglass. As he observed the southern tower, he witnessed one guard come behind another and belt him on the head and tip him over the guardrail. Shortly after, there was a lot of yelling from the courtyard drifting across the open space on the light breeze. It had begun. He turned, headed back to the horses, and ignited the brush and dead wood bundles tied by long tether to the horses. Slapping them on their rumps with a loud, "Yeaah," the horses sped off in opposite directions to each other, setting small fires along the path as they galloped wide-eyed in fear from the fire following behind them. As the horses left, Locke picked up his pack and weapons and broke cover. He ran at full pelt straight for the main gate. The tower guards and those in the ramparts were all giving attention to the events happening within the walls. The hundred-and-fifty-pace run to the gates up the gentle slope left Locke panting heavily but not inattentive to his surroundings. He looked back to the woods to see small fires and smoke palls rising steadily and drifting toward the prison. He crouched by the left side of the gate and waited. He could hear the commotion on the other side clearly, and somewhere inside was the sound of a shotgun going off. He immediately thought of Merv. There was a yell from above his head, and just as a whiff of smoke caught his own nostrils, a guard on the ramparts yelled, "Fire!"

Attention was once again diverted, and there were noises on the other side of the thick oak gate that sounded like some kind of bar and metal chain work were being manipulated and slid back. Without warning, the gate swung inward, and a mass of children and women ran out. Locke shouted, "Stay close to the walls! Don't run into the open. Head round to the south side." Locke recognized a couple of guards in uniforms running out with them and grabbed an arm, "Where's Abalus?"

Jack stopped while still urging the fleeing prisoners to keep running by waving his arm across to point the direction to go. "He's in the gatehouse with a girl and his mother. Simon, one of the guards, is with them. They're pinned down by the guards on the northern tower and ramparts."

"Thanks, OK, get the others into the woods as fast as you can."

Locke put his hand into his cloak behind his back and unclipped a Nighthawk Talon 45-caliber handgun. This was his most treasured weapon, but it had up to now never been fired in anger. He had only three clips. It was going to be interesting to see how effective it was.

He rounded the gate entrance and looked over to the north tower and ramparts. The two guards seemed to be focused on the rear of the courtyard. He raised his arm, looked down the sight, and squeezed the trigger. A loud, sharp noise was followed by the recoil flicking his wrist up. The projectile splintered one of the upright posts of the lookout roof. One of the guards in the tower turned his way, pointed in his direction, and shouted, "At the gate!" More eyes on the north wall looked his way. He ducked back behind the outer wall for cover.

Wow, some kick this weapon has, he thought to himself. He gripped the handle with both hands and rounded the gate a second time, arms locked, the Talon raised. As soon as he caught sight of a guard in the tower, he trained the weapon and fired. A second loud crack was followed by the sight of the guard in the tower dropping his crossbow and collapsing to his knees with a large red patch spreading across his chest. Then, he fell out of sight to the floor of the tower. A crossbow bolt embedded itself in the oak post of the gate close to his right ear. Locke looked down from the tower and to the left. On the rampart stood a guard reloading his crossbow. Locke trained the weapon for the third time and fired. The man staggered back, clutching his left shoulder and swearing loudly in pain. A second man on the rampart dropped over the edge with a crossbow bolt in his neck. Locke looked to his right and saw Shaun in the far southeast corner of the yard moving down the southern wall and disappearing into one of the guards' quarters out of sight. So, he was still alive. In the courtyard were several injured children and women who had been fired at from ramparts. Locke looked around the entrance further and peered into the gatehouse. Simon appeared round the half-closed door and fired a bolt up toward the rampart above Locke's head. Locke whirled round and looked up to see a small firearm dropping from a limp hand. He sidestepped and threw himself to the ground just as a body landed where he had just been standing. Simon grabbed his arm and dragged him into the gatehouse.

"Locke, you made it!" said the familiar, young voice of Abalus.

"Hi, kid, you OK?"

"I'm all right apart from my ankle." Abalus turned to the two women sitting under the window counter. "Mum, Mags, this is Ranger Locke, the man who has helped me since we escaped."

"The Lord Master bless you, sir. Thank you so much for bringing my boy back to me."

"We are not out of danger yet, Mrs. Rider. But, I'm pleased to meet you."

Abalus gestured toward Mags, "And this is Mags, a friend." Locke nodded cordially to the young girl. She smiled and nodded but seemed somewhat too frightened of their current predicament to speak.

Locke raised his head to look out of the window and take stock the remaining threat. There was no one left on the north rampart, and a guard in the south tower seemed to have taken care of those on the south rampart. There was one man on the far east wall with his arms raised in the air, clearly surrendering. No one had come out of the mess hall as yet. It would need to be checked. Just as Locke was casting his eye across the south wall where the mess hall and sleeping quarters were, two guards were backing out of one of the sleeping quarters followed a few paces by Shaun armed with a crossbow in one hand and a firearm in the other. While Locke was watching Shaun, he missed the movement in the radio room. The guard called Mac had recovered consciousness, and although in much pain with a broken jaw, his intent was clear. He had a crossbow raised and aimed toward Shaun.

"Don't!" The yell came from the left of Locke; Simon was eyeing the gap of the partially open door of the gatehouse.

Mac, startled by the shout, looked away from Shaun and across to the gatehouse entrance. Recognizing the exposed half of Simon's face as the man who'd broken his jaw, Mac began to move the crossbow around toward the gatehouse door.

Simon repeated, "Don't!"

The crossbow bolt released. Simon slammed the door shut and heard the thud as the bolt embedded in the wood where his face was an instant before. Simon flung open the door and was across the gate entrance before Mac was able to reload and train the bow a second time. Simon careered forward and raised his right forearm to head height, and as Mac looked up from trying to reload, Simon's elbow connected with his right cheekbone. Mac went down, knocked out for the second time. As Simon turned round to view the damage and see if Mac was to offer any further resistance, a bolt appeared in the side of his right thigh. Simon's knees buckled under him as he looked down in shock and grasped the bolt with his left hand. He did not have the strength to withdraw the bolt and simply fell back looking up to the west rampart. Locke flung open the door to the gatehouse, raised the Talon, and let off three shots toward the figure of a guard running toward the northwest corner. The guard arched his back as if stung by a wasp between the shoulder blades, fell forward, and started to crawl for a few paces only to collapse facedown.

Locke rushed over to Simon, closely followed by Mags, who cried out, "Uncle Simon, Uncle Simon." She reached her uncle and cradled his head in her arms with tears in her eyes.

"I'm OK, Mags. I'll live. I just can't walk right now." Simon tried to make light humor to calm his niece down. He hid the pain well, and Mags calmed down, and her tears dried. Locke did another scan of the courtyard and looked back outside the gates to see that the other prisoners were clear. Abalus and his mother joined them outside.

Locke knelt beside Simon. "Where do I find Alucious right now?"

"It was his job to delay and trap the Cardinal in his chambers. Alucious wants to find the Cardinal's library. Go to the elevator in the radio room. I've left power on to operate it. Power to the security cameras and alarms is cut. Hopefully, the Cardinal is confined to his living quarters."

"Mrs. Rider, please can you take care of Simon as much as you can until I get Father Alucious up here? He has more experience with injuries."

Shaun joined them without a word, and as Locke took Simon's right arm to assist him to walk, Shaun leaned forward to hook Simon's left arm over his shoulder. Between them, they walked Simon into the interview room where Abalus was confined a while earlier. They settled Simon on the bare table. Locke, without warning, yanked out the bolt. Simon lost consciousness. Locke left Evey to set about cleaning the wound. Mags looked on in concern for her uncle and grasped Abalus's hand while he stood by her side. Shaun and Locke entered the elevator and went down to the main access corridor.

* * *

Alucious heard the single, "GO," on his intercom and felt his heart pick up pace as fear and adrenalin took hold. He took a couple of deep breaths to calm his nerves and clasped the modified fork with a single prong for assurance. Alucious opened his door into the front passageway that connected the men's sleeping quarters along the south wall. The stairs down to the lower level was at the southeast end of the passageway. As he entered, a couple of guards awoken by the falling body on the tiles close to their bunk space were staggering down the passageway half dressed and attempting to weapon up as they took in the scene outside in the courtyard through the window. Alucious ignored them and walked briskly down into the stairwell, taking two steps at a time, until he was in the lower passageway. The main lights were out, and the small emergency wall lights embedded in the brickwork were on. Alucious looked up at the passage security camera and saw that the little red light was out.

"Good work, Simon," he mumbled to himself in a low tone and continued down the passageway to the Cardinal's chambers at the end. Alucious knocked and announced himself, and the door opened. The Cardinal sat at his desk, tapping keys on his desk control panel for the security monitors. Without looking up, he said, "Why has the power gone down on the security system?"

The doors closed behind Alucious. The Cardinal looked up from his panel and gave Alucious a cold, piercing stare that bored right into his being. Was he going to survive this encounter? Would he be able to complete his part of the plan?

The Cardinal continued, "I know you have been planning this day, Alucious. How far did you think you would get?"

Alucious looked around the room and noted that the main lights in here were still on. So, the power to these chambers was on a separate source to the rest of the prison accommodations.

Alucious played dumb and ignored the question. "Your Eminence, I came to inform you that there has been a main power failure in the radio room. The duty watch are attempting to locate the source of failure, but we don't fully understand the circuits and have no drawings to isolate the problem."

The Cardinal gave a wan smile to himself. "My dear Father, the game is up. You don't need to pretend anymore."

Alucious's heart missed a beat, and he felt his throat go dry. He replied without observable pause, "I'm sorry, your Eminence. I don't understand what you mean."

"Come now, my dear Father, you've started a mutiny and are freeing the women and children. Did you think I did not know?"

Alucious breathed out in resignation. He was not going to attempt to lie; it was pointless. "Why have you not imprisoned me?"

"What makes you think I won't?" came the sharp reply. He continued, "I knew that you were planning something, but I did not know precisely who else was involved. However, I am sure that, without you to encourage them, I shall have things back to normal very soon."

Alucious knew he was now trapped in the chamber and in mortal danger. He fingered the one-pronged fork in his pocket and began to think of options. He could do what he set out to do to prevent the Cardinal leaving and probably die in the process. However, if he left the door mechanism alone, the Cardinal could get out and of course someone else could get in to help him if he raised the alarm somehow.

Above them, somewhere, was a loud crack of a firearm. The sound was not familiar to Alucious. It was not a guard's gun that he had heard. This had a sharper crack to it. Locke maybe? The intercom—if he could just get to the intercom on the Cardinal's desk, maybe he could shout for help.

The Cardinal rose from his chair; his eyes never left Alucious' face. "Well, Father Alucious, what did you possibly hope to gain by this treachery?"

Alucious did not need to manufacture an answer to this question. He responded with rising courage from his desire to find the truth, "I want access to the library and archive that I know you have been putting together over the years. I know your knowledge extends beyond what the rest of us are taught. The knowledge you have is the source of your power over the citizens. Fear is what you use as a weapon in the face of our ignorance. It is wrong of you to keep these from us. It is wrong to use the Lord Master's Holy Writings to suppress our natural curiosity to learn more about the truth of our past."

"Excellent speech, Father." The Cardinal moved round to the front of the desk and continued, "What you do not realize is that I have been saving humanity from itself. I was witness to the devastation caused by your ancestors."

Father Alucious eyes widened. "That makes you about one hundred and fifty years old!"

Both men were distracted by three more sharp cracks from somewhere above them. Alucious moved casually off to the right toward the monitors, the screens now black and lifeless. The Cardinal was staring up at the ceiling and appeared to be listening for further clues as to what was transpiring above him. Alucious continued to edge toward the desk to get close enough to activate the intercom switch. He got within one pace of the desk when the Cardinal turned toward Alucious. "Don't go any closer, Father, or I will kill you where you stand." The Cardinal's voice was a sharp command, filled with a cold emotionless timbre. It left no doubt.

Alucious froze obediently, one hand partly outstretched, hovering fearfully toward the intercom.

Alucious attempted to keep the conversation going. "Where is the archive? Does it really exist?"

The Cardinal seemed to muse over the question before deciding to respond, "Oh, yes, it exists, but you will never see it now. You are, in fact, standing over it."

Alucious looked down at his feet and thought to himself, *So, it is here, but how to get down to it?*

It was now or never. Alucious decided to make a bid for the intercom and took the remaining pace toward the desk. His finger found the intercom button, and he blurted, "Help! I'm in the Cardinals Chamb—"

That was as far as he got. The Cardinal closed the three-pace distance, withdrew his red, jeweled short dagger, and thrust it into the back of the Father's outstretched right hand. The force drove the knife through his hand and into the panel of the intercom. Alucious yelled out in pain as blood started to free flow from his trapped hand. The slightest movement of his fingers sent shock waves up his arm. The tendon to his middle finger was severed. He hoped to the Lord Master that someone outside had heard his cry for help. The Cardinal looked impassively into the screwed-up face of Alucious, gripped the knife handle, yanked it out of the table, and shook the impaled hand off the knife blade. Alucious collapsed onto his knees, head bowed, clutching his wounded hand close to his chest, waiting for a second knife thrust to end his life. It did not come. He looked up in pain and found himself staring into the Cardinal's pale, lifeless face.

"I think a trial for treason against the Lord Master's commandments is out of the question, don't you?"

The Cardinal raised the dagger, the jeweled handle catching the light, the blood from his hand dripping from the blade. Alucious closed his eyes and relaxed in the finality of this moment knowing that he had done the right thing by those incarcerated in this place. He hoped to the Lord Master that the freed women and children would remain clear of the Cardinal's clutches and were able to spread the word about what transpired in this place.

There was a loud, deep explosion, and the door became pockmarked with indentations, then another in rapid succession. The Cardinal lowered the dagger, turned away from Alucious, and moved toward the door. There was another double volley of shot pounding on the door, and in a concentrated area, the metal panel began to show shafts of light from the other side of the door. Alucious struggled to his feet, still holding his injured hand to his chest. He looked across the desk and spied what he was looking for, the door remote.

The Cardinal, now halfway between the door and the desk, realized the dilemma he was in as soon as he saw Alucious reach for the remote. Alucious raised the remote and pointed it toward the door. It began to slide away, revealing

Shaun and Locke. Shaun stood with Merv's double-barreled shotgun poised for another double volley. Shaun caught the movement of the Cardinal as he turned and headed for the rear wall of his chamber. He trained the twin barrels in his direction and released a double volley in the Cardinal's direction. The Cardinal's cloak shredded with small holes, but apart from a faltering step, the Cardinal continued his dash for the rear of his chamber. Then, as if the floor opened up, he dropped from sight. Locke and Shaun ran toward Alucious, who had now slumped into the Cardinal's chair at the desk, his pain clear on his face.

"I'm all right. Quick, go after him. Don't let him get away."

Locke responded by dropping to his knees beside the Father to get a closer look at Alucious's hand covered in blood. He ripped a section off his cloak and wrapped it round the Father's hand to stem the flow.

"Father, your assistance with the injured is needed above. Are you able to provide guidance to Mrs. Rider, who is doing as much as she can for one of your guards?"

"Who's been hurt?" Alucious asked through clenched teeth.

"Simon had a crossbow bolt in the leg. It has been removed, but he's now unconsciousness. There are some of the prisoners who got caught in the crossfire. They need help."

Alucious forgot about his own discomfort, and his resolve steeled to a new task before him. The result of his plan had meant innocent people had gotten hurt. He was on his feet and heading for the door.

He turned briefly, "Thank you, my son; I shall do what I can. Don't let him get away," Alucious nodded toward the hole in the floor and the narrow staircase downward.

Shaun had already disappeared from view down the staircase. Locke reloaded his Nighthawk Talon and moved off to the dim aperture in the floor. Alucious made his way back up the passage toward the light of day.

Locke descended into a narrow, gloomy passageway only illuminated by small, embedded wall lights not much larger than a pea. Ahead, Locke could hear footfalls echoing back up the passage to his position. He doubled his pace to catch up with the sounds of footsteps. In the gloom, he saw Shaun's back disappear around a bend in the passageway. As he reached the bend, it became apparent that it was a T junction rather than a bend. Shaun had gone to the right, so Locke took the left. The passage opened out into a small anteroom with a wooden door in each wall. One door was ajar. Above the door was a sign, "A to J". Locke moved up to the side of the doorframe and put his back against the wall. His eyes were becoming accustomed to the gloom, but the room seemed to be dimmer than out in the anteroom. There was no sound coming from inside. Locke craned his head round the door and peered into dark recesses. He could make out shelves lined with books creating narrow walkways between each shelf. Locke advanced into the library, stooped low in a crouch; he penetrated deeper into the nearest walkway.

From somewhere in the darkness, a low voice broke the calm solitude of the room, "Well, Mathew Locke, I underestimated you. You are indeed persistent in life."

"Your Eminence, I've no wish to kill you, but be sure I will if you force me to. I would prefer it if you would give this up and allow me to escort you back upstairs."

"I don't think I'll take your offer, Locke."

"Your rule is over, your Eminence. Please don't make this difficult."

There was no reply. The silence was suddenly pierced by the sound of a rush of air. Instinctively, Locke ducked and turned toward the direction of the whoosh of air. In a brief flash, Locke caught sight of the Cardinal's robe and a glint of shiny metal in the shaft of light from the doorway. The blade flashed downward toward Locke's right shoulder. He rolled to his left, and the blade smashed with a metallic clang on the stone floor. Locke banged into a shelf that prevented him from getting clear of a second swipe of the sword. He scrambled to his feet, ready to run deeper into the dark, and felt the blade brush down the side of his left arm, ripping his cloak and shirtsleeve and taking a thin slice of flesh, like carving a rasher of bacon. His flesh burned with pain, but he continued to run into the darkness, deeper into the library. He withdrew the Talon from its holster, turned, and let three shots go back down the aisle of books. But, the Cardinal seemed to have disappeared again.

"You can't harm me with that," the voice of the Cardinal mocked him.

Locke removed his cloak, ripped a section off, and wrapped it around his left upper arm.

A silhouette appeared in the shaft of light of the doorway. Shaun's lithe shape stood with shotgun raised. "Maybe he can't, but I can."

Two bright flashes and a shower of book pages responded to the blast of shot. In the light of the flash, the outline of the Cardinal appeared to fragment into a cloud. Shaun reloaded another two shells and let them go in a thunderous blast toward the Cardinal. In the flash, the Cardinal seemed to fragment further, but as soon as the shot had shredded into his body, the fragmentation began a process of coagulation to rebond. Shaun loaded two more shells, took two steps forward, stood point blank in front the Cardinal, raised the barrels to eye level, and let both barrels go at the same time. Bits of paper from shredded books and a cloud of ignited nanomas that were the Cardinal's head and shoulders vaporized. The body of the Cardinal initially stretched out arms and tendrils toward Shaun in a desperate effort to latch on and combine with the hand holding the shotgun. But, every part of the body dropped to dust. Shaun took a step back and watched the mass on the floor, making sure enough damage and separation had taken place to prevent rebonding. Locke came up beside Shaun, clutching his left arm.

"Thanks, Shaun, I am indebted to you."

"It's done. He won't be passing any more sentences of death in the name of the Lord Master." Shaun's tone emphasized the last two words.

"This seems to be the library section. What was down the other passageway Shaun?"

"It opened out into another three rooms, much like this only much bigger. One room was small and held mounds of metal money. It seems the Cardinal was consuming it to stay alive."

Puzzled, Locke responded, "What do you mean? I don't understand."

"He and I are alike. We are both remnants of the disaster that happened a long time ago. I am not human. Abalus can tell you all about it later. But now, I think we had better get back up top and let the others know what we have found."

"What have we found?" Locke replied, returning to the secrets behind the other two doors.

"The second door seemed to be some kind of power generating room. It contained a large set of black blocks—batteries I believe they are called. They can store energy called electricity. That's what seems to power much of the equipment in this prison." Shaun paused. "The third chamber I know Abalus will like. The room beyond is huge, and it contains all manner of technology and things from years ago. Much of it looked in good condition, but whether anything works, I'm sure Abalus will love to find out."

Locke reholstered his Talon, "Well, let's go see how things are up top."

* * * *

Mags leaned over close to my ear and whispered, "Abalus, I am so pleased to see you again."

I squeezed her hand tightly in mine; the warmth of her breath on my face made my blood rush faster through my veins. My heart pounded a little faster. I looked into her eyes, and the depths of her soul smiled back at me. I raised my hand to touch her grubby cheek and stroke her hair; she mirrored my action. Mother turned from her attentive cleaning of Simon's impaled thigh and smiled up at both of us. In her grief of loss of my father, she seemed to take comfort in the bond she could see being forged between myself and Mags.

Father Alucious stepped out of the elevator and seemed to be on rather shaky legs. I dropped Mags's hand, rushed over to him, and helped him to a seat.

"The Cardinal, is he . . . dead?"

Alucious looked up and replied weakly, "I am not sure, my son. Locke and Shaun have chased him down into a tunnel below his chambers."

My excitement must have shown, "That must be where the library is hidden."

"I think you might be right on that one," he replied, and then he continued, "Get your mother here to help me bind this wound, and we'll start attending the other injured."

As I assisted the Father to stand, the doorway to the radio room became crowded with people. The imprisoned women and children who earlier had run free into the woods had returned. My mother beckoned to them, and between herself and Father Alucious, they set about getting injured people over into the mess hall for aid. Albie crossed from the mess hall with another guard and helped transport Simon into one of the guards' quarters. As he passed me, he stopped, looked me straight in the eye, and said, "See, I told you to have faith, didn't I?" By then, Mags had come up to my side and folded her hand in mine once more. Albie continued, "So, introduce me to this nice young lady of yours."

I blushed a little and glanced sideways to see Mags's reaction. She had a playful smile across her face as she tugged on my hand as if to cajole me into a reply.

"Albie, this is Mags. She was imprisoned here next to my cell. Mags, this is Albie, a good friend of mine. He took care of my ankle on the journey back here."

Mags gave Albie one of her beaming smiles and a gracious curtsy. It seemed so out of place here in a prison, with her all grubby with tangled hair and in a ripped skirt, but the effort was not wasted on Albie.

Albie took one foot back and, with a sweeping gesture, imitated the removal of a hat and bowed deeply.

"I am pleased to make your acquaintance, young miss." He then stood up, leaned forward, and whispered in her ear, "Take care of this one. He'll go far." With that, he took up Simon, whom he had left leaning on the other guard, and continued on to guards' quarters.

"Mags, I want to go down to the library. The Cardinal took my notebooks. I must find out what he did with them."

"Abalus, wait. It's not safe yet. The Cardinal's still down there somewhere."

Just as Mags had finished her sentence, as if on queue, Locke and Shaun stepped back out of the elevator and appeared in the radio room doorway. I saw Locke's arm moist red with blood, but Shaun seemed unhurt. They walked across the courtyard to where we stood. Locke smiled calmly at me and said, "It's done. The Cardinal is no more." Shaun nodded in agreement.

"Can I go down to the library now?" I asked.

Shaun replied, "You'll have to wait some. There's very little light down there. You'd better wait until power is restored so you can see."

"I'll take a torch. Mags, you coming?" Mags nodded.

"Shaun, go with them just in case." Locke knew I would want to go anyway. He added, "I'll go and get myself patched up and check on the brush fires." Locke left us to make our way down.

Mags and I walked hand in hand down the passage toward the Cardinal's chambers; Shaun was a few paces ahead of us showing the way. We entered the chambers, and my eye was drawn to the monitor bank on the wall to my right and the damaged control panel on the desk. Mags spied the small screen with letters on the keyboard and immediately recognized it.

"Abalus, do you remember I described something we found on our farm buried in a wooden box and wrapped in bag of stretchy cloth?"

I turned my attention to where she was standing. "Yes, I remember."

"Well, it looked very much like this." She pointed at the oblong object on the desk.

There was an amber blinking light in the top right of the keyboard section. I touched a letter on the keyboard tentatively. The screen section burst into a rich blue color with a small box with the word "Windows" at the top in the middle and a blinking black line winking next to the words "User name." I typed "Abalus" and waited, but nothing happened. I turned to Mags, "What's a password?"

"No idea."

"This thing seems to be waiting for one."

"Never mind now—let's go figure it out later. Perhaps we'll find a book about it somewhere in the library."

"Good thought, Mags."

Shaun had continued on down the stairwell, and we followed into the dimly lit passageway. I turned on the flashlight I found in the radio room equipment cupboard and illuminated the passage with a strong light. The passage was of regular square stones much like the construction of our cells. Small dim lights shone a pale light toward the floor. The walls were bare with some green mosses gripping some of the upper and lower corners. Shaun had turned left, and we followed. The passage opened into an anteroom. I shone the torch on three doors in turn. A simple sign of embossed metal above each— "A to J," "K to Q," and the third "R to Z." Shaun beckoned us to A to J. I shone my touch through the doorway and let out a deep breath.

"Whoah! Look at the size of this room." The door appeared to be at the top end of a long room lined with shelves. Down the first aisle was a pile of brown-grey ash that seemed to scintillate in the light of the torch; all around were bits of paper and the hard backs of several books. I picked up one of the broken covers and shone the torch on the gold-embossed title, "The Holy Writi." The rest was disintegrated. Shaun pointed to the scintillating ash and said one word, "Cardinal."

I understood. Mags looked puzzled but did not press for further explanation. We turned and opened the other doors to find rooms of similar size just filled with books. My eyes recognized the enormity of the treasures that existed down here, and I had no idea where to start. Shaun tapped me on the shoulder.

"Follow me, Abalus. I'll show you something that will make your head spin."

Mags clasped my hand, and we followed the beam of light back down the passageway past the T section onward to a second anteroom laid out the same as the other. Shaun opened the door on the far wall and beckoned us in. I passed through the door and scanned my torch in front of me. My jaw became weak and dropped, and my eyes opened agog at the sight before me. The room was full of all sorts of objects large and small. The largest was a four-wheeled vehicle with the word "Ford" written on the front and back. The smallest that I could see from this vantage point by the door was a flat pad with the word "iPad" written on the top of it. The room was huge and stretched back beyond the strength of the light beam.

I turned to Mags with an overwhelming sense of awe. "We have a lot to discover and learn, Mags. Where do we start?"

My eyes were filling with tears from the culmination of everything that had happened to me over the last few weeks—the Cardinal's visit, the loss of my father, the incarceration of my mother and myself, the trials of the journey, and now the discovery of all this.

"How about we start here?" Mags said in a low voice as she leaned forward and kissed me full on the lips.

The tears flowed freely, and I smiled weakly through them. "That's a good place to start."

The End (almost)

Epilogue

It was a month ago now since the prison was extricated from the Cardinal. Alucious put down the pen he had been learning to use with his left hand. His writing was becoming quite legible. He had spent a few evenings putting down in writing much of the events over the last couple of months with the help of Locke, Shaun, and particularly Abalus. Abalus had spent several evenings giving his account of the recent weeks. Abalus and Mags had become inseparable and were here in his chambers, having given their last account for his journal.

"Well, Abalus, I think I have most of it now. Anything else you can think of?"

Barkley pricked up his ears and whined long and low, completing his contribution with a single woof.

Abalus and Mags looked at each other then toward Barkley, who was patting his tail on the rug, then back to toward the Father.

"No, I don't think so, Father. I guess we should make plans for the future. There is so much here to learn and many people to teach."

"That is true, my son. This prison can be put to far better use as a house of learning."

This was true enough. Over the last month, Abalus and Mags had spent many days searching through the artifacts and books that had been amassed here over the years. Many of the books were to do with their ancestors' inventions and discoveries, but there were some storybooks as well. They had realized this when, on closer investigation, they found the library split into what was called fiction and nonfiction sections. Finding a dictionary had helped.

Many of the women and children returned to their homes to be reunited with loved ones; some like Abalus and Evey stayed, having lost husbands to the Cardinal. Some returned with their partners and parents whose curiosity had been fueled by one or two books they had guarded and hidden in their own homes for so long, now drawn to the fact that the prison was a font of treasures beyond their imagination. This place was to have a new lease of life. The open pasture that surrounded the old prison was beginning to become a temporary home for people using makeshift tents and the stream for water. Locke had begun mobilizing the remaining guards and arriving people to repair and convert the prison into accommodations and classrooms. The Father, a teacher of the Holy Writings, was to become the guiding influence on what was to be taught alongside the good book.

* * *

Abalus had not taken long to retrieve the notebooks of Professor Geoffrey Short. He resolved to search the southern region for the third notebook the Professor had said he would write. Undoubtedly, Mags would go with him.

Locke and Shaun had become close friends, and Shaun was persuaded to stay and help once Abalus had promised not to tell anyone of his origins.

Simon, Mags's uncle, decided he wanted to stay and help the Father teach some of this stuff. He had a natural fascination for the power used to drive the instruments and equipment around the prison. He hoped to learn more and help others learn about it as well. The power source, they found out, was called electricity. The dictionary had come in handy here as well to interpret some words printed on labels of some of the equipment in the big room of artifacts. Many of them had 240Vac or 5Vdc or some other numbers. Simon had spent some time searching through stuff, reading, and worked some of this out. He spent a lot of effort in the battery room and with the panels on the roof, his interest fueled by fascination and curiosity.

* * *

The remains of the Cardinal, the grey scintillating dust, was collected up and sealed in a container, clearly labeled and locked away in the coin room. Alucious, earlier, had decided to cremate the remains as was expected of the Lord Master. There was some protest from many others, considering the lack of respect the Cardinal had had for those he sentenced in the Lord Master's name. Alucious decided not to press the point, nerves and emotions still raw. Perhaps some time in the future . . .